S

Sin Bin 4

Bev

Keith Miles

An Armada Original

Bev was first published in Armada in 1989

Armada is an imprint of the Children's Division,
part of the Collins Publishing Group,
8 Grafton Street, London W1X 3LA

© 1989 Keith Miles

Printed in Great Britain by
William Collins Sons & Co. Ltd, Glasgow

Chapter One

It all began as a joke. The two girls were helping to smarten up the classroom with the rest of 4C and feeling mutinous because they were being kept in after school. They had much better things to do than tidy their desks.

'I'll miss my telly!' wailed Abbie.

'Mum's waiting for me in the precinct,' said Bev.

'Iss the larst flippin' episode!'

'She'll wonder where I've got to.'

'I hate thar Froggy!'

'Why pick on *us*?'

The headmaster was to blame. Froggy Parsons was having one of his Keep Woodfield Tidy campaigns, touring the premises for signs of litter and conducting snap inspections of the classrooms. It was 4C's turn to be made the scapegoat. Froggy interrupted an English lesson that afternoon to run a beady eye over the place. He was horrified by the filth, graffiti and general untidiness. The room had to be spick and span before they were allowed to go home.

Abigail Reynolds had a surprisingly strong character for a short, small-boned girl of fifteen. Her long fair hair hung straight down to frame her large-lensed glasses. Her usual expression of cheerful indifference had been replaced by a frown of indignation.

'Gor no right to keep us in,' she protested.

'Try telling him that,' sighed Bev.

'Froggy's the worst 'eadmaster in Britain.'

'In the world.'

'Iss 'igh time someone tort *'im* a lesson.'

'How, Abbie?'

5

It was a harmless enough question but Bev would live to regret that she ever asked it. Those two words sealed her fate.

Beverly Kington was a tall, shapely, handsome girl whose poise made her seem much more mature than she really was. Her straw-coloured hair curled attractively around her face. Even in school uniform of dull grey skirt, grey cardigan and white shirt, she contrived to look elegant. Bev stuck out from the others. Woodfield was an inner city comprehensive whose pupils were drawn from deprived areas. Most of those kids came from problem families. Bev's problem was that she didn't. It made her the odd one out.

'Really wanna know?'said Abbie.

'Yes.'

'First thing I'd do with Froggy is to sling 'im back in the pond where 'e come from. Then I'd smash thar stupid car of 'is to pieces. Then I'd nick 'is dirty big briefcase and bury it where 'e'd never find it. Then . . .'

'Go on.'

'I'd ger to work on 'is study.' Abbie was into her stride now. 'Empty all 'is drawers. Tip them books orff 'is shelves. Tear up all our record cards. Pour ink over everythin'. Stick glue on 'is chair. Then leave a coupla messages on the walls with a spray can of paint.'

'That would show him,' agreed Bev.

'You 'avenn 'eard the best bit yet,' continued her friend, with cheeks aglow. 'Juss wenn ole Froggy'd finished cleanin' it all up, I'd set fire to Woodfield and burn the soddin' place to the ground!'

Her fantasy was cut short by the man who inspired it.

'Come along, come along! You can do better than this.'

Froggy Parsons appeared in the doorway. Short, squat and bow-legged, he peered through the black hornrimmed spectacles that helped to earn him his nickname. Desks had been tidied and straightened, the floor had been mopped and some of the graffiti had been sponged off the walls, but the

6

headmaster was still not satisfied. He clicked his tongue in disapproval.

'Put your backs into it, 4C,' he urged. 'Cleanliness is next to godliness. Take a pride in your classroom. You *live* here. Make it gleam and glisten. An environment determines the quality of work you produce. Nobody can be at their best in a pigsty!'

'Aw, shurrup,' muttered Abbie.

'Did you say something, Abigail?' he challenged.

'No, sir.'

'Then keep at it. The lid of your desk needs attention. Look at all those stains and squiggles.'

'They're drorin's, sir.'

'Wipe them off. I'll be back in ten minutes.'

A concerted moan went up as he swept off down the corridor. They had already been at it for the best part of half an hour. Grumbling noisily, they made one last effort to make the room presentable. When Froggy returned, he marched up and down the rows of desks and checked every nook and cranny. He went back to the front of the class.

'That's more like it, 4C,' he congratulated them. 'I want it like this all day and every day. Understand?'

'Yeah, sir,' they chorused.

'Good. You may go now.'

With a muted cheer, they grabbed their bags and surged towards the exit like a tidal wave. 4C had never been so glad to escape from the school. They poured out into the hazy sunshine and scurried across the playground.

Abbie was usually the friendliest girl in the school but now she was brooding on revenge.

'Thass it, Bev!' she decided.

'What are you on about?'

'Wor I said earlier. Teachin' Froggy a lesson.'

'Oh, forget him,' advised Bev.

'Arfter wor he juss done to us? No fear!'

'So what are you going to do?'

7

Abbie giggled so much that her whole body shook. 'Wait till I tell you! Iss a fantastic idea!'

Bev was all ears.

Fifty yards from the school stood a detached Edwardian town house with a gracious solidity to it. Unlike many of the buildings in the road, it was in a good state of repair. The Ainsley Annexe was an important and much-used part of Woodfield. It was the place where unruly kids were sent to be ground into submission. The Sin Bin. Home of the school hard cases.

Don Sheen was in the back bedroom, which was used as the staff room. Slumped in a decaying armchair, he was marking some essays with a black biro. Don wore jeans, an open-necked red shirt and a pair of trainers. His long hair looked like a vandalized bird's nest. He believed in the casual approach and it often brought him into conflict with older members of the staff.

The huge figure of Basher Bowen came into the room.

'Some people don't have homes to go to,' he said.

'Oh, hello, Bryn.'

'Still here, boyo? Gone five o'clock.'

'Thought I'd stay behind and finish these essays.'

'You must be a glutton for punishment.'

Basher Bowen was a genial Welshman who might have been carved out of granite. A massive, powerful man with a craggy face which had survived many rounds in a boxing ring, Basher was the Dean of Discipline at the school. It made him the automatic choice to run the Sin Bin. Don Sheen was his assistant there, the only other member of staff to work at the Annexe on a regular basis.

'Anyway, what are you doing here?' asked Don.

'Came back for these,' explained Basher, taking a plastic box out of a sports bag. 'Tuna sandwiches. Got to have some grub before I can face my evening class.'

'Badminton?'

'That's Thursdays. Tonight it's weight training. The local lads pumping iron in the hope of becoming Mr Universe.'

Basher had been Head of P.E. before taking over responsibility for discipline at Woodfield. He was still involved with a number of sports and kept himself in prime condition.

'Expected you to have buzzed off by now, Don.'

'Not tonight.'

'Aren't you seeing whatsername?'

'Katie. No, I'm afraid not.'

The Welshman raised a bushy eyebrow in surprise.

'Eh, you two haven't split up or anything, have you?'

'Of course not, Bryn.'

'So what's the problem?'

'Katie's gone away on a course. For six weeks.'

'Dieu! No wonder you're hanging around here with nowhere to go. Six weeks is a long time. Where is the course?'

'Southampton.'

'And what's it on?'

'Remedial education.'

'Katie should've come *here*, mun,' argued Basher. 'We could have shown her our brand of remedial education. Learning by ordeal!' He clapped his colleague on the shoulder. 'Never mind, Don. You'll be able to go and see her for weekends.'

'Not allowed. The course is residential.' Don heaved a sigh. 'Besides, I don't think my motorbike would make it to Southampton and back. It rattles like mad when I go above thirty.'

Basher was sympathetic. He knew that Don spent a lot of time with his girlfriend. They would miss each other while they were apart.

'That mean you're going to be mooning around the Sin Bin every evening?' asked the Welshman. 'Because we can't have that.'

'What do you suggest?'

'A game of snooker with me now and again.'

'You're on, Bryn.'

'And you're welcome to call round to our house any evening. If you bring the beer and crisps, I'll supply the telly and the intellectual conversation.'

Don Sheen grinned. He and Basher got on remarkably well for two people who had such different views on how the Sin Bin should be run. Don promised to take his friend up on his offer.

'One thing,' added Basher.

'What's that?'

'If you want female company, there's an easy answer.'

'Is there?'

'Yes, mun. Go across to the main school and chat up Lambo.'

'No thanks!'

Don paled at the thought. Mrs Lambert was the fearsome Head of Science and her imperious manner cowed most of the staff as well as the pupils. Don would be giving her a wide berth.

'I'll just throw myself into my work,' he said.

'Don't overdo it.'

'The Sin Bin is the most valuable part of Woodfield.'

'Hadn't noticed.'

'This is where the *real* education takes place,' insisted Don. 'There's a limit to what you can do with classes of thirty-five or more. Over here, we only deal with a handful of kids. Ideal situation. We can give them individual attention.'

'A boot up each backside.'

'You have your way, Bryn. I have mine.'

'Well, don't get carried away,' warned the Welshman. 'Know what your trouble is, boyo? You take your job too seriously. This is a punishment block not a rehabilitation centre.'

'It should be both,' insisted Don. 'I'll prove it.'

* * *

It seemed like a good idea at the time. When Bev had slept on it, however, she started to have doubts. The plan was too dangerous. It could easily go wrong. Besides, she was not sure that she wanted to get her own back on Froggy Parsons. She was annoyed when he kept the class in and made her miss a shopping expedition with her mother, but that annoyance had worn off now. Left to herself, Bev would much rather put the incident behind her.

As she strolled along a busy Woodfield Road next morning, she hoped that Abbie had second thoughts as well. Then they could call the whole thing off. It was the only sensible thing to do.

Her hopes were doomed as soon as Abbie ran up to her.

'Hi, Bev! Ready?'

'Well . . .'

'Come on – quick! The phone box is empty.'

Before she could protest, Bev was hustled along the pavement and into the telephone box that was within sight of the school. Abbie was in a state of high excitement. She had clearly been looking forward to their little adventure.

'I'm not sure that we should do this,' said Bev hurriedly.

'Why nor?'

'It's going too far.'

'Wass gor into you, then? Scared?'

'No!'

'Sounds like it to me.'

'Look, let's talk it over, Abbie.'

'Nothin' to say,' declared the other girl, sweeping aside her objections. 'Now, pick up the phone and ger on with it.'

'*Me?*' Bev was horrified.

'Who else?'

'I can't do it.'

'You'll 'ave to, Bev. You're the one with the voice. You sounds much older than me. Iss gorra be you.'

Abbie was right about the voice. It sounded deep and

almost adult. Bev was the most well-spoken girl in the fourth year. Moreover, her voice had only a faint trace of the local accent. Everyone else spoke with the unmistakable Midlands vowels but not Bev. It was one of the things that set her apart from the other kids and made her unpopular. Abbie was her only close friend and she valued the friendship a great deal.

Fear of losing it kept her in the telephone box.

'Go on, Bev. Gerra move on.'

'You do it.'

'Stop messin' about or we'll be too late.'

'Abbie . . .'

But there was a glint in the other's eye which told Bev that argument was useless. She had to go through with it now. All she could do was to grit her teeth and get it over as quickly as possible.

'What if they find out it was us?' she whispered.

'Norra chance.'

'I don't know what to do.'

'Pick up the phone and dial 999.'

'And then?'

'We agreed all this larst night. Juss do it!'

Bev nodded. Her hands were trembling now and she felt herself begin to perspire. Taking a deep breath, she lifted the receiver and dialled the number. The response was immediate. A crisp female voice came on the line.

'Operator. Which service do you require?'

'Uh . . .'

'Can you hear me, caller? Which service do you require?'

'Fire brigade,' said Bev.

'I'm trying to connect you . . .'

After a momentary pause, there was a click and then a man's voice came on the line. It was calm and business-like.

'Central Fire Station . . .'

'Hello . . . I, uh, want to report a fire.'

'Where exactly is it, please?'

'Woodfield School,' replied Bev, almost gabbling now. 'I can see smoke going up from the main building. And flames. It looks serious.'

'Can I have your name and number, please.'

'What?' Mild panic set in.

'Your name and number.'

'I'm Wendy Brown and I work at the Royal Hotel,' mumbled Bev. 'I'm ringing from the phone box in Woodfield Road. We can *see* the fire from here. Hurry!'

She slammed the receiver down and put a hand to her thumping heart. It had shaken her to her roots. Abbie kissed her on the cheek.

'You were terrific, Bev!'

'Was I?'

'Thar bit about bein' Wendy Brown. Dead clever.'

'I had to say something.'

'Come on. Less go see the fun.'

'I'm still not happy about this, Abbie.'

'Where's the 'arm?' retorted the other. 'Iss nor as if we really did set fire to the school. We only *pretended* to.'

They left the telephone box and walked down to the next corner. Their first lesson that morning was swimming which meant that they had to report to the public baths, but they could not turn their backs on the school yet. They wanted to see if their hoax had worked. As other pupils streamed past them on their way to the main gates, they stood on the corner and waited impatiently.

'Wass keepin' 'em?' demanded Abbie.

'I don't know.'

'Fire Station's only a coupla blocks away.'

'Maybe they didn't believe it was a real alarm.'

Inwardly, she was hoping that this was the case. It would let Bev off the hook completely. Under pressure from Abbie, she had made the emergency call but she now prayed that it would not be heeded.

Her prayer went unanswered. The telltale klaxon soon

13

wailed above the buzz of traffic. An urgent fire engine soon came charging around the corner at the other end of Woodfield Road.

'Whoopee!' yelled Abbie.

'We did it,' murmured Bev.

'Not one, not two . . . but *three*!'

'Oh dear!'

'I'd love to see Froggy's face when they rolls in!'

The three fire engines caused a stir along the road. Traffic stopped to let them past, people came out of their houses to stare and Woodfield pupils were mesmerized. When the first of the vehicles swung into the school premises, a spontaneous cheer went up from the kids. Was the place *really* on fire?

'Well done, Bev!' said Abbie, patting her back.

'It was your idea.'

'Told you it'd work.'

'Let's walk down to the baths,' suggested Bev nervously.

'No 'urry.'

'Someone might see us.'

'With three fire engines to goggle at? Doan be stupid.'

'I'd still rather go, Abbie.'

'We gor nothin' to worry about.'

'Are you sure?'

'Yeah!' came the confident reply. 'No way they can trace thar call to us. We nor only gor our revenge on Froggy, we're in the clear. I feels great! Doan you?'

'I suppose so . . .'

But Bev's mind was in a turmoil. Fear, guilt, remorse, amusement and elation were all jumbled together. She simply did not know what to think. Her instinct was to get away from the scene. Only when she reached the baths did she feel safe.

They could not touch her now.

Froggy Parsons was quivering with rage. Confronted with the fire brigade in the playground, he realized immediately that they must have come in response to a hoax call. He apologized profusely to the helmeted Captain Riggs and promised that the culprit would be caught. The fire chief was able to give him a vital clue as to the identity of the miscreant. When the fire engines had gone, the headmaster rushed off to his study and summoned two people – Mrs Craig, his deputy, and Basher Bowen. While they sat in chairs, Froggy paced up and down like a caged animal.

He addressed them as if conducting a murder inquiry.

'This is a black day in the annals of Woodfield School.'

'So is every other day,' murmured Basher cynically.

'The person or persons responsible for this criminal act must be tracked down and punished immediately.'

'Yes, headmaster,' said Mrs Craig.

'Fortunately, that should not be too difficult.'

'How come?' asked Basher. 'Did the mystery caller leave his name, address and a set of fingerprints?'

'We are dealing with a young woman here, Mr Bowen,' replied Froggy. 'That makes it even more disturbing. With a bit of luck, Mrs Craig can tell us who the girl is.'

'Can I?'

Mrs Craig was a big, well-groomed woman in her fifties. Always impeccably dressed, she had a weakness for strong perfume. She and Basher watched as the headmaster strode behind his desk and lifted up a cassette recorder like a magician pulling a rabbit from a top hat.

'This is our secret weapon!' he announced.

'Her voice is on tape?' said Basher.

'They have so many hoax calls at the fire station that they now record all messages as a matter of course. I've only heard it through once but the voice is vaguely familiar. Mrs Craig will know it, I'm certain. Listen.'

He depressed the switch and the message was replayed. Bev's voice was hollow and distant but quite recognizable. Mrs Craig had taught the girl for the last three years. She shook her head in disbelief. It was the very last voice she had expected.

'That's Beverly Kington of 4C.'

'Are you certain?' pressed Froggy.

'Absolutely. What other pupil is so well-spoken?'

'That false name she gave,' noted Basher. 'Rings a bell.'

'It should do,' continued Mrs Craig. 'Wendy Brown was in the sixth form a couple of years ago. And she *does* work at the Royal Hotel. I remember doing a reference for her. Nice girl, if a trifle precocious. When she was here, she seemed to spend all her time canoodling in a corner with her boyfriend – Philip Kington.'

'Beverly's brother!' observed Froggy triumphantly.

'I believe they're now engaged,' added the deputy.

'That clinches it,' decided the headmaster. 'When she gave a false name, Beverly obviously chose the first one that came into her head. Wendy Brown. Easy to see why she selected that particular name.'

'Is the girl a troublemaker?' asked Basher.

'Far from it,' answered Mrs Craig. 'I'm astonished she's mixed up in anything like this. Beverly is a model pupil. And she comes from such a good home.'

'That means nothing these days,' remarked Froggy.

'Quite,' agreed Basher. 'And whatever kind of home she comes from, she can't be allowed to call out the fire brigade for fun.'

'I will impress that upon her,' asserted the headmaster, pounding the desk with his fist. 'You will be having a new guest at the Annexe, Mr Bowen. Show her no mercy. This is a shameful episode in Woodfield's history. I will exact full payment.' He put a hand on his hip and struck a pose. 'Miss Beverly Kington of 4C will not know what hit her.'

16

Chapter Two

The main pool was a bubbling cauldron of noise and laughter. Shrieks, giggles and yells echoed as the girls splashed about in the water. Some of the keener swimmers took part in races up and down the pool, while others put in some diving practice on the springboard. But most of them just flailed happily about and enjoyed themselves.

Miss Whitnall, the lithe, young gym teacher, patrolled the edge of the pool in a green tracksuit. Occasionally, she would blow her whistle to stop the pandemonium or to establish control while she organized another race. There was a wide range of ability and she tried to cater for it all. When she was not supervising the mini gala, she was coaching the weaker swimmers, building up their confidence in the water and getting them to work on some elementary exercises. They all liked Miss Whitnall. She was friendly, easy-going and genuinely interested in them.

Bev and Abbie were enthusiastic divers. After ten minutes on the springboard, they graduated to the highboard where they could attempt more ambitious dives. Abbie was bolder, hurling herself into all kinds of positions before spearing her way into the pool. It was Bev, however, who had the real style. Far more graceful while executing a dive, her entry was always markedly cleaner.

She did a backward somersault from the highboard and hit the water at a perfect angle. Her impetus took her right to the bottom. When she surfaced, she found Abbie waiting for her.

'Why carn *I* do it as good as thar?' she complained.

'It's only a question of practice, Abbie.'

'Iss the way I'm built. Too short and skinny.'

'You're a smashing diver,' encouraged Bev.

'Thanks.' She smiled wickedly. 'First to the far end.'

'Right.'

But it was not a fair contest. Before Bev could move, Abbie's hand pushed her head under the water. The shorter girl then stole a lead of three or four yards.

'Come back, you cheat!' Bev spluttered.

She set off in hot pursuit. Abbie's breaststroke was smooth and steady but it was no match for her friend's crawl. Bev soon overhauled her and won the race. They shared a breathless laugh.

Swimming was always a favourite period for the two girls. It took them out of themselves. For Bev especially it worked wonders that morning. She forgot all about her trial in the telephone box. Doubts and apprehension vanished. She was having a whale of a time.

A shrill blast on the whistle brought her back to reality.

'Bev!' called Miss Whitnall. 'Bev Kington!'

'Yes, miss?'

'Over here, please.'

Bev shrugged then swam across to the side of the pool. The gym teacher was now standing on the side with a chubby girl from the upper sixth. Bev recognized her as a prefect.

'Come on out, Bev,' said Miss Whitnall.

'OK.'

Bev hauled herself out of the water and straightened up. She was dripping freely. Pulling off her bathing cap, she shook out her hair. Then she gave a polite smile to the teacher.

'What's wrong, miss?'

'Get dressed, Bev.'

'*Now*?'

'You have to go back to school.'

'Why?'

18

'Mr Parsons wants to see you in his study.'

The prefect could not resist a podgy grin.

'Iss urgent,' she said.

Bev reeled. Her face went bright crimson. She guessed what must have happened. The practical joke had somehow backfired.

They knew.

Don Sheen liked to get to know the pupils under his charge. When a new boy or girl was sent to the Annexe, he always made time to be alone with them. By chatting informally, he found, he could often break down some of their defensive barriers and get through to the root of their problems. It was a productive exercise.

'First time in the Sin Bin?'

'Yeah, sir.'

'Afraid?'

'No, sir.'

'Think you'll survive?'

'Dunno, sir.'

'Did you really smash up a desk?'

'Sort of. Bur it was an accident.'

'Tell me about it.'

Thick thought it over. He studied the teacher warily as he tried to weigh him up. Don Sheen had a reputation for dabbling in psychology. Though he was not really sure what psychology was, Thick was nevertheless frightened of it. He elected to clam up.

Don shifted to another tack.

'Why do they call you Thick?'

'Dunno, sir.'

'Do you mind?'

'Nor really.'

'Doesn't it get to you sometimes?' pressed the teacher.

'Eh?'

'Isn't that what happened with the desk? They goaded

19

you until you lost your temper. Am I right?'

Barry Dobrowski retreated into silence again. He was a sturdy boy of medium height with a big, flat, scowling face. The close-set eyes and the crew cut gave him a slightly menacing appearance. Polish by birth, he still had the vestiges of an accent. Because he was broad of body and slow of mind, he had been assigned his demeaning nickname. Thick. It was unkind but it suited him.

'What are your plans for the future, Barry?'

'Gor none, sir.'

'Have you no idea what you'd like to be?'

'No.'

'What does your father do?'

The boy shrugged. Don understood. Mr Dobrowski was unemployed.

'Any brothers or sisters at Woodfield?' asked the teacher.

'One sister.'

'What class?'

'2B.'

'Then I daresay she looks up to her big brother in the fifth form. How does she feel about this? You being sent to the Sin Bin?'

'Who cares?'

'I do, Barry.'

Thick regarded him with suspicion. He did not trust teachers. They were all the same. Only interested in the bright kids. They either ignored him or treated him with amused contempt. Why should Don Sheen be any different?

The door opened and Basher came in.

'What's this, then? New member of staff?'

'Barry Dobrowski, 5D,' explained Don. 'Just joined us.'

'I thought he would sooner or later,' said Basher, beaming down at the boy. 'Thick by name and thick by nature. You're just my weight, sunshine. I'll soon sort you out.'

'He's in my class,' Don reminded him.

'Then what's he doing here in the staff room? He ought

to be in the cage with the rest of the monkeys. Feeding time at one o'clock.'

Thick Dobrowski was all too used to this kind of sarcasm. Don could see the boy's resentment deepen. There was no point in talking any further to him. Certainly not while Basher was present. Don sent the lad back to the classroom and told him to get on with the work that was set. Then he turned back to his colleague.

'Don't ride him, Bryn. He needs help.'

'That thug? All he needs is sitting on – hard! And I'd be grateful if you didn't bring him into the staff room for one of your little chats. This is *our* territory. He's a trespasser.'

'You got that message across to him.'

Don looked towards the door and shook his head. Thick Dobrowski was going to be a problem. He could sense it. The boy had erected so many barriers it was impossible to get through to him. One of the main things to do was to keep him away from Basher. Effective as the Welshman's methods were with some kids, they were quite wrong for someone like Thick. He needed understanding.

Basher Bowen flopped into a chair and chuckled.

'Never learn, do you, boyo?'

'I won't browbeat my pupils, if that's what you mean.'

'Discipline never hurt anybody.'

'It's not the complete answer, Bryn.'

'Know what your trouble is?'

'What?'

'You always feel *sorry* for them. Fatal.'

It was true that Don had a lot of compassion. This was often mistaken for weakness and it earned him the nickname of Mister Softee. He refused to write any pupil off as a hopeless case. He believed that there was some good in all of them. Finding it and bringing it out was his mission.

Thick Dobrowski was his latest recruit.

He knew the boy would present a challenge for him.

*   *   *

21

'I'm Wendy Brown and I work at the Royal Hotel. I'm ringing from the phone box in Woodfield Road. We can *see* the fire from here. Hurry!'

Bev was condemned out of her own mouth.

As she listened to the cassette recording, she went numb all over. It never occurred to her that her emergency call would be taped at the fire station. She was trapped. The irony was that the hoax hadn't even been her idea. Forced into it against her will, she would now have to suffer the consequences.

Froggy Parsons sat behind his desk. Mrs Craig stood beside him. Their expressions were grim and judgmental. Bev felt as if she were in the dock in a court of law. The headmaster looked as if he was about to pronounce a death sentence.

'This is a truly appalling offence,' he began.

'We're disappointed in you, Beverly,' scolded Mrs Craig.

'Profoundly disappointed,' said Froggy. 'Before I go into the full implications of this outrage, I have two questions to ask you. First – why did you do it?'

Bev lowered her head in embarrassment and shifted her feet.

'Come along, girl,' he prompted. 'Why?'

'It was . . . a sort of joke, sir.'

'A joke! A *joke*!' Froggy stamped a foot for emphasis. 'Is this the kind of thing that amuses you? Wasting the time of the fire brigade with a false alarm?'

'Sorry, sir,' whispered Bev.

'It's no good saying that now.'

'I didn't mean any harm.'

'Well, you created plenty,' he said in an aggrieved tone. 'I've had the education office on to me three times already. And the local newspaper wants to send a photographer around.'

Bev shuddered. The thought of publicity terrified her. She had done wrong and expected to be punished, but her one

22

hope was that she could somehow keep it from her parents. If her name appeared in the paper, she was doomed.

'Let's come to my second question,' resumed Froggy. 'Who was involved apart from you?'

'Nobody, sir.'

'Don't lie to me, girl. You had an accomplice. Somebody put you up to this, didn't they?'

'No, sir.'

'You're shielding someone. I know it.'

'Was it Abigail Reynolds?' probed Mrs Craig.

Bev bit her lip and shook her head. On the journey from the swimming baths, Bev had vowed that she would not tell on Abbie. Even though her friend had got her into trouble, Bev was going to protect her. It was a duty.

'Tell the truth,' urged Froggy.

'You'd never do a thing like this by yourself,' argued the deputy. 'My guess would be Abigail Reynolds.'

'She's nothing to do with this,' said Bev quietly.

'Then who is?' pressed Froggy.

'No one, sir.'

'Heavens above, girl! You just gave yourself away in that taped message. You said that "we" can see the fire from here. Who is "we"? You and whom else?'

'I was on my own, sir.'

'Give us the name!' he howled, jabbing an accusing finger at her. 'Unmask your accomplice.'

Bev was frightened but her lips were sealed. Apart from anything else, if she gave Abbie away, the friendship between the two girls was over. Bev could not risk that. She would endure any punishment rather than confess the truth.

'We shall find out,' cautioned the headmaster. 'We have other means of detection. Dozens of people were passing along Woodfield Road while you were in that telephone box. There must be witnesses.'

'Let me have a word with Abigail,' suggested Mrs Craig. 'I'll get to the bottom of this, headmaster.'

Froggy nodded then turned to glare vengefully at Bev.

'You have let the whole school down, girl.'

'Yes, sir.'

'You have forfeited the right to stay within it.'

Bev almost fainted. Were they going to expel her?

'Until further notice,' he said darkly, 'your education will continue at the Ainsley Annexe. That is where we send the criminal element at Woodfield. When you leave this study, you will report to Mr Bowen. He will be expecting you.'

Bev nodded. Her mouth had gone dry.

'One last thing,' added Froggy, consulting a record card that lay on the desk in front of him. 'I understand that your father is the manager of a building society.'

'Yes, sir,' she admitted, tensing with anxiety.

'Which one?'

'The Halifax.'

'I intend to ring him to explain the situation.'

'Oh, please don't do that, sir,' she begged. 'He hates being contacted at work.'

'He's entitled to know about his daughter's misbehaviour.'

'*I'll* tell him, sir,' she lied. 'When I go home.'

'It's not quite as straightforward as that, I'm afraid. Your father and I need to discuss a financial matter. This little escapade has a cost attached to it.'

'Cost?' Bev's mind was racing.

'You alerted three fire engines, each with a full complement aboard. Their time is money. Captain Riggs estimated that your alarm call occupied his men for a total of twenty minutes. Then, of course, there is the cost of the petrol for the vehicles. When it is all added up, it could come to a substantial amount.'

Bev wished that the floor would open and swallow her up.

'Count yourself lucky, Beverly,' advised Mrs Craig. 'Thanks to Mr Parsons, this has remained a school matter. He persuaded the fire brigade not to hand you over to the police. Otherwise, you might have faced prosecution and a hefty fine. Imagine how your parents would have reacted to that.'

It did not bear thinking about. Bev did not know how she was going to face them as it was. They would be mortified.

That one short phone call had ruined her life.

Abbie had been worried when her friend was summoned out of the swimming pool but she was very skilled at hiding her feelings. When the other girls asked her about Bev, she came up with a plausible excuse for her sudden departure. The important thing was to keep calm. When they had got dressed again, the girls headed towards the school in a crocodile. Abbie trailed at the rear.

Miss Whitnall made a point of walking beside her.

'Why was Bev hauled off like that?'

'Dunno, miss.'

'Come on, Abbie. There's not much you don't know about Bev. You two live in each other's pockets. Now, what's going on?'

'Search me.'

'And we'll do without the cheek, thank you.'

'Yeah, miss.'

'What have you and Bev been up to?'

'Nothin'! 'oness!'

'Mr Parsons wouldn't send for her unless it was something really serious.' Miss Whitnall started fishing. 'I don't suppose it has anything to do with those fire engines, has it?'

'Wor fire engines, miss?'

Abbie looked as if butter would not melt in her mouth. The teacher found it impossible to dislike the girl. She was lively, cheerful and good company. But she was also strong-willed. Miss Whitnall would not break her down easily.

'OK,' said the teacher resignedly. 'Play it your way. But don't think I'm fooled by that innocent face. I know you too well.'

As the crocodile wended its way in through the main gates,

two figures were coming across the playground. A crestfallen Bev was being escorted by the chubby prefect. The picture told its own story. Eager classmates pressed for gory details.

'Wass up, Bev?'

'You in trouble?'

'Wor did Froggy wann you for?'

'Where you goin'?'

The prefect allowed herself a smirk of self-importance.

'The Sin Bin.'

Shock and amazement spread. Beverly Kington was one of the best-behaved pupils in the class. What could she have *done*?

Abbie wanted another question answered. She traded a brief glance with Bev and got her reply. Her friend had not implicated her. Relief flooded through Abbie. She was off the hook.

Still speculating wildly about Bev's punishment, the girls went into the main block and made for their classroom. Abbie was the last through the door. The stately figure of the deputy head awaited her.

'Ah, there you are, Abigail!'

'Wass up, miss?'

'Perhaps I could have a word with you . . .'

When they crossed the road and reached the Annexe, the building seemed to loom above Bev like a prison. Everything she had ever heard about the Sin Bin had served to make her glad she had never been sent there. That fate had now befallen her. Was it really as tough and painful as was claimed? Were the rumours about corporal punishment true? Bev was stricken with cold terror.

The prefect led the way up the steps and in through the front door. They went along a passageway then stopped outside the door of what had once been the spacious living room. Bunching her fist, the prefect knocked hard.

'Come in!' roared Basher.

The prefect opened the door, ushered in Bev then withdrew. Eight or nine youths were seated at their desks. They looked up from their work. Seeing Bev, they gave her a few wolf whistles.

'Belt up, you sex maniacs!' ordered Basher. He rose from his seat and tossed his *Daily Mirror* aside. 'Let's go outside.'

It was a small mercy but Bev was grateful. She hated having to stand there while the boys leered at her. Basher closed the door behind them then appraised her carefully.

'So you're Beverly Kington.'

'Yes, sir.'

'What's a nice girl like you doing in a nasty place like this?'

'Mr Parsons sent me, sir.'

'I know. You been playing naughty tricks, haven't you? Making a hoax call to the fire brigade.' His bushy eyebrows arched in concern. 'I know you thought it was fun but let me ask you this. How would you feel if *your* house was on fire and they didn't get there in time to save it because they were out answering a false alarm? Get my point? Instead of wasting their time at Woodfield, those fire engines might have been needed at a *real* fire.'

'Yes, sir.' Bev was contrite.

'Think twice next time.'

'I will, sir.'

'Right,' he said briskly. 'Let's get you sorted out. I won't have you in my class. That's reserved for the old lags. You'll be in with Mr Sheen. Ever had him before?'

'No, sir.'

'Treat in store for you.' He pointed to the staircase. 'Go on up and turn right. Front bedroom.'

'Yes, sir.'

Basher watched her go. The real reason she was not in his class was that he felt uneasy when imposing discipline on girls. His jovial violence worked best on boys. He went back to his morning crossword.

Bev, meanwhile, hovered outside the front bedroom and

tried to pluck up enough courage to knock. The decision was taken out of her hands because the door suddenly opened from within. She stepped back as a rather scruffy individual faced her.

'Thought I heard someone out here,' said Don Sheen.

'I'm, uh . . . I'm Beverly Kington, sir.'

'Ah, yes. Mr Bowen mentioned you. Step on in.'

The atmosphere of this classroom was very different. No sense of hard grind and strict discipline. Only four pupils occupied the room. All boys. None of them ogled her or whistled. They just stared in blank surprise.

Don's manner was much gentler than that of Basher Bowen. He had none of the Welshman's towering physical presence or heavy-handed humour. Don actually smiled at her. Bev relaxed slightly.

'This is Beverly Kington,' he introduced. 'I'm sure you've all seen her around Woodfield. She'd brighten up any school. For the time being, she's come over here to spend some time with you. I hope you'll all make her welcome.'

There was some general muttering and a few nods.

'I think we'll put you over here, Beverly,' said Don.

He took her across to a desk in the corner of the room. What pleased her most was that everyone else now had his back to her. She would not be under scrutiny. Bev put her bag on the floor and sat down. It was rather odd being the only girl on the premises.

The four boys resumed their work. Bev knew three of them by name. Calvin Hubberd had been in her class lower down the school. Steve Sadler and Greg Escott were seasoned troublemakers from 4B. She did not know what the thickset Polish boy was called but she had seen him around. His muscular intensity was a little unsettling.

'Do you have some paper?' asked Don.

'Yes, sir,' she said, taking a loose-leaf pad from her bag.

'Then you can start by writing something for me. When people come here for the first time, it can be a shock to the

28

system. I try to help them come to terms with it. Tell me three things, Beverly. Why you were sent here. What your preconceptions are about the Sin Bin. And whether or not you think your punishment is just.' He smiled again. 'Never met a kid yet who felt that it was, mind you, but there's always hope. OK, get weaving. I don't want a thesis. A page will do.'

Bev took out a pen and chewed the end of it as she searched for her opening sentence. It was more difficult than she thought. To put down the details of her crime was humiliating. She had to force her pen into action. It was hard going.

Don let her get on with it. He went from one boy to another, helping each with his assignment, talking in a low, coaxing voice that still preserved its Midlands accent. Don was a local boy who had returned from university to work in his home town. It helped him to identify with the kids and most of them appreciated that.

It was almost an hour before Bev finally finished. She blushed as she read through what she had written. On impulse, she wanted to tear the paper into tiny shreds but she resisted the temptation. She had come to the Annexe for punishment. This was part of it.

Don glanced across at her. His tone was casual.

'By the way, Beverly. Can you make tea?'

'I think so, sir.'

'Then we're going to get along famously.'

His words were to be prophetic.

Chapter Three

Martin Kington was a tall, slim, angular man in his late thirties. He ran the local branch of the Halifax building society. His customers found him efficient and reliable but his staff thought him too fussy. He had thinning hair and a habit of stroking his natty moustache. Always smartly dressed, he looked as if he had been born in a grey pinstripe suit.

When the headmaster rang him, Martin was interviewing a young couple about their mortgage requirements. Froggy threw him into a spin. He could not believe that his daughter was responsible for the hoax call. When he finished with the young couple, he telephoned his wife and broke the news to her. Sheila Kington, a rather fraught woman at the best of times, was scandalized. Her first thought was for herself.

'How can I hold my head up after this?' she moaned.

'Let's keep it in perspective, dear.'

'What will the neighbours say?'

'Who knows?'

'I won't be able to cope, Martin. I just won't.'

'Calm down, Sheila. We'll get through this somehow.'

His wife was aghast. 'Did Beverly really do such a thing?'

'I'm going around to the school to find out right now,' he told her. 'I want chapter and verse on this. Yes, and I want to know how much this so-called joke is going to cost me.'

The manager rang off and told his staff that he was slipping out of the office. Ten minutes later, he was being shown into Froggy's study at Woodfield. They went painstakingly through the details of what had happened and Martin was forced to accept that his daughter was indeed to blame.

'But there are extenuating circumstances, headmaster.'

'Are there?'

'Beverly did not act of her own volition.'

'That is our feeling, Mr Kington.'

'Someone talked her into this. Abbie Reynolds, probably.'

'Almost certainly,' agreed the headmaster. 'The difficult thing is to prove it. Mrs Craig tackled the girl this morning but got nothing out of her. Abigail is a rather defiant creature at times.'

'I've never liked her myself,' said Martin.

'But you see our problem, don't you? Unless we get a confession from one or other of them, we can't actually tie Abigail in with this deplorable episode.'

'Beverly will tell the truth!' insisted her father.

'She has not managed to do so as yet, Mr Kington.'

'Wait till *I* have a talk with her.'

'Your assistance would be appreciated. In the meantime . . .'

'Yes, yes,' conceded Martin. 'I'll gladly settle the bill from the fire brigade. And I'll make sure that Beverly writes to this Captain Riggs with an apology.'

'It's heartening to hear you say that,' observed Froggy. 'So many of our parents take a very hostile attitude when we have to discipline their children. I'm glad to know that you approve of what we have done.'

'I do, headmaster. You were right to send her to the Ainsley Annexe. A short, sharp shock is exactly what she needs.' He stroked his moustache absent-mindedly. 'And it's exactly what she'll get when she comes home today.'

'Don't forget to ask her about her accomplice.'

'Leave it to me.'

Froggy sighed. 'I'd hoped we could find eye-witnesses who saw the two girls together in the telephone box. We asked every class in the school. But children have this ridiculous sense of false loyalty to each other. Nobody would come forward.'

31

'Beverly will. I promise you.'

'Her corroboration is vital.'

'You'll get it, headmaster. I know my daughter.'

But Martin did not know her as well as he imagined.

When the bell sounded to end the school day, Abbie was the first to pack up and rush out through the door. It took her just over a minute to get across to the Sin Bin. She waited impatiently until the pupils began to trickle out. Calvin Hubberd was among them.

'Eh, Cal!' she called. 'You see Bev?'

'Yeah. She's in my clarss.'

'Where is she?'

'Makin' tea for Basher and Mister Softee.' He gave her a gap-toothed grin. 'Thar used to be *my* job. Bev's welcome to it.'

Calvin was a short, stubby Jamaican boy with a happy-go-lucky attitude to life. A natural rebel, he drifted in and out of the Annexe all the time. Its strictures had no real effect on him.

'See you, Ab!' he said, bounding off down the road.

'Yeah. Cheerio, Cal.'

Abbie waited for several more agonizing minutes. Pleased to have eluded punishment herself, she was very worried about how Bev would take it. She feared that her friend would crack under the pressure of the Sin Bin. Bev was altogether too sensitive.

When the girl finally came out of the house, she looked pale and haggard. Abbie leapt forward to embrace her.

'At larst!'

'Hi, Abbie.'

'Well? 'ow was it?'

'Not very nice.'

'Who you gor? Basher Bowen?'

'Mr Sheen.'

'You're larfin', then. 'e woan 'urt you.'

'It still wasn't very pleasant in there.'

'Tell us all about it, Bev . . .'

They fell in beside each other and strolled up Woodfield Road. Bev gave a halting version of what had occurred since she had been unceremoniously yanked out of the swimming baths. Abbie listened intently and put a consoling arm around her friend's shoulders.

'Iss all my fault,' she admitted.

'I shouldn't have let you talk me into it.'

'The idea was OK. Wor I never thort about was gerrin' caught. I mean, fancy recordin' your voice like thar. Of all the dirty, rotten, stinkin' tricks!'

'I nearly died when they played me the tape.'

'Doan blame you. I'd 'ave 'ad kittens.'

'Froggy kept on at me about my accomplice.'

'Wor did you say?'

'Nothin'.'

'Good girl!'

'I'd never split on you, Abbie.'

'Thanks! You're a real friend.'

'Has anyone questioned you about it?'

' Oh, yeah,' said Abbie blithely. 'Bur they were wastin' their time. Miss Whitnall 'ad a go at me first. Then ole Sweetness and Light pounced on me.'

'Mrs Craig?'

'Took me orff to 'er room for interrogation. Thar perfume of 'ers doan 'alf pong! Anyway, I juss denied everythin' an' so she 'ad to give up. They'll never ger me!' She tightened her grip on Bev's shoulder. 'I feel awful about you being caught. 'ow long they gonna keep you in the Sin Bin?'

'Indefinitely.'

'Sadists!'

'The Sin Bin is not what I'm worried about, Abbie.'

'Then wor is?'

'My parents. They'll go mad.'

'Ignore 'em. Thass wor I do.'

'It'll be terrible,' predicted Bev. 'I bet they're waiting at home for me right now. All ready to tear me apart.'

'Then lerrem wait.'

'What?'

'If you're gonna ger a bollockin', why nor 'ave it when you feels up to it. Come on. We'll go into town an' 'ave a coffee somewhere. Do us the world o' good.'

'But my parents will expect me back straight away.'

'Thass exactly why you gorra 'ave a few larfs with me first. OK, they'll ger narsty 'cos you're late but – so wor? Iss time you 'ad a birrof independence.'

'Fat chance of that with Mum and Dad.'

'Purrit this way, Bev. Do you wanna spend the rest of your schooldays frightened of wor they're gonna do an' say? Sooner or later, you gorra stand up to 'em. Start right now!'

Bev thought it over. On any other day, fear of her parents would have outweighed all else. But she had been through a lot in the last six hours. She had been made to feel shame and disgrace. If she went home, she would only get more of the same treatment. She needed to get up her strength before subjecting herself to that.

'Where shall we go for coffee?' she asked.

'Thass the spirit!'

Basher Bowen potted the yellow into the top pocket and got perfect position on the green. He sank it with another decisive shot. This time, however, he was not so fortunate.

'Bloody hell! I've snookered myself!'

'I was hoping you would,' said Don Sheen.

'All the colours were there for the taking.'

'Tough.'

Needing to pot the brown, he was instead trapped behind the blue. Escape was difficult. It required a tricky shot off two cushions. Basher played it with care but he was inches off target.

'Damn!' he groaned. 'Four more for you.'

'And the rest,' remarked Don with a quiet grin.

He potted the brown, blue and pink in succession then fluked the black into one of the baulk pockets. Against all the odds, Don had actually won the game.

'*I'm* supposed to be the snooker player!' complained Basher.

'I got lucky, that's all.'

'Set 'em up again.'

'Oh, no. I always quit while I'm winning.'

'One frame. You've got to give me that.'

'Just one, then . . .'

The snooker hall was almost adjacent to the school and Basher was a regular visitor. It enabled him to keep a friendly eye on any pupils who sneaked in there and to make sure there was no under-age drinking at the bar. Don Sheen had for once agreed to join him. Expecting an easy victory, the Welshman was stunned by his defeat.

The two colleagues set the balls up for the next game.

'How was the plodding Polak today?' asked Basher.

'Much the same.'

'Give him up, Don.'

'I could never do that.'

'Kid's nothing but a hooligan,' argued the other. 'You can see it written all over him. Today, it's punch-ups at soccer matches. Tomorrow, it'll be bashing old ladies and stealing their handbags. Thick Dobrowski is your classic psychopath.'

'Only if he's pushed along that road.'

'What choice has he got?'

'None at all if we turn our back on him. I've got faith in the lad. All he really needs is someone to talk to.'

'But you can't get a bloody word out of him!'

'That's because I haven't won his trust yet.'

'Daro! You ask for trouble.'

Basher split the pack to begin the next game. Don chalked

35

his cue and assessed the possibilities. He opted for a safety shot.

'Anyway,' he said. 'Thick Dobrowski is not my main concern.'

'I can guess who is.'

'Beverly Kington.'

'Lovely-looking girl. Decorates the place nicely.'

'She should never be in the Sin Bin at all.'

Basher snorted. 'So what are you supposed to do with a kid who gets three fire engines racing round to the school? Tap her over the knuckles with a ruler and tell her not to do it again?'

'First thing is to understand why she made that call.'

'Obvious, mun. For kicks.'

'Wrong. She got no bang out of it.'

'How do you know?'

'Because I asked her to write an essay about it,' explained Don. 'Talk about conflicted motives. That girl is all churned up.'

Basher played a safety shot of his own then looked up.

'So why did she make that hoax call?'

'She was afraid not to, Bryn.'

'Somebody else pulled the strings?'

'Beverly won't name her. Rather take the rap herself.'

He addressed himself to his next shot.

'Serves her right,' said Basher airily. 'Spoiled middle-class girl thrown in with the yobbo contingent. Open her eyes for her. Show her how the other half lives.' Anguish came into his voice. 'Hey! You just potted two reds with one shot!'

'I was wondering when you'd notice.'

Don Sheen was enjoying his visit to the snooker hall.

Martin and Sheila Kington had plenty of time to work themselves up into a lather of irritation. Not only had their daughter done something dreadful at school, she had failed to come home on time. The couple sat in the lounge of their neat, modern, well-appointed home and became more and more agitated. Bev was almost an hour late.

'Where on earth is she?' demanded Martin.

'I wish I knew,' said his wife.

'This is intolerable!'

'I can't take much more.'

Sheila Kington was a thin, pale, nervous woman with the same straw-coloured hair as her daughter. She wore a dark blue dress with a small handkerchief tucked up one sleeve. Her attractive face with its careful make-up was furrowed by anxiety.

'Oh, Martin,' she gasped. 'You don't suppose anything could have happened to her, do you?'

'No. She's just avoiding us.'

'How can you be so sure?'

'If there had been an accident or anything like that, we'd have heard by now. Beverly is deliberately staying out of our way.'

'But that's not like her.'

'Nor is ringing up the fire brigade!'

His wife reached for the glass on the coffee table and sipped some more of her gin and tonic. She had a talent for making a drama out of almost anything. Her relationship with her children had never been easy and now she feared the worst.

'I do hope it's not going to happen all over again,' she moaned.

'What do you mean?' he asked.

'Philip.'

'That was quite different,' he said curtly.

'He got into trouble at school as well.'

'Only because we didn't stamp hard enough on him at the very start. We won't make that mistake with Beverly. We'll come down on her like a ton of bricks.'

'Whatever got into Beverly?'

The distraught mother drained her glass before putting

it aside. Staring blankly in front of her, she became wistful.

'I wish Philip still lived at home.'

'Don't start all that again,' he snapped.

'I miss him.'

'He left of his own accord, Sheila.'

'That's not quite true.'

'Look, let's keep Philip out of this,' he snapped. 'All we're concerned with now is Beverly.'

Sheila Kington got up from the sofa and roamed aimlessly around the room. She suddenly stopped dead, clenched her fists and let out a small yell of desperation.

'This is too much! Yesterday, she kept me waiting outside Marks and Spencer's for three-quarters of an hour. Today, it's even worse. Where *is* she?'

Before she could burst into tears, they heard the sound of a key in the lock. Martin stood up in readiness. They listened as the front door opened and closed. Seconds later, Bev came into the lounge with her bag over her shoulder.

She was making an effort to be calm and self-possessed.

'Hello,' she said casually.

'Where the hell have you been?' asked Martin.

'I went to McDonald's with Abbie.'

'McDonald's!' He was horrified.

'You are supposed to come straight home,' said Sheila.

'Abbie suggested a coffee.'

'You should have come back *here*, Beverly,' repeated her mother.

Martin fiddled with his moustache and tried to control his temper. He pointed to an armchair.

'Sit down, young lady. We have a lot to discuss.'

Bev perched on the edge of the chair, fearing the worst. Her mother went back to the sofa but her father remained on his feet.

'Mr Parsons rang me this morning,' he said with subdued anger. 'You can imagine how I felt when he told me what you had done. I was appalled. Frankly appalled.'

38

'It was a dreadful blow to us,' recalled Sheila.

'Shaming,' continued her husband. 'I could not believe what I was hearing about my own daughter. Whatever possessed you to do such a thing, Beverly? You must have known it was wrong.'

Not trusting to words, Bev gave an apologetic nod.

'Then there's the money,' said Sheila.

'Exactly,' resumed Martin. 'Do you know how much your hoax call is going to cost me?'

'I'll pay back every penny out of my pocket money,' said Bev.

'*What* pocket money?' retorted her father. 'As of now, you don't get any. And that's only for starters.'

'You've brought it upon yourself,' Sheila pointed out.

'The one tiny consolation in this sorry affair is that you're not entirely to blame.' Martin had another go at his moustache. 'You were persuaded to make that call by someone else.'

'No,' said Bev.

'Abbie Reynolds.'

'No.'

'She's behind this, isn't she?'

'No, Dad.'

'Admit it!' he insisted.

'There's nothing to admit.'

'It was Abbie.'

'But it wasn't.'

'She forced you into it, didn't she?'

'NO!'

Bev's exclamation silenced her father and made him back off. She seized the chance to turn defence into attack, reeling off some of the things that she had rehearsed with Abbie over the coffee.

'Anyway, what's all the fuss about?' she asked. 'OK, I did something stupid but it's not the end of the world. You should see what some of the others get up to at Woodfield.

Lots of girls in my class smoke and quite a few of them go drinking in pubs. That's not to mention all the thieving and swearing and vandalism that goes on.' She shrugged helplessly. 'All I did was to ring the fire brigade.'

'It was enough!' growled Martin.

'We're the ones who have to suffer,' said Sheila.

'And what about me in the Sin Bin?' asked Bev. 'They didn't send me there for a rest cure.'

'Shut up!' snarled her father. He took a deep breath and tried to reason with her. 'Beverly, you are a privileged girl. Unlike most of the children at Woodfield, you come from a very good home.'

'An exceptionally good home,' supported his wife.

'Don't throw those advantages away,' he urged. 'People look up to us. We have a nice house, two cars, foreign holidays. We set the standard. Why do you have to go and spoil it all?'

'It wasn't deliberate,' said Bev.

'Well, it won't happen again,' he asserted. 'I should have seen this coming. It all dates back to the time you became friendly with Abbie Reynolds.'

'She's a bad influence on you,' said Sheila.

'No, she's not,' argued Bev.

'She is,' reinforced her father. 'But she won't be any more. You're to stop being friends with her, Beverly, do you hear?'

'That's cruel!' wailed the girl.

'It's necessary,' he said firmly. 'No walking to school with her, no going out with her and – most definitely – no bringing her into this house. Abbie Reynolds is banned. For good. All right?'

Bev could not even bear the thought of it. Jumping to her feet, she raced out of the room and up the stairs. The door of her bedroom was slammed dramatically after her.

Down in the lounge, Sheila Kington was disturbed.

'Are you sure we've done the right thing, Martin?'

'Quite sure.'
'You said that about Philip.'
A flicker of doubt came into his eyes.

Chapter Four

Thick Dobrowski awoke at six o'clock on a damp, grey morning and rubbed at his eyes with the backs of his hands. Heaving himself out of the narrow bed, he padded off to use the toilet and have a quick wash. When he came back, he pulled off his pyjamas and clambered into his school uniform. His shirt was soiled, his tie was crooked, his trousers were crumpled and his pullover was darned in a very amateurish way on both elbows. Thick didn't believe in mirrors.

He went downstairs to the tiny kitchen and made some breakfast. He was still munching the last of his toast as he wheeled his bicycle out through the front door. Rain was falling in a fine drizzle but he wore no coat. He tucked his trousers into the tops of his socks.

Vale Road was a bleak and battered cul-de-sac off Railway Street. It consisted of twenty houses in competing stages of collapse. Built at the turn of the century, the terraced dwelling had known better days and kinder owners. Since they were all scheduled for demolition, nobody bothered to maintain them. Cracked windows were left. Missing slates were ignored. Fading paintwork was the norm. The overwhelming impression of decay was endorsed by the cluster of second-hand cars along each side of the road. They, too, had given up the ghost.

The Dobrowski household was at the far end. It was joined to its opposite number by the high brick wall which closed off the cul-de-sac and which offered itself as a sitting target to aspiring young artists. Painted slogans, crude drawings and plaintive declarations of love were studded by the ball marks of a thousand soccer matches. Vale Road was simply worn out by overuse.

Thick glanced up at the bedroom of one of the houses then cycled off. His wheels hissed on the wet surface and sent up a delicate spray. Turning into Railway Street, he went all the way down to the bridge then swung left. The newsagent's shop was on the next corner. Thick parked his bicycle and went in. Mr Cappanini was already sorting out the papers. Mumbling a greeting, Thick helped him. Two other paper boys soon joined them. They shared a couple of sniggered jokes at Thick's expense.

It was a long round but it could not be hurried. By the time he had gone back to the shop to leave his bag then cycled home again, it was well past eight o'clock. His father was still in bed. His mother, a round, red-faced woman who was perpetually short of breath, was making breakfast for her daughter and her youngest son. Mrs Dobrowski had just returned from her early-morning stint as a cleaner at the council offices. When the children were off her hands, she would go round to the local fruiterer's where she served part-time.

Thick did not need to go back to Vale Road at all. He could have gone straight to school from the paper shop. His sister, Josie, always dropped young Tom off at his junior school on her way to Woodfield. It was not family duty which brought Thick back to base.

Mrs Dobrowski waddled into the living room and found her eldest son lurking near the window. She gave him a tired smile and held up the letter which had arrived that morning.

'Good news, Barry!' she said.

'Eh?'

'Neil's comin' 'ome on Sat'day.'

'Oh.'

'Woan thar be nice? We'll all be together again.'

'Yeah.'

'Cheer up your Dad, thar will.' She thrust the envelope

into the pocket of her apron. 'Wor shall we do with Neil?'

But he was no longer listening. His attention was fixed on one of the houses opposite. As his mother burbled happily on, he cut right across what she was saying.

'Gorra go, Mum. See you.'

He left in a flash.

After two sessions in the gymnasium, Miss Whitnall was ready for her mid-morning break. It offered her the prospect of a cup of herbal tea and a chat with her colleagues. She flopped into a chair in the staff room and felt better at once. Then Mrs Craig descended upon her. The gym teacher groaned inwardly. She did not get on too well with the deputy head.

'May I join you?' gushed Mrs Craig.

'Please do,' said the other without enthusiasm.

Miss Whitnall recoiled from the aroma of strong perfume as the older woman sat beside her. The deputy head was wearing a beautifully-tailored brown suit with a diamanté brooch on its right lapel. In her old tracksuit, the gym teacher felt shabby by comparison.

'How are you, Miss Whitnall?' said Mrs Craig sweetly.

'Fine, fine.'

'I ought to make more effort to get down to the gymnasium to see some of the excellent work you do there.'

'Thank you.'

'Tell me. Did you teach 4C this morning?'

'First period.'

'What's your view of Abigail Reynolds?'

'Good gymnast when she puts her mind to it. Useful netball player, too, despite her lack of inches. Plenty of aggression.'

'I was thinking more of her character.'

'Ah.' Miss Whitnall understood. 'The hoax call.'

'We feel that Abbie was involved.'

'No doubt about it,' said the other firmly. 'It's exactly

44

the kind of thing Abbie would do. She's always playing practical jokes only she's too clever to get caught. Beverly Kington was obviously set up by Abbie Reynolds.'

'How do we verify that fact, though?' sighed Mrs Craig. 'All we get from both girls is a vehement denial. I just couldn't break Abbie down. She really is a most . . . self-assured young lady.'

'Cocksure is the word I'd use, Mrs Craig.'

'I wondered if you might help us.'

'Me?'

'You seem to have such a rapport with that kind of girl, Miss Whitnall. You talk their language. I don't, I'm afraid. Something about me always makes pupils like that shrink away.'

The gym teacher knew what it was but said nothing.

'You tackle Abbie,' suggested the deputy. 'See if you can catch her off guard. It's awful that she should get away with this.'

'I'll do what I can,' promised the other. 'Abbie is the one who belongs in the Sin Bin. Not Beverly.'

'I do wish you wouldn't use that unfortunate nomenclature,' complained Mrs Craig. 'It is not a Sin Bin. The Ainsley Annexe is a withdrawal centre. We take disruptive pupils out of the system and give them special treatment.'

'Yes,' conceded Miss Whitnall, 'but I don't think that Beverly Kington is robust enough for that special treatment. Bryn Bowen can be something of a slave-driver.'

'Beverly has been assigned to Mr Sheen.'

'Ah, that's different.' She was pleased. 'Don has a much softer approach. He's there to save their souls.'

'If only the man would wear a suit while he's doing it,' said Mrs Craig with disdain. 'Have you *seen* him recently? He doesn't even wear a tie. He looks like Worzel Gummidge.' She rolled her eyes. 'I suppose we ought to be grateful that he doesn't wear an earring.'

Miss Whitnall laughed but only out of politeness.
She rated Don Sheen as the best teacher in the school.

Bev put some hot water into the teapot and swilled it around before pouring it out again. Having warmed the pot, she spooned in three measured quantities of tea. Hot water was added then she put the lid on.

Don Sheen breezed into the staff room at the Annexe and saw what she was doing. He grinned amiably.

'Thank goodness Miss Finch is not here!' he remarked.

'Why, sir?'

'Because she's a keen feminist. Be up in arms if she saw what you're doing now. You're the only female in the building and we've assigned you to tea-making. If that's not sex-typing, what is?'

'I like it, sir.'

'And we like your tea.'

Something told Don that the girl was not yet ready for the kind of long, probing interview he tried to have with each pupil. He had wandered into the staff room so that he could talk to her in a more relaxed, off-duty setting. Opening his battered old briefcase, Don pretended to search about inside.

'So how do you like it here, Beverly?'

'It's all right, sir.'

'That means you prefer the main school.'

'Yes, sir.'

'GCSE next year, isn't it? Then what? Sixth form?'

'I hope so,' she said, rather sheepishly.

'Let me see,' he mused. 'Didn't we have your brother in the sixth form a year or so ago? What was his name – Philip?'

'That's right, sir. He dropped out.'

'Why?'

Bev shrugged. It was clearly a sore point with her.

'Do you make the tea at home?' he asked.

'I never get the chance. Not with Mum around.'

46

'Waits on you hand and foot, does she?'

'A bit, sir.'

While Bev busied herself at the table, he pulled a sheaf of papers out of his briefcase and leafed through them. Don chuckled.

'Ambitious lot, I'll say that for them.'

'What's that, sir?'

'Your four colleagues in the front bedroom.'

'Oh?'

'I asked them to write about what they'd like to do when they leave school.' He glanced down at the papers and grinned. 'Those lads in there certainly think big.'

'Do they?'

'What do *you* see them as in ten years' time, Beverly?'

'I don't really know them, sir.'

'Go on first impressions. Start with Calvin Hubberd.'

'I've no idea, honestly.'

'You've met the kid. Have a guess.'

'A comedian?'

'That's what I would have said but we're both wide of the mark. Calvin wants to own a racing yacht and win the America's Cup in it.'

'A *yacht*?' She laughed involuntarily.

'Amazing, isn't it? Here we are in the heart of England – miles from the nearest coastline – and yet he has set his heart on becoming a champion sailor! Good for him, I say.' He picked out another sheet of paper. 'What about Steve Sadler?'

'Not a clue, sir.'

'Would you believe it if I told you that young hooligan wants to be the next Bruce Springsteen?'

'All boys want to be that,' she noted.

'But he's quite serious about it. Seems he's already got a band going. They practise regularly and have had some bookings locally. Now we come to Greg Escott. I'd pegged him as a cardsharp.'

'What does *he* want to be, sir?'

'Brace yourself.'

'Why?'

'Prime Minister.'

Bev giggled. The idea was totally ludicrous.

'I did warn you,' said Don.

'But Greg isn't politically-minded, is he, sir?'

'Not in the slightest. It's the other aspects of the job that appeal to him. The fame, the fortune, the travelling around the world and being on the telly. Everyone paying attention to him. It's a power fantasy.'

'PM Greg Escott!' She giggled afresh.

'Finally – Barry Dobrowski.'

'Oh.'

'Why do you say that?'

'Well, I've never even heard him open his mouth, sir.'

'He is a boy of few words,' agreed Don, looking down at the relevant sheet of paper, 'and he's not happy expressing himself on paper. But Barry didn't need many words to say what he wants to achieve.'

'What did he say, sir?'

'The most sensible thing of the lot, Beverly. I was unfair on him. At first glance, you'd put him down as a nightclub bouncer. But he's got a serious ambition. He might even fulfil it.'

'Fulfil what, sir?'

Don read out the single sentence in front of him.

' "I want to go back to Poland to help my people." '

'Gosh!'

Bev was quietly impressed. The hulking boy whom the others mocked had a real purpose. They were chasing dreams of glory. He wanted to help someone else. From that moment, Bev stopped being afraid of Thick Dobrowski. He had earned her respect.

'Now for the big question,' said Don.

'Sir?'

'What do *you* want to be?'

Bev was covered in confusion. Blushing with embarrassment, she waved her hands about in the air and shook her head.

'I don't know, sir.'

'You must have some idea, Beverly.'

'No, sir. None at all.'

It was a lie and he knew it. The girl was holding something back. Before he could even begin to find out what it was, however, the door opened and Basher Bowen marched in.

'Where's my tea?' he demanded. 'I like it strong, dark and with three sugars. That's the way to keep old Basher sweet.'

Bev was grateful for the interruption.

Don was determined to resume the conversation another time.

Abbie Reynolds had not realized how much she would miss her friend. There was nobody else like Bev. The two of them were inseparable. As she sat at the back of the class during a maths lesson, she became progressively more bored. Wally Walters was trying in vain to teach them and getting the usual teasing. Weak and ineffectual in front of a class, he was always fair game for the troublemakers. Abbie always played noughts and crosses with Bev during maths but now she was on her own. She decided to manufacture her own fun.

Taking a sheet of paper from her pad, she tore off two strips and folded them carefully into pellets. Then she got an elastic band and stretched it between her thumb and forefinger. Wally was doing his best to interest them in geometry. Abbie waited until he turned to the blackboard then she took aim. The pellet sped through the air towards the teacher with venomous intent. Missing its target, it hit the lampshade above his head with a comical ping. Wally shook the pellet off as it landed in his hair.

The whole class dissolved into laughter.

'You gor dandruff, sir!' yelled someone.

'Who did that!' demanded the teacher.

He faced a sea of sniggering faces. It was quite impossible to pick out the culprit. His voice explored a new octave of despair.

'Someone fired a pellet at me! Who was it?'

Fingers were pointed at random around the class.

' 'im, sir.'

' 'er, sir.'

'Them, sir.'

'Us, sir.'

'You, sir.'

The mockery was completely out of control now.

Abbie added to Wally's miseries. She had already removed the elastic band and slipped it back into her pencil case. She now put the second pellet in the palm of her hand, slapped it against her cheek and let out a piercing scream.

'What is it, Abbie?' asked the teacher in alarm.

'They fired one at *me*, sir!' she said, holding up the pellet. 'It came from over there.' She pointed to the right hand corner. 'One of those aimed it at me.'

The boys in question denied it hotly. Accusations and counter-accusations now flew everywhere. Wally threatened them with all kinds of dire punishments but his words went unheard in the general hubbub. Only the bell stopped the lesson from degenerating into utter chaos.

Abbie was pleased with the way she had livened things up.

But she still missed her best friend.

Life at the Ainsley Annexe was designed to be tough. The pupils were kept under constant supervision and lost all privileges. Discipline for the majority of them was rigidly enforced. Work was unremitting. Being sent to the Sin Bin was not a way to dodge the normal curriculum. As well as doing assignments set by Basher Bowen and Don Sheen, pupils had to keep abreast of their subjects. Classwork and homework was sent over from the main school every day.

One result of all this was that they had to work longer hours in the Sin Bin. There was no mid-morning or mid-afternoon break. Lunch was reduced to half an hour in the cramped back garden. Even then, they were under surveillance. From the vantage point of the back bedroom, the teachers could look down and watch them.

Bev found it a long day but she would still rather have missed out on the lunch time break. Being the only girl among so many boys was unnerving. They had glared and muttered on the first day. When she came out to eat her sandwiches on the second day, her problems were more acute.

A tall, dark-haired swarthy boy ambled across to her.

' 'ello, darlin',' he said familiarly.

Tim Roach of 5A had a reputation to keep up.

'Wor you doin' this evenin', then?'

'Why?' asked Bev uneasily.

'Thort we might go for a jar or two. OK?'

'I don't drink.'

'Thass all right, Bev. I'll teach you.'

'No thanks.'

'You gorra start some time, darlin'.'

'Yeah,' urged another boy. 'An' nor only at boozin'.'

Guffaws went up. Tim Roach was being egged on by his mates. They encircled Bev so that she could not get away. When she looked anxiously upwards for help, she saw that there was nobody in the staff room window. She was on her own.

Tim Roach stepped in closer. He had a greasy complexion and his teeth were snaggly. Bev found him repulsive. There were lots of boys like him at Woodfield. Nuisances who tried to pester the girls whenever they could. But Bev had always been safe before because she was with Abbie. Her friend's acid tongue could see off any boy but it could not come to Bev's aid now.

The mates wanted some action. They threw in some advice.

'Go on, Tim.'

'Gerrin there, mate.'

'Wor you waitin' for?'

'She's mad for you.'

The self-appointed suitor waved them to silence. He would do it his way and at his pace. Putting a hand on the fence behind her head, he leaned in even closer. He had an arrogant charm that did not work on Bev at all. It disgusted her.

'Wor do you say to a film tonight, then?'

'No thanks,' stuttered Bev.

'Doan mean in the flicks. A video. Round at my place. Juss you, me and a dirty big sofa. Worrabout it, Bev?'

'Just leave me alone.'

'But I likes you.'

'Well, I don't like you!'

'Thass 'coss you doan know me proper.'

'Go away!'

'Give us a kiss first.'

'No!' she cried.

'Come on . . .'

Bev tried to push him away but he grabbed her arms. It was hopeless. She struggled hard but Tim Roach was far too strong for her. He bared his teeth in an oily grin.

'I'll give you one of my specials!'

Bev closed her eyes in horror but the kiss never came. As he pushed his head towards her, Tim Roach was grabbed roughly from behind and yanked backwards. He spun round in surprise and a fist connected with his jaw, sending him sprawling to the ground.

Thick Dobrowski glared at the others, daring them to take him on but they did not have the courage. They slunk back to help their friend up from the floor.

Thick moved to stand in front of Bev.

She had a protector now.

Chapter Five

Thin Lizzie was the fattest member of the Woodfield staff. She was also one of the most popular. Young, keen and tireless, she brought a dynamism to the teaching of English that made the subject come alive. A cosily attractive woman with long hair and rimless glasses, she favoured voluminous cardigans and huge, sweeping skirts. When Thin Lizzie was on the move, she was like a galleon in full sail.

She surged along the corridor with a set of exercise books under her arm. As she passed the headmaster's study, Froggy emerged and dived after her ample frame.

'Miss Finch! The very person!'

'You wanted me, headmaster?'

'This is fortuitous.'

He walked beside her as they headed for the staff room. Against her bulk, he looked small and insignificant. He tried to counteract this by stretching up on his toes and raising his voice.

'It's about that debating contest.'

'I think we should enter it, Mr Parsons.'

'No question. Woodfield's banner must be flown.'

'We said that last year,' she admitted, 'and our banner got rather tattered. But only because we met Cardinal Newman School in the first round. They had a cracking team.'

'Ours must be better this year, Miss Finch.'

'It will be.'

'Plenty of talent in the fourth year?'

'I think so.'

'Let's put it on show. These inter-school contests are

valuable shop windows for us. An opportunity to display our wares.'

'I prefer to see it from the kids' point of view,' she said.

'In what way?'

'Wonderful experience for them.'

'Quite so.'

'They can test themselves against schools with supposedly better catchment areas than ours. OK, they may come adrift but they *learn*. That's what it's all about.'

'I couldn't agree with you more.'

Froggy stood aside so that she could go into the staff room first. Then he went after her and joined her by her locker.

'I want us to push the boat out this year.'

'How, Mr Parsons?'

'By taking more time with the preparation,' he explained. 'I've had a word with Mrs Craig and she thinks we can rejig the timetable so that you can have a free period last thing on Thursday and Friday.'

Thin Lizzie chuckled. 'Tell me more.'

'That would be your rehearsal time for the debate. I'd give you *carte blanche* to haul any pupil you require out of his or her class. You can really work on them.'

'At that rate, we'd be bound to win.'

'I've set my heart on it, Miss Finch. Woodfield needs that kind of triumph to brighten up its image. We look to you to provide it.'

'Any pupils, headmaster?'

'Take your pick.'

'I know who my first choice would be.'

'Who?'

'The only girl in the fourth year who can speak properly,' she told him. 'Beverly Kington of 4C.'

'Oh dear!'

'What's the problem?'

'She's not available, I'm afraid.'

'Why not?'

'Because the girl has been sent to the Annexe.'

'Makes no difference.'

'It does to me, Miss Finch. She is in disgrace. We will not have someone like that representing the school.'

'Beverly Kington is the best debator in the whole year.'

'She is also the one pupil you can not have on the team.'

Froggy was adamant. Thin Lizzie was flabbergasted.

When they were let out of the Ainsley Annexe at the end of the school day, they ran off with evident relief. Abbie Reynolds stood guard outside the house, exchanging words or nods with pupils whom she knew. Eventually, Bev came out through the front door. When she saw Abbie there, she gave a little gasp and stepped backwards.

'Wass wrong?' said her friend.

'Nothing.'

'I gor leprosy or somethin'?'

'Of course not, Abbie. It's just that . . .'

Bev came over to her then looked furtively up and down Woodfield Road. Taking Abbie by the elbow, she hustled her around the corner and into the nearest shop doorway.

'Wass goin' on?' protested Abbie.

'It's my parents,' explained Bev.

'Eh?'

'They don't want me to see you any more.'

'*Wor*!' Abbie was deeply hurt.

'Mum and Dad think that you were behind that hoax call.'

'Thar wor you told 'em?' accused the other.

'No!'

'Sure?'

'Dead sure.'

'I hopes you're tellin' the truth.'

'Abbie, you're my *friend*!'

'Nor if your parents 'ave their way. Tell us wor 'appened.'

55

Bev related the story, editing the facts slightly to spare Abbie's feelings. She was downcast at first but soon rallied. All they needed was a plan of campaign.

'Do you wanna see me again, Bev?'

'Yes!'

'Then wass to stop us?'

'They won't let you in the house.'

'So? We meet somewhere else. My 'ouse, swimmin' pool, McDonald's, disco, flicks, park, dozens of places. They'll be none the wiser.'

Bev had reservations. Her parents were very determined.

'We'd have to be ever so careful, Abbie.'

'Add to the fun of it.'

'They must *never* see us together.'

'Easy enough.'

Bev nodded excitedly then checked her watch. She gulped.

'Look at the time. I must fly.'

'Gorra clock in at 'ome, 'ave you?'

'Dad said I've got to go straight back every day.'

'Fine,' agreed Abbie. 'I'll come with you.'

'You can't!'

'Doan mean to the 'ouse, silly. Juss part of the way.'

'Too dangerous!'

'No, iss nor.'

'We could be spotted, Abbie.'

'Who by? Your dad works in thar buildin' society till five-thirty and your mum's at 'ome 'ooverin' those bloomin' carpets she's always on about. We gor nothin' to fear.'

'Well . . .'

'Come on. We gorra make plans.'

They went back into Woodfield Road and walked up it. Bev was nervous and hesitant but Abbie was quite unconcerned. The shorter girl gave her characteristic giggle.

'Bev . . .'

'Yes?'

'Know wor?'

'What?'

'Iss juss like ole Sweetness and Light said. Remember? In thar 'istory lesson? She said thar religions always thrives when they try to stamp 'em out. Same with us, Bev. Your parents are out to persecute us an' our friendship is gonna thrive. Right?'

'Right,' said the other, without conviction.

'You can do berra than thar.'

Bev thought it over. As usual, Abbie was talking sense. It was simply a case of working around her parents. Her primary duty was to her friend not to them. They need never know what was going on. It was a way of attesting her freedom and independence. The more she considered it, the more appealing it became.

'Less try again,' suggested Abbie. 'Right?'

'*Right*!' shouted the other.

They walked happily along Woodfield Road together.

Their friendship was stronger than ever now.

He was always glad when he reached Richards Terrace. The block of flats enabled him to get rid of a large proportion of the papers left in his bag. Most of the inhabitants read the *Sun* or the *Star* or the *Daily Mirror*. A few people took *Today* and there was a man on the top floor who liked the *Daily Express*. Human beings were defined by the papers they bought. He found that out. It interested him.

It took him several minutes to get around all the flats and it was not the kind of area where a bicycle could be left unlocked for a second. Thick Dobrowski therefore chained his machine to the railings on the ground floor before he went up the steps. He also made sure that he pushed the newspapers right into the homes. If you left a copy of the *Sun* protruding from a letterbox, it would either be stolen by a neighbour or pulled out by some pop-eyed youth who wanted to gaze in wonder at the nude on page three.

Thick went through his established routine then began

to descend the steps again. When he got to the bottom, he unlocked his bicycle and mounted it. As soon as he tried to pedal, he became aware of the problem. Both his tyres were now flat.

The bicycle had been sabotaged.

Don Sheen spluttered along the road on his motorcycle then turned in through the main gates of the school. He drove to the staff car park and brought his vehicle to a halt beside a gleaming Renault 15. It belonged to Mrs Craig. Like its owner, it had been polished to a high gloss and gave off an aura of cleanliness. Don removed his crash helmet and put his gauntlets into them. He then unhooked his briefcase from the pannier and tucked it under his arm.

A distinctive and welcome figure bore down on him.

'Good morning, Don!'

'Hi, Liz.'

'How's it all going?'

'Ask me when I've woken up properly.'

Thin Lizzie cast an amused eye over his decrepit motorcycle.

'When are you going to put four wheels on the road?'

'I could do that today,' he boasted. 'It's the car that goes with them that I can't afford.'

They shared a laugh then she became serious.

'Glad I bumped into you, Don. Want some help.'

'Ask away.'

'Beverly Kington.'

'What about her?'

'I need her.'

Thin Lizzie told him of her encounter with the headmaster and of the latter's refusal to consider the girl for the debating team. Don heard her out then responded warmly.

'Do all I can,' he promised. 'But you know what Froggy's like when he digs his heels in. We'll have to work on him. Meanwhile, I can make sure the girl gets some practice. As it happens, I was planning to hold a debate for my lot.'

'Beverly has got style and that's rare at her age.'

'Some of it may be a trifle dented,' he warned.

'What do you mean?'

'Being sent to the Sin Bin. It's rocked her.'

'Has it affected her confidence?'

'Shattered it.'

'Oh no!'

'Froggy never thinks of the psychological damage that place can do to some people. Beverly is one of them. I've tried to make it easier for her but she's going through hell. For someone like her, the Sin Bin is a process of continuous humiliation.'

'We must get her out!' decided Thin Lizzie.

'Easier said than done.'

'I can't have my champion debator rotting away over there.'

'That won't happen,' he reassured. 'And I'll do everything I can to rebuild her confidence. Don't worry, Liz. Beverly won't go far astray with me holding her hand.'

'Thanks, Don. Keep me posted.'

'I'll send bulletins on the hour.'

She laughed and sailed off to the main block.

Another fateful day at Woodfield was about to begin.

The house was only a quarter of a mile away from the city centre but Martin Kington still elected to drive to work. He felt that a professional man like the manager of a building society had to arrive by car if only to impress his staff. It was part and parcel of his image.

He was climbing into the vehicle when Sheila came out.

'What did you make of all that?' she wondered.

'All what, dear?'

'The way she behaved over breakfast.'

'Beverly was bound to be subdued.'

'There was more to it than that, Martin.'

'I don't follow.'

'She was hiding something from us.'

'How do you know?'

'I have a sixth sense. It was the same with Philip.'

'Stop dragging him into it all the time,' he said with some exasperation. 'Philip thought he'd be better off if he left home and where has he ended up? Living in two rooms over a Wimpy bar with that hotel receptionist.'

'I rather liked Wendy,' she confessed.

'As a daughter-in-law?'

'Well, no . . . that's different.'

Martin turned on the ignition and the engine came to life.

'I still say that Beverly is being secretive,' argued Sheila.

'This is not the time to discuss it.'

'She won't look you in the eye. Did you notice?'

'I'm sorry, Sheila, but I really must go.'

'This is our daughter we're talking about.'

'I have to be on time. I'm the manager.'

'You can spare me two minutes.' She gripped his arm through the open window. 'Martin, I'm worried about her. Are we doing the right thing?'

'No question about that.'

'Does Beverly resent us for it?'

'She'll come to appreciate the wisdom of our stand in time.'

'Philip never did,' she said.

'For the last time, keep him out of it!'

He released the handbrake and put the car in gear.

'We don't want to drive our daughter away as well.'

'There's not an earthly chance of that, Sheila.'

'She's all we've got left.'

'I'll ring you if I get the chance,' he mumbled.

Then he drove off before she could say anything.

Sheila felt tense and bewildered. She went back into the house in search of something to do. The breakfast things had been cleared away and the dishwasher was purring contentedly. The beds had been made and the bathroom was spotless. She did not even have an excuse to hoover the carpets again.

Walking into the lounge, she took down the large photograph of Beverly that stood on the mantelpiece. She looked so composed and mature. She had been everything they had wanted her to be. Until this had happened. Sheila held the photograph to her bosom and wrapped both arms around it.

The tears began to trickle down her cheeks.

Miss Whitnall had to wait for the right moment. It was not something that could be rushed. Abbie Reynolds would not co-operate at all if she was tackled head-on. Another method was required. The chance came that morning. Miss Whitnall was on playground duty. She noticed the girl leaning against a wall. It was time to move in.

'Hello, Abbie.'

'Oh, hello.'

'All alone?'

'I was thinkin', miss.'

'What about?'

'Nothin'.' She shrugged and pulled a face. 'I hate school.'

'That why you give us all such a tough time?'

'Bur I doan!'

'I was only teasing, Abbie.'

'Oh.'

Miss Whitnall stood beside her and realized what the girl had been staring at. The Ainsley Annexe on the other side of the road. Gazing at it herself, the teacher spoke softly.

'I don't think Beverly's come out of this too badly.'

'Wor?'

'The Sin Bin. I bet she enjoys it over there.'

'*Enjoys* it?'

'Why not?'

'It's supposed to be a terrible place.'

'Work it out for yourself, Abbie,' said Miss Whitnall. 'It's a much nicer building than this one. Staff-pupil ratio is excellent. And you get to miss the daily horrors of this place such as morning assembly and school dinners. The Annexe has got a lot going for it.'

'Bev says it's awful, miss.'

'Well, she would, wouldn't she?'

'Eh?'

'It probably was on her first day. Now that she's settled down, it's another story. Only five of them in the class with Mr Sheen able to devote a lot of individual time to them. Bev is the tea monitor, apparently. That gives her the run of the staff room. She has a pretty easy berth over there, by all accounts.'

'Then why doesn't she like it?'

'I don't know. I would.' She looked around the busy uproar of the playground. 'Better than being in this jungle. Of course, it takes real guts.'

'Wor does?'

'Facing up to the Sin Bin. Beverly had what it takes. That's why she'll come through. Most girls wouldn't.'

'I dunno . . .'

'She's really tough.'

'*Bev*?'

'Not on the surface,' said the other, 'but she has hidden strengths. Those quiet ones are all the same. It's the bigmouths who turn out to be the cowards and the cheats.'

Miss Whitnall did not want to labour the point. Having planted an idea, she was ready to let it grow of its own accord. She excused herself and went off to break up an argument between a group of second formers.

Abbie's eyes returned to the Annexe. What was happening at the Sin Bin? How was Bev coping? Why had she changed slightly since she'd been there? Something had been troubling Abbie all morning and she had been unable to work out what it was until now. After her chat with the gym teacher, it suddenly became clear.

Abbie was jealous.

When they finished their written work, Don Sheen collected it in. Then he sat on the edge of the table and flashed them a smile.

'I'm going to give you a little test,' he explained. 'Chance to talk your heads off. I want you all to think of something and concentrate on it. Choose a subject that's dear to your heart.'

Steve and Greg sniggered. Calvin whooped.

'Ideally,' continued Don, 'you should choose an abstract – love, hope, freedom, art, something like that. Give it your full and undivided attention because I'm going to ask each of you to talk on his or her subject for five minutes. Chosen yet? Think *hard*. I'll give you time.'

The five of them did as they were told. Brows wrinkled, eyes narrowed, teeth clenched, they concentrated for all they were worth. Don could almost hear their minds clanking away. None of them looked at the others. They were in a world of their own.

It was time to begin.

'What's your subject, Calvin?'

'Sex.'

Steve and Greg sniggered again. The Jamaican beamed.

'OK,' said the teacher, calling his bluff. 'Talk about sex for five minutes. Though I'd be surprised if you know enough to hold our attention for thirty seconds. Off you go, Calvin.'

The boy opened his mouth but no words would come.

'We're all waiting,' nudged Don.

'I, er . . . that is . . . anyway . . .' Calvin gave up and looked hopefully up at the teacher. 'Can I talk about reggae instead?'

'Yes,' said Don. 'But go to the end of the queue.'

'Right, sir.'

'Steve?'

'Bruce Springsteen, sir.'

'I might've known!' moaned Don. 'Greg?'

'Sir?'

'What's your subject?'

'War films, sir.'

'Bit gruesome.'

'Thass why I likes 'em.'

'I see,' said Don. 'Barry.'

'Poland,' grunted Thick.

'That'll be interesting. What about you, Beverly?'

'Friendship, sir.'

'Now, that's the most promising of all. Right – ladies first.'

'Shall I start now, sir?' she asked.

'When you're ready.' Don looked at his watch. 'Talk for five minutes. Longer, if you wish.'

Bev cleared her throat and ran her tongue over her lips.

'Friendship!' she announced. 'Friendship is the most important thing you can learn at school. Much more important than all the other subjects they teach us. There's two parts to it, really. You've got to learn how to make friends and how to keep them. Because friendships change as we grow up. They develop. You all have friends so you'll know what I'm talking about. The great thing about a friendship is that it can break through any barriers. Barriers of race, for instance. Or religion. Or class . . . yes, and barriers of age . . .'

She spoke for over twenty minutes.

Don and the other kids were spellbound.

Chapter Six

The conspirators met at lunch time in the yard at the back of the Annexe. They gathered around Tim Roach whose chin now bore an ugly bruise. There was no shortage of suggestions.

'Less smash up his bike, Tim.'

'Rough 'im up a little.'

'Throw 'im in the canal.'

'Gerrim arfter school and do 'im in proper.'

Tim Roach silenced his mates with a wave of his hand. He was bent on revenge but he was in no hurry. He would take his time. His victim would suffer much more that way.

Thick Dobrowski had caught him with a sneak punch when he was not looking. Tim Roach was not afraid of him. With his three mates to back him up, he would take on anybody. The Polish boy would be paid back for what he did. With interest. Nobody laid a finger on Tim Roach and got away with it. He always caught up with them somehow.

'Wor we gonna do next?' asked Mooser.

'Make 'im sweat,' said Tim.

'Yeah. Turn the screw on 'im,' sneered Keach.

'Nice an' slow, like,' added Vinny.

They were an assorted bunch. By virtue of his height, strength and pushy nature, Tim was their natural leader. Mooser was a skinny, loose-limbed boy. Keach was big, lazy and running to fat. Vinny was a small, sly, treacherous youth. Individually, they were no trouble. Their bravado came from the gang.

'Look out!' hissed Mooser. ' 'ere 'e comes!'

'Lemme do the torkin',' commanded Tim.

'If you wann some muscle, we're 'ere,' said Keach.

'No point,' observed Vinny. 'Basher's on the lookout.'

They glanced up. The Welshman was sitting in the window of the staff room, devouring a sandwich and chatting to Don Sheen. A fight in the yard was out of the question.

Thick saw them and walked off into a corner. His lunch consisted of two bags of crisps and a Diet Coke bought from the paper shop. As he took his first drink, the gang sidled over to him.

'Well, well, well,' began Tim Roach. 'If it issen ole Thick-as-two-short-planks. Wor you gonna be wenn you grows up, then, Thicko? Nuclear scientist or a brain surgeon?'

Thick tried to remain calm as they baited him.

'I thort the Irish were stupid,' said Tim, 'but they gor nothin' on the Poles. They're *stupid* stupid!'

'Know any good Polish jokes, Tim?' asked Keach.

'Dobrowski!'

The four mates laughed harshly. Thick felt his hackles rise.

Tim Roach had his old swagger back now. He grinned at the Polish boy and tapped him on the chest with his finger.

'Juss to ler you know, Thick'ead. Wherever you goes and worrever you does, we'll be watchin'. Gorrit? An' wenn it suits us, you'll ger a tap on the shoulder. Know wor I mean?'

'Shall I spell it out to 'im?' suggested Keach.

Vinny smirked. 'No use, mate. Thick doan even know 'is alphabet yet. 'e thinks ABC is thar cinema in town.'

They laughed at him again. Thick was fighting hard to control his temper in the face of the provocation. He stiffened as they moved in menacingly. He was not frightened.

But the explosion was checked before it happened.

Basher Bowen stood in the window and pounded on the glass with the flat of his hand. Tim Roach and his mates pulled back at once. They did not want any trouble with the teacher. A former Welsh ABA heavyweight champion, Basher could lick them all with one hand tied behind his back. They would bide their time.

Thick Dobrowski had been warned. He was now certain that they had let his tyres down that morning. He was equally certain that it was only the start of their campaign against him.

There would be lots more to come.

Bev came bouncing down the steps of the Sin Bin as if she had really enjoyed her day there. Her fatigue and guilt had evaporated. There was a new sparkle to her. Abbie Reynolds was peeved. She herself had had a particularly tiresome day. All the fun seemed to have gone out of school for her. She was jaded and resentful.

'Hello, Abbie!'

'Hi,' murmured her friend.

'What's wrong? You look down in the dumps.'

'One o' those days.'

'You should've been here. It was great!'

'The Sin Bin? I thought they were supposed to punish you.'

'Oh, yes, there is that side to it as well,' conceded Bev, 'but I'm getting used to that. It's just that we had this marvellous lesson with Mr Sheen. He's a smashing teacher.'

'No such thing,' said Abbie disconsolately. 'All teachers are rotten. Even Thin Lizzie. She tore strips off me this afternoon.'

'Don doesn't work that way.'

'Oh? It's "Don" now, is it?'

'I've never met anyone like him, Abbie.'

'Wor do you mean?'

'I know this is going to sound silly but . . . he's on our side.'

Abbie was unconvinced. 'You're right. It does sound silly.'

The two girls began to walk up Woodfield Road. There was a spring in Bev's step but her friend was dragging her feet. They were silent for a minute or two then Abbie rose to a grudging invitation.

'Go on, then.'

'Eh?'

'Tell us why Mister Softee is such a Mister Wonderful.'

'He's so *understanding*,' said Bev. 'You don't have to explain things to him. He sees them for himself and takes action.'

'Does 'e?'

'Yes. For instance, I'm the only girl there and that makes it a bit hairy during the lunch break. All those yobs lounging around. Yesterday, one of them gave me a lot of hassle.'

'Who was it?' demanded Abbie.

'Tim Roach.'

'Thar long streak o' nóthin'! Tim Roach 'as a go at every girl. Tried to pur 'is 'and down my blouse once. I almost bit 'is finger orff. Next time 'e touches you, stick your knee where it'll 'urt 'im the most.'

'There won't be a next time, Abbie. That's the point.'

'Wor is?'

'Well, Don could see how uncomfortable it was for me in that yard so I don't have to spend my lunch break there any more. He's given me this little office of his upstairs. Really cosy. I even get to use his radio.'

'I see,' commented Abbie. 'All mod cons.'

'Don's been so good to me.'

'I bet he has! I suppose he keeps popping into that office of his to make sure that you're all right.'

'He does, actually.'

'And I bet he always manages to wander into the staff room when you're alone in there making the tea.'

'He does it deliberately.'

'You can say that again!'

'It's because I'm new to the Sin Bin,' argued Bev. 'Don says there's bound to be a period of adjustment.'

'Is thar wor 'e calls it?' said Abbie with scorn.

'He's helping me through it with these private chats.'

'Grow up, Bev!'

'What?'

'You're nor *thar* stupid, are you?'

'Well . . .'

'There's only one reason that "Don" is 'angin' round you.'

'Because he's kind enough to help me.'

'No. Open your eyes, will you?'

'My eyes?'

'Don Sheen *fancies* you!'

The idea had never occurred to Bev and it hit her with the force of a thunderbolt. She was stunned at first but she quickly recovered and a complete change took place. When she thought about it, she saw that it was indeed a possibility. Don had been excessively helpful and attentive. A *teacher*? Interested in *her*?

She felt a warm glow of hope deep inside her.

Basher Bowen took the chalk from his pocket and drew a face on the punchball. It was a passable likeness of Froggy Parsons. When he added the famous hornrimmed spectacles, the resemblance was even stronger. Pulling on the boxing gloves, he held out his arms while Miss Whitnall tied the laces for him. Then he squared up to the punchball as if taking part in a title fight.

'Seconds out – Round One!' she declared.

Basher opened his account with a straight left which sent the punchball over at an acute angle. When it sprang back at him, he met it with a powerful left hook. Dodging, weaving and timing his punches carefully, he kept the leather ball squeaking and swaying for the best part of ten minutes. By the end of the session, the face of Froggy Parsons had been knocked to oblivion.

Miss Whitnall untied the laces for him.

'Honestly, Bryn. You're worse than the kids sometimes.'

'Froggy deserved it.'

'Oh, I can believe that.'

'Know what his latest is?'

'What?'

'Woodfield is going in for some inter-school debating contest. Big prize at stake. Good publicity if we win.'

'And?'

'The best speaker in the fourth year is Beverly Kington.'

'I think I can guess the rest.'

'Exactly,' confirmed Basher, raising his eyebrows. 'Because the girl is in the Sin Bin, she's been forbidden to take part. Our esteemed bloody headmaster says it's all part of her punishment.'

'But Woodfield suffers as well.'

'That point is too subtle for him to grasp.'

'So you decided to punch it into him.'

'Had to get rid of my aggro somehow, Maureen.'

Basher Bowen was due to take an evening class in the gymnasium. He had come ahead on his own to have a short workout. Miss Whitnall had been putting some apparatus away and stayed to watch him.

'How's Beverly getting on in the Sin Bin?' she said.

'Ask Don.'

'Why?'

'He's taking her under his wing.'

'Didn't the job appeal to you?'

'I'm a married man,' he joked.

'She's certainly a lovely girl.' Miss Whitnall handed the boxing gloves to him. 'She may be having company over there.'

'Who from?'

'Her best friend.'

'The one who helped her make that hoax call?'

'Abbie Reynolds.'

'I've heard of her. Bit of a handful.'

'In every sense, Bryn. Watch out.'

'So why is she coming to us? Signed a confession?'

'That's too much to hope for,' admitted Miss Whitnall. 'No, it's just a hunch I have. Abbie's one of those kids

70

who hates anyone to have something that she doesn't. She was glad enough when Bev got shipped off to the Annexe instead of her but she's got a sneaking envy now. Don't be surprised if she rolls up.'

Basher gave the punchball one last shuddering blow.

'We'll be waiting for her . . .'

Thick Dobrowski kept his eyes peeled as he did his paper round the next morning. Instead of chaining his bicycle to the railings on the ground floor of the Richards Terrace flats, he locked it to the lamppost on the opposite side of the road. That meant that he was able to keep it in vision as he delivered the papers along each level of the building. He got to the end of his round without incident. Evidently, they were not going to strike against him that morning.

Mounting his bicycle, he pedalled home as quickly as he could so that he would not miss his morning ritual. As he came freewheeling at speed around the corner of Vale Road, his mind was on that special little moment which started off each school day for him. He simply did not see the two figures lurking behind a parked car.

When he was almost level with them, they hurled a large piece of timber into his path. His front wheel hit it, twisted and buckled. Thick was thrown headfirst over the handlebars. He was too late to get a glimpse of his enemies as they ran off but he heard their derisive laughter. They had got him, after all.

Dragging himself up, he carried his bicycle over to his house and propped it against the wall. He was bruised and shaken but nothing seemed to be broken. When he went into the house, however, his mother gasped in horror.

'Dear God, Barry! Your face is covered in blood!'

Froggy Parsons did not like having his decisions questioned. He expected everyone else to put his orders into practice without delay. When Mrs Craig came to see him, therefore, he was less than pleased. Because she towered over him, he invited her to sit down. That gave him the position of advantage. He stood with his legs braced apart like a sailor on deck in a high wind.

His deputy gave her saccharine smile. Always a bad sign.

'Well, Mrs Craig?'

'I've been talking with Miss Finch.'

'Ah!'

'This forthcoming debating contest . . .'

'My views on the matter are well known.'

'I beg you to reconsider.'

'Out of the question,' he said, with a dismissive gesture.

'But headmaster,' she persisted, 'surely it's our duty as a school to field the best team possible.'

'And that is what we shall do.'

'But Beverly Kington will be omitted.'

'She is not the only pupil who is skilled in public debate.'

'Perhaps not,' agreed Mrs Craig, 'but she happens to be the only one who can speak the English language properly. We can't rest our hopes on the adenoidal Woodfield voice.'

'I find that remark patronizing.'

'It was not intended to be.' She attacked from another angle. 'There has been widespread concern over this business. I feel it my duty to warn you that several members of staff are against you.'

'And where do *you* stand, Mrs Craig?' he accused.

'Oh, well, naturally, I support you . . .'

'No more discussion is needed.'

'Wait a moment,' she said hurriedly. 'I must represent to you what Miss Finch has said. She is supported by the entire English department. They are talking of getting up a petition.'

'Don't they have anything better to do?'

'There is the principle of double jeopardy,' she reminded him.

'Is there?'

'We feel so . . . er, that's to say, Miss Finch feels so.'

'Go on,' he said wearily.

'Beverly transgressed and we sent her to the Ainsley Annexe.'

'The punishment fitted the crime.'

'Quite so, headmaster. But you now want to inflict a *second* punishment on her. It does seem unfair.'

'Not in my opinion.'

'Isn't the girl entitled to a chance to redeem herself?'

'In time.'

Mrs Craig masked her exasperation behind a sigh. She was getting nowhere. He was deflecting every argument she used against him. She reached for her last weapon.

'Supposing they *do* organize that petition . . .'

'Yes?'

'And supposing the vast majority of the staff sign it.'

'Yes?'

'Will you bow to the will of the majority?'

'I shouldn't dream of it, Mrs Craig,' he said airily. 'Besides, it would be a complete waste of time if I did.'

'I don't follow.'

'Fearing that this would be a contentious issue, I took the trouble of contacting the girl's father to sound him out. He sided with me. Beverly should not compete.' He smiled benignly. 'My hands are tied, Mrs Craig. Even if *I* said the girl could take part in that debating competition, her parents would stop her.' The smile broadened. 'Was there anything else?'

'No.'

Anyone who knew the two girls would have said that Bev Kington was entirely dependent upon her friendship with Abbie Reynolds. It was Abbie who decided what they would do and where they would go.

Yet it was not Bev who was suffering from their enforced separation. During school hours, they had to get along without each other. Amazingly, it was Bev who was turning out to be the more self-sufficient. Abbie, the one with the drive and initiative, was almost in mourning. She trailed from lesson to lesson without a vestige of interest. All she could think about was what she had lost.

Another mid-morning break found her loitering near the main gates. Traffic surged past to obscure her view. When it cleared, she was able to stare at the Ainsley Annexe once more, a building whose every external detail she now knew by heart. The Sin Bin was a symbol of oppression. It was not only punishing Bev for something which had not really been her fault, it was robbing Abbie of her friend. She was mesmerized by the place and would have stayed there longer if someone had not shaken her by the shoulder.

It was Charlie, the school caretaker.

'Wake up, girl,' he said.

'Wor?'

'Didn't you hear the bell? They've all gone in.'

Abbie turned round. The playground was empty.

After one more wistful glance across the road, she ran off.

The office was like Don himself. Untidy, disorganized but comfortable. Bev was already sitting down when he came in with the tray.

'My turn to make *you* a cup of tea, Beverly.'

'Oh! Thank you, sir.'

'Don't mention this to the others, will you?'

'No, sir.'

'We're not supposed to fraternize with the pupils.'

He was breaking the rules for her. Bev was pleased.

Don put the tray on the table, closed the door behind him then sat down. It was very cramped. Their knees were almost touching. He indicated her tea then took his own and sipped it. Bev spooned sugar into her cup and stirred.

'What do you think of us so far?' he asked.

'Think of you?'

74

'This madhouse called the Ainsley Annexe.'

'Oh, well, it's . . . not as bad as I thought.'

'So you've learned to like us.'

'Yes, sir.'

'Up to a point, anyway.' He put his cup down. 'Beverly, I like to have a session with everyone who gets sent here. It's not so much for my benefit as yours. I hope I can help you understand certain things about yourself. You are, after all, a very mature young lady.'

It was a compliment. She was touched. When she sipped the tea, it was too hot. She put the cup aside then crossed her legs. Her toe brushed against his. Don smiled. She could see that he liked her.

'Do you like Woodfield?' he asked.

'Yes, sir.'

'Be honest.'

'I like some things about it.'

'Such as?'

'English, swimming, geography, art . . .'

'And what are the things you don't like?'

'Maths, physics, chemistry . . . oh, and the rules. There's so many of them. Mr Parsons has a rule for everything.'

'I had noticed.'

'We don't get much freedom here.'

'Do you get a lot at home?'

'Oh, yes!'

'How much?'

'As much as I like, really. Except on Sundays.'

'Sundays?'

'We always visit my Gran in Stourbridge. Takes up the whole day.'

'And Saturdays?'

'Help Mum with the washing in the morning. Usually we go into town shopping in the afternoon. In the evening, I usually see Abbie.'

'That's Abbie Reynolds.'

'Yes, sir.'

'Weekdays? What do you do in the evenings?'

'Homework, most nights. Watch the telly.'

'But you stay in?'

'Yes, sir.'

Why was he so interested in what she did with her time? Did he have a personal reason for wanting to know about her evenings?

'No boyfriend?'

'No!' She stifled a giggle.

'Don't you like boys?'

'Of course, sir.'

'But you haven't met the right one yet.'

Bev was out of her depth. She could not tell if his questions were loaded. And she was not sure how she was supposed to answer them. The only thing she did know was that she liked being with him. Don Sheen was restful and unthreatening. She could not say that about any other male member of staff. Most of them frightened her.

'So what do you want to be, Beverly?'

'Sir?'

'I asked you this once before. You said you didn't know.'

'I don't, sir.'

'I believe you do.'

'No, honestly . . .'

'You're too embarrassed to say, that's all. You think you've blotted your copybook by being sent here and that we won't take your ambitions seriously.' He leaned forward. 'What do you want to be?'

'Well . . .'

'Can't be any more unrealistic than what some of the lads chose.'

'I have this vague idea . . . but not now . . .'

'Why not?'

'It seems . . .'

'Don't be afraid,' he coaxed. 'This is strictly confidential.

I happen to think you've got a lot of ability. I'd like to feel that you were going to use it properly.'

There was a long pause as she searched his face. He was kind and reassuring and gentle. That was what she appreciated the most. And he seemed to be able to read her thoughts. That was worrying but it was also heartening in a way. It showed that he cared.

'Shall I tell *you* what you want to be?' he whispered.

'What, sir?'

'A teacher.'

He knew. She felt a sudden upsurge of affection for him.

Chapter Seven

There was one big disadvantage to being the manager of a building society. It kept Martin Kington in the public gaze. At a time when he wanted to keep discreetly out of the way, he was forced to greet or chat to dozens of customers every day. Convinced that they all knew about his daughter's disgrace, he was upset by even the most well-meant enquiries.

'Hello, Mr Kington.'

'Good afternoon, Mrs Runyard.'

'How is Mrs Kington keeping?'

'Oh, very well, thank you.'

'And the children?'

The question brought him two stabs in the heart now.

'Oh, they're fine,' he lied.

'Beverly is still at Woodfield, isn't she?'

'That's right.'

'How is she finding it?'

Martin imagined things that were not in fact there. He thought that a simple question was a concealed laugh at his expense. He thought that people wanted to rub salt in the wound. Because he was so obsessed with what Beverly had done, he believed that everyone else was as well. It was very lowering.

He left early that afternoon to keep a dental appointment. A fine day had broken up into a squally shower. As he ran to the car park and got into his vehicle, it struck him that he would be driving along Woodfield Road at about the time that his daughter came out. She would appreciate a lift home in the bad weather and it would not make him late for his appointment.

Martin got on to the ring road which skirted the city and made his way around it. His stomach lurched as he drove past the fire station. It brought all the bad memories flooding back to haunt him. He accelerated and left the ring road by the next exit.

The worst was over. That was what he kept telling himself. He and his wife had suffered a cruel blow but they had survived it. With the help of Mr Parsons, they had made the right decisions and pulled their daughter back from any further mishap. They were going to watch her more closely now. It was the only way.

Breaking her friendship with Abbie Reynolds had been the key factor. They should have done it much earlier. The girl had led Beverly astray. Their daughter would be far better off now that her former friend had been wiped out of her life.

Martin waited at the traffic light then turned into Woodfield Road. His timing was good. The mass exodus was just beginning from the main school. He could not see the Annexe properly yet. A stream of traffic held him up and he inched painfully along. When he finally approached the Annexe, he saw something which made his blood freeze. Beverly was walking along with Abbie Reynolds. They were deep in animated conversation. His daughter had disobeyed his orders.

Martin felt desperately hurt and betrayed.

'You certainly covered a lot of ground with her, Don. How long were the two of you at it?'

'About an hour, Bryn.'

'Dieu! Wouldn't dare to leave my class for an hour.'

'They'd wreck the place.'

'In two minutes flat!'

They were gathering up their things in the staff room at the Sin Bin. Basher had had a fairly routine day with nothing of interest to report. It was Don who seemed to have had all the fun.

'What else did Beverly tell you?' asked the Welshman.

'Lots. Once she got going.'

'You certainly know how to loosen a woman's tongue.'

'I listen, that's all.'

'And what did you learn?

'That she's the spoiled child of over-controlling parents. According to her, she had all the freedom she wanted. When we broke down her week and analysed it day by day, she came out looking like a robot.'

'How did she react to that?'

'Shock. Disbelief. Annoyance.'

'The usual.'

'She just hadn't realized how much her life was programmed by Mummy and Daddy. Talk about disillusion.'

'At least she has parents who show an interest,' noted Basher. 'That's something. Most of my kids come from homes where one or other of the "parents" keeps changing all the time. How does a growing boy cope with the idea that his mother has an endless string of boyfriends? Or that his father likes picking up teenagers at a disco?'

'Beverly's problems are rather more sophisticated than that,' said Don. 'There's the brother figure for a start. She blames him for leaving home yet she admires him for standing up to her parents. It's not only the working-class families who have confused kids.'

'Let's get out of this dump, boyo.'

The rain had stopped by the time they came out of the building. They waited for a break in the traffic, crossed the road and sauntered towards the staff car park.

Something was still puzzling Basher.

'How did you guess?'

'Guess what?'

'That she wanted to be a teacher.'

'Two things,' explained Don. 'She was very uptight about the whole subject. Wouldn't admit what she wanted to be. Understandable. The girl's just been disciplined for bad

80

behaviour. Last thing she wants to talk about is her ambition to teach.'

'You said there were two things.'

'Friendship.'

'Come again.'

'It's what Beverly talked about when I gave them this verbal test. She could have gone on for an hour. The kid's a born teacher.'

'Not many of *those* about these days!'

'You're right, Bryn.'

'So what's the next stage with her?'

'Beverly? She has a lot of repressed hostility. We'll have to work through that first. But we'll do it, I'm sure. She was a different girl today. Willing to co-operate.'

'Must be your aftershave.'

'I never wear any.'

They reached Basher's car. He unlocked the boot and tossed in his briefcase and sports bag. Slamming down the lid, he turned to his colleague again.

'And how's old Silent Sid coming on?' he wondered.

'Dobrowski was a revelation today.'

'I'm glad I wasn't there to see it.'

'You missed something astonishing.'

'Thick actually completed a sentence unaided?'

'I'm serious!' said Don. 'We had this discussion about Russia, you see. The other lads came out with the most fatuous rubbish, all of it straight out of the James Bond films. But not Dobrowski. It had real meaning for him. Half his family still live in Poland.'

'So what was this great revelation?' pressed Basher.

'The kid was dying to contribute but he couldn't get the words out. You could see the frustration in his face. So much to say and no way of saying it. Then Beverly hit on the solution.'

'What was it?'

'She told him to speak in Polish.'

81

'Can he?'

'Like an express train. Once he got going, we couldn't stop him. It was wonderful to hear the words pouring out of him. We couldn't understand any of them, of course, but that didn't matter. He had his say and he was *so* pleased about it.'

'It was Beverly's idea?'

'Told you she was a born teacher . . .'

They sat there in silence without moving a muscle. Bev stared down at the carpet. Martin watched her. Sheila wrung her hands. The lounge of her own home seemed like the most alien place on earth to Bev. She would have given anything to be able to walk out.

'We're waiting,' said Martin.

'Say something!' hissed his wife.

Bev shook her head. She understood about Philip now.

'I was staggered,' recalled Martin. 'Strolling along the pavement with the girl as if nothing had happened.'

'What made you do it, Beverly?' asked her mother.

'Why did you defy us!' snarled her father.

But their daughter remained motionless and said nothing.

Sheila Kington reached for a packet of cigarettes, took one out and slipped it between her lips. She used a match to light it then inhaled deeply. Smoke drifted across the room.

'You will not see that girl again,' ordered Martin.

'Listen to your father, dear.'

'You will have no further dealings with Abbie Reynolds.'

'We mean it.'

'I will drive you to the Annexe every morning and your mother will collect you at four.' A note of smugness crept in. 'That'll put a stop to your little game.'

'Abbie is no good for you, Beverly.'

'As of now, she doesn't exist in your life. Do you hear me?'

Bev raised her head and looked from one to the other. Years of slavish obedience to them counted for nothing now.

She had been caught on the raw. She had to strike back.

'You can't stop me seeing Abbie,' she said levelly.

'Who can't?' threatened her father.

'We'll speak to Mr Parsons about it,' added Sheila.

'To the girl's parents, if need be.'

'It still won't work, Daddy.'

'And why not?'

'Ask Phil.'

'Don't *you* start dragging him into it as well!' shouted Martin, jumping to his feet. 'Philip is irrelevant.'

'No, he isn't,' returned Bev. 'The reason he left school was that you told him he couldn't see Wendy again.'

'She was a nice enough girl,' said Sheila wistfully.

'She was *common*!' snapped Martin.

'Phil chose her,' reasoned Bev. 'You had no right to —'

'I had every right as long as he was living under my roof!' insisted Martin. 'We've set our children a good example. Is it too much to ask them to follow it?'

'It's not as easy as that, Dad.'

'Of course it is!' He waited until he had calmed down then he repeated his decision. 'Abbie Reynolds belongs to your past, Beverly. Make that clear to her in every way.'

'But I don't want to,' she said.

'Do as you're told!'

'We know best, dear,' soothed her mother.

'Then why did you drive Phil out?'

'I think you'd better go to your room,' suggested Martin, glaring down at her. 'Come back when you're able to talk sensibly about this.'

Bev was about to answer but she bit back her words. Grabbing her bag, she went out and wearily climbed upstairs. Once inside her bedroom, she locked the door and flopped down on the bed.

Just as things seemed to be getting better, the new crisis had blown up. It was a complete accident and could not have been avoided but it was going to worsen relations all round. Abbie was such a vital part of her life that Bev could not imagine what it would be like without her. Nor could she bring herself to tell her friend some of the unkind things her parents had said.

She put her hands to her head and rolled over on to her back. All this because she made one foolish telephone call. It killed off almost everything of value in her life. As she reflected on the last few days, the sense of pain and loss was overwhelming.

Slowly, however, something else seeped into her mind. It eased the pain and soothed the loss. It began to fill the great emptiness which she felt inside her. She thought about help she had been given. About trust, patience and tenderness. She thought about being rescued when she had been drowning.

There *was* something of value in her life.

Don Sheen.

Calvin Hubberd lived by his wits. A wild, amiable, anarchic boy, he tended to get into trouble through over-exuberance. He did not run with any gang. By the same token, he made sure that he did not upset any. Calvin aimed to be a friend to all. It saved a lot of bother. An underdog himself, his sympathy was always with his kind. It was this sympathy which took him in the direction of Vale Road that evening. He bounced a white plastic football as he walked along.

Thick Dobrowski was mending his bicycle. The new front wheel had taken most of his savings but he had to have the vehicle for his paper round. The damage to his face was less dramatic than his mother had at first feared. A good wash and two pieces of elastoplast had transformed him. He worked slowly and carefully.

Calvin Hubberd checked that the coast was clear then turned into Vale Road. Seeing the blank wall, he swung a foot at the ball and sent it screaming towards the brickwork. It bounced off and landed up near Thick.

'Wor you doin'?' asked Calvin.

'New wheel,' muttered Thick.

'Accident?'

'No.'

'Thort nor.' He reclaimed his ball. 'Fancy a game?'

'Now?'

'Yeah.'

Thick did not want to leave his task but he sensed that Calvin had come for a purpose. He went along with the suggestion. Standing a few feet apart, the boys took it in turns to boot the ball at the wall so that it rebounded hard. They played for a few minutes before Calvin spoke.

'Doan come tomorrer.'

'Why?'

'Juss doan.'

As the ball rolled towards him, he flicked it up with his toe, bounced it on his knee, then headed it four times before letting it drop to the ground. He smashed it against the wall once more.

'Wenn round the snooker 'all,' he said.

'By the school?'

'Yeah. Lorra kids there. Your friend was one of 'em.'

'Ah.'

'I 'eard wor they said. Stay 'ome.'

'Carn.'

'S'nor worth it, mate.'

'They doan worry me.'

'Four to one. Gonna ger you at lunch time. In the bog.'

Calvin treated his companion to another piece of artistry as he kept the ball in the air, using alternate feet. When he finally lost control, he had one final strike then caught the ball in his hand.

'Gorra shove off, mate.'

'Right.'

'See you.'

'An' thanks.'

'Wor for?'

'Oh . . . yeah.'

'Never said a dickybird, did I?'

Thick nodded. Calvin Hubberd was covering his tracks.

With a sudden burst of speed, the Jamaican went off down the road like a basketball player, dribbling the ball with impressive control. He shot into an imaginary basket then disappeared around the corner.

Thick was grateful. It was a timely warning. He was not sure what he could do about it but one thing was certain. Calvin was a friend. It meant a lot.

He went back to his work, removing the damaged wheel and replacing it with the new one. He was just tightening the bolts when he heard a door open and slam behind him. Thick turned around hopefully but he was out of luck.

Wrong house. Wrong girl.

Abbie Reynolds had never seen the first former before. When the girl ran up to her and thrust an envelope into her hand, Abbie was taken aback. She looked down at the freckled messenger.

'Wass this?'

'I gor twenty p. to bring it over.'

'Where'd you gerrit?'

'Over by the Sin Bin. This girl came out.'

'OK. Buzz off.'

As the first former raced away, Abbie opened the envelope and took out a single sheet of Basildon Bond. It was a hasty message in Bev's handwriting. The tidings were bleak.

They went mad. I'm not to see you at all. Don't come at four. Being picked up every day now. Will write again soon.

Abbie was desolate. It was bad enough only seeing Bev for a brief chat at the end of the school day. Even that limited access had been taken from her. Bev's parents were trying to burn Abbie off completely. It made everything much more difficult.

She could not survive without her friend.

There had to be a way to get to Bev.

Tim Roach went through the plan once more. His mates clustered around him in the classroom on the ground floor. Other pupils kept well out of the way. Tim and his gang ruled the roost.

'Iss gorra be done real quick,' stressed the leader.

'It will be,' assured Vinny.

'OK. This is the drill. Mooser and Keachy grab 'im by the arms. I lay into 'im and show 'im who's gaffer.'

'Worrabout me?' asked Vinny.

'You're watchin' the door,' said Tim.

'Doan I gerra punch?'

'Yeah – this one.'

Tim Roach thumped him playfully in the stomach and he doubled up. The real punches were being saved for someone else. They were sure that their plan would work. It was foolproof.

'Wor 'appens to the girl?' wondered Mooser.

'Less ger ole Thick outa the way first.'

'Then wor, Tim?'

'Me an' 'er can ger acquainted, like.'

'Leave somethin' for me,' cried Vinny.

'You an' whose army?'

Derisive laughter filled the room. They were in good spirits.

The day of reckoning had arrived.

When she first saw him, it took a few moments before she realized that it was indeed him. The change was remarkable. Don Sheen had altered his appearance in one move. He had been for a haircut. The new, shorter style took years off him and gave him an almost adolescent look. Bev was more drawn towards him than ever.

'Miss Finch is going up the wall,' he said.

'Yes, sir.'

'And you can see why, Beverly.'

'Yes, sir.'

'It's such a ridiculous decision. I mean, you do *want* to represent Woodfield in the debating team, don't you?'

'Of course, sir.'

'Then we'll have to pool our resources and come up with a solution. Froggy is not the only problem, apparently.'

'Who else, sir?'

'Your parents.'

'Oh!' said Bev gloomily.

'They've put their weight behind Froggy's decree.'

'They would!'

'Any suggestions?'

'I'm afraid not, sir.'

They were in the upstairs classroom at the Sin Bin. The other pupils had not yet arrived and Don had seized the opportunity to discuss the debating contest. He racked his brains to find a way out of the dilemma. An idea formed.

'How would your parents react to a direct approach?'

'What do you mean?'

'Well, supposing Miss Finch actually went around to see them and put her case?' He smiled at the thought of Thin Lizzie in action. 'She can be very persuasive. I remember her tackling Melanie Judd's parents when they refused to let the girl appear in the school play.'

Bev had immediate reservations. Much as she herself liked the English teacher, she could not see Thin Lizzie getting on too well with her parents. The woman was too forthright and Bohemian. Martin Kington would take against her on sight.

'No go?' asked Don.

'It's a good idea in principle, sir,' said Bev. 'But Miss Finch may not be the ideal person.'

'We could send Basher. He'd pound them into agreement.'

'What about you, sir?'

She asked the question with apparent innocence but a

complex manoeuvre was taking shape in her mind. Bev had so far only met Don at the Sin Bin on his terms. She wanted him to come to her house where the rules would be different.

'I suppose I could,' he agreed.

'How about tomorrow evening, sir?' she proposed quickly.

'Saturday? Won't you be going out?'

'No, we'll be there. Could you make five-thirty?'

'Probably.'

'I'll check with my parents.'

'Fine.' He mulled over the plan. 'I feel very strongly about it. It's criminal to suppress someone's talents like this, especially when they might benefit the school.'

'I'd be terribly grateful, sir.'

'That's reason enough to come.'

He smiled fondly at her and she felt another swell of emotion. Bev was amazed how calm and collected she had been about it all. It was not as if she had any experience in these matters. But instinct had guided her.

Don Sheen's visit to her home could change everything.

Chapter Eight

Thin Lizzie was in no mood for interruptions. When she was in full flow, she liked to surge on unchecked at her own pace. *Twelfth Night* was one of her favourite plays. She had firm views about it and a determination to get those views across to 4C.

'The use of disguise here is very clever,' she noted. 'Viola is a woman who dresses up as a man and who is then asked to woo another woman on behalf of the man with whom she falls in love. In Shakespeare's day, of course, the female parts would have been played by boys so we have another dimension of disguise. It also makes for a lot of dramatic irony . . .'

'Dramatic wor, miss?' said Abbie cheekily.

'Irony!'

'Never 'eard of it.'

'Then you were not listening in the last lesson, Abbie. We looked at the concept in some detail.'

'I doan remember.'

'That is your problem.'

'Could you explain it again, miss?'

'No,' sighed Thin Lizzie. 'Now, let me get on, will you?'

'Didden unnerstand thar about disguise either,' confessed Abbie. 'Think you could go over it again, miss?'

'If you say another word, I shall get very cross.'

'Bur I only —'

'Very cross indeed!'

A mild-tempered Thin Lizzie was a formidable creature. The Very Cross version was to be avoided at all costs. The English teacher could steamroller you flat when roused. 4C all expected Abbie Reynolds to give up while she still could. She was on a hiding to nothing. But that did not deter the girl.

'Iss nor much of a play, miss, is it?'

'Shut up, Abbie.'

'The men are such wimps. All of 'em.'

'Are you *asking* for trouble, girl?'

'I thort it was s'pposed to be a comedy, like.'

'That's enough,' said the teacher. 'Out you go.'

'Wor?'

'OUT! If you want to play games, you will not do so in one of my lessons. Go on. Stand outside! Serves you right if Mr Parsons happens to be passing.'

Abbie broke into a song just loud enough to be heard.

' "Mr Froggy went-a-wooing and he did ride . . ." '

The explosion of mirth carried Abbie to the door. Thin Lizzie waved her out then admonished the class. A minute later, she was back in Illyria. There were no interruptions this time.

Abbie, meanwhile, hung about in the corridor and prayed that the headmaster would come along. Every so often, he trawled around the school and collected all the children who had been sent out from their classes. Abbie was keen to be part of a trawl but she was out of luck. When the bell went, Thin Lizzie came out and gave her a roasting.

'Since you don't understand what dramatic irony is, you can do an additional essay on it. By tomorrow, please.'

Abbie winced. It was not what she had had in mind.

Basher Bowen waited until the stroke of one o'clock before he dismissed his class. They stood politely until he himself had left then dispersed in haste. Tim Roach and his mates got to the boys' toilets first. They took up their appointed positions. Vinny lurked at the bottom of the stairs. Mooser and Keach hid behind the door. Tim Roach himself pretended to be using the urinal.

It was not long before they heard footsteps on the stairs. Vinny sent word that their prey was at hand. The others tensed in readiness. Tim remembered the punch on his chin and savoured the prospect of revenge. As Thick Dobrowski walked into the toilets, Tim swung round to confront him. Mooser and Keach leapt in to pinion the boy's arms.

' 'old the bastard tight!' said Tim.

But Thick was not to be taken as easy as that. Lifting a leg, he put it on Tim's chest and pushed hard. The gang leader was catapulted backwards against the wall. Thick lurched heavily to the left and crushed Keach against the door, causing him to release his victim. The Polish boy now swung his free hand round to punch Mooser who also let go.

Vinny came running, Tim got up, Keach rallied and Mooser closed in. They would not let him get away so easily this time.

'What's going on here, then?' boomed a Celtic voice.

Basher saw the situation at a glance and grinned.

'What's this, Dobrowski?' he said jocularly. 'Taking on four of my class? Unfair odds on your part. I'll see you after school.' He looked around the gang. '*All* of you . . . Now get out of here and let those who need the place have use of it.'

Tim Roach and his gang trooped off with their tails between their legs. They had failed. And they did not relish the idea of meeting Basher Bowen after school. His tone had been ominous.

During the lunch break, Bev was given the use of the telephone in the little study upstairs. With a confidence borne of regular use of the instrument, she rang her father at his office. Martin Kington was at first annoyed that she had contacted him but he changed his tune when he heard what she had to say.

'First thing I want to do is to apologize, Dad.'

'Ah . . .'

'I shouldn't have said those things last night.'

'Your mother was very upset.'

'Maybe I should finish with Abbie.'

'You have, Beverly. Completely.'

She mollified him even more then worked around to a mention of Don Sheen. Bev did not say that he wanted to talk about her involvement in the debating contest because she knew that her father would probably not even agree to see him. When she explained that he wanted to have a chat about her general behaviour at the Annexe, Bev got the response she wanted.

'I'll be leaving here around five-thirty tomorrow,' said Martin. 'Your mother's hair appointment finishes around the same time. Why not fix Mr Sheen for six o'clock?'

'I will, Dad.'

'And thanks for ringing.'

'I wanted to clear the air.'

'I'm glad you've come to your senses.'

'So am I.'

She put the receiver down and rubbed her hands. It was all coming together nicely. If she rearranged Don for five o'clock, that would give them a whole hour alone before her parents got back. Quite what they would do in that hour she did not as yet know, but she was profoundly excited. Don Sheen beside her on the sofa.

Fantasies began to take hold.

She left the office and went through to the classroom where she had left her bag. Thick Dobrowski had returned to collect his lunch. Bev gave him a welcoming smile.

'Hello . . .'

'You in 4C?' he asked.

'Yes.'

'Know Abbie Reynolds?'

'Very well.'

He stood there and appraised her, wondering if she was fit

93

to receive the secret he wanted to pass on to her. Eventually, he took her into his confidence. With his eyes twinkling, he told her something she had never known before.

'Me an' Abbie live in the same road.'

It was the longest conversation she had ever had with him. Bev was touched. Evidently, he trusted her a great deal now. And if he lived in Vale Road, he might act as a messenger between her and Abbie. His address was a happy coincidence.

Wally Walters did not let her down. He always began a lesson on the brink of a nervous breakdown. It did not take much to push him into gibbering hysteria.

'Leave the room at once, girl!' he said.

'Why, sir?' asked Abbie, feigning surprise.

'You know quite well why.'

'I was only askin' for some guidance.'

'You were trying to undermine my whole lesson.'

'Truth is, it was sendin' me orff to sleep, sir.'

4C gave her a resounding cheer for this flash of honesty.

'Quiet!' shrieked Wally.

'Didden say anythin', sir.'

'Not you, Abigail. The whole class.'

'I see.'

'Now, outside!'

'Me or the 'ole clarss, sir?' she teased.

'You!' he affirmed. 'Report to Mr Parsons at once.'

Abbie had made it at the second attempt.

She found Froggy Parsons going through the timetables with Mrs Craig. The study was a solid fug of perfume. Abbie was invited in and explained that she had been sent there for punishment.

Froggy passed sentence in a quivering voice.

'We will not have disrespect to our staff, Abigail,' he said. 'You will report to Mr Stanley at four. Detention.'

'Bur thass nor fair!'

'You are getting off rather lightly.'

'Thass my point,' she complained. 'I wanna be sent to the Sin Bin.'

'The Ainsley Annexe,' corrected Mrs Craig. 'Why do you wish to go there, child?'

'Because I do, thass why.'

'Detention with Mr Stanley,' insisted Froggy.

'Iss a swizz!'

'You may go now, Abigail.'

'Wor do I 'ave to do to ger to the Sin Bin!' she cried.

The headmaster traded a shrewd glance with his deputy.

'Quite simple, Abigail. Confess.'

'Eh?'

'The hoax call,' Mrs Craig reminded her.

'Admit that you were behind it,' said Froggy, 'and you can go across to the Annexe this very moment.'

It was a serious temptation but Abbie resisted it. There was a principle at stake here. She could never confess to something when she had got away with it. They could lock her up in the Sin Bin for anything – except telephoning the fire brigade.

'Detention with Mr Stanley.'

'Aw, sir!'

'Goodbye, Abigail.'

'I been cheated!'

'I'm sorry you feel that way.'

'Iss downright rotten!'

She withdrew from the study and closed the door.

They were deliberately trying to stop her reaching the Sin Bin.

It was a conspiracy.

The problem was that she was not quite sure what to buy. She took the advice of the beautician at the shop and bought a range of cosmetics. Bev came out and headed straight for home, walking briskly through the precinct. She was just about to take a shortcut through an alleyway when she saw him. It was Thick Dobrowski.

He was pushing a wheelchair. Its occupant was a youth of twelve or thirteen. Severely handicapped, the boy was twitching and turning in his seat as they moved along. Thick wheeled him over to the water fountain in the centre of the precinct. The youth was entranced by it and got such simple pleasure out of it that Bev was moved. Her admiration for her classmate went up even more. He was anything but a stupid and insensitive thug. Clearly, the boy had finer feelings.

She watched them for a few minutes. When she studied the figure in the wheelchair, she could detect a family likeness. At a guess, it was Thick's brother. The Woodford boy treated him with a blend of care and understanding. Bev saw her slow, ponderous classmate in a new light.

Tearing herself away, she continued on her journey. The long walk gave her the opportunity to think everything right through. It was Abbie who first put the idea to her. Don Sheen fancied her. Ludicrous as the suggestion might have seemed, it was backed up by substantial evidence. Don went out of his way to be with her alone. He bent the rules to help her and he favoured her openly.

Abbie was right. The question for Bev was what she should do about it. Having started to look for certain signs, she had found them in profusion. Don's interest was serious. Hers had begun as curiosity and intensified in a very short period. She thought about him all the time. She longed to be with him again. She had to make a deeper commitment.

She was only fifteen but that did not deter her. She was advanced for her age and patently able to secure the attentions of an older man. Where those attentions would lead was a separate matter. What Bev was keen to do was to explore the possibilities.

It would be a crucial experience in her life.

Tim Roach and his mates sat on a bench in the park and

drank cans of lager beer. They leered at passing girls, told crude jokes, nursed their resentment. The attack on Thick Dobrowski had earned them all a four-page essay for the weekend. That cut deeply into their leisure time. It gave them fresh cause to get their own back on Thick Dobrowski.

'It'll 'ave to be away from school,' said Tim.

'Late at night's best,' argued Vinny. 'Then 'e woan see us to identify us.'

'I think we should really work 'im over,' mused Keach.

'Yeah,' added Vinny. 'With baseball bats!'

'Bare 'ands'll do,' said Tim.

'Round 'is bloody neck!' urged Mooser.

'Where's 'e live?' wondered Keach.

'Vale Road,' said Tim. 'Me an' Vinny fetched 'im orff 'is bike there. Abbie Reynolds lives there an' all.'

Mooser beamed. 'Eh, she's a birra awright, thar Abbie.'

'Nice little mover,' endorsed Keach.

'Juss my style,' boasted Vinny.

'Forgerrit,' warned Tim Roach. 'Abbie's pure wildcat. Nearly bit my finger orff when I tried to be friendly once.'

They finished their cans and hurled them recklessly into the pond. Ducks scattered and the stately swans moved out of reach. The gang hardly noticed. One by one, they were dropping off to sleep. Tim Roach was still plotting revenge as his eyelids closed.

Thick was still their number one priority.

The first hour in front of her bedroom mirror had been fruitless. Bev wanted to look more sophisticated but her early experiments were bungled. She started afresh and had more success. When she added mascara, she felt that she was really getting somewhere. In a subdued light, she could easily pass for twenty.

Bev tried five dresses before she settled on the right one. It was a rust-coloured sheath dress which highlighted her figure and set off her shock of hair. Black patterned tights and black shoes completed the outfit. She was ready for him.

Don arrived bang on time. She showed him into the lounge.

'Hi, Beverly.'

'Lovely to see you.'

'You look different somehow.'

'Do I?'

'Yes!' he said approvingly.

She was immensely encouraged. He cared. He had also made an effort to smarten up his own appearance and that was a large undertaking. Corduroy trousers replaced his usual jeans and an open-necked checked shirt gave him a hint of a holiday-maker. It was so much more relaxed than at the Annexe. The teacher-pupil barriers vanished.

'Can I offer you a drink, sir?'

'Call me Don, please.'

'Yes, Don.' It was a thrill to use his name. 'What will you have? We've got whiskey, gin, vodka.'

'An orange juice will be fine.'

'Is that all?'

'It's a bit early for booze.'

She brought his drink along with a bitter lemon for herself, then she motioned him to the sofa. They talked about the Sin Bin, about the other pupils, about their own ambitions. Don did not seem at all worried that her parents were not there.

Trembling with nerves, she tried to sound alluring.

'I'm so glad you came, Don.'

'Delighted to be here.'

'I've been looking forward to this all day.'

'Me, too.'

'You've been wonderful this week.'

'All part of the service,' he said briskly.

'I mean it. You kept me going.'

'That's nice to know.'

She sipped her drink and edged closer to him on the sofa.

'My parents are delayed,' she said airily. 'Won't be here for at least half an hour.'

'Suits me.'

'And me.'

It was exactly as she had envisaged it. Bev was the entrancing young girl and he was the experienced man of the world. There was an electricity between them. She felt it coursing right through her.

'Tell me about yourself,' she asked.

'Nothing much to tell.'

'Yes, there is. How did you start teaching?'

'Very badly.'

'You're great now!'

'Thanks. Where did it all begin? I'll tell you . . .'

He held her fascinated as he gave her a brief history of his career in teaching. It was a vocation for him. Nothing less would do. As she heard him sounding off, he touched responsive notes in her own heart. His passion, his commitment and his honesty swept her away. She was drawn to him like a magnet.

The words eventually tumbled out of her.

'Don . . .'

'Yes?'

'There's something I want to say.'

'Fire away.'

'I *wanted* you to come here.'

'Only too pleased to help, Beverly.'

'I don't mean the debating contest.'

'Oh . . .'

'That was just an excuse really.'

'Was it?'

'Yes. I had to see you. Simple as that.'

She moved closer to him and waited. At this point in her fantasy, he leaned over to cradle her in his arms and kiss her. Unfortunately, Don did not act like a fantasy lover. He crossed his legs and finished his drink instead.

Bev put it down to hesitation. Her tender age was both an attraction and a warning. He wanted her but was afraid to reach out. She had to help him. Bev mustered a smile and put a hand on his thigh. It gave her confidence to go on.

'Don't be afraid.'

'Of what?' he asked.

'You know.'

'Bev . . .'

'I want us to be friends.'

'We are.'

'Proper friends.'

'Maybe this is not such a good idea.'

'Don . . .'

'What?'

'I think I love you,' she said dreamily.

She did not so much embrace him as fall against him in the hope that he would take over. Instead, he eased her gently aside and stood up. Bev was hurt. She got to her feet and put her hands on his shoulders. His eyes were cold and wary now.

'What's wrong?' she whispered.

'How did we get into this?'

'Does it matter?'

'Of course it matters.'

'But I thought . . .'

'If I did anything to give you the wrong idea, I'm sorry. I really am. Now why don't we just forget all this ever happened?'

But Bev could not. His rejection of her was so total that she was deeply wounded. She turned away and crossed to the sideboard. Inside a drawer, she found a box of tissues and took one out. He came up behind her and tried to console her.

'Don't touch me,' she said weakly.

'Beverly . . .'

'Just go.'

Don weighed up the situation and decided to leave. The mood which had brought him there had changed. He was shy, awkward and clumsy. With a resigned shrug, he crossed to the door and let himself out. She ran to the window to watch him go and the last of her fantasy fell into pieces. Bev was utterly dejected.

She flung herself on the sofa and let the tears come. They streamed down her face and ruined her make-up. She was inconsolable. How long she lay there she did not know, but she eventually heard the car arrive outside. Her parents got out and let themselves into the house. When they walked into the lounge, they were met with the sight of a hysterical young girl full-length on the sofa.

Sheila dashed to kneel beside her.

'Beverly!'

'What happened?' asked her father in concern.

'Where's Mr Sheen, dear?'

'Didn't he come?'

Bev had no control over what she said.

'Yes, Mr Sheen came. He tried to grab me . . .'

She took refuge in another outburst of tears.

Chapter Nine

Even in a crisis-laden school like Woodfield Comprehensive, emergency sessions in the headmaster's study on a Sunday morning were unusual. Froggy Parsons was in a state of dithering panic. Mrs Craig was shaking with moral outrage. And Basher Bowen was downcast because he had been forced to miss his usual pint at the local. Scandal threatened the school and their immediate duty was to keep it at bay.

'We must keep this under wraps at all costs,' said Froggy querulously. 'If the tabloids got hold of this, we'd be ruined.'

'What about the office?' asked Mrs Craig.

'I'm trying to hold them at arm's length as well. Until we resolve this matter. Ideally, I'd like to do that today.'

'There's not much chance of that, headmaster,' she said.

'I fear not!'

'Let's start with the facts,' asserted Basher loyally. 'One – Don Sheen is innocent. Two – Bev Kington is lying her head off. And three – we're making a mountain out of a molehill.'

'This is a highly serious matter, Mr Bowen,' said Froggy.

'Only if it's true. And it's not.'

'How can you be so sure?' asked Mrs Craig.

'Because I know Don Sheen.'

'He did *go* to the girl's house,' Froggy reminded him.

'No, Mr Parsons. He went to the home of Mr and Mrs Kington in the hope of persuading them to allow their daughter to compete in an inter-school debating contest.' Basher snorted. 'The girl was on her own, all dolled up to the nines. Talk about provocation!'

'Did he succumb, I wonder?' mused Froggy.

'No!' insisted Basher.

'I'm keeping an open mind,' said Mrs Craig.

'That'll be a change!' said Basher under his breath.

'We can do without snide comments,' she said.

'We must pull together on this,' emphasized Froggy.

'What's the state of play, headmaster?' asked his deputy.

'I've put the Kingtons on hold, thank goodness!' He mopped his brow with a handerkchief. 'When this happened yesterday, they were all for bringing the police in.'

'The police!' repeated Mrs Craig.

'The girl is under age,' Froggy reminded her.

'That means nothing in this day and age,' offered Basher.

Froggy nodded dolefully. He tried to impose order on chaos.

'Right. Here's my suggested list of priorities. Interview Mr Sheen. Interview Beverly Kington. Interview the parents.'

'I would make one amendment to that,' said Mrs Craig. 'Suspend Mr Sheen on full pay while the investigation goes on.'

'No!' bellowed Basher.

'He's under suspicion.'

'But he's done nothing wrong.'

'That remains to be seen.'

They argued for a further hour before they broke up. Opinions were divided. Basher supported his colleague. Mrs Craig thought he did it. And Froggy was torn between the two. It was going to be a long and bitter controversy.

Don Sheen stared at the empty coffee cup in front of him as if it held the answer that he sought. Thin Lizzie sat beside him. They were in his flat in one of the tougher parts of the city.

Thin Lizzie was sympathetic.

'How do you feel now, Don?'

'Lousy.'

'Kids!'

'It was my own fault, Liz.'

'But you didn't know the girl would turn out to be a Lolita.'

'I should've been more suspicious when the parents weren't there.'

'Easy to say that after the event.'

'What event? Nothing happened, Liz.'

'Except in Beverly's mind.'

'That's what I'm up against. The over-heated imagination of a fifteen year old. Her word against mine.'

'I know which one I'd take.'

'Thanks.'

Don had had a long, sleepless night. News of the allegations against him had arrived late the previous evening. He had asked to see the girl in person to rebut the charges but her parents had refused to let him anywhere near her.

'Frightening,' he said.

'What is?'

'How easy it all was.'

'In what way, Don.'

'I walked into that house as a respected member of the teaching profession. I walked out as Jack the Ripper.'

'That kid needs help,' decided Thin Lizzie.

'Professional help,' added Don. 'Not two neurotic parents who'll stoke up her emotions.'

'Another coffee?'

'Why not?'

'Another job?'

'Yes, please!'

They shared a laugh. It helped to relax Don slightly.

'If only Katie had been here!' she said.

'Perhaps it's just as well she isn't.'

'What do you mean?'

'I wouldn't fancy having to tell her about this.'

'But you're the innocent party.'

'No such thing in cases like this. Some mud always sticks.'

'You're being far too pessimistic,' chided Thin Lizzie robustly. 'When this whole business is cleared up in twenty-four hours, you'll wonder what all the fuss was about. As for Miss Beverly Kington, I wish *I* could have five minutes alone with her.'

'Look what it did for me.'

He gave a mirthless laugh.

Bev lay on her bed in a darkened room. The strain of the last eighteen hours had been too much for her. She was close to fatigue yet beyond sleep. Her mind kept replaying what had happened. Or what she said had happened. She had told the lie so many times now that it had taken on a patina of truth for her.

Don Sheen *had* touched her, hadn't he? Because she had wanted him, that is what he must have done. How could he possibly reject her in those circumstances?

Other images came into her mind. A handicapped youth in a wheelchair. Cosmetics scattered in front of a mirror. Her father's angry face when he caught her with Abbie Reynolds. Her mother's inability to think of anyone but herself. Greg Escott as Prime Minister. A boy with greasy skin trying to steal a kiss from her. Someone holding her arms as his lips came towards her.

Three fire engines converging on the school. Miss Whitnall hauling her out of the swimming baths. Froggy Parsons interrogating her. 4C watching as she was marched off to the Sin Bin. A classroom of wolf whistles. Basher Bowen's cheerful welcome.

Someone being kind to her, being considerate to her, gentle to her.

Friendship.

It was Abbie's turn to take the dog for a walk. The park was the best place. He could roam at will through the trees and sniff to his heart's content. Abbie did not have to keep

Gip on a lead in the park. He could run where he wished. Catching him was the problem.

'Gip! Come 'ere, Gip!' she yelled.

The animal ran in circles as it chased its tail.

'Wait till I get my 'ands on you, Gip! Come 'ere!'

Abbie broke into a run but the dog only thought she was joining in the game. Off he bounded at even greater speed. Abbie slowed to a walk and trudged after the animal. She had known better Sundays.

'There you are, you bad boy!'

He was sniffing around a wheelchair.

'Now stand still and wait for me!'

Gip stood still long enough to lift his back leg against the side of the wheelchair. Abbie dashed forward with apologies.

'Doan, Gip, you dirty thing! Oh, I'm so sorry. Thass awful!'

'Iss OK,' said Thick.

He was pushing his brother through the park.

'Iss you,' murmured Abbie. 'Never realized.'

'Neil's 'ome for the weekend.'

'Saw 'im yesterday.' She raised her voice. 'Hello, Neil. 'ow are you, love?'

The boy in the wheelchair nodded away at her and gave her a toothy grin. His arms and legs were constantly on the move as he twisted about. Thick put a brotherly hand on Neil's shoulder.

Though they lived in the same road, Abbie had very little to do with the Dobrowski family. She had always found Thick rather creepy. But she was starting to reassess him now.

'Bev told me wor you did.'

'Eh?'

'At the Sin Bin. Punchin' thar Tim Roach for 'er. Well done.'

'Thanks.'

Gip returned to sniff the other wheel of the chair. Abbie

106

took the opportunity to grab his collar and snap the lead on to it. Thick looked at her in wonderment. He built up to a declaration that took her quite by surprise.

'I follows you to school every day.'

'Do you?'

'I leaves juss arfter you and follows.'

'Oh.'

'Thar other mornin', with the fire engines. I was there.'

'Were you?'

'Yeah. You wenn in the phone box with thar girl. Saw you both. Then the fire engines come. Thar girl got cort.'

'Hey!' she said in alarm. 'Doan tell anyone you saw me in thar phone box, will you?'

'No. Norra word.'

'You're a friend.'

Thick beamed as if she had just given him five pounds.

'See you, Barry . . .'

'Yeah!'

Abbie scampered off with Gip.

Sheila Kington was much calmer now. Several glasses of gin and some sedatives had enabled her to have a modicum of sleep. She was still highly disturbed by the alleged attack on Beverly but she was no longer in a condition of frothing hysteria. Martin was just very tired.

'Should I go up and see how she is?' asked Sheila.

'Let her rest, dear.'

'Such a terrible thing to happen!'

'We're over the worst.'

'What will they do to the man?'

'They have to establish the facts first.'

'But you heard what Beverly said. *Those* are the facts.'

'Maybe.'

'I still think we should have contacted the police.'

'That may not be necessary.'

'He's got to leave the school, Martin,' she insisted. 'He

107

must be sacked. Or he could do it to some other poor girl.'

'Yes, dear.'

'What time is Mr Parsons coming?'

'He's on his way now.'

'They mustn't be allowed to see Beverly. We must protect her.'

'I'll handle everything, Sheila.'

She nodded and stared unseeing at the blank television screen.

'She told the truth about him.'

'I know, I know,' he soothed.

'Beverly doesn't lie. Our daughter's not a liar.'

Martin was thinking just the opposite. She had lied about her motive for making the hoax call. She had lied about Abbie's part in it. She had lied about her continuing friendship with the girl. She had lied about 'the arrangements for Mr Sheen's visit. She had lied about why she was wearing make-up.

Caught up in the general panic the previous evening, he had been only too willing to believe what she had told them. It was dreadful but it was plausible. Beverly had shown them the marks on her arms where she had been held as she struggled. She *had* to be telling the truth. She was their daughter.

He heard the sound of a car on the drive.

'That will be Mr Parsons and the others.'

'They must sack the man.'

'We'll discuss all that.'

'Make him pay. Make him *pay*!'

Don Sheen sat in the little office at the Sin Bin and sorted through piles of papers. He singled out certain items and put them aside on the desk. He worked fast with the subdued panic of a man who may have to face a firing squad if he does not hurry. When he had finished, he took the items he had collected through into the staff room. Dropping into an armchair, he began to read through the material.

It represented everything that Bev had written since she came to the Sin Bin. He searched it for clues. It was his last hope.

Froggy Parsons belonged in a headmaster's study. It was a stage set in which he gave his best performances, strutting and fretting in his inimitable way. Put him in the lounge of an executive home and he was diminished. He was away from his natural environment. It was Basher Bowen who came into his own. His sheer physical presence enabled him to dominate the proceedings.

'One other point,' he stressed. 'It was Beverly who invited Mr Sheen here. He suggested that Miss Finch would be more suitable but your daughter was keen that *he* should come here.'

'That proves nothing,' snapped Sheila.

'It proves she had a strong desire to get him here.'

'Good point,' noted Froggy.

'See it from Mr Sheen's position,' urged Basher. 'If he *did* have designs on your daughter, wouldn't he be more likely to take her somewhere else? The Sin Bin? His flat? A hotel, even. I mean, let's be realistic, shall we? What man is likely to assault a girl in her own house when he knows the parents are due back?'

'Sheen lost control,' argued Martin. 'A man doesn't stop to think in those circumstances. He just makes an impulsive grab.'

'You don't know Don Sheen,' said Basher. 'He's never lost control in his life. It's not as if he'd been drinking or anything. It was five o'clock and he was stone cold sober. How does he get from there to jumping on your daughter?'

'He's trying to talk his way out of it,' complained Sheila. 'Stop them, Martin. Don't let them do it.'

'We have to consider all aspects, Mrs Kington,' said Froggy.

Mrs Craig spoke for the first time.

'Then perhaps it's the moment to consider an aspect that we've ignored so far. I'm talking about Mr Sheen's private life.'

'Steady on,' warned Basher.

'This could be relevant,' she maintained. 'I understand that Mr Sheen has a long-term relationship with a young lady. It just so happens that she is away for some weeks on a course. He is –if you like – a carefree bachelor again.'

'Mrs Craig,' said Basher firmly, 'carefree bachelors do not pick on fifteen year old schoolgirls. Neither does Don Sheen.'

'Beverly knows otherwise,' insisted Sheila.

'We always come back to that,' added Martin. 'Our daughter was the person who *had* the gruesome experience. No amount of clever arguments can get away from that.'

'We want this pervert sacked,' said Sheila bluntly.

'He's no pervert,' defended Basher.

'Besides,' argued Froggy, 'there would be no question of sacking at this early stage. The most we could do would be to suspend him until investigations have been completed.'

'Tell them, Martin,' urged his wife.

'We want this man kicked out.'

'On unproven charges?' Basher was aghast.

'They're proven to us, Mr Bowen,' said Martin. 'Look, let's cut through all this amateur detection, shall we? Our position is simple. If Don Sheen is not sacked, we go straight to the police.'

It was a savage ultimatum.

It was good to have Neil back in the family again but it was only a short visit. On Sunday afternoon, he got back in the van with the others and went off. Thick and his parents waved Neil off. Much as they wanted to keep him, they knew that he was extremely well looked after at the home. Vale Road could not hope to compete with the sort of facilities that Neil enjoyed.

With some of the afternoon still left, Thick decided to call on a friend who lived on the other side of the park. While his parents trundled back home, he jogged across the green acres of the Memorial Park. It had been an exceptional day so far for Thick. Not only had he spent a lot of time with his younger brother, he had met Abbie and had a proper conversation with her. He was still replaying their chat in his mind when he cut through the trees.

His reverie was brutally interrupted.

'Thass far enough, clunk'ead!'

'You juss come to the end of the line, mate.'

'Should've looked where you're goin'.'

'OK. Gerrim!'

They came at him from four sides and gave him no chance. Tim Roach got the first punch in. Mooser landed the first kick. Their victim did not submit easily. Shrugging off Keach's first lunge, he managed to catch Vinny with a solid punch that floored him. But he could not keep them all at bay.

Mooser jumped on his back, Tim pounded away at his chest and the others lent their power. It was only a matter of time before Thick went down. Luck favoured him. A group of people were coming through the trees as he was scythed to the grass.

'Smash 'im, lads.'

'Doan lerrim ger back up!'

'Pur the boot in!'

The newcomers saw the commotion and hurried towards it.

'Come on!' shouted Vinny. 'Less go!'

Thick was left moaning on the ground.

Half-a-dozen bodies bent solicitously over him.

'OK, mate?'

'Who were they?'

'Dirty sods!'

'Four against one.'

'Come on. We'll give you an 'and up.'

'Easy does it.'

Thick was able to give them a smile of thanks before he lapsed back into unconsciousness.

Chapter Ten

Bev stood at the window of her bedroom and watched the visitors departing. They did not look pleased. Froggy Parsons was harassed. Mrs Craig was rueful. Basher Bowen was throbbing with anger. They got into a car and Froggy drove them away. Their mission had clearly failed. Bev felt vindicated.

She lay on the bed once more and gazed up at the ceiling. It was extraordinary. Twenty-four hours earlier, she had almost persuaded herself that she was in love with Don Sheen yet she could not even remember in any detail what he looked like. Having come into her life and made such an impact, his exit had been equally dramatic. Bev's feelings towards him now were completely neutral.

Feet ascended the carpeted stairs. Someone tapped on her door.

'Beverly?' It was her mother.

'Yes?'

'Are you all right in there?'

'A little better.'

'Anything you need?'

'No thanks.'

'Something to eat, drink?'

'Nothing.'

'OK, darling,' said Sheila Kington comfortingly. 'By the way, they've just gone.'

'I saw them.'

'They didn't get any of the things they came for. Your father and I sent them packing. They got the message.'

'Good . . . What about Don – er, Mr Sheen?'

'Don't worry,' promised her mother. 'We'll have him out of Woodfield if it's the last thing we do.'

There was a long pause as Bev absorbed the information.

'Mum?'

'Yes, darling?'

'I won't have to see him again, will I?'

'Mr Sheen? Never. We've stipulated that.'

'Thanks.'

'Try to rest now. I'll come back later.'

'OK.'

The footsteps faded away and Bev was left alone once more. Her anxieties had been soothed now. She could begin to think rationally again. It was even possible that she could feel sorry for Don Sheen.

But that was all she felt.

Back in the study at the Sin Bin, Don pored over the collection of her writings. He had telephoned several of her teachers to discuss her work and character. An interesting profile had emerged and it did not conform with first impressions of the girl. He reached for the directory, looked up a number in a new housing development then dialled it. The voice which answered was brusque and strained.

'Mr Kington?'

'Yes,' said Martin.

'My name is Don Sheen.'

'You've got a damn cheek ringing here!'

'I simply had to talk to you.'

'Listen, Mr Sheen —'

'I haven't come to apologize or justify or anything like that, Mr Kington. In fact, I don't want to speak about myself at all.'

'We really have nothing to say to —'

'Please don't hang up,' implored Don. 'Just hear me out for two minutes, that's all I ask. Less, probably. Is it a deal?'

'What do you want?' said Martin suspiciously.

'To try a little experiment.'

'Experiment?'

'My whole career is at stake here and that's why I have to take this one chance. It's my last resort.'

'I'm not with you.'

'Well, what it comes down to is this, Mr Kington. I'm being hanged, drawn and quartered on the unsubstantiated word of one person. You won't even listen to my version of the story.'

'Correct.'

'So take a closer look at Beverly's version.'

'Look?'

'Put it to the test.'

'And how do I do that, Mr Sheen?'

'Very simply. You use a lie detector.'

'A what?'

'I'm not talking about a machine. I'm talking about a person. It's the only kind of lie detector that will work.'

'You've got me baffled.'

'Then please let me explain . . .'

In view of the severity of the attack, Thick Dobrowski had come off relatively lightly. His body was a mass of bruises but no bones were broken. One of his eyes was puffed up, one of his ears enlarged and he had six stitches inserted in a cut on his forehead. Apart from that, he was in surprisingly good condition. He would certainly be able to go to school the next day. It was important to do that. As a show of strength.

Mrs Dobrowski brought him a cup of coffee and sat down beside him in the living room. When she looked at his injuries again, tears welled in her eyes.

'Who did it, Barry?'

'Dunno.'

'You're only sayin' thar.'

'No, I'm nor.'

'You *know* them, doan you?'

Thick shook his head but he knew them all too well. And he would get even with them somehow. The attack on him had not made him fear the gang. It had just steeled his resolve to stand up to them. They had a lot to answer for and he would call them to account.

Bev was flicking idly through a pop magazine in her bedroom but it could not hold her attention. Her mind was elsewhere. Things had got out of control and it unnerved her. She had not intended to get Don Sheen dismissed. That prospect made her feel slightly ashamed. Throwing the magazine aside, she reached for the glass of water on the bedside table and sipped it.

The doorbell rang. Someone was admitted to the house and muffled voices rose from below. Feet then came up the stairs. Knuckles tapped on the timber.

'Beverly?'

'Yes, Mum?'

'You've got a visitor.'

'Oh.'

Bev looked up with a mixture of alarm and curiosity. Who could possibly be calling on her? She got her answer when the door opened and she was quite stunned.

'Abbie!'

'Hi, Bev.'

'Whatever are *you* doing here?'

'Came to see 'ow you were, like.'

'Mum and Dad let you in?' Bev was astounded.

'Yeah.'

Abbie closed the door behind her and sat cross-legged on the floor. It was just like old times. Alone together, they had spent hours listening to records in that room. It had been their refuge.

They plunged straight into a mass of small talk. Abbie did not mind. There was a lot of news to catch up on and

116

the chat was helping Bev to relax. It was twenty minutes or more before there was a lull in the conversation. The visitor seized her opening.

'So wass all this, Bev?' she probed.

'All what?'

'You, hidin' away up 'ere. Your parents bein' all funny. Wass 'appened? You can tell me.'

Bev nodded. Abbie was the one person she could tell.

'It was terrible, honestly.'

'Wor was?'

'Don Sheen called round here yesterday.'

'To the 'ouse?'

'Yes.'

'Why?'

'Something to do with the debating contest,' said Bev. 'He was trying to persuade Mum and Dad to let me represent the school.'

'You'd be great!' encouraged Abbie.

'That's what Thin Lizzie and Don Sheen thought.'

'An' 'e actually came 'ere?' The other girl was impressed. 'Muss be keen to ger you if 'e gives up 'is spare time like thar.'

'Yes, I suppose so.'

'Nor many teachers would bother thar much.'

'No.'

'Anyway, he comes round. Wor then?'

'My parents were both out.'

'You an' 'im were alone?'

'Yes,' said Bev, concealing the fact that she had arranged it that way. 'Nothing happened at first. We just chatted about this and that. Had a drink together.'

'A *real* drink?'

'No, no. Just soft drinks.'

'And?'

'He was really nice to me at first. Showing an interest in my work and that. I thought he meant it all. Then . . .'

117

'Go on.'

'It was awful, Abbie! Really frightening!'

'Wor did 'e do?'

'Jumped on me. In the lounge.'

'Mister Softee? Thass nor 'is style.'

'I was *there*, Abbie. I know what he did.'

'Oh, sure.'

Bev worked herself up into a state of mild hysteria. Her face had a tortured expression and the words came tumbling out of her.

'One minute, he was OK. Like he is in class. The next ... I mean, it was the last thing I expected. He's a *teacher*. I trusted him. It was dreadful, Abbie. I fought him off and he gave up but I was shaking like a leaf. He tried to calm me down and asked me not to tell anyone. Then he left. I cried my eyes out. It was the worst thing that's ever happened to me.'

'This was Don *Sheen*?' Her friend was sceptical.

'Yes. He caught me off guard.'

'Actually pounced on you?'

'I've just told you.'

'Bur 'ow?'

'What do you mean?'

'Did 'e grab 'old of you or wor?'

'He grabbed my arms,' insisted Bev, rolling up her sleeves to reveal some ugly blotches. 'I've still got the bruises.'

'Tim Roach gave you those.'

'Mm?'

'I remember you tellin' me. Tim wanned a kiss so 'e cort 'old of your arms and gave you them bruises. Thick Dobrowski saved you.'

Bev fell silent. Her evidence was not as convincing as she had thought. Abbie had a good memory. She also had a nose for the truth.

'Why doan you tell me wor *really* 'appened, Bev?'

'I have!'

'Pull the other one.'

'Why should I lie?'

' 'cos you felt cheated.'

'What?'

'When Don Sheen was 'ere, you *wanned* 'im to jump on you.'

'No, Abbie!'

'Bur 'e didden touch you.'

'Yes, he did.'

'So you thort you'd ger your own back, like, by makin' up thar story. You felt cheated, didden you?'

'It wasn't like that!'

'It was Bev,' argued the other levelly. 'Less face it. Don Sheen's a teacher. A grown-up. Why's 'e gonna bother with a fourth former like you?'

'Because he fancies me!' wailed Bev. 'You said so.'

Abbie was halted for a moment. She began to see that a chance remark of hers might have been instrumental in the whole episode. It sobered her. It also made her feel more sympathy for Bev who was now on the verge of collapse. Abbie went over to her friend and put an arm around her.

'Look, I'm sorry,' she whispered. 'I did say 'e fancied you but nor like thar. You're only fifteen, Bev. Don Sheen's norra cradle snatcher. Anyway, 'e's already gor a girlfriend. I seen 'er. Looks a bit like Miss Whitnall only darker.' She squeezed Bev's shoulder. 'Come on. Less 'ave the truth. 'e didden lay a finger on you, did 'e?'

Bev gestured helplessly. She could not deceive her friend. Seasoned in the art of lying herself, Abbie was not fooled for a second. Don Sheen had been absolutely right to send the girl along to the house.

Abbie Reynolds was a lie detector.

Sheila Kington was on her second gin and tonic. Her husband opted for a brandy and soda. Having nothing to say to each other, they said it a dozen times. Their conversation went round in circles.

'I'm wondering if we've been too hasty,' admitted Martin.

'We did the right thing,' insisted his wife.

'Yes, yes. Even so . . .'

'You can't *doubt* Beverly, can you?'

'I'm not sure.'

They heard the bedroom door open. Bev and Abbie came downstairs, holding hands. White, nervous and hesitant, Bev kept her eyes on the floor. Abbie was more composed. She looked from one parent to another.

'She told me the truth.'

'Did she?' asked Martin.

'You're nor gonna like this, Mr Kington.'

'Why?'

'Don Sheen never touched 'er.'

Shocked faces turned to Bev. She confirmed with a nod.

Martin and Sheila flew into a joint panic.

'But you accused the man!' he said.

'We made a formal complaint,' added his wife.

'The headmaster came to the house.'

'We *believed* you, Beverly.'

'My God!' The full implication hit Martin. 'We might have destroyed that man's career. On your say-so! Just think what he must have gone through.'

'And look at the position *we're* in,' groaned Sheila.

'This is no time to think of ourselves,' snapped her husband. 'Mr Sheen is the person we should be concerned about.' He turned on his daughter. 'Why ever did you lie to us, Beverly?'

'I don't know,' she said.

'Couldn't you see how much damage you'd do?'

'No.'

'This is terrible!'

Martin ranted on at her with support from his wife. Bev took it on the chin. She knew that she deserved it. As the torrent of criticism died down, Abbie came to her aid.

'Lemme try an' explain,' she offered. 'Iss nor all Bev's fault. I'm to blame, really. None of this would've 'appened if I 'adden torked Bev into makin' thar call to the fire brigade.'

Martin took a deep breath and tried to stay calm.

'Now we're getting somewhere . . .'

Don Sheen sat by the telephone for a call that never came. Convinced that his last shot had failed, he gave up. There was no point in staying at the Sin Bin any longer. It was hours since he had rung the Kington household. They were patently not going to ring back. Looking sadly around his office, he got up then went out.

He was leaving the building when they came up to him.

'Could we have a few moments, please?' asked Martin.

'Yes. Of course.'

'Beverly has something to say to you.'

The girl was going through agonies. Standing between her parents, she was tense and pained. Martin and Sheila were obviously embarrassed but Bev was positively writhing with guilt.

'Well?' prompted her father.

'I'm sorry, sir,' she murmured.

'Beverly admits she made it all up,' said Sheila.

'It was a rotten thing to do,' confessed the girl. 'Sorry, sir.'

'We owe you an apology as well, Mr Sheen,' said Martin. 'We were grossly unfair to you. I suppose every parent likes to think that their child is honest. We certainly did. Beverly told an appalling lie and we swallowed it. We can't tell you how sick that makes us feel now.'

Don Sheen was overcome with relief. He gave a half-smile.

'It's very good of you to come here like this,' he said.

'The least we could do,' continued Martin. 'Beverly has caused you an enormous amount of trouble and worry. She must be punished for it.'

'I like to understand *why* people do things before I think

121

about a punishment.' Don looked down at Bev, who was squirming in discomfort. 'Let's forget all about it for today, shall we? There'll be time for talking during school hours. No real harm done.'

'That's very generous of you, Mr Sheen,' said Sheila. 'I don't think I'd be quite so forgiving if I were in your shoes.'

Bev stood there in torment as her parents continued to apologize. Now that she was confronted with Don Sheen again, she realized just how vicious her lie had been. Because of her claim, he had been on the verge of losing his job at Woodfield. And all because he had taken the trouble to help her. It was a poor way to reward his interest. She was glad when the discussion finally broke up. All she wanted to do was to get away.

'Just one thing,' recalled Don.

'Yes?' said Martin.

'We'd still like Bev in that debating contest. Any chance of it?'

The girl's spirits lifted. She was wanted.

Basher Bowen read the situation as soon as the boys trooped into the Sin Bin on Monday morning. Thick Dobrowski bore the scars of battle. Tim Roach and his mates strutted in with a smug arrogance. The teacher made some time for a chat with the victim. At the end of the school day, he kept the gang in and talked idly about the art of self-defence. The four of them had no idea what he was on about. When the main school had emptied, he took the quartet across to the gymnasium. They were startled to find Thick Dobrowski already there, wearing a boxing strip and using a skipping rope.

'Now we'll have a real fight!' announced Basher. 'Marquess of Queensberry rules. Vinny – get some gloves on. You're first.'

'Bur 'e's bigger than me!' yelled the boy.

'I'm bigger still, boyo. Rather take me on?'

Vinny stepped into the ring with Thick and lasted less than a minute. The thickset Polish boy anticipated every move the puny youth made and ran circles around him, humiliating and demoralizing his opponent. Thick repeated the process with Mooser and Keach, displaying more innate skill and ability than Basher could ever have suspected.

Tim Roach put up a more spirited defence but he was essentially a streetfighter. Deprived of his dirty tricks, he was largely disarmed. Thick deftly blocked every attack the Sin Bin bully launched, and dispatched a few swift jabs. Within moments Tim Roach was defeated.

Basher Bowen stood among the four fallen heroes.

'Next time you lot set on him – whether it's inside school or outside – *I'll* come looking for you. OK?'

They nodded ruefully. Basher lifted Thick's gloved hand up.

'The champion!'

Dreading her return to school, Bev found it far less daunting than she had feared. Don Sheen played down what had happened over the weekend. Completely exonerated, he wanted nothing more than to carry on as usual. Bev slotted back into the class and she was pleased to see that Calvin had superseded her as the official tea-maker. Later in the day, there was a sticky interview with Froggy Parsons but it was not as traumatic as it might have been. Abbie was beside her. Having owned up to her part in the hoax call, Abbie was chastised alongside her friend.

Froggy ran through the whole gamut of his tricks. He slapped the desk, stamped his foot, punched the air, waved his arms about like a miniature windmill and told them that they had committed the worst crime in the history of education. Bev weathered it all with comparative ease. The real test had been to face Don Sheen the previous day. Both girls were to continue the term in the Sin Bin. Bev was thankful. Having Abbie beside her would make everything so much easier to endure.

Don Sheen made no attempt to talk about the incident. He realized what had happened. He had been the subject of an adolescent infatuation that had got out of hand. Under intense pressure from all sides, Bev had seen him as her saviour. In her confused emotional state, she had imagined a relationship that was simply not there. When Don Sheen – as she saw it – disappointed her at her home, she lashed out wildly at him. The best course for him was to forgive and forget.

After all the trouble it had cost him, however, he did take an interest in the debating competition. When the Woodfield hopefuls were auditioned by Thin Lizzie, he sat at the back of the classroom. There were a dozen or more pupils and the English teacher was putting them through a series of short debates.

'OK,' she said. 'Let's get under way.'

She held out a small cardboard box and shook it vigorously. Inside the box were slips of paper that had been folded into pellets. Thin Lizzie walked across to where Bev and Abbie were sitting.

'Right,' she decided. 'You two will make a good team. Bev, you choose a subject then you propose the motion. Abbie, you second her.'

She shook the box again. Bev put in her hand.

'Wor is it?' said Abbie eagerly.

'Give me a chance to open it,' replied Bev.

'Read it out,' suggested the teacher.

Bev flattened the piece of paper then glanced at it. A blush threatened but she tried to keep it at bay. This was no time to be oversensitive. The choice of subject was pure luck.

'Well?' nudged Thin Lizzie.

'This House Believes that Honesty is the Best Policy.'

The momentary silence was broken by a giggle from Abbie.

'They picked the right pair for this one,' she said.
'Yes,' agreed Bev.
Everyone joined in the laughter. Including Don Sheen.
Bev felt an upsurge of happiness.
A load was lifted from her.

Hairline Cracks
John Robert Taylor

Sam Lydney's mother knows too much. She has realized that a public inquiry into the safety of a local nuclear power station has been rigged and, despite his father's assurances, Sam is certain she's been kidnapped. He can trust no one except his resourceful friend Mo. They must work alone to piece together the clues and discover who has taken his mother and where she may be kept.

An Armada Original

Run With the Hare
Linda Newbery

Elaine, a sixth-form pupil, becomes involved in an Animal
Rights group through her more forceful friend Kate. She
also forms a romantic attachment with Mark, an Adult
Education student at school and one of the more
sophisticated members of the group. Partly in an attempt
to win Mark's approval, Elaine finds herself painting
slogans, sabotaging a fox hunt and breaking into a veal
production unit. But then she and her friends uncover a
dog fighting ring – and things turn very nasty.

An Armada Original

STEVIE DAY SUPERSLEUTH
(that's me!)

I'm on my way to being the first female Commissioner of the Metropolitan Police. It's true I have a few personal problems: for a start I'm small and skinny and people are always mistaking me for a boy. I'm 14 – though you wouldn't think so – and my younger sister, Carla, not only looks older than me but she's much prettier too. Not that that really matters. You see, she doesn't have my brains.

If you want to see my razor-sharp mind in action or have proof of my brilliant powers of deduction then read about my triumphant successes in:

STEVIE DAY: Supersleuth
STEVIE DAY: Lonely Hearts
STEVIE DAY: Rat Race
STEVIE DAY: Vampire

ARMADA

THE E
E

Two brand-n
stories from two stars.

Betty Neels

&

Liz Fielding

**Get caught up in
The Engagement Effect**

**Two gorgeous men
carry their brides-to-be over the threshold
into a world of wedded bliss...**

Betty Neels spent her childhood and youth in Devonshire before training as a nurse and midwife. She was an army nursing sister during the war, married a Dutchman, and subsequently lived in Holland for fourteen years. She lives with her husband in Dorset, and has a daughter and grandson. Her hobbies are reading, animals, old buildings and writing. Betty started to write on retirement from nursing, incited by a lady in a library bemoaning the lack of romantic novels.

Betty Neels has written more than 130 novels, with books translated into more than 25 languages and published in over 100 international markets. Betty is a global bestselling author.

Born and raised in Berkshire, **Liz Fielding** started writing at the age of twelve when she won a hymn-writing competition at her convent school. After a gap of more years than she is prepared to admit to, during which she worked as a secretary in Africa and the Middle East, got married and had two children, she was finally able to realise her ambition and turn to full-time writing in 1992.

She now lives with her husband, John, in West Wales, surrounded by mystical countryside and romantic crumbling castles, content to leave the travelling to her grown-up children and keeping in touch with the rest of the world via the Internet.

Visit her website at www.lizfielding.com

First Published 2001
First Australian Paperback Edition 2002
ISBN 0 733 53494 5

THE ENGAGEMENT EFFECT

AN ORDINARY GIRL
by
BETTY NEELS

A PERFECT PROPOSAL
by
LIZ FIELDING

Mother's Day Special

CONTENTS

AN ORDINARY GIRL

by
Betty Neels

CHAPTER ONE

PHILOMENA SELBY, the eldest of the Reverend Ambrose Selby's five daughters, was hanging up sheets. It was a blustery March morning and since she was a small girl, nicely rounded but slight, she was having difficulty subduing their wild flapping. Finally she had them pegged in a tidy line, and she picked up the empty basket and went back into the house, where she stuffed another load into the washing machine and put the kettle on. A cup of coffee would be welcome. While she waited for it to boil she cut a slice of bread off the loaf on the table and ate it.

She was a girl with no looks to speak of, but her face was redeemed from plainness by her eyes, large and brown, fringed by long lashes beneath delicately arched brows. Her hair, tangled by the wind, was brown too, straight and fine, tied back with a bit of ribbon with no thought of fashion. She shook it back now and got mugs and milk and sugar, and spooned instant coffee as her mother came into the kitchen.

Mrs Selby was a middle-aged version of her daughter and the years had been kind to her. Her brown hair was streaked with silver-grey and worn in a bun—a style she had never altered since she had put her hair up as a seventeen-year-old girl. There were wrinkles and lines in her face, but the lines were laughter lines and the wrinkles didn't matter at all.

She accepted a mug of coffee and sat down at the table.

'Mrs Frost called in with a bag of onions to thank your father for giving her Ned a lift the other day. If you'd pop down to Mrs Salter's and get some braising steak from her deep-freeze we could have a casserole.'

11

Philomena swallowed the last of her bread. 'I'll go now; the butcher will have come so there'll be plenty to choose from.'

'And some sausages, dear.'

Philomena went out of the house by the back door, and down the side path which led directly onto the village street. When she reached the village green she joined the customers waiting to be served. She knew that she would have to wait for several minutes. Mrs Salter was the fount of all news in the village and passed it on readily while she weighed potatoes and cut cheese. Philomena whiled away the time peering into the deep-freeze cabinet, not so much interested in braising steak as she was in the enticing containers of ice cream and chocolate cakes.

Her turn came, and with the steak and sausages wrapped in a not very tidy parcel she started off back home.

The car which drew up beside her was silent—but then it would be; it was a Bentley—and she turned a rather startled face to the man who spoke to her across the girl sitting beside him.

'We're looking for Netherby House, but I believe that we are lost...'

Philomena looked into the car, leaning on the window he had opened.

'Well, yes, you are. Have you a map?'

His companion thrust one at her and she opened it out, pausing to smile at the girl as she leaned further in.

'Look, this is Nether Ditchling—here.' She pointed with a small hand, reddened by the cold wind. 'You need to go through the village as far as the crossroads—' her finger moved on '—go right and go to Wisbury; that's about three miles. There are crossroads at the end of the village. Go right, and after a mile you'll see a lane signposted to Netherby House. Can you remember that?' she asked anxiously.

She looked at him then; he had a handsome, rather rugged face, close-cropped dark hair and blue eyes. They stared at each other for a moment, and she had the strange feeling that something had happened…

'I shall remember,' he told her, and smiled.

Philomena gave her head a little shake. 'People often get lost; it's a bit rural.' She withdrew her head and picked up her steak and sausages from the girl's lap, where she had dumped them, the better to point the way on the map. She smiled as she did so and received a look of contempt which made her blush, suddenly aware that in this elegant girl's eyes she was a nonentity.

'So sorry. It's only sausages and steak.'

She didn't hear the small sound which escaped the man's lips and she stood back, hearing only his friendly thanks.

Her mother was still in the kitchen, peeling carrots. 'Philly, you were a long time…'

'A car stopped on its way to Netherby House; they'd got lost. A Bentley. There was a girl, very pretty and dressed like a fashion magazine, and a man driving. Mother, why is it that sometimes one meets someone one has never met before and it seems as though one has known them for always?'

Mrs Selby bent over the carrots. She said carefully, 'I think it is something which happens often, but people don't realise it. If they do then it is to be hoped that it may lead to happiness.'

She glanced at Philly, who was unwrapping the sausages. 'I wonder why they were going to Netherby House. Perhaps their eldest girl has got engaged—I did hear that it was likely.'

Philly said, 'Yes, perhaps that's it. They weren't married, but she had an outsize diamond ring…'

Her mother rightly surmised that the Bentley and its occupants were still occupying her daughter's thoughts. She said briskly, 'Will you make your father a cup of coffee? If he's finished writing his sermon he'll want it.'

So Philly went out of the kitchen, across the cold hall and along a passage to the back of the house, which was a mid-Victorian building considered suitable for a vicar of those days with a large family and several servants. The Reverend Selby had a large family, but no servants—except for Mrs Dash, who came twice a week to oblige—and the vicarage, imposing on the outside, was as inconvenient on the inside as it was possible to be.

Philly skipped along, avoiding the worn parts of the linoleum laid down years ago by some former incumbent, and found her parent sitting at his desk, his sermon written. He was tall and thin, with grey hair getting scarce on top, but now, in his fifties, he was still a handsome man, with good looks which had been passed on to his four younger girls. Philly was the only one like her mother—something which he frequently told her made him very happy. 'Your mother is a beautiful woman,' he would tell her, 'and you are just like she was at your age.'

They were words which comforted Philly when she examined her face in the mirror and wished for blue eyes and the golden hair which framed her sisters' pretty faces. But she was never downcast for long; she was content with her lot: helping her mother run the house, helping with the Sunday School, giving a hand at the various social functions in the village. She hoped that one day she would meet a man who would want to marry her, but her days were too busy for her to spend time daydreaming about that.

The driver of the Bentley, following Philomena's instructions, drove out of the village towards the crossroads, listening to his companion's indignant voice. 'Really—that girl. Dumping her shopping in my lap like that.' She shuddered. 'Sausages and heaven knows what else...'

'Steak.' He sounded amused.

'And if that's typical of a girl living in one of these godforsaken villages—frightful clothes and so plain—then the less we leave London the better. And did you see her hands? Red, and no nail polish. Housework hands.'

'Small, but pretty, none the less, and she had beautiful eyes.'

He glanced sideways at the perfect profile. 'You're very uncharitable, Sybil. Ah, here are the crossroads. Netherby is only a mile ahead of us.'

'I never wanted to come. I hate engagement parties...'

'I thought you enjoyed ours.'

'That was different—now we're only the guests.'

The house was at the end of a narrow lane. It was a large, rambling place, and the sweep before the front door was full of cars.

Sybil sat in the car, waiting for him to open the door. 'I shall be bored stiff,' she told him as they walked to the door, and he looked at her again. She was more than pretty, she was beautiful, with perfect features and golden hair cunningly cut. But just now she looked sulky, and her mouth was turned down at the corners. 'That stupid girl and now this...'

But once she was inside, being greeted by their host and hostess and the various friends and acquaintances there, the sulky look was replaced by smiles and the charm she switched on like a light. She was in raptures over the engagement ring, laughed and talked, and was the picture of a dear friend delighted to join in the gossip about the wedding. At the luncheon which followed she kept her end of the table entranced by her witty talk.

'You're a lucky fellow, James,' observed a quiet little lady sitting beside the rather silent man. 'Sybil is a lovely young woman, and so amusing too. When do you intend to marry?'

He smiled at her. 'Sybil is in no hurry, and in any case we're short-staffed at the hospital. I doubt if I could find the time. She wants a big wedding, which I understand takes time and organising.'

Kind, elderly eyes studied his face. There was something not quite right, but it was none of her business. 'Tell me, I hear that there is a scheme to open another ward...?'

'Yes, for premature babies. It's still being discussed, but we need more incubators.'

'You love your work, don't you?'

'Yes.'

She saw that she wasn't going to be told more and asked idly if he had enjoyed the drive down from town.

'Yes, it's a different world, isn't it? Last time I saw you, you were making a water garden. Is it finished?'

They turned to their neighbours presently, and then everyone left the table to stand around talking, or walked in the large formal garden, and it was there that Sybil found him presently.

'Darling, we simply must leave. I'm so bored. Say that you take a clinic this evening and that you have to be back by seven o'clock.' When he looked at her, she added, 'Oh, darling, don't look like that. It's such a stuffy party.'

She had a lovely smile, so he smiled back and went in search of their hostess.

Having got her own way, Sybil was at her most charming self, keeping up amusing talk as they drove back to London. As he slowed through Nether Ditchling she said with a laugh, 'Oh, this is the place where we talked to that plain girl with the sausages. What a dull life she must lead. Shall we be back in time to have dinner together some-where I can dress up? I bought the loveliest outfit the other day—I'll wear it.'

'I must disappoint you, Sybil. I've a pile of paperwork, and I want to check a patient at the hospital.'

She pouted prettily, clever enough to know that he wasn't to be persuaded. She put a hand on his knee. 'Never mind, darling. Let me know when you can spare an evening and we'll go somewhere special.'

He drove her to her parents' flat in Belgravia and went

straight to the hospital—where he forgot her, the luncheon party and the long drive, becoming at once engrossed in the progress of his small patient. But he didn't forget the girl with the sausages. That they would meet again was something he felt in his very bones, and he was content to wait until that happened.

March had come in like a lamb and it was certainly going out like a lion. Winter had returned, with wind and rain and then the warning of heavy snow. Professor James Forsyth, on his morning round one Saturday morning, was called to the phone. 'An urgent message,' Sister had told him.

It was Sybil. 'James, darling, you're free this afternoon and tomorrow, aren't you? I simply must go to Netherby. I've bought a present for Coralie and Greg and it's too large to send. Will you be an angel and drive me down this afternoon? I promise you we won't stay, and we can come straight back and dine somewhere. I thought tomorrow we might go to Richmond Park. The Denvers are always inviting us to lunch and I'm dying to see their new house.'

Professor Forsyth frowned. 'Sybil, I have asked you not to phone me at the hospital unless it is an urgent matter.'

'Darling, but this *is* urgent. I mean, how am I to get this wretched present down to Netherby unless you drive me there?' She added with a wistful charm which was hard to resist, 'Please, James.'

'Very well, I'll drive you down there and back. But I can't take you to dinner this evening and I need Sunday to work on a lecture I'm due to give.'

He heard her murmured protest and then, 'Of course, darling, I quite understand. And thank you for finding the time for poor little me. Will you fetch me? I'll have an early lunch. I can be ready at one o'clock.'

As they left London behind them the dark day became darker, with unbroken cloud and a rising wind. Their journey was half done when the first idle snowflakes began to fall, and by the time they were driving through Nether Ditchling it was snowing in earnest.

Sybil, who had been at her most charming now that she had got what she wanted, fell silent.

'Will ten minutes or so be enough for you to deliver your gift? I don't want to linger in this weather.'

She was quick to reassure him. 'Don't come in; I'll only be a few minutes. I'll explain that you have to get back to town.'

At the house she said, 'Don't get out, James. If you do they'll want us to stay for tea. I'll be very quick.'

She leaned across and kissed his cheek, got out of the car and ran up the steps to the front door, and a moment later disappeared through it.

The doctor sat back and closed his eyes. He was tired, and the prospect of a quiet day at home was very welcome. Peaceful hours in his study, making notes for his lecture, leisurely meals, time to read...

He glanced at his watch; Sybil had been gone for almost fifteen minutes. He could go and fetch her, but if he did they might find it difficult to leave quickly. He switched on the radio: Delius—something gentle and rather sad.

Sybil was sitting by the fire in her friend Coralie's sitting room. The wedding present was open beside them and there was a tea tray between them. Another few minutes wouldn't matter, Sybil had decided, and a cup of tea would be nice. While they drank it details of the wedding dress could be discussed...

She had been there for almost half an hour when she glanced at the clock.

'I must go. It's been such fun and I quite forgot the time. James will be wondering what's happened to me.' She gave a little trill of laughter. 'It's such a good thing he always does exactly what I want.'

She put on her coat and spent a few moments examining

her face in her little mirror. She added a little lipstick and
went down to the hall with Coralie. Saying goodbye was a
leisurely affair, too, but the butler had opened the door and
she hurried out into the blinding snow.

The doctor had the door open for her. He leaned across
to shut it as she got in and asked in a quiet voice, 'What
kept you, Sybil? A few minutes was the agreed time.'

'Oh, darling don't be cross. I haven't been very long,
have I? Coralie insisted that I had a cup of tea.' She turned
a smiling face to him.

'You were half an hour.' His voice was expressionless.

Her smile disappeared. 'What if I was a bit longer than
I said? I won't be ordered around and I won't be hurried.
Now for heaven's sake let's get back to town.'

'That may not be possible.'

He drove carefully, for the snow was drifting and visi-
bility was almost non-existent. The big car held the road
well, but it was now pitch-dark and there was no lighting
on the narrow country roads. He came to the crossroads,
drove through Wisbury and onto the crossroads after it. It
was as he drove into Nether Ditchling that a flashing blue
light from a police car parked on the side of the road
brought him to a halt.

A cold but cheerful face appeared at the window. The
professor opened it and a policeman, muffled against the
weather, poked his head in.

'Road's closed ahead, sir. Are you going far?'

'London.'

'Not a chance. They'll have the snowploughs out on the
main roads, but they won't get here much before tomorrow
afternoon.'

'Is there no other way? We've come from Netherby.'

'Just had a message that the crossroads at Wisbury are
blocked. You'd best put up here for the night.'

Sybil said suddenly, 'I won't. I must be taken to London.
Of course there's another road we can use...' Both men

looked at her, and she added furiously, 'Well, do something, can't you?'

A tall figure in a hooded cape had joined them.

'Officer Greenslade? Can I be of help to you?'

'Reverend—I've suggested that these folk put up in the village, for they can't go anywhere else tonight.'

'Then let me offer them a meal and a bed.'

The Reverend Selby poked his head through the window in his turn. 'You car will be safe enough here. My wife will be delighted to help you.'

Professor Forsyth got out and made his way round to Sybil's door. 'That's most kind of you—we shan't be too much trouble?'

'No, no—and Greenslade, if anyone else needs shelter send them along to the vicarage.'

Sybil, for once mute, was helped up the short drive to the vicarage door and into the hall, where she stood watching the men shed their coats and cloak. She looked forlorn and very pretty, but the only feeling the professor had for her was one of exasperation. Nevertheless he unbuttoned her coat and took it off her, and then held her arm as they followed their host through the hall and into the kitchen.

This was a large room, with an old-fashioned dresser, a vast table with an assortment of wooden chairs around it and an elderly Aga giving out welcome warmth.

Mr Selby led the way to the two shabby Windsor chairs by the Aga, gently moved a cat and kittens from one of them, and said, 'My dear, we have guests. The road is closed and they can go no further.'

Mrs Selby gave them a warm smile and said, 'You poor things. Sit down and I'll make tea—you must need a hot drink.'

Professor Forsyth held out a hand. 'You're most kind and we're grateful. My name's Forsyth—James Forsyth. This lady is my fiancée, Miss Sybil West.'

Mrs Selby shook hands and turned to Sybil. 'This is horrid for you.'

Sybil lifted a lovely wistful face. 'Yes, I'm so cold and hungry, and we should be in London. If I could go to bed, perhaps I could have a small meal on a tray...'

James said evenly, 'You'll warm quickly here, and you have no need to go to bed.' He stopped speaking as the door opened and two girls came in, both fair-haired and pretty and smiling.

'We heard the car. Are you cut off from the outside world?' One girl offered a hand. 'I'm Flora and this is Rose. There are three more of us, but Lucy's spending the weekend with friends and Katie's finishing her homework. And Philly...'

A door at the back of the kitchen opened, letting in a great deal of cold air, and Philomena, wrapped in a variety of coats and scarves, with her head tied in some kind of a hood, came in.

'I got the chickens in, but we'll have a job to get to them by morning.'

She cast off some of the garments and looked across the kitchen at the tall man standing beside her father. 'Oh, hello, you were in that car...' She smiled at him and then saw Sybil, crouching by the Aga. 'And you, too,' she added cheerfully. 'Are you going to spend the night?'

She had taken off the last coat and pulled the hood off her head. 'I'll go and make up some beds, shall I, Mother? Rose will give me a hand.'

'Yes, dear.' Her mother was pouring tea into mugs and inviting the professor to sit down. 'Let me see. Miss...' She turned to Sybil with a smile. 'West, isn't it? You had better have Katie's room; she can go in with you. Rose and Flora can share, and Mr Forsyth...' Her eye fell on the bag he was carrying. 'Are you a doctor?' When he nodded, amused, she said, 'Doctor Forsyth can have the guest room.'

As Philly and Rose left the room she added, 'They'll put clean sheets on the beds, and if you're tired, which I expect you are, you can go to bed when we've had supper.'

'We are putting you to a great deal of trouble. Is there anything I can do?'

'No, no. It's stewed beef and dumplings, and there is plenty of it. Also there's an egg custard in the Aga.'

'Then if you've no need of Doctor Forsyth's services, my dear,' observed her husband, 'I'll take him along to my study while you and the girls get supper.'

There was the table to lay, more potatoes to peel, plates and cutlery to get from cupboards and drawers. Mrs Selby and Flora talked as they worked but Sybil stayed silent, fuming. A spoilt only child in a wealthy household, she had never done anything for herself. There had always been someone to wash and iron, cook meals, tidy her bedroom, to fetch and carry. Now she was dumped in this ghastly kitchen and James had left her with no more than a nod.

He would pay for it, she told herself silently. And if he and these people expected her to sit down and eat supper with them, they were mistaken. Once her room was ready she would say that she felt ill—a chill or a severe headache—and they would see her into bed and bring her something on a tray once she had had a hot bath.

Her thoughts were interrupted by a bang on the front door and voices. Philly ran to open it and returned a moment later with an elderly couple shedding snow and looking uncertain.

'Officer Greenslade sent them here,' announced Philly. 'They are on their way to Basingstoke.'

She began to unwind them from their snow-covered coats. 'Mother will be here in a moment. Our name's Selby—Father's the vicar.'

'Mr and Mrs Downe. We are most grateful…'

'Here's Mother.' Philly ushered them to the Aga and introduced them, and Flora pulled up chairs.

'A cup of tea to warm you?' said Mrs Selby. 'There'll be supper presently, and you'll sleep here, of course. It's no trouble. Here's my husband…'

The vicar and the professor came in together, and over mugs of tea the Downes reiterated their gratitude and, once warm, became cheerful.

Philly and her mother, busy at the Aga, rearranged the bedrooms.

'Rose and Flora can manage in Lucy's room; Mr and Mrs Downe can have their room.' So Rose went upstairs again, and then led Mrs Downe away to tidy herself and find a nightie.

It was time she dealt with her own comfort, decided Sybil, since James was doing nothing about it.

'I feel quite ill,' she told Mrs Selby. 'If I'm not being too much of a nuisance I do want to go to bed. If I could have a hot bath and just a little supper?'

Mrs Selby looked uncertain, and it was Philly who answered with a friendly firmness.

'No bath. There'll be just enough hot water for us all to wash—and if you go to bed now, I'm afraid we wouldn't be able to do anything about your supper for a bit.' She smiled, waving a spoon. 'All these people to feed.'

'But I'm ill…' Sybil's voice was lost in a commotion at the door again.

It was PC Greenslade again, this time with a solitary young man, his short jacket and trousers soaking and caked with snow.

'Got lost,' said the policeman. 'On his bike, would you believe it? Going to London.'

There was a general reshuffle as everyone moved to give the young man a place near the Aga. More tea was made and then the policeman, suitably refreshed, went back to his cold job while the young man's jacket was stripped off him.

He thanked them through chattering teeth. He was on his

way to see his girlfriend in Hackney, he explained. He was a seasoned cyclist, rode miles, he added proudly, but like a fool he'd taken a shortcut recommended by a friend and lost his way...

'You poor boy,' said Mrs Selby. 'You shall have a hot meal and go straight to bed.'

Professor Forsyth said quietly, 'After a good rub down and dry clothes. You said that there will be no chance of a hot bath? He does need to get warm...'

The vicar spoke. 'If everyone here will agree, we will use the hot water for a bath for this lad. There will still be just enough for a wash for the rest of us.'

There was a murmur of agreement and he led the young man away.

'But *I* wanted a bath,' said Sybil furiously.

'But you're warm and dry and unlikely to get pneumonia,' said James, in what she considered to be an unfeeling voice.

The electricity went out then.

He told everyone to stay where they were, flicked on the lighter he had produced from a pocket and asked Mrs Selby where she kept the candles.

'In the cupboard by the sink,' said Philly. 'I'll get them.'

There were oil lamps, too, in the boot room beyond the kitchen. He fetched them, lighted them, and carried one upstairs to the vicar and his charge. The people in the kitchen were surprised to hear bellows of laughter coming from the bathroom.

Philly had filled a hot water bottle, and when the Professor reappeared thrust it at him. 'He'll have to sleep in your bed,' she told him, and when he nodded she went on, 'I'll bring blankets down here and when everyone has gone to bed you can have the sofa. You won't mind?'

'Not in the least. Shall I take some food up? Clive—his name's Clive Parsons—is ready for bed.'

'Mother has warmed some soup. Katie can bring it up—

she's the youngest. She's been doing her homework; she's very clever and nothing disturbs her until it's finished. But she should be here in a minute.'

'Homework in the dark?' he asked.

'She'll be reciting Latin verbs or something. I told you she was clever.'

The professor, beginning to enjoy himself enormously, laughed, received the hot water bottle and, presently back in the kitchen, devoted himself to improving Sybil's temper.

This was no easy task, for she had taken refuge in a cold silence, which was rather wasted as everyone else was busy relating their experiences in the snow and speculating as to what it would be like in the morning.

Presently the vicar came to join them. Katie had taken a bowl of soup with a dumpling in it up to Clive and had left him to enjoy it while they all gathered round the table.

The beef, stretched to its limits, was eked out by great mounds of mashed potatoes and more dumplings and was pronounced the best meal eaten for years. There was more tea then, and everyone helped to clear the table and wash up. Sybil's wistful excuses that she would like to help but she had to take care of her hands went unheeded. The professor, in his shirtsleeves, washed the dishes while Mr Downe dried them and Mrs Downe and Mrs Selby found more candles and candlesticks.

Philly had her head in the kitchen cupboard and the girls were laying the table for breakfast.

'Porridge?' queried Philly to the room at large. 'For breakfast,' she added.

There was a general murmur of agreement but Sybil said, 'I thought porridge was what poor people in Scotland ate. I've never eaten it.'

The doctor said briskly, 'Well, now will be your chance. It's the best breakfast one can have on a cold winter's morning.'

She glared at him. 'If no one minds, I'll go to bed.'

Philly gave her a hot water bottle and a candle. 'I hope you feel better in the morning,' she said kindly. 'Remember about the hot water, won't you?'

The doctor abandoned the sink for a moment and went to the door with Sybil.

He gave her a comforting pat on the shoulder. 'You'll feel better in the morning,' he told her bracingly. 'We are very lucky to have found such generous kindness.'

He smiled down kindly into her cross face, aware that the feeling he had for her at that moment wasn't love but pity.

Sybil shook off his hand and turned to Katie, waiting to show her the way, and followed her without a word.

There had been a cheerful chorus of 'goodnight,' as she went, now followed by an awkward silence. The professor went back to the sink. 'Sybil has found everything rather upsetting,' he observed. 'She will be fine after a good night's sleep.'

'Which reminds me,' said Philly. 'Clive's in your bed. I'll get some blankets and a pillow for the big sofa in the sitting room. You're too big for it, but if you curl up you should manage.'

Everyone went thankfully to bed, leaving the professor, with one of the reverend's woolly sweaters over his shirt, to make himself as comfortable as possible on the sofa. As he was six foot four inches in his socks, and largely built, this wasn't easy, but he was tired; he rolled himself in the blankets and slept at once.

He opened his eyes the next morning to see Philly, wrapped in an unbecoming dressing gown, proffering tea in a mug.

Her good morning was brisk. 'You can use the bathroom at the end of the passage facing the stairs; Father's left a razor for you. The water isn't very hot yet, so I've put a jug of boiling water on the kitchen table for you.'

He took the mug, wished her good morning, and observed, 'You're up early.'

'Not just me. Rose has gone to wake the Downes, but we thought we'd better leave Clive until you've seen him—in case he's not well.'

'Very well. Give me ten minutes.'

In a minute or two he made his way through the quiet cold house. Someone had drawn the curtains back and the white world outside was revealed. At least it had stopped snowing...

He found the bathroom, shaved with the vicar's cutthroat razor, washed in tepid water, donned the sweater again and went to take a look at Clive.

He had recovered, except for the beginnings of a nasty head cold, and professed himself anxious to go to breakfast.

'No reason why you shouldn't. If you're still anxious to get to London as soon as the road's clear I'll give you a lift. We can tie your bike on the roof.'

With the prospect of the weather clearing, breakfast was a cheerful meal. The porridge was eaten with enthusiasm—although Sybil nibbled toast, declaring that she hadn't slept a wink and had no appetite. But her complaining voice was lost in the hubbub of conversation, heard only by the doctor sitting next to her.

'If the snowplough gets through we will be able to leave later today,' he told her, and then, hearing Philly saying in a worried voice that the hens would be snowed in, he volunteered to shovel a path to their shed.

So, in the vicar's wellies and with an old leather waistcoat over the sweater, he swung the shovel for a couple of hours. When he had cleared a path Philly came, completely extinguished in a cape, carrying food and water to collect the eggs. 'Enough for lunch,' she told him triumphantly.

The worst was over; the sun pushed its way through the clouds, the snowplough trundled through the village and they lunched off bacon and egg pie with a thick potato crust to conceal the fact that six eggs had been made to look like twelve.

The Downes were the first to go, driving away carefully, hopeful of reaching Basingstoke before dark. Half an hour later the doctor left, with a transformed Sybil, wrapped in her coat and skilfully made up, bestowing her gratitude on everyone.

The doctor shook hands all round and held Philly's hand for perhaps a moment longer than he should have, then ushered Sybil into the car, followed by Clive. They had roped the bike onto the roof and Clive, despite his cold, was full of gratitude to everyone. Well, not Sybil. He had taken her measure the moment he had set eyes on her, and why a decent gent like the doctor could be bothered with her he had no idea. He blew his nose loudly and watched her shudder.

The Bentley held the road nicely, but travelling at a safe speed they wouldn't reach London before dark. The doctor settled behind the wheel and wished that they had been forced to spend a second night at the vicarage, although he wasn't sure why.

CHAPTER TWO

SYBIL forgot her sulks as they neared London, and she ignored Clive's cheerful loud voice, too. She said softly, 'I'm sorry, darling. I did behave badly, didn't I? But, really, I did feel ill, and it was all so noisy. No one had any time for poor little me—not even you...'

She gave him a sidelong glance and saw with disquiet that he wasn't smiling. He was going to be tiresome; she had discovered that he could be. He assumed a remoteness at times which was a bit worrying. She was used to being admired and spoiled and she was uneasily aware that he did neither. Which was her reason for captivating him and—eventually—marrying him. She didn't love him, but then she didn't love anyone but herself. She was ambitious, and he had money and enjoyed a growing reputation in his profession, and above all she wanted his unquestioning devotion.

The doctor didn't take his eyes off the road. He said evenly, 'Yes, you did behave badly.'

Clive thrust a friendly face between them. 'Can't blame you, really,' he said. 'Not like the rest of us are you? I bet you've never done a day's work in your life. Comes hard, doesn't it?'

He trumpeted into his handkerchief and Sybil shrank back into her seat.

'Go away, go away!' she screeched. 'I'll catch your cold.'

'Sorry, I'm sure. Where I come from a cold's all in a day's work.'

'Do something, James.' She sounded desperate.

'My dear, I don't care to stop the car. What do you wish me to do?'

'Get him out of the car, of course. If I catch a cold I'll never forgive you.'

'That's a risk I shall have to take, Sybil, for I don't intend to stop until we get to your place.' He added gently, 'You will feel better once you have had a night's rest. Can you not look upon it as an adventure?'

She didn't reply, and very soon he was threading his way through London streets to stop finally before the terrace of grand houses where Sybil's parents lived.

He got out, warned Clive to stay where he was and went with her up the steps. He rang the bell and when a man-servant opened the door bade her goodnight.

'Don't expect to be asked in,' said Sybil spitefully.

'Well, no,' said the Professor cheerfully. 'In any case I must get Clive to his friends.'

'I shall expect you to phone tonight,' said Sybil, and swept past him.

Back in the car, the Professor invited Clive to sit beside him. 'For I'm not quite sure where you want to go.'

'Drop me off at a bus stop,' said Clive, 'so's you can get off home.'

'No question of that. Which end of Hackney do you want? The Bethnal Green end or the Marshes?'

'Cor, you know your London. Bethnal Green end— Meadow Road. End house on the left.' He added gruffly, 'Me and my girl, we've got engaged, see? We're having a bit of a party...'

The doctor drove across the city's empty Sunday streets and stopped before the end house in a narrow road lined by small brick houses.

They got the bike down off the roof and Clive said, 'You will come in for a mo? Not quite your style, but a cuppa might be welcome?'

The doctor agreed that it would and spent fifteen minutes

or so drinking a strong, dark brown drink which he supposed was tea while he made the acquaintance of Clive's girl and his family.

It was a pleasant end to a long day, he thought, driving himself home at last.

Home was a ground-floor flat behind the Embankment overlooking the Thames. The doctor parked the car, and before he could put his key in the house door it was opened by a short sturdy man with grizzled hair and a long, mournful face. Jolly—inaptly named, it had to be admitted—was the manservant whom the doctor had inherited with the flat, along with a charming stone cottage in Berkshire and a croft in the Western Highlands.

With the respectful familiarity of an old servant Jolly greeted the doctor with some severity. 'Got caught in all that snow, did you? Car's not damaged?'

'No, no, Jolly, and nor am I. I'm hungry.'

'I guessed you would be. It'll be on the table in fifteen minutes.' He took the doctor's coat and case from him. 'Found shelter, did you?'

'Indeed we did. At a place called Nether Ditchling—at the vicarage. Charming people. There were others caught in the snow as well—a houseful.' He clapped Jolly on the shoulder. 'I enjoyed every minute of it.'

'Not quite Miss West's cup of tea. She's not one for the country.'

'I'm afraid she disliked it, although we were treated with the greatest kindness.'

He picked up his letters and messages from the tray on the console table. 'Did you ring the cottage?'

'Yes. Plenty of snow, Mrs Willett says, but she's snug enough—hopes you'll be down to see her soon, says George misses you.'

The Professor was going down the hall to this study. 'I'll try and go next weekend. George could do with a good walk and so could I.'

Presently he ate the splendid meal Jolly had ready, then went back to his study to consider his week's work ahead. He had fully intended to phone Sybil, but by the time he remembered to do so it was too late. He would find time in the morning.

It was gone midnight before he went to his bed and he didn't sleep at once. He had enjoyed his weekend and he had enjoyed meeting Philomena. He smiled at the memory of her small figure bundled in that old hooded cape—and there had been a feeling when they had met—as though they had known each other for a long time…

Miles away, at Nether Ditchling, Philly turned over in bed, shook up the pillow and thought the same thing.

The snow disappeared as quickly as it had come. March came back with chilly blue skies and sunshine, and the banks beside the roads were covered with primroses. The vicarage became once again an orderly household.

There had been thank-you letters from the Downes, and a colourful postcard from Clive, and from Professor Forsyth a basket of fruit, beribboned and sheathed in Cellophane, with a card attached expressing his thanks. It expressed thanks, too, from Sybil—although she had told the doctor pettishly that she saw no reason to thank anyone for such a ghastly weekend.

'But you do what you like,' she had told him. Then, seeing his expressionless face, she had instantly become her charming self, coaxing him to forgive her. 'And take me out to dinner,' she had begged him. 'I've the loveliest dress, which I'm simply longing to wear…'

He had agreed that he would do that just as soon as he had an evening to spare. She was a woman any man would be proud to take out for the evening; he had no doubt that she would attract men's glances and he would be looked upon with envy.

The Professor, driving himself to the hospital later, told himself that he must make allowances for Sybil; she neither knew nor wished to know how the other half lived.

It was as though the weather had decided to apologise for that sudden return of winter. The fine weather continued, and even if the sunshine wasn't very warm it was bright. Philomena dug the garden, saw to the chickens, and ran various errands round the village for her mother. There was always someone who needed help or just a friendly visit.

Rose and Flora left home each morning, sharing a lift to and from the market town where Rose worked in a solicitor's office and Flora in an estate agent's firm. Dull jobs, both of them, but since Flora was engaged to the eldest son of a local farmer and Rose was making up her mind about one of the schoolmasters at the local prep school they neither of them complained since they had their futures nicely planned. Lucy was always busy with her friends, and as for Katie—the brightest of the bunch, the vicar always said—she had her sights set on university. It was a good thing, he often remarked to his wife, that Philly was so content to stay at home.

It was Monday morning again. The girls had left already and Philly had put the first load into the washing machine when someone thumped the front door knocker. Her mother was upstairs making beds, and her father was in his study, so she went to the door. It was someone she knew: young Mrs Twist from a small farm a mile outside the village. Philly had been there only a week before because Mrs Twist had needed someone to keep an eye on her twins while she took the baby to the doctor.

Philly swept Mrs Twist into the house. She had been crying and she clutched Philly's arm. 'Miss Philly, please help us. The doctor says the baby must go to London to see a specialist—but there isn't an ambulance and he's been called away to Mrs Crisp's first. Rob can't leave the farm, so if you could watch the baby while I drive...'

'Give me five minutes. Go and sit by the Aga while I tell Mother and get a coat. What did the doctor say was wrong?'

'Possible meningitis. And there aren't any beds nearer than this hospital in London.'

Philomena raced upstairs and found shoes, coat and gloves, all the while telling her mother about the baby.

'You'll need some money. I'll tell your father...'

The vicar was in the kitchen comforting Mrs Twist and went away to get the money. 'You may not need it, but it is better to be safe than sorry,' he said kindly. 'I'll go to Mrs Frost and see if she knows of anyone who would go to the farm and give a hand. They had better not have anything much to do with the twins...'

Mrs Twist nodded, 'Yes, the doctor told me not to let them be with anyone.'

In the car she said, 'You're not afraid of catching it, Miss Philly? I shouldn't have asked you... Rob's got the baby at home, waiting for me.'

'Not in the least,' said Philly. 'Don't worry about a thing. Once baby's in hospital they'll give him all the right treatment.'

He certainly looked very ill and the small shrill cries he gave were pitiful. Philly sat in the back of the car with him while Mrs Twist drove the seemingly endless route to London.

Since neither of them knew the city well, finding the hospital took time, and although the rush hour was over there seemed endless stop lights and traffic queues. At the hospital at last, Mrs Twist thrust the car keys at Philly. 'Lock the car,' she said breathlessly. 'I'll take the baby.'

She disappeared into the emergency entrance and Philly got out, locked the car and followed her. Here at least there was speedy help; the doctor's letter was read, and the baby was borne away to a small couch and expertly undressed. Since Mrs Twist refused to leave him, it fell to Philly's lot to answer the clerk's questions. In no time at all there was a doctor there, reading his colleague's letter and then bending over the couch.

'Get Professor Forsyth here, will you, Sister? He hasn't left yet...'

Philly was making herself small against a wall. She supposed that she should find the waiting room, but she didn't like to leave Mrs Twist. She stood there feeling useless, hoping that she wouldn't be noticed: very unlikely, she reflected, since it was the baby who had everyone's attention. She admired the way Sister and the nurses knew exactly what they were doing, and she liked the look of the doctor, bending over the baby and talking quietly to Mrs Twist...

There was a faint stir amongst them as they parted ranks to allow a big man in the long white coat to examine the scrap on the couch.

Philly stared, blinked, and looked again. She had never expected to see him again but here he was, Doctor—no, Professor Forsyth, who had shovelled a path to her father's chickens wearing an old sweater of the vicar's and his wellies, looking quite different from this assured-looking man listening to the doctor.

He looked up and straight at her, but there was no sign of him recognising her. She had expected that; the baby had his full attention.

Please, God, let the baby get well again, begged Philly silently.

It seemed a long time before Professor Forsyth straightened his long back and began to give instructions. His patient was borne away in the arms of a nurse. He didn't go with them, but led Mrs Twist to a chair and leaned against the wall and began to talk to her. She was crying, and he looked across to Philly and said quietly, 'Will you come

here, Miss Selby? I think Mrs Twist would be glad of your
company while I explain things to her.'

He did this in a calm reassuring voice; the baby was very
ill, but with immediate treatment there was every hope that
he would make a good recovery. 'I shall stay with him for
the next hour or so and he will be given every help there
is. You will wish to stay here, near him, and that can be
arranged. Do you need to go back home?'

'No, my husband can look after the twins. Can I leave
my car here?'

'Yes. I'll get someone to see to that for you.'

Mrs Twist dried her eyes. 'You're so kind.' She turned
to Philly. 'You don't mind? You can get a train, and someone could fetch you from the nearest station. And thank
you, Miss Philly. Rob'll let you know if—if there's any
news.'

'Good news,' said Philly bracingly. 'I'll go and see Rob
as soon as I can.'

The Professor said nothing, but took Mrs Twist with him.
Philly sat down to think. She would have to find her way
to Waterloo Station, but first she must phone her father, for
the nearest station to Nether Ditchling was seven miles
away—and had she enough money for the fare?

She was counting it when a stout woman in a pink over-
all put a tray down on the chair next to her. 'Professor
Forsyth said yer was ter 'ave this and not ter go until 'e'd
seen yer.'

'He did? Well, how kind—and thank you for bringing
it. It looks lovely and I'm hungry.' Philly smiled, prepared
to be friendly.

'Yer welcome, I'm sure. Mind and do as he says.'

Philly ate the sandwiches and drank the tea, then went
in search of the Ladies' and returned to her seat. There was
no one else in the waiting room, although there were any
number of people going past the open door and the noise
of children crying and screaming. She wondered how Baby

Twist was faring, and whether she would see Mrs Twist before she left the hospital. She looked at her watch and saw that she had been sitting there for more than an hour. But she had been asked to wait and it was still only mid-afternoon. There was no point in phoning her father until she knew at what time she needed to be fetched from the station. Besides, she was afraid to spend any money until she knew how much the fare would be...

It was another hour before the Professor came, and by then she was getting worried. She had been forgotten, the baby's condition was worse, and what time did the last train leave?

The Professor folded his length onto the chair beside her.

'Getting worried? I'm sorry you have had this long wait, but I wanted to make sure that the baby would be all right...'

'He is? He'll get better? Oh, I am so glad. And Mrs Twist, is she all right, too?'

'Yes. How do you intend to get home?'

'Well, I'll go to Waterloo Station and get the next train to Warminster, and Father will come for me there.'

'Have you enough money for the fare?'

'Oh, yes,' said Philly airily. 'Father gave me ten pounds.'

He perceived that he was talking to someone who travelled seldom, and then probably not by train. He discarded his intention of a few hours of quiet at his home before going back to the hospital; he could be there and back in five hours at the outside.

He said, 'I'll drive you back to Nether Ditchling.'

'But it's miles away! Thank you all the same,' she added quickly.

'Not in the Bentley,' he observed gently. 'I can be back to take another look at Baby Twist later on this evening. He's in the safe hands of my registrar.' And when she opened her mouth to protest, he said, 'No, don't argue. Wait here for a little longer; I'll be back.'

She flew to the Ladies' once more, and was sitting, neat and composed, when he got back.

'Ready? Mrs Twist has asked me to speak to her husband; perhaps I might phone him from the Vicarage?'

'Of course you can.' She trotted beside him out of the hospital and got into the Bentley in the forecourt. She would have liked a cup of tea but she didn't dwell on that; he was wasting enough of his time as it was.

He had very little to say as he drove, only asked her if she was warm enough and comfortable. She made no attempt to talk; he was probably preoccupied with the baby's condition—probably regretting, too, his offer to drive her home.

It was a clear dry day, and once clear of the city he drove fast and she sat quietly, thinking her own not very happy thoughts: the poor little baby and his mother—and how would Rob manage with the twins? She would have to go and see him. And how she longed for a cup of tea and something to eat. That was followed by the even sadder thought that the Professor didn't much like her. Though I like him, she reflected, and it's a great shame that he's going to marry that awful Sybil. I wish I were as lovely to look at as she is...

The Professor turned off into the maze of narrow roads which would lead to Nether Ditchling. He was enjoying the drive, although he wasn't sure why. Philly, sitting like a mouse beside him and not uttering a word, was nevertheless the ideal companion, not distracting his thoughts with questions and trivial chatter. He slowed the car and turned into the Vicarage drive.

'You'll come in for five minutes and have a cup of coffee? We won't keep you, but you must have a few minutes' rest before you go back.'

He smiled at the matter-of-fact statement as he got out and opened her door. The Vicarage door was already open and her father stood there, telling them to come in.

'Come into the kitchen. Your mother's there, getting things ready for supper, Rose and Flora are upstairs, Lucy's at choir and Katie's seeing to the hens.'

He led the way and her mother looked up from her saucepans. 'Philly and Forsyth. Sit down. Coffee in a minute. Is the baby going to be all right—and why is Forsyth here?'

She put two mugs on the table and smiled at him.

'He's a professor,' said Philly.

'Is he now? But that doesn't make him any different,' said Mrs Selby, and he smiled at her.

'The baby will, I hope, recover. I work at the hospital where he is being treated. His mother is staying with him and it seemed a good idea, since I had an hour or two to spare, to bring Philly back home.'

Mrs Selby darted a look at Philly. 'We're very much in your debt...'

'No, no. Nothing will repay you for your kindness in the snow.' He drank some coffee and bit into a slice of cake. 'May I use your phone and talk to Mr Twist? He's been kept informed, but he might like a more detailed account of what's being done for his son.'

'In my study,' said the Vicar. 'Can we offer you a bed for the night?'

'No, thanks all the same. I want to get back and keep an eye on the baby.'

He took his coffee and the cake with him to the study and Mrs Selby said, 'What a very kind man...' She paused as Flora and Rose came into the room.

'We heard a car, and it's too soon for Lucy to be back from choir practice.' Rose sat down by Philly. 'Do tell, Philly. It's not the Twists' car, is it? The baby...?'

Philly, who had hardly spoken a word, explained, and Katie, who had just come into the kitchen with a pile of school books, exclaimed, 'Why ever did he bring you back home? He could have put you on a train. Is he sweet on you?'

Rose and Flora rounded on her, but Philly said calmly, 'No, Katie. He was kind, that's all, and I expect he feels he's now repaid Mother and Father for looking after him and Sybil when we had all that snow.'

The Professor, an unwilling listener as he left the study, had to smile at the idea of his being sweet on Philomena!

He left shortly afterwards, scarcely giving Philly time to thank him, brushing her gratitude aside with a friendly smile.

'You will get Baby Twist better, won't you?' she asked him.

'I shall do my utmost,' he assured her, as he took his leave.

The Vicar, after escorting him out to his car, came back indoors to observe warmly, 'Now there goes a man I should like to know better.'

Me, too, thought Philly.

She went the next morning to the Twists' farm and found Rob cautiously cheerful. He was a stolid young man, a splendid farmer and a hard worker, but he was unused to illness. He told Philly that he had had a phone call from his wife and that the baby was responding to treatment. 'I've got me mum coming today, to keep an eye on the twins and do the cooking. And the doctor's been to have a look at them. He says they should be all right. They mustn't play with their friends, though, and they've got to stay here on the farm.'

'Well, I'll take them for a walk,' volunteered Philly. 'We can go picking primroses and violets. Has the Professor phoned you?'

'Late last night—must have been nigh on midnight—and then this morning at seven o'clock.'

He'd been up all night, thought Philly. He was a big powerfully built man, but all the same he needed his sleep like anyone else. She hoped that he would be able to snatch a few hours of leisure…

*   *   *

The Professor, despite a wakeful night, went about his usual
hospital routine. He had gone home briefly, to shower and
change, and returned looking as though he had had a good
night's sleep to do his rounds, discuss treatments and talk
to anxious parents.

Baby Twist, in a small room away from the other children, was holding his own; it wasn't for the first time that
the Professor marvelled at the capacity of tiny babies to
fight illness.

He left the hospital in the late afternoon and found Jolly
hovering in the hall, his long face set in disapproving lines.

'Did you have your lunch?'

The Professor, leafing through his post, said casually,
'Yes, yes. A sandwich.'

Jolly pursed his lips. 'And your tea?'

'Tea? I had a cup with Sister after the clinic.'

'Dishwater,' said Jolly with disdain. 'There'll be tea in
the sitting room in five minutes…'

The Professor said meekly, 'Yes, Jolly. How well you
look after me.'

'Well, if I don't who will?'

The Professor didn't answer. He was very aware that
Jolly disliked his future wife, although, old and trusted servant that he was, he would never allow his feelings to show,
and his manner to Sybil was always correct. As for Sybil,
she seldom noticed Jolly; he was part and parcel of James'
life, a life which she had every intention of changing to
suit herself once they were married.

A week went by. March gave way to an April of blue
skies and warm sunshine and Baby Twist recovered; a few
more days and he would be allowed home.

Mrs Twist had stayed at the hospital. How would she go
back home? Sister wanted to know.

'Well, my car's still here, but I'm a bit scared to drive
home without someone with me…'

Sister mentioned it to the Professor. 'She's a sensible young woman, but nervous of being alone with the baby—it's quite a long drive.'

'Perhaps she could contact the friend who came in with her?'

'Yes, of course. I'll see what she says. Had you a discharge date in mind, sir?'

'Four or five days' time—Wednesday. The baby will have to come back for a check-up. See to that, will you?'

It would be pleasant to see Philomena again. He hadn't forgotten her; indeed he thought about her rather more often than his peace of mind allowed. Her ordinary face and lovely brown eyes had a habit of imposing themselves upon his thoughts at the most awkward times: when he was dining with Sybil, listening to her light-hearted talk—gossip, tales of her friends, the new clothes she had bought—and dining with friends, listening to Sybil's high clear voice once more, her laughter... He avoided as many social occasions as he could, which was something she was always quick to quarrel about.

'And don't suppose that you can expect me to stay home night after night waiting for you to come home from the hospital or out of your study.' Then, seeing his frown she had added, 'Oh, darling James, how horrid I am. You know I don't mean a word of it.' And she had been all charm and smiles again.

On his way home from the hospital he made a note to himself to see Philly when she came to collect Mrs Twist and the baby.

Wednesday came, and with it Philly, very neat and tidy in a short jacket a little too big for her, since it was one of Lucy's, and last year's tweed skirt. But her shoulder bag was leather and her shoes were beautifully polished. The Professor saw all this as he watched her coming along the wide corridor to the ward. He saw her cheerful face too, damping down a strong feeling that he wanted to go and meet her and wrap his arms around her and tell her how beautiful she was.

'I must be mad,' said Professor Forsyth aloud, and when she reached the cot he greeted her with chilly politeness so that her wide smile trembled uncertainly and disappeared.

There was no reason to linger. Mrs Twist had her instructions and advice from Sister and an appointment to see the Professor in a few weeks' time.

The Professor shook Mrs Twist's hand and told her in a kind and reassuring voice that her baby had made a complete recovery. He stood patiently listening to her thanks before asking Sister to see them safely into the car and walking away. He gave Philly a cool nod as he went.

Sitting in the back with the baby as Mrs Twist drove back to Nether Ditchling, Philly wondered what she had done to make him look at her like that. She hadn't forgotten the strange feeling she had had when they had first met, but she didn't allow herself to think about it. She had been sure that he had felt the same, but perhaps she had been mistaken. And a good thing too, she told herself. She and Professor Forsyth lived in separate worlds.

In due course Baby Twist went back to London to be examined. Sloane, who had his surgery at Wisbury, was satisfied as to his progress, but the check-up was still advisable.

This time Mrs Twist took her mother, who was staying with them, on the journey to the hospital. Philly had hoped that she would be asked to go again. Even if she didn't speak to him, it would have been nice just to see the Professor again...

Professor Forsyth, giving last-minute instructions to Mrs Twist, firmly suppressed his disappointment at not seeing

Philly. He really must forget the girl, he told himself, and dismissed her from his thoughts—although she persisted in staying at the back of his mind, to pop up whenever he had an unguarded moment.

He must see more of Sybil. He took time off which he could ill spare to take her out to dine and dance, to see the latest plays and visit friends and found that nothing helped. Sybil was becoming very demanding: expecting him to spend more and more of his leisure with her, scorning his protests that he had his own friends, lectures to write, reading to do...

Jolly, disturbed by the Professor's withdrawn manner, gave it as his opinion that he should go to his cottage. 'You've got a bit of free time,' he pointed out. 'Go and see Mrs Willett. She's always complaining that she doesn't see enough of you. And that George will be pining for you too.'

The Professor went home on Friday evening with the pleasant knowledge that he had two days of peace and quiet to look forward to. Sybil had said that she would be away for the weekend and he planned to leave early on Saturday morning. He ate a splendid dinner and went to his study; there was plenty of work for him on his desk.

He hadn't been there more than ten minutes when the phone rang.

It was Sybil's querulous voice. 'The Quinns phoned. That wretched child of theirs has got chicken pox—they told me not to worry, as she's in the nursery anyway, but I'm not risking catching it. So I'm here at a loose end, darling. Take me out to dinner tomorrow evening and let's spend the day together first. Come for me around midday. We can go to that place at Bray for lunch and drive around. And on Sunday you could drive me up to Bedford. We can spend the day with Aunt Bess. It will be a dull day, but she's leaving me the house when she dies and we shall need somewhere in the country as well as your place here.'

'I have a cottage in Berkshire, Sybil…'

She gave a little crow of laughter. 'Darling! That poky little place! There would barely be room for the two of us, let alone guests.'

The Professor pondered a reply but decided not to say anything. Instead he said, 'I'm sorry about your weekend, Sybil. I'm going out of town early tomorrow morning and I shan't be back until Monday. A long-standing invitation.' Which was true. Mrs Willett, his one-time nanny and housekeeper at the cottage, reminded him almost weekly that it was time he spent a few days at the cottage.

'Put them off,' said Sybil.

'Impossible. As I said, it's a long-standing arrangement.' She hung up on him.

He left early the next morning, taking the M4 until he had passed Reading, then turning into a side road running north to the Oxfordshire border. The villages were small and infrequent, remote from the railway, each one with its church, main street and a handful of small houses and cottages. And each with its manor-house standing importantly apart.

The country was looking beautiful in the bright morning sun and the Professor slowed his pace the better to enjoy it. He didn't come often enough, he reflected. But Sybil didn't like the cottage and the quiet countryside, and she didn't like Mrs Willett who, for that matter, didn't like her either.

The cottage was on the edge of a village lying between two low tree-clad hills, round the bend of the road so that the sudden sight of it was a pleasure to the eye. Beyond a narrow winding street bordered by other cottages stood his own: redbrick and thatch, with an outsize door and small-paned windows. It stood sideways onto the road, with a fair-sized garden, and beyond it were fields and, beyond them, the wooded hill.

He drove round the side of the cottage to a barn at the

end of the track, its doors open ready to receive him, and parked the car and went into the cottage through the open kitchen door.

The kitchen was small, with a tiled floor, a small bright red Aga and shelves along its walls. There was a table in the centre, with a set of ladder-backed chairs round it. There were bright checked curtains at the window and a kettle was singing on the stove.

The Professor went through the door into the narrow hall, threw his jacket and bag down on one of the two chairs and hugged his housekeeper, puffing a little from her hasty descent of the narrow stairs.

'There you are, Master James, and about time too!' She eyed him narrowly. 'You look as though you could do with a few days here. Working too hard, I'll be bound.'

'It's good to be here,' he told her. 'I'll stay until early Monday morning. Where's George?'

'Gone to fetch the eggs from Greggs' farm with Benny.' Benny was the boy who walked George each day, since Mrs Willett was past the age of a brisk walk with a lively dog.

'I'll go and meet them while you get the coffee.' He grinned at her. 'We'll have a good gossip.'

'Go on with you, Master James! But I dare say you'll have plenty to tell me.' She gave him a questioning look. 'Fixed a date for the wedding yet?'

His soft, 'Not yet, Nanny,' left her with a feeling of disquiet.

Later, with George the Labrador pressed up against him, the Professor gave Mrs Willett a succinct enough account of his days. 'Rather dull, as you can see,' he told her. 'Except for that weekend at the Vicarage.'

She had watched his face when he told her about it, and had been quick to see the small smile when he'd told her about Philly.

'A real country girl,' she had observed mildly.

'You would like her, Nanny.'

'Then it is to be hoped that I'll meet her one day,' said Nanny.

CHAPTER THREE

AT DAYBREAK on Monday morning the Professor, with George at his heels, let himself out of the cottage, opened the little gate at the bottom of his back garden and started to climb the gentle hill beyond. Halfway up it he stopped and turned to look behind him. It was a bright morning and the sun was going to show at any moment. The cottage sat snugly in its garden and the white curtains at his bedroom window waved gently to and fro in the light breeze. A little haven, he reflected, and one to which he should come far more frequently. But Sybil had been adamant about not going there, always coaxing him to stay in town when he had a free weekend—'For I see so little of you,' she had said, beguiling him with one of her charming smiles.

The Professor turned to continue his walk. There was a tractor starting up some way off, a herd of cows leaving the milking shed from the farm across the fields, everywhere birds, rabbits in the hedges and, sneaking across the field ahead of him, a fox. He wanted to share it all with someone—with Philly, for this was her kind of world.

'I don't even know the girl!' said the Professor testily, and resumed his walk.

He drove himself back to London after breakfast, thinking of the busy day ahead of him, and the days after that, and at the weekend he and Sybil were going to Coralie's wedding at Netherby. Perhaps on the way back he could persuade her to go to the cottage for an hour or two…

But Sybil was adamant about that, too; she had bought a new outfit for the wedding and she had no intention of ruining it by paying a visit to the cottage with a chance of tearing it on hedges or having George's dirty paws all over it. 'And it was wickedly expensive, darling. I want to be a credit to you, and I've gone to a great deal of trouble.'

So on Saturday morning the Professor, elegant in morning dress and top hat, bade Jolly goodbye and drove to collect Sybil—who wasn't ready.

The butler, a sympathetic man, ushered him into a small room and offered coffee, assuring him that Miss Sybil would be down directly. And half an hour later she did indeed come downstairs. She stood in the doorway, waiting for the Professor's admiration. Her dress was white, with a vivid green pattern calculated to catch the eye, but it was her hat which kept him momentarily silent.

Of bright green straw, it had an enormous brim and the crown was smothered in flowers of every colour.

'Well?' said Sybil. 'I told you the outfit was gorgeous, didn't I? It's charming, isn't it?'

The Professor found his voice. 'All eyes will be upon you.'

She smiled happily. 'That is my intention, James darling.'

'I thought the bride was the principal attraction on her wedding day.'

'There's nothing like a little healthy competition, darling.'

They drove for the most part in silence: the Professor deep in thought, Sybil contemplating the pleasures ahead of them. They must get seats in the church where she would be easily seen, and stand well to the front when the photos were taken...

Approaching Nether Ditchling, the Professor slowed the car; there was the chance that he might see Philly. And the chance was his; there she was, standing outside the village shop. No hat on her head, but wearing what he suspected was her best dress: blue, simply cut, and off the peg.

He pulled the car across the road and stopped beside her.

He rolled the window down. 'Hello, Philomena. Are you going to the wedding too?'

Philly beamed at him; thinking about him was one thing, to see him was an added bonus. 'Hello.' She looked past him to Sybil, and her eyes widened at the sight of the hat. She met the Professor's gaze and it was as though they shared the same thought. Philly looked away from him and wished Sybil good morning.

'Oh hello, nice to see you again. We're in rather a hurry…'

'Are you going to the wedding?' asked the Professor again.

'Well, yes, but not really to the wedding. I promised Coralie that I'd look after her sister's small children. There are four of them, much too small to go to the church and the reception.'

'In that case we'll give you a lift.' The Professor got out of the car and opened the door.

Philly held back. 'I was going to get a lift from the postman; he'll be along any minute now…'

'Leave him a message,' said the Professor easily, and did it for her, charming Mrs Salter standing at the open shop door, listening to every word.

She nodded and smiled. 'You go, Miss Philly. Not often you get the chance to travel so grand. I'll tell Postie.'

The Professor made small talk during the brief journey to Netherby and Philly said, 'Yes' and 'No' and 'how nice,' and admired the back of his head, and then turned her attention to Sybil's hat. Wedding hats, she knew, were always outrageous, but Sybil's took one's breath…

'Go straight to the church,' said Sybil. 'We want decent seats…'

The Professor said mildly, 'We are in plenty of time, my dear. I'll drop Philly off at the house on the way to church.'

'There's no need. It's only a short walk…'

He disregarded that. 'How will you get back?' he asked
Philly.

'Father will fetch me.'

At the house there were a number of cars being loaded
by the family on their way to the church, so Philly nipped
out smartly. 'Thank you very much—I hope you'll have a
lovely day.'

She whisked herself away and in through the open doors,
and Sybil said, 'Oh, for heaven's sake, let's get to the
church.'

Seedings, the butler, bade Philly a dignified good morning.
'Miss Coralie would like you to go to her room, Miss
Philly, as soon as you get here.'

So Philly went up the grand staircase and tapped on a
door. She was admitted, to spend five minutes admiring the
bride and the bridesmaids, before going up another flight
of stairs to the nursery wing with Coralie's sister.

'Just like Nanny to become ill when she's most needed.
I'm very grateful, Philly.' She opened a door. 'Mother's
maid is with them...'

There were twins, not quite four years old, Henry and
Thomas, Emily, almost two and the baby, a mere eight
months. At the moment they looked like small angels, but
it was still early in the day. Philly, though she liked small
children, braced herself for the task ahead.

The wedding was at eleven o'clock. She heard the church
bells pealing at the end of the service and presently the
slamming of car doors as everyone returned to the house.
There would be any number of guests, she knew. Friends
and family would come from far and near to enjoy the
occasion. She hoped that Coralie would be very happy; they
could hardly be described as friends, they didn't move in
the same circles, but Philly had been at school with
Coralie's sister, the eldest of the three girls, so they were
on friendly terms.

A maid brought the children's lunch, and soon the baby was due for another bottle. Philly assembled her small companions round the nursery table and for the moment forgot about the wedding.

No one came, but she hadn't expected anyone. She had told the maid to tell the children's mother that everything was going well, and now she settled the eldest three little ones to an afternoon nap. She set about seeing to the baby, who refused to be settled but lay on her shoulder, bawling his small head off.

The opening of the door brought his crying to an abrupt halt. He burped, puked on her shoulder, and smiled at the Professor entering the room.

'I'll have him while you clean up.'

'You can't possibly—look at you in your best clothes. You ought not to be here.'

He grinned at her, wondering why it was that when he was with Philly he felt life was such fun. 'I'm on an official visit,' he told her. 'I had the twins in for a few days with bad chests, and I've come to see if they're fit and well again.'

'They're asleep.' She nodded to where they lay, tucked up in one of the cots. 'They've been as good as gold and they ate their lunch.'

The baby was taken from her. 'Good. Go and wash while this monster's quiet.' He took the baby from her in the manner of a man who knew exactly what he was doing. But then he would, she reflected, scrubbing at her dress; he was a children's doctor.

'Was it a lovely wedding?' she asked.

'Yes. The bride looked beautiful, as all brides do.'

'Shouldn't you be at the reception?'

'The cake's been cut and toasts have been drunk, and everyone is standing around waiting for the happy couple to leave. How are you going home?' he asked again.

He was sitting on the arm of a chair, the baby peacefully asleep against his waistcoat.

'Father will come for me.'

'Better still, we'll drop you off as we go.' He had a phone in his hand and was dialling a number. Philly, aware that she should remonstrate with him at such high-handed behaviour, said nothing, listening to him telling her father that she would be returning in about an hour or so.

'I can't go until someone comes to look after the children,' said Philly, finding her voice.

'There'll be someone,' he assured her, and smiled, handed back the baby and went away.

'Well, really. I don't know,' said Philly to the baby, who stared back at her and went to sleep again.

Philly longed for a cup of tea, but she had no doubt that she had been forgotten with the house full of guests and everyone run off their feet. She drank some water and looked at the nursery clock; in less than an hour the children's tea would be brought up, and then hopefully someone would come to take her place.

She worried a bit about the Professor giving her a lift. For one thing Sybil wouldn't like it, and for another she might keep them waiting unless someone took over promptly.

The children woke up, and she washed their faces and hands, brushed their hair and sat down on the floor with them to play the nursery games she remembered from her childhood, thankful that the baby remained soundly asleep. Their teatime came and went, and after another ten minutes she picked up the phone. Just as she did the door opened and a maid came in with a tray.

'Sorry I'm a bit late, Miss. Everything's a bit rushed downstairs. The guests are leaving. Here's a pot of tea for you.'

Philly beamed at her. 'Thank you. I'm sure you are

rushed off your feet. I expect someone's coming to take over?'

'I don't rightly know, Miss.'

Which wasn't very satisfactory. Philly sat the children at the table, put the baby's bottle ready to warm and handed out mugs of milk and egg sandwiches, much cheered by the sight of the teapot, but before she could pour herself a cup the door opened and the children's mother came in.

'What a day! I'm exhausted, but it all went off splendidly. Are you ready to go?'

An elderly woman came in behind her. 'We'll see to the children now. Have they been good? We are so grateful, Philly. Now do run along; James and Sybil are waiting for you.'

They bustled her away. She bade the children a hurried goodbye, with a regretful look at the teapot, smiled away their mother's thanks, and hurried down to the hall. The Professor was there, talking to a group of guests, but when he saw Philly he made his goodbyes and crossed the hall to meet her.

'I've kept you waiting?'

He smiled down at her. She looked tired and dishevelled, and her hair badly needed a comb; he found it disturbing that she outshone all the attractive women he had seen that day. And that included Sybil.

'The car is outside,' he told her. 'You must be tired.'

'Well, a bit.' She smiled in the general direction of everyone else there and walked to the door, feeling very out of place. At the door she was stopped by the butler, who handed her a neatly wrapped package.

'Wedding cake, Miss—I was to be sure and give you a slice. For good luck, you know.'

She thanked him and got into the car, where Sybil said, 'There you are at last. James, I'm exhausted...'

'Not nearly as exhausted as Philly after most of the day spent with a handful of toddlers and a baby.' He looked over his shoulder. 'All right? We'll have you home in no time.'

Philly had settled on the back seat, bringing with her a strong whiff of baby talcum powder, milky drinks and soap. There were sponged stains on her dress, which from time to time gave off an unavoidable tang. Sybil gave an audible sigh and the Professor bit back a laugh.

No one spoke on the brief journey. At the Vicarage he got out and opened her door. Not sure if she would receive a snub, Philly offered tea.

'I know Mother will be delighted...'

'In that case we would be delighted; a cup of tea is just what I need. Don't you agree, Sybil?'

She shot him a look which boded ill for the future, but she got out of the car and Philly ushered them into the Vicarage.

She took them not to the kitchen but into the drawing room, which was seldom used because it was always damp, even in the height of summer. It was a splendid room, with wide windows, and furnished with the good pieces her mother had inherited when her parents died. A fitting background for Sybil's hat, thought Philly naughtily.

'I'll tell Mother,' said Philly, and sped to the kitchen.

Mrs Selby, being a vicar's wife, was unflustered by sudden demands on her hospitality.

'Fetch your father,' she said, and went to welcome her visitors.

Leaving the Vicar to entertain them, Mrs Selby hurried back to the kitchen, where Philly was putting cups and saucers onto a tray.

'That's the most extraordinary hat,' she observed, getting a cake from its tin, and added, 'She's not at all suitable...'

Philly giggled, and then said, suddenly sober, 'But she does look gorgeous, Mother.' Adding matter-of-factly, 'She doesn't like me.'

'No, dear. But of course that is only natural.'

Philly made the tea. 'Is it? Why?'

Her mother didn't answer. 'Bring the teapot, dear. I'll take the tray.'

The Professor had quite a lot to say about the wedding, but Sybil hardly spoke and refused Mrs Selby's fruit cake with an, 'Oh, God no,' which made the Vicar draw a breath and bite back the rebuke on his tongue.

Mrs Selby filled an awkward moment by observing cheerfully, 'I expect you had too much wedding cake. A wedding wouldn't be one without it, though, would it?' She turned an artless gaze onto Sybil. 'Have you planned your own wedding? I dare say it will be a big one?'

'Oh, I suppose so. We have very many friends. Though we don't intend to marry yet...' Sybil's vague reply, from Mrs Selby's point of view, was reassuring...

They didn't stay long, but their departure was delayed for a few minutes by the arrival of Lucy and Katie, back from their schools. They wanted to hear about the wedding, and Katie remarked with all the candour of a teenager upon Sybil's hat. It was fortunate that Sybil, confident of her splendid appearance, took Katie's, 'Now that's what I call a hat...' as a compliment.

Sybil said, in the voice she used to those beneath her notice, 'I'm glad you like it. I had it specially made...'

The Professor, looking amused, shook hands all round and ushered her into the car.

Driving away, Sybil said, 'I can't think why you had to stop. There was no need to give that girl a lift—she smelled...'

'Philly has spent most of the day looking after three toddlers and a small baby. They needed to be fed and washed and cuddled and amused. A hands-on job, Sybil, without regard to what one is wearing.'

'You should have considered me. I hate anything like that...'

'Would you even with your own children?'

'We will have a highly qualified nanny—and anyway, I consider four children to be excessive. One is more than enough. Shall we be back in time to go out to dinner? A pity you can't join me at the Reeves' for lunch tomorrow. Really, you take your work too seriously, James.'

The Professor reflected that falling in love with a lovely face had been a mistake. One which he would have to rectify if he could think of a way of doing so.

Sybil didn't love him; he had thought at first that she did, but now he realised that loving someone was very low in her priorities. There were things which mattered more: comfortable living, money, being popular amongst the society in which she moved, a husband with money to spend on her—and one who was at the top of his profession—and the leisure to enjoy her life without worry.

He said now, 'It will be eight o'clock before we're home, and I want to go to the hospital. And I'm sorry about tomorrow but there's this meeting…'

'How tiresome you are, James. But we'll change all that when we're married.'

'Am I to give up my work?'

'Don't be silly, of course not. But you can give up all this hospital work and keep your private practice. Do some consulting work, if you must, but you're well enough known to pick and choose.'

'I'm a children's doctor, Sybil, and that's what I intend to remain.'

Sybil gave a little laugh. 'Darling, I'll change your mind for you.'

The Professor didn't answer.

After leaving Sybil at her home, he drove straight to the hospital. There was a premature baby he wasn't happy about, and he spent the next hour or so discussing treatment with his registrar.

It was ten o'clock before he got home and Jolly, coming into the hall as he let himself in, said, 'There you are then, and high time too. It's a good thing your dinner's one that won't spoil.' He peered at the Professor. 'Fed up with the day? Weddings, leastways anyone else's but yours, aren't much cop.'

The Professor had one foot on the stairs. 'Give me five minutes to get into other gear. I could eat a horse, Jolly.'

'Not in this house, you won't. I don't hold with horse-flesh!'

The professor laughed. Five minutes later he was back again, in casual trousers and a sweater, pouring himself a whisky.

No one looking at Jolly would have thought of him as being an excellent cook. But he dished up a splendid meal, and the Professor, whose large frame needed more than the bits and pieces usually offered at weddings, enjoyed every morsel of it.

'That's the ticket,' observed Jolly. 'Be in for lunch to-morrow, will you?'

'As far as I know. I think I'll drive down to the cottage in the afternoon. If you want to go out, leave something cold for me, Jolly. I'll probably stay there for tea.'

'Miss West going with you?'

The Professor said, 'No,' in a voice which warned Jolly not to say any more.

Sunday was a dry day, but cold under a grey sky. The cottage looked charming, with daffodils spilling from the banks around it and great clumps of primroses. There were early tulips in the flowerbed and forsythia in abundance. George was delighted to see him and Nanny, roused from an afternoon nap, bustled about getting tea. The Professor, greeting them both, wished that Philly was there, too. It was becoming increasingly evident to him that she fitted very nicely into the kind of life that he enjoyed...

Easter had been early and May Day wasn't far away. Nether Ditchling was preparing for the annual children's fête which would be held on Bank Holiday Monday. It was held in the village hall, lavishly decorated with balloons, and was an old-fashioned event, its traditions untouched by modern ideas.

There would be Punch and Judy, in the disguised persons of the primary schoolmaster and his wife, a bran-tub, presided over by Mrs Salter, a trestle table loaded with buns and ices, lemonade and bags of crisps donated by Lady Dearing, wife of the Lord of the Manor, and served by herself and her two daughters, while at the other end of the hall her son would be in charge of target shooting with toy rifles.

Since the children would have their mothers and fathers with them, the Vicar and his wife always took charge of a vast tea urn, rows of cups and saucers and a great variety of cakes. As for Philly and her sisters, they helped out wherever they were needed: consoling crying children, taking toddlers to the lavatory, clearing up after one of them had eaten too much. It was an event which never varied from year to year and no one would have wanted it otherwise. This year there was to be a fancy dress parade with prizes, which meant a good deal of searching in trunks and attics and a run on the crinkle paper which Mrs Salter had remaining in stock from Christmas.

The church was full on the Sunday before. The Lord of the Manor with his wife and family sat in their high-walled pew, and the Vicar's wife and his five daughters were on the other side of the aisle. Rose and Flora had their fiancés beside them, and Lucy's current boyfriend sat there too. Only Katie and Philomena were unaccompanied, and as usual the village craned its neck to see if Miss Philly had found a man yet. The nicest of the bunch, everyone agreed, but likely to die an old maid.

Philly, unaware of the village's concern for her future, sat quietly, listening to her father's sermon, while hidden away at the back of her mind she wondered what the Professor was doing.

He, just as she was, was in church. Sybil had gone to Italy for a week to stay with friends who had a villa in Tuscany. It was an invitation she couldn't ignore, she had told him. She had sounded regretful, peeping at him to see if he minded, but his face had told her nothing and she had been careful to beg him to go with her. 'I see so little of you, darling, and we could have a lovely time. There'll be several people we both know there, and there'll be plenty of amusement.'

When he had said patiently that a holiday for him was out of the question she had made a charming little face and said, 'Surely you can take a holiday when you want to?'

'Perhaps a day now and then. I could manage to be free for a day or so. If you stayed here we could spend a few hours at the cottage.'

'But there's nothing to do there and no one to talk to—only Mrs Willett.'

He had wanted to tell her that if they loved each other there would be plenty to talk about, just the two of them: their wedding and their future together, and the delight of just being together.

He had said mildly, 'Go and enjoy yourself, Sybil. Tuscany should be lovely at this time of year.'

And so Sybil had gone, with a case of new clothes and a rather careless goodbye, confident that James would be waiting for her when she came home, placid and tolerant of her demands upon his time.

He went early to the hospital on Bank Holiday Monday, and then, with the rest of the day free, went back to tell Jolly that he wouldn't be home until the late evening.

He drove first to the cottage, where he persuaded Mrs Willett to put on her hat and spend the day with him.

George was to come with them, of course, and the three of them set out in the best of spirits.

Mrs Willett asked, 'Are we going somewhere nice?'

She peered at the Professor, in a sweater and casual trousers and looking years younger.

'Remember I told you of that charming family who were so kind to Sybil and me in that freak snowstorm? And the baby who was so ill? A ward sister was telling me about a children's fête to be held in the village where he lives. An old tradition, his mother told her, especially held for them on May Day. I thought we might go and have a look.'

Nanny straightened the hat which George had inadvertently nudged to one side as he poked his head between them. 'That sounds nice,' she said placidly, and wondered what Master James was up to. He had mentioned, very briefly, the girl who had collected eggs from the hen house he had freed from the snow.

Nanny, who couldn't abide Sybil, allowed herself a few hopeful thoughts.

Nether Ditchling was *en fête* and since it was a fine day there was a good deal of activity in the street as well as the village hall. Mrs Salter had put a table outside her shop, laden with bottles of fizzy lemonade and pastries, hoping to catch any passing trade, and there were balloons hanging from all the windows. The street was filled with children being coaxed into order for the fancy dress parade, and coaxing them was Philly.

The Professor, edging the Bentley into the Vicarage gateway, saw her at once, already a bit untidy, patiently and cheerfully creating order out of chaos. He watched her, smiling, and Nanny watched him. So this was the girl. Nothing to look at, but a happy laughing face and pretty hair, and a nicely rounded shape under that cotton dress.

'Now this is what I call a nice day out,' said Nanny, and James, his eyes on Philly, continued to smile. 'Shall we have a look?'

Philly came to meet them. 'How lovely to see you.' She beamed up at the Professor. 'Have you a day off? Mother and Father will be so pleased...'

'This is Mrs Willett, a family friend and my house-keeper.'

Philly shook hands, still beaming, and said, 'How do you do? It's a bit of a muddle at the moment—the children are getting ready for their parade. Then everyone goes to the village hall. Would you prefer to sit down somewhere quiet? Mrs Salter at the shop won't mind a bit if you have a chair in her window.'

'I'll stay here and have a good view.' Nanny, not given to easy smiling, smiled now.

Philly had bent to stroke George's head, suddenly shy because she had greeted the Professor too warmly. 'Is he your dog?' she asked, not looking higher than the Professor's chin.

'Yes. He lives at the cottage with Mrs Willett.'

'Oh, I thought you lived in London.'

'I escape to the cottage whenever I get the chance.'

He stood looking down at her, half smiling, and after a moment she said, 'I must go and sort out the children. If I see Father I'll tell him you are here.'

She slipped away and was lost in the melee of excited children.

The Professor ushered Nanny and George across the street, and Mrs Selby, coming from the village hall, saw them.

'Well,' she said, 'this is a lovely surprise.' She looked round. 'Is Miss West with you?'

'I'm afraid not. This is Mrs Willett, family friend and housekeeper, and this—' indicating placid George '—is my dog. We had a fancy to come and see you.'

'How delightful. I'll find Philly...'

'We have already met. We have been told to watch the fancy dress parade.'

'Some of us older ones are having coffee outside the shop. May I take Mrs Willett with me? We can have a cup of coffee together and watch the children at the same time. If you go to the village hall—' Mrs Selby nodded over her shoulder '—you'll find the Vicar there, arranging cakes on plates.' She added, 'The rest of the girls are here somewhere, and they will all be in the hall presently, to help with the amusements and the food.'

She took Nanny with her, and the Professor strolled along the crowded narrow pavement and into the village hall. The Vicar, with a handful of ladies to help him, was piling cakes and sandwiches on plates and stacking cups and saucers. He looked up as the Professor went in.

'This is a delightful surprise! Yes, yes, do bring your dog in. Is Miss West with you? You're on your way to Netherby, perhaps?'

'No, no. Sybil isn't with me. I've brought my housekeeper and George. We all fancied some fresh country air.'

'There's plenty of that. But isn't it coals to Newcastle? I understand that you're a paediatrician.'

The Professor laughed. 'I like children, especially when they're happy and bursting with good health. Can I do anything to help you?'

'No, no. Indeed, you give me a good reason to leave these good ladies to finish getting everything ready.'

He led the way out of the hall and the two of them leaned against the churchyard wall and watched the children marching through the village while the grown-ups on the pavements clapped and cheered. Prizes were given at the end, of course, with the Lord of the Manor handing out picture books, paintboxes and boxes of sweets. Everyone had a consolation prize too, so that it all took some time, and the Professor, listening to the Vicar's gentle conversation, didn't take his eyes off Philly. She was oblivious of his gaze, darting here and there, blowing noses, adjusting wobbly headgear, dealing firmly with belligerent little boys who were finding the whole thing was taking too long.

Finally everyone began to make their way to the village hall, and Mrs Selby reminded the Vicar that he had promised to man the tea urn.

The Professor unfolded his great length. 'Perhaps there is something I can do? I see that Mrs Willett is happily engaged with some ladies.'

'Someone she knew years ago; they're so pleased to meet again. If you really would like to help would you mind the bran-tub? Mrs Salter's son had promised to do it, but he's just phoned to say that he's missed the train...'

So the Professor folded himself up again, onto a wooden stool, and helped small eager hands poke the sawdust in the tub in the hope of finding something they really wanted. This entailed a good deal of surreptitious feeling of the parcels in the tub, and their return when not wanted.

'You're cheating,' said Philly, and put a hand on his shoulder when he would have stood up.

'But in such a good cause. I had no idea I was so good at it!'

'Ben, our milkman, will be coming to relieve you so you can have a drink and something to eat. Rose and Katie are making more sandwiches, but there's cheese and pickles and rolls and beer.'

'Perfect. Are you going to keep me company?'

'Well, on and off I can. Almost everyone is busy eating and drinking for a little while, before the games start.' She looked up at him. 'There's a tug-o'-war; they could use you against the farmers.'

The Professor, who would willingly have walked on hot coals to please her, assured her that there was nothing he'd like better. 'But first that beer. There's nothing like a bran-tub to give one a thirst.'

Nanny, sitting with a group of older ladies, took an active part in their conversation while at the same time managing to keep her eyes on the Professor and Philly. Very happy together, she could see that, but in a strictly friendly way. Yet when their eyes met they smiled together for all the world as though they were the only two people there...

I always knew that Sybil wasn't for him, reflected Nanny, deeply satisfied.

By late afternoon people were beginning to go home, to get supper and put tired children to bed. The day had been a great success, observed the Vicar, bidding people from the Manor goodbye and then walking with the Professor to his car.

'I'm sorry you are not able to stay for supper; it would have been a pleasant ending to the day.' He shook hands and bade Nanny goodbye, then stood patiently while his wife and all five daughters made a more prolonged leavetaking. The Professor's goodbye to Philly was brief, but only she saw the look in his eyes as he glanced down at her.

It was as Mrs Selby dished out second helpings of macaroni cheese later that Katie looked across the table at Philly. 'Professor Forsyth is sweet on you, Philly. Even if he's going to marry that awful Sybil. Aren't you a lucky girl? I wouldn't mind being in your shoes...'

Philly got up from the table. 'I'll see to the hens,' she said. She left her half-empty plate and had gone before anyone could speak.

CHAPTER FOUR

THERE was a moment's silence, then everyone spoke at once. Mrs Selby hushed them. 'Katie, we all know that you didn't mean to upset Philly. She regards the Professor as a friend. Remember that he is to marry Sybil—she hasn't had much opportunity to meet people—men—as you and your sisters have had, and I'm quite sure that she thinks of him as a friend and nothing more. She's a sensible girl, long past teenage daydreams.' Of course Mrs Selby was wrong there. 'But you did embarrass her, making a joke of a casual acquaintance whom she will probably never see again.'

'I'm sorry,' burst out Katie. 'I was only teasing her a bit. And he did stare at her a lot, and when she's with him she sort of lights up...'

The Vicar said thoughtfully, 'I'm afraid that we've taken Philly for granted. Perhaps we can arrange for her to meet more people—young people. I am ashamed to own that I have always thought that Philly was content to stay here in the village, but of course she needs young society—which she would have if she had a job and met other people.'

He looked round the table. 'You all agree with me, I'm sure.'

There was a chorus of assent. 'If she could just go away and stay with someone?' suggested Rose. 'It doesn't have to be a job; she would hate that after village life. Don't we know anyone she could visit?'

After several minutes' cogitating they had to admit that there wasn't anyone. True, there was Aunt Dora, who lived in Balham, but she was in her seventies, deaf, and unlikely to know anyone younger than sixty. Then there was Cousin Maud, recently widowed and unsociable by nature—even more so now. That left Cousin Elizabeth, quite young still, never in a job for more than a few months and boasting a host of unsuitable friends. Besides, she had only last week written to the Vicar and asked him to lend her five hundred pounds. This was an impossibility, for the heavy snow in March had damaged the roof and Noakes, the builder, had shaken his head over it and sent an estimate which precluded lending a farthing to anyone...

So it was the general regretful opinion that, for the time being at least, Philly would have to stay at home.

And then, the very next day, the unexpected happened.

Mrs Selby had a letter from a friend with whom she had kept in touch since they had been at school together. After they married—she to the Vicar, Mary to a wealthy businessman—they had remained firm friends, exchanging news several times a year.

Mrs Selby opened the letter at the breakfast table and read it slowly. When she had finished she said, 'Listen to this—a letter from Mary Lovell.' She waited until they were all looking at her. 'Her daughter Susan—remember her—a bit younger than Philly?—well, Mary's husband has to go to America on business and Mary is going with him. Susan was to have gone, too, but she has been very ill with shingles and the doctor won't allow her to go. Mary's mother is going to stay with Susan while they are away but she asks if we could spare one of you to go and stay with her for company until they return—in a few weeks, she says.' She paused to re-read the page. 'Susan isn't ill—indeed the doctor says that it will do her good to get out and about a bit. Her grandmother's too elderly...'

Mrs Selby looked round the table and exchanged speaking glances with the Vicar and four of her daughters. Philly had bent to give Casper, the family Labrador, a crust of toast and missed it, but as she sat up she found everyone looking at her. She said, 'Let Lucy go. It's half term next weekend.'

'Not long enough—and she mustn't miss school with all those exams in another month. Philly, dear...? Just for a few weeks...you like Susan.'

'What about the hens and the garden?'

'I'll do the hens,' said Katie quickly.

'And I'll keep the garden going,' said Lucy.

'I haven't the right clothes...'

'You can have my blue dress. We can make it shorter and take it in. I dare say Susan goes to the theatre and so on.'

'I'm sure your father will give you some money, dear,' said Mrs Selby comfortably. 'A nice jersey two-piece—they always look right at any time of day—and a light raincoat, perhaps.'

Katie, anxious to atone for her ill-timed joke, offered the dressing gown she had had for her birthday, a vivid silky garment which dazzled the eyes. But she was almost the same size as Philly, and Philly, understanding why it was being offered, accepted it with gratitude.

She didn't particularly want to go. She had visited Susan and her mother once or twice over the years, but although they had been kindness itself she had missed village life and the more or less peaceful day-to-day routine. Obviously there was no one else available. And she would be back before spring slipped into summer.

'All right, I'll go,' said Philly. 'You're sure it's only for a week or two?'

'I'll ring and make sure about that.' Mrs Selby re-read the letter. 'Mary says that they will fetch you in the car next Tuesday. Goodness, I had better phone her, and then we must go shopping.' She looked at the Vicar. 'If we might have the car for an hour or two Philly can drive us— Shepton Mallett or Yeovil or Sherborne...'

So Philly found herself on the following Tuesday, sitting beside Mr Lovell in his Jaguar car, listening to his rather loud voice explaining that he wasn't sure how long he would be in the USA— 'But certainly not more than three weeks,' he told her, laughing heartily. 'We can't leave Susan for longer than that time. Her grandmother won't be much company for her.' He added hastily, 'Of course she will have you...'

Philly wasn't sure whether that was meant as a compliment or not.

The Lovells had a large Victorian house in Fulham in a prosperous-looking street obviously lived in by people of substance. As Philly got out of the car she felt sure that a maid would answer the door, not a modern version in a pinny, but one wearing a uniform and a white apron.

She was right. An elderly silent woman, in a black dress and a small white apron, opened the door to them, acknowledged Mr Lovell's greeting with a slight movement of the lips and gave Philly a quick appraising look. Philly smiled at her, which was a waste of time. London, thought Philly. Everyone's a stranger.

Mrs Lovell welcomed her warmly, though, and Susan was glad to see her. Grandmother Lovell, sitting in a high-backed chair with her feet on a stool, offered a hand and observed in a dry old voice that she hoped that Philly would enjoy her stay. 'I must depend upon you to keep Susan amused.'

Which remark made Philly wish that she was back at home.

It took her only a few days to discover that Susan's grandmother wanted nothing to do with Susan's activities— indeed they saw very little of her, since she breakfasted in bed and they were almost always out for lunch. Only in the evenings did they dine together, and then the old lady talked a great deal about herself and her youth and evinced no desire to know what they had been doing all day.

Philly might miss village life, but there was a lot to be said for London's attractions. There were the shops; Susan, with plenty of money to spend, would spend the morning at Harrods, poring over the cosmetics counter or trying on clothes. 'Mother and Father like me to look smart,' she explained complacently to Philly. She cast a not unkind look at Philly's knitted two-piece. 'Of course you don't need to have a lot of clothes, do you? Don't you ever want to live here in London?'

Philly said that no, she didn't, but added politely that she was enjoying her visit. 'There's so much to see—the shops and the parks and seeing the Horse Guards riding...' She hesitated. 'Do you ever visit any of the museums?'

'Well, only if Mother and Father have been invited to something special at one of them. Did you want to go to one? I tell you what, there's an exhibition of Chinese porcelain—I can't remember where, but we can easily find out... I don't mind going—it's the fashionable thing to do. We might even get our photos in one of the society magazines.'

'I'd like that,' said Philly. She didn't know anything about Chinese porcelain but she was willing to learn, although she didn't like the idea of having her photo in the papers. It was not very likely, she told herself. Hers was the kind of face that people passed over without even seeing it.

Susan was as good as her word. She was not a clever girl, and was too lazy to do anything about it, but she was kind and she liked Philly and felt vaguely sorry for her since she lived buried in the country and had no fun. It puzzled Susan that she seemed content to dwindle into middle age without even the prospect of marrying. Susan, at twenty-three, thought of thirty as being the end of youth and beauty, and Philly was twenty-seven, although she didn't seem to mind in the least.

It was a fine morning; it would have to be the knitted two-piece again. The saleswoman who had sold it to her had commented that it was a well-bred outfit, suitable for any occasion. Philly, looking around her once they were in the museum, hoped that she was right. At least it was so unassuming that it passed unnoticed amongst the elegant outfits surrounding her.

The porcelain was magnificent. Philly forgot about everything else and went slowly from one showcase to the next, reading all the little tickets and trying to appreciate what she read. They had been there about half an hour when Susan nudged her. 'I've seen some friends of mine over there. Do you mind if I go and talk to them?'

Philly, bent double over a fragile dish in its own glass case, nodded absently, to be brought upright by a voice behind her.

'The last person I would have expected to see here.'

Sybil West, the picture of elegance, was smiling at her as she stood up.

'Surely this isn't quite your scene?' went on Sybil, and turned to smile at the woman with her. 'My dear, imagine! This is the Vicar's daughter—the one with the sausages.'

They both laughed, but Philly, red in the face, nonetheless said politely, 'Hello, Miss West. I'm surprised at meeting you here, too. But life's full of surprises, isn't it?'

'Pleasant ones, too.'

Philly turned round smartly. The Professor was standing there. There was nothing in his face to tell her whether he had heard their brief exchange. He smiled down at her and then he nodded at Sybil. 'Sorry, I couldn't get here earlier—and I can't stay. I'm afraid I'll have to break our date for this evening.'

Sybil said angrily, 'That's the second time this week...'

Philly edged away. The woman who had been with Sybil had already turned her back to talk to someone else, but the Professor's hand was suddenly on her arm.

'You're not on your own?'

'No. With a friend.'

'You're staying in London?'

'Yes.' Philly was very conscious of the hand, so she

smiled at Sybil. 'It was nice meeting you again. I must find my friend. Goodbye.'

She looked at the Professor and then wished him goodbye, too, in a stiff little voice, and met his eyes for a brief moment. He dropped his hand from her arm and she slipped away to lose herself in the crowd.

When she found Susan she was forced to explain who the tall good-looking man was. 'I saw him talking to you, but I didn't dare interrupt. Who is he? Someone important? And there was a girl with you, too. She looked cross.'

So Philly explained sufficiently to satisfy Susan's curiosity.

'A pity—I thought just for a moment that he was keen on you, Philly.'

She laughed, and Philly laughed with her, and wished that she was back home where she would be able to forget Professor Forsyth and the way he had looked at her.

Wishful thinking, reflected Philly, never did anyone any good.

When they left the museum a few minutes later the Professor was at the door, talking to the porter, and what was more natural than that he should speak to Philly?

'Are you staying long in London?' he asked her and looked at Susan.

'Just for a week or two, to keep Susan company. Susan, this is Professor Forsyth. Susan Lovell—Professor Forsyth.'

They shook hands and Susan, as she would tell her mother later, had the instant and urgent feeling that Philly and this professor wanted to be alone. A girl of impulses, she didn't hesitate.

'Philly, I've just remembered. I promised Granny that if I saw Lady Savill here I would ask her about the bridge party. And she is here. I must go back and talk to her, and she'll be so long-winded she might even invite me to lunch. You go on back and tell Granny, will you? Get a ninety-three bus.'

She had gone before Philly could speak.

'I'm going the same way as the ninety-three bus,' said the Professor, deceptively casual. 'I'll give you a lift.'

'Really? You wouldn't mind? I'm not quite sure about the buses. Susan lives in Fulham—if you're going that way?'

He assured her that he was and led the way to the car. Fulham wasn't all that distance, but the lunch hour traffic was building up and he had no intention of taking the quickest route. Philly was constantly in his thoughts and now she was here with him, sitting beside him, answering his carefully casual questions with all the openness of a child.

London, she told him, was very interesting, and parts of it were really very pleasant. 'But some of the side streets look very depressing. Rows and rows of little brick houses with no gardens. I do hope that the people who live in them go for holidays to the sea or to the country...'

'I think a good many of them do.' The Professor turned down a side street which would lengthen their drive considerably. 'But you would be surprised to know how many of them dislike the country, even for a holiday—country such as Nether Ditchling, with no shops or cinemas or amusement arcades. You see, they don't need to walk for miles to get eggs; everything is on the doorstep or at the supermarket.' He glanced at her. 'Mrs Salter's shop is hardly a fair exchange to them.'

'Well, yes, I dare say Nether Ditchling is a bit dull...'

'But you wouldn't wish to leave it?'

'I'm very happy there.' She didn't say more, thinking wistfully that she would leave the village and go to the ends of the earth if he asked her to.

They were nearing their journey's end.

'Do you know where we are?'

'Yes. It's the second road on the left and then the first road on the right,' said Philly. She added, 'It was lovely to see you again. I didn't think we would—I mean, you living here and being important and me living at home.'

As he drew up before the house which she had pointed out she asked, 'When are you getting married?' She had her hand on the door and he got out to open it for her. On the pavement she added, looking up at his calm face, 'You mustn't marry her; she'll make you very unhappy.'

The street door had been opened by the severe maid and Philly skipped up the steps and into the house, so appalled at what she had said that she forgot to say goodbye or thank you.

She avoided the maid's astonished stare and ran upstairs to her room. Her tongue had run away with her with a vengeance, and the faint hope that the Professor might not have heard her wasn't worth a second thought. Would it be best to write and apologise? Or ignore the whole regrettable happening? She stared at her face in the mirror and wished that she was at home; that today was still yesterday, that she had never gone to the museum...

She went downstairs to join Susan's granny in the sitting room and give an account of her morning. She explained why Susan had gone back to talk to Lady Savill, and then listened politely to the old lady's long-winded account of her friendship with her.

Philly, listening with half an ear, was startled when she was suddenly asked sharply why she wasn't married or at least engaged.

'I don't know,' she said. 'No one has ever asked me...'

'You have never met a man whom you wish to marry?'

Philly went a bright pink. Incurably honest, she said, 'Oh, yes, but he doesn't know.'

'There are ways of letting a man know,' said Granny Lovell, 'and you're no fool.'

'That isn't possible. There are circumstances...'

'In that case you must hope that fate will intervene, as

she so often does.' Granny Lovell heaved herself up against her cushions. 'Pour me another glass of sherry, child.'

Philly, reflecting that elderly grannies should never be written off as dim old ladies, filled her glass obediently.

Susan came back then, with messages from Lady Savill.

'Did you get a bus? You knew where to get off?'

'Well, Professor Forsyth said he was coming this way so he gave me a lift.'

'I thought perhaps he would. He looked nice. Known him long, Philly?'

'And who is this professor?' asked Granny, and fixed Philly with a beady eye not to be ignored.

'Well,' began Philly, 'he's not really a friend, only some-one I met by accident, and then again when we had that snow.' She added soberly, 'He's engaged to a very beau-tiful girl. Susan, you saw her at the museum. You said she looked cross.'

'And so she did! Do you know her, Philly?'

'We've met several times, but only because we were both in the same place at the same time, if you see what I mean.'

'Well, she didn't look your sort,' said Susan. 'Granny, if you've finished your sherry may we have lunch? I'm simply starving.'

Going to bed that night, Philly wondered if the Professor would come to the house now that he knew where she was staying. There was no reason why he should—indeed, he had probably forgotten where she was staying by now, and he had evinced no wish to see her again. Remembering the way they had parted, she conceded that it was highly un-likely that the idea would even cross his mind.

I am behaving like an idiot, Philly told herself, and any-way I don't want to see him ever again after what I said. Half-asleep, she muttered, 'I'm bewitched. The sooner I go home the better.'

*   *   *

The Professor was still smiling as he let himself into his flat, and Jolly, coming to meet him in the hall, said, 'Come up on the pools, have you? Haven't seen you look so pleased with yourself for a month of Sundays, sir.'

The Professor tossed his bag on a chair and picked up his post from the console table. 'The pools, Jolly? No, no— I have discovered nirvana, glimpsed a future.'

He went to his study and shut the door and Jolly went back to his kitchen.

'And what's got into him?' he asked Tabby, his cat. 'It certainly isn't that Miss West. He's never smiled like that for her…'

The following week the Lovells came back and Philly was driven home, clasping a tee shirt emblazoned with American slogans which she didn't think would go down well in Nether Ditchling, her ears ringing with the Lovells' thanks. Granny had bidden her goodbye in her tart manner, with the hope that she had taken advantage of her visit, which had made her feel that she was the one who should be thanking them. London had been interesting, she admitted, but the only reason she would wish to return there was because Professor Forsyth lived and worked there. But that was a thought she kept to herself.

It was lovely to be home again. She gave the tee shirt to Lucy, who had been looking after the hens for her, and then handed round the small presents she had bought and gave a detailed account of the pleasures she had had, the places she had been to and the shops she had visited.

'But everyone's in a hurry,' she explained. 'Going somewhere or coming back from somewhere…'

'So you wouldn't want to live there?' observed her father.

'Only if I had a very good reason, Father. I am very happy to be home again.'

Something in her voice made her mother look at her

sharply. Perhaps she had met someone—a man—while she was in London. But Philly was a grown woman, not a young daughter to be questioned...

The Professor, meanwhile, was in his study working. But after half an hour or so of writing, he sat back in his chair and allowed his thoughts free rein. He allowed his thoughts to dwell pleasurably on Philly until they were interrupted by the phone. It was Sybil...

A friend of hers had told her with concealed spite that James had been seen talking alone with that funny little creature who had been at the museum. What was more, the friend had added, he had put her in his car and driven off— 'They seemed to know each other very well...'

'Someone we both know,' Sybil had said sweetly. 'A girl we met earlier this year. We're both rather sorry for her. She lives in the country—a very dull life...'

'When you spoke to her in the museum you didn't sound sorry for her,' the friend had pointed out. She'd laughed. 'You'd better watch your back, darling.'

Sybil had laughed too, then, but when she had gone home she'd sat down to think.

Perhaps she was a bit too sure of James. Perhaps she had been away too much, not wanting to spend her time with him at that boring cottage. This girl might be a real danger. Sybil was shrewd enough to know that James might want something more than a glamorous companion on an evening out, and the girl was bright enough to see that. 'The stupid creature,' Sybil had hissed aloud.

But Sybil had a good deal of charm when she wished to use it, and said now, 'Darling, am I interrupting you at work? Only I wanted to tell you how glad I was that you gave Philly that lift last week. It was such a surprise to see her at the exhibition, and she wasn't a bit happy about being there. I quite forgot to ask her where she was staying—I thought I might take her out to lunch, somewhere rather chic. I don't suppose she gets out much when she's home. Have you her address?'

'Somewhere in Fulham. I didn't notice the street or the house. But she will be back home by now.'

Sybil was too clever to press the point. James sounded as calm and composed as he always did, but that wasn't to say that he wasn't intending to see Philly. She said sweetly, 'What a pity. I hope she had a good time; her friend looked rather nice. I won't keep you, darling, but I hope I'll see you at the Mastertons' dinner party. Don't work too hard!'

Sybil put down the phone and sat down to think once more. She had every intention of marrying James, but in her own good time. In the meantime, though, she must make sure that his eye didn't wander.

She had a great belief in her ability to charm him; she was lovely to look at, dressed beautifully, and hid a keen intelligence beneath effortless conversation and the ability to be amusing. She was also greedy and selfish, quick-tempered, and quite uncaring about anyone or anything which didn't concern her personally, and, knowing this, she was careful to conceal the true side of her nature. Just once or twice she had allowed it to show and she knew that James had seen it.

Philly must be made to be out of reach, but how? It seemed that she had no boyfriends, no prospect of marrying anyone at Nether Ditchling. A boyfriend must be found— better still a man who professed himself to be serious about her. She knew James well enough to know that he would accept that, whatever his own feelings were.

There must be someone who would play the part of devoted admirer. Someone who enjoyed a joke at someone else's expense and wasn't too scrupulous about hurting feelings…

And there was. Her cousin, a young tearaway with too much money and too much time on his hands. She had had a phone call from him recently, deploring his dull life while he recovered from a skiing accident. He was, she judged, ripe for some amusement…

Wasting no time, she drove herself down to the country house in Norfolk where he was staying with his parents until he was fit enough to return to his London flat.

Her aunt and uncle, who didn't like her particularly, nevertheless welcomed her as someone who would relieve Gregory's boredom, and she had ample opportunity to spend hours with him as he limped around the gardens, grumbling, ripe for any mischief offered to him.

It would be a joke, she told him. No one would get hurt—not that either of them cared about that.

'James is getting impatient to marry,' she told him, 'and I don't want to tie myself down yet. James has everything, you know that, but we don't see eye to eye about some things. I'm still working on him, and while I'm doing that I can't have him being distracted by another woman. This girl's a walk-over, a real country miss—keeps hens and teaches Sunday School, full of good deeds. One look at you limping into the village and she's yours.'

'What's her name?'

'Philomena, believe it or not! Everyone calls her Philly. She's quite plain and wears the most awful clothes.'

'You don't suppose James has fallen for her?'

'Not for one moment. She just happened to turn up at the right moment, though. Do say that you'll help me out, Gregory. Besides, it will keep you amused while you get fit again.'

'What's in it for me?'

'A bit of fun to keep you amused, as I said, and I'll wangle an invitation to the Strangeways', on their yacht. Everyone would give their eye teeth to get asked…'

She looked sideways at him; he was a good-looking young man, and could be charming when he had his own way. And he was quite as heartless and as selfish as she was. Absolutely ideal for her plan.

'It's on,' said Gregory. 'When do I start?'

'You know the people at Netherby, don't you? You couldn't go to the wedding because of your accident, but you're well enough acquainted with them for me to drive you down there. There should be a chance of getting a weekend invitation. Nether Ditchling is only a few miles away. You could run out of petrol, or some such thing, and contrive to get yourself into the Vicarage.'

The Professor was going to Birmingham, to the children's hospital there, in a week's time. There was ample time before that to drive to Netherby with Gregory.

It all went splendidly. The newly-weds weren't back from honeymoon and everyone was feeling a bit flat; new faces were welcome and Gregory could be charming and amusing. They were glad of a diversion, and he was invited to stay for a week or so.

Sybil drove him back to London, delighted with the success of her plan.

'I can't stay for more than a week or ten days,' observed Gregory. 'I mean, I know the family slightly, but not enough to outstay my welcome.'

'Then you'll have to put up at a pub somewhere close.'

When he demurred, she said slyly, 'I met Joyce Strangeway a day or two ago—you'll get your invitation...' She went on, ignoring his pleased grin, 'There's a good pub at Wisbury; that's only about three miles from Nether Ditchling. It's only for a few weeks,' she added coaxingly, 'Just long enough for James to be told about it. I'll do that, and get him to drive me down to Nether Ditchling. You can be there, being very possessive about Philly.'

'Supposing she doesn't like me?'

'Don't be a fool, Gregory. You can make anyone like you if you choose.'

The Professor, dining with Sybil on the evening before he went to Birmingham, found her in a charming mood, ready to amuse him, prepared to listen to his infrequent references to his work, talking with smiling vagueness about their future.

In this compliant mood, he reflected, perhaps they could talk seriously, discover if their feelings for each other were deep enough, and perhaps agree mutually to free each other from an engagement which had gone on too long and become meaningless.

But Sybil, wary of such talk, gave him no chance to start a serious conversation. When at length he said, 'Sybil, I think we should have a talk,' she pretended not to hear, but waved to friends at a nearby table and suggested that they should join them for coffee.

The Professor, whose good manners prevented him from not welcoming her friends, resolved to go and see Sybil when he got back from Birmingham.

The following day Sybil drove Gregory down to Netherby House, spent a few hours there, and then drove back to town. There was nothing more she could do until James came back; her plan depended on Gregory now.

Gregory was the perfect guest when he exerted himself. On the third day of his visit he proposed talking himself off for the day— 'So that you won't get too tired of me around the house,' he told his hostess.

When she protested about his lame leg he told her that he could drive quite easily in his small sports car, and besides, there was almost no traffic.

He set off after breakfast, saying that he might drive down to the coast and wouldn't be back before the late afternoon, and then he idled his way to Nether Ditchling, a half-formed plan in his head. He drove into the village slowly and stopped at Mrs Salter's shop. He went inside, exaggerating his limp, aware that it aroused friendly sympathy. He wished her a sunny good morning and bought a newspaper, and then took the local paper as well.

'Haven't seen you before,' observed Mrs Salter. 'Touring, are you?'

'Hardly that. I'm looking for somewhere to live. I've been told that there are several places for sale in this part of the country.'

It was a shot in the dark that found its mark.

'Well, now,' said Mrs Salter, delighted to have a good gossip. 'You're right there. There's Appletrees at the end of the village. Nice little place—a bit pokey though, if you have young children.'

Gregory smiled. 'I'm not married yet, but I'd want a place where there was plenty of room.'

'Well, there's Old Thatch, between here and Wisbury, and the Old Manor, a mile or so from this end of the village. Nice place with a good big garden.'

'That sounds just right. There's an agent?'

He couldn't believe his luck when Mrs Salter said, 'Mr Selby, the Vicar, has the keys. It's a bit out of the way and the agent has to come a long way. Besides, no one has been to see it for months.'

Gregory gave her a winning smile. 'It may be just what I'm looking for. Bless you for telling me about it. Where is the Vicarage?'

Mrs Salter beamed. 'See the church? It's that redbrick house just beyond it. The Vicar will take you round the Old Manor. He's a very nice gentleman.'

Gregory smiled again. 'I hope we shall meet again,' he told her, and went back to his car. This was going to be his day…!

CHAPTER FIVE

THE Vicarage door was open. Gregory pulled the old-fashioned bell and listened to the distant sound of voices and then hurrying feet. The girl who opened the door wider had to be Philly—Sybil's description of her had been accurate and, he had to admit, spiteful. No looks, but a lovely smile, a mouth which turned up at the corners and beautiful eyes. And her friendly, 'Good morning,' was uttered in a soft voice.

For a moment Gregory felt mean, but then he remembered the Strangeways' yacht, and he returned Philly's smile.

'Good morning. I do apologise for bothering you, but Mrs Salter told me that perhaps the Vicar could help me.'

'Come in. I'll fetch him for you.' She ushered him into the drawing room. 'Do sit down. Father won't be a minute.'

Gregory sat, but got up as soon as she had left him. The room was large and the furniture in it was good solid stuff, worth quite a bit. There were some good pictures on the walls too, although the armchairs and the sofa were shabby. He went to the window and looked out, then turned round as the door opened and the Vicar came in.

Gregory smiled his charming smile. 'Good morning, Sir. I hope I'm not disturbing you, but Mrs Salter at the shop sent me to you. I'm looking for a house and she was telling me about the Old Manor and that you had the keys. I should very much like to look over it at your convenience. If you would suggest a time?'

A polite young man and I don't like him. I wonder why? thought the Vicar.

'Why not now? I am free for an hour or so, and it is only a couple of miles from here. Do you have a car?'

'Yes, I'm staying at Netherby House for a week or so.' Gregory held out a hand. 'Gregory Finch.'

The Vicar shook hands. 'Then let us go at once. I'll get the keys. The house has been empty for some time. It's a delightful place, but needs some refurbishment.'

He went away for the keys, and they were going down the path to the car when Philly called from the door. 'Father, the Armstrongs have phoned. Mr Armstrong's worse; they ask if you'd go right away...'

'Of course.' The Vicar turned back to the house. 'You must forgive me. An elderly parishioner, gravely ill. I must ask you to come at some other time.'

Philly had joined them. 'I'll take this gentleman, Father. Now he's here he might just as well have a look at the house. He can come back if he likes it and discuss it with you. It's the Old Manor, isn't it? I saw you take the keys...'

'Very well, my dear. Lock up well, won't you? I may possibly be back within an hour or so, and Mr Finch is welcome to wait here if he wishes to know more about the house.'

He hurried into the street and Philly said, 'Will you wait a minute while I tell Mother?' and she went back into the house.

Mrs Selby had been looking at them from the drawing-room window. A good-looking young man, she considered, obviously recovering from some injury to his leg. She turned her attention to the sports car, and as Philly came in she said, 'He looks all right, but don't let him drive too fast.'

Gregory, seeing her watching him from the window, exaggerated the limp. Older ladies, he had discovered, had a soft spot for the lame.

He was careful to be politely formal with Philly as they drove the short distance to the Old Manor, and once there he inspected the place slowly, asking all the right questions, discussing the garden at some length, asking about the neighbourhood and the village.

'It is delightful,' he told her. 'I should very much like to come again and inspect the place more thoroughly. When is it most convenient for me to come?'

'Well, Saturday afternoons are mostly free for Father, or any time on Monday. He might be called away, of course...'

He stood aside politely while she locked the house door. 'Then if I come on Monday around eleven o'clock? I can wait if the Vicar is engaged. I'm able to please myself until my leg is quite fit again and I shall enjoy looking round the church and the village.'

He gave her a quick look and saw that he was behaving exactly as she would expect him to behave.

Philly nodded. 'If you don't mind having to wait Mother will be glad to give you coffee. You won't want to walk too far with that leg.'

Back at the Vicarage they found that the Vicar was still away. Mrs Selby offered coffee and suggested that Gregory might like to wait, but he was satisfied with his morning's work. He mustn't rush things. Certainly he must phone Sybil. He thanked her, got into his car and drove away.

'Was he interested?' asked Mrs Selby.

'He seemed to be. He didn't say much but he wants to go again and talk to Father about it. He was very polite...'

Mrs Selby agreed, ignoring the vague thought that she didn't like him.

Gregory had said that he must drive back to Netherby for lunch, but he had no intention of doing so; he had told his hostess that he would be away all day and he intended to drive to Bath.

He had had enough of the country already, and a civilised pub and a decent restaurant would help him to while away the hours. He hoped that Sybil's plan could be carried out quickly, before he got too bored. He pulled into a lay-by and dialled her number on his mobile phone. She would probably not be home…

But she was, and avid to hear if he had been able to meet Philly.

He told her, and listened to her delighted praise. 'Gregory, you're a marvel. Now I must get James to go to Nether Ditchling and you must manage to be there… I'll phone you as soon as I know something. What did you think of Philly?'

'I don't know why you're making such a fuss, Sybil.' When she made an impatient sound, he said, 'Oh, all right, I'll help you out. It will give me something to do in all this boring country, and it shouldn't be too hard to fix up something. I'm already on good terms with the Vicar and his wife, and it'll be amusing to get Philly interested in me.'

'I knew you'd help me,' said Sybil, and added cunningly, 'I met David Smale yesterday; he's been invited by the Strangeways to join them on their yacht. He had heard that you had been invited too.'

Gregory smiled to himself. 'Let me know what you plan to do and give me as much warning as you can.'

It seemed as though the fates were on Sybil's side. A carefully casual wish that James might drive her to Netherby so that she could see Coralie met with willing agreement.

He would be free on Saturday. They could have lunch on the way and get to Netherby in the early afternoon, he suggested. Perhaps if he and Sybil saw more of each other—and she had been very sweet and undemanding lately—they could talk about their future. Their separate futures. Her vagueness about it forced him to think that she had no wish to settle down to married life, with a husband and children, and if she would admit that, then they could part amicably with no hard feelings.

He told Jolly that he would be driving Miss West to

Netherby on Saturday afternoon, looking so pleased about it that Jolly went to his kitchen and brooded over a future dominated by that lady.

But the Professor was looking pleased because there was a good chance that he might see Philly as they drove through Nether Ditchling.

Which, of course he would.

Gregory couldn't believe his luck. Primed by Sybil that she and James should be at the village around two o'clock, he had had no difficulty in asking the Vicar to arrange for him to see the Old Manor again. There was the chance that something would upset their timetable, but he thought it unlikely. They both had their phones; Sybil could ring him when they stopped for lunch and give him a good idea at about what time they should reach Nether Ditchling.

He made his own plans and spent the best part of the morning playing the dutiful guest.

'Such a charming young man,' observed his hostess. 'So thoughtful and so amusing. I shall miss him when he goes.'

Her husband, in the habit of keeping his own opinions to himself, grunted in a non-committal manner which allowed her to think that he agreed with her.

Saturday was a busy day for Philly: typing her father's sermon, since he could never read his own notes, making up beds for Rose's and Flora's fiancés, picking the broad beans for Sunday lunch, going to do the church flowers with whichever of the village ladies whose turn it was.

It was warm for the time of year. 'Likely it's a taste of 'an 'ot summer,' the milkman had said early that morning, a remark which had encouraged Philly to put on a cotton blouse and a denim skirt before going to lay the table for lunch.

Her mother and father, Katie and Lucy and herself would

be there. It was to be omelettes and a salad, with rolls warm from Mr Brisk's bakery in the next village.

They all had a great deal to say over their simple meal, for they liked to talk, airing their views, encouraged by the Vicar, who found small talk a waste of time, so that it was later than usual when they got up from the table.

'What time is Mr Finch coming?' asked Katie.

Mrs Selby looked at the clock. 'Goodness, it's almost two o'clock. He said between two and half past…'

But there was no sign of him when Katie went to look.

They washed up and put the tea tray ready, and Philly went to the hen house to cast an eye over a broody hen. By that time it was almost half past two.

As James slowed the Bentley when they reached the village Gregory slid to a halt outside the Vicarage. Things couldn't be better; now it was up to Sybil…

She had seen him; she put an urgent hand on James' sleeve. 'Stop, James, do stop. That's my cousin by the Vicarage gate—remember I told you he was staying at Netherby? I must say hello.'

They greeted each other as though they hadn't seen each other for months. Sybil introduced the men and asked, 'Whatever are you doing here, Gregory?'

'Waiting for Philly,' he told her with a smile. 'I'm driving her to Bath to do some shopping. Of course—you know her?' His glance swept from Sybil to the Professor. 'We met over at Netherby and we rather fell for each other.' The lies tripped off his tongue with easy assurance. 'Forgive me if I don't stay talking; I'd better see if she is ready.'

He got out of his car and started up the Vicarage path with an airy wave of the hand. Of course if the Vicar or his wife were to come out now he would be in an awkward spot…but no one came. He turned at the door and waved again, and saw the Bentley slip away.

He spent a tedious afternoon with the Vicar, inspecting

drains and walls and discussing the need for roof repairs, and towards the end of the afternoon his mobile phone rang.

It was Sybil, phoning from Netherby, and he said at once, 'You're in town? This evening? May I phone you back?' He glanced at the Vicar and said, 'An old friend in town for a couple of days. Wants me to meet him for dinner.'

'Well, I think you have inspected this house very thoroughly. Suppose we go back to the Vicarage and have a cup of tea and you can drive to town from there? You will want to warn them at Netherby…'

Gregory hid a grin. Everything was going splendidly. 'I'll phone them now.'

'I'll go and turn the car and start locking up,' said the Vicar, and wandered off.

Gregory dialled and said loudly, 'It's Gregory. Would you forgive me if I go straight to town?' and then softly, once the Vicar was out of the room, 'Sybil, we're just leaving; I'm having tea at the Vicarage. Any chance of you getting there? There's nothing to stop you knocking on the door and paying a friendly visit. Bring the Professor with you, of course, and I'll do my stuff with Philly.'

He heard her delighted giggle. 'I can't promise anything, but I'll do my best.'

It wasn't difficult to suggest getting back to London. Sybil made her excuses in her charming way, and in the car again she said coaxingly, 'You don't mind, darling? I do love the country, but after an hour or so I've had enough. We can get tea on the way. Where shall we go this evening?'

'We'll stop for tea, but I'm speaking at a dinner this evening…'

'Tomorrow we could go to Henley—go on the river.' When he hesitated, she said, 'Oh, all right, you don't want to go. You never do what I want to do, do you? But you expect me to trail down to that cottage of yours and be bored to tears.'

It seemed as good a time as any. The Professor said quietly, 'We must talk, Sybil...'

They were nearing the Vicarage and she shouted, 'Well, I don't want to talk. Stop—I want a cup of tea and I'm going to the Vicarage. After all, they seem to keep open house.'

'We can have tea further along the road. You can't interrupt their afternoon.'

She pointed her finger at Gregory's car. 'Why not? It looks as though Gregory has.'

Against his better judgement, the Professor stopped the car. Sybil flounced out and up the path to the Vicarage door, half-open as usual. Since they were having tea in the drawing room the entire Selby family saw her—and the Professor coming more slowly.

Mrs Selby got up and went to meet Sybil. 'Just in time for tea,' she said kindly. 'And your cousin is here on his way up to London. Come in. I think you know nearly everyone here.' She turned to smile at the Professor. 'This is a delightful surprise. The girls are always asking when they will see you again.'

'This is an intrusion, Mrs Selby.'

'Nonsense. We love visitors, especially unexpected ones.'

Sybil was already sitting by the Vicar, being offered tea and cake, and in the general upheaval Gregory took care to sit next to Philly, joining in the general talk and at the same time contriving to pay her special attention.

Philly, being polite by nature, smiled at his joking description of getting lost, and answered him when he asked her something, speaking in a low voice which the Professor was quick to note. He made civil conversation with the Vicar and stifled the desire to wring Gregory's neck and then Philly's.

Mrs Selby, apparently unobservant, said quietly, 'Philly, fill the teapot, will you, dear? You'll need more tea.' And,

after a few moments, 'James—I may call you James?—
would you go to the kitchen and tell Philly to bring the
other cake? It's in the cupboard by the Aga.'

Philly was sitting on the kitchen table, swinging her legs
and watching the kettle boil. Part of her felt happy, for the
Professor was here in the house and she hadn't expected
that, and part of her was unhappy because Sybil looked so
beautiful and so sure of herself, glancing at him from time
to time and smiling. She wasn't surprised that he was in
love with her…

He walked in and stood in front of her. 'Your mother
wants the other cake. Did you have a pleasant afternoon…?'

'Oh, yes. We went walking; it's so nice being with someone you like, isn't it?' Indeed it had been nice; she hadn't
seen Mrs Twist's elderly father for some time, and there
had been such a lot to talk about now that Baby Twist was
once more a bouncing infant, the apple of his grandfather's
eye. She went on, wishing that he didn't look so cross,
'He's staying here for a week or two, so we shall see each
other quite often. He doesn't care for London and he's
looking for somewhere to live round here.'

The Professor glowered and said, 'Indeed?' in a voice to
freeze any attempt at light conversation.

It was a good thing that the kettle boiled just then. She
made fresh tea and fetched the cake and gave it to him to
carry.

Sybil gave them a sharp glance as they went back into
the drawing room and a few moments later got up to go.

'We're going out this evening,' she said, and apologised
prettily for leaving so quickly, waiting with ill-concealed
impatience as James made his more leisurely farewells.

When they had gone Mrs Selby said, 'What a beautiful
young woman she is,' and everyone agreed, although Katie,
remembering how upset Philly had been when she had
voiced her opinion once before, held her tongue.

*   *   *

Sybil broke the silence in the car. 'What a nice family—and the girls are so pretty. Not Philly, of course, although she's quite sweet. And what a surprise to find Gregory almost one of the family. They certainly seemed on excellent terms, he and Philly. It's time he settled down.'

'Aren't you being rather premature?' James spoke casually, but, glancing at his profile, Sybil noted its grimness.

'Perhaps, but you must admit that Philly looked happy.'

'How long is Gregory staying at Netherby? He's going up to town this evening, isn't he?'

'He's meeting a friend for dinner...'

'Does he work?'

'Oh, yes. Something in the City. But he's got leave until his leg is quite better. He has money of his own, of course. My uncle's got a small estate in Norfolk.'

All of this was said with an air of such honesty, yet somehow the Professor's handsome nose smelled a rat...

With only vague plans made for a future meeting, he dropped Sybil off and drove to his flat, where Jolly took one look at his face and retired discreetly to the kitchen.

'In a mood,' he told his cat. 'Best leave him for a bit and then dish up something tasty. No doubt that Miss West's been upsetting him again.'

The Professor wasn't upset, he was in a towering rage. He had taken an instant dislike to Gregory, and to his air of possessiveness each time he looked at or spoke to Philly. If he had been a decent fellow, James told himself, he would have accepted the situation, but Gregory was the very last man for Philly. Besides, he wasn't sure that she liked him, let alone loved him...

He went in search of Jolly presently. 'I'm going down to the cottage tomorrow. Have the day off—I'll not be back until early evening.'

'I thought that was what you might be doing. There's a marrow bone in the fridge for George.'

Mrs Willett was delighted when he phoned her. 'There'll be roast pork and apple sauce, and one of my treacle tarts, and we can have a good gossip.' Which meant that she would ask innumerable questions without once probing his private life, knowing that if he wished to he would tell her anything he wanted to.

She knew that he was a very reserved man—he had many friends, but they knew very little about him other than his work. Not one of them approved of Sybil, but they liked him too much to say so, even in the vaguest way. Mrs Willett didn't like her either, but she was prepared to do her best to do so if that would make her Master James a happy man.

He wasn't happy; she saw that at a glance although she said nothing. He had a problem and she hoped that he might tell her about it. And sure enough, the pork and apple sauce disposed of, the washing up done and the pair of them sitting in the garden with George at their feet, the Professor said, 'Nanny, I need your advice...'

'If I can help, I will,' said Nanny, 'and I'll listen.'

When he had finished, he added, 'You see, Nanny, I love her, and if she loves this Gregory and wants to marry him I'll not see her again. But, whether or not she does love him, I know that I cannot marry Sybil. I suppose that I should feel very much to blame for that, but I have known for some time now that she doesn't love me. She is beautiful and charming, but behind that there is nothing. And before I say goodbye to Philly I want to make sure that she will be happy. Do you know, Nanny, I think that something is not quite right about this Gregory? Though Sybil told me that his home is in Norfolk and that he has a job in the City.'

Nanny was brisk and matter-of-fact. 'Find out where this man lives and go and see where it is—perhaps manage to meet his father or family. Find out where he works, discover his friends. And don't tell me that you can't, for you know any number of people who could help you. If he's a good man and loves Philly, and you're satisfied about him, then you can bid her goodbye and take up your life again. If there's something wrong, you can put it right.'

'That is what I've been thinking. I needed someone to tell me that I wasn't behaving like a fool.'

It was a few days later, discussing a small patient's complicated fractured leg, that the Professor's colleague remarked, 'Uncommon case this. Only seen one other. A young man some months ago. Private patient and gave a good deal of trouble so I understand—chatting up the nurses, having drinks smuggled in and so on. Told me that he had an executive job in the City; turned out to be a job in name only, working in the family firm whenever her felt like it. Didn't pay his bill, either. His father settled it finally, explained that though his son had money of his own he was still sowing his wild oats.'

The Professor listened to this with an expressionless face and finally said, 'I seem to have heard about this—was it Finch…?'

'Very likely. The father has a small estate in Norfolk; not liked in the neighbourhood. I made it my business to find out before I sent in my bill.'

'I wonder why I remember the name?' observed the Professor guilelessly. 'A village not too far from the sea?' It was a lucky guess.

'That's right—inland from Great Yarmouth. Limberthorpe. A dozen houses and a church.' He glanced at his watch. 'I must go. Let me know how that leg does…'

The Professor went home and got out a road map. He would be free on Sunday. From what he had heard his dearest Philly had fallen in love with a man who would make her unhappy, but he must give the fellow the benefit of the doubt. He might not be as black as his colleague had painted, and the only way to find out was to go and see for himself. Surely someone in a village as small as Limberthorpe would let drop a hint or two.

He set off early in the morning and reached Limberthorpe in time to join the handful of men in the bar of the village pub. They paused in their talk as he went in. He ordered a pint and sat at the bar, making no attempt to join in their conversation.

Presently one of the men said, 'You're strange to these parts?'

'Just passing through. This village looked so pleasant I stopped for a while.'

''Tis pleasant enough,' said an old man, 'for them as passes on their way.'

He paused, and the Professor recognised this as a strong hint that a round was called for. This done, he said casually, 'Why do you say that?'

'Being sold up lock, stock and barrel, the big house. The old man wants to go and live with his daughter, and young Mr Finch he can't be bothered with the place, you see. Likes London and racketing around. Can't be bothered with the house, never been interested in the village.'

The Professor signalled another round. 'Does that affect the village?'

'Course it does. We rent our cottages from old Mr Finch, but the young 'un, he doesn't want to know. The new owner, when they get one, will probably put up the rents or turn us out.'

'But you could talk to young Mr Finch...'

'Him? Smooth, he is. Always smiling and wouldn't lift a finger to save his granny.'

Driving back home later, the Professor reflected that, even allowing for exaggeration, Gregory Finch was the last man in the world he would allow Philly to marry...

He had a busy week ahead of him, so there was no chance to go and see Philly before the following weekend. Sybil was clever enough not to demand to be taken out, being charmingly sympathetic over his long days at the hospital and only once mentioning Gregory.

'He seems so happy,' she told James. 'He sees Philly most days—he's moved into the local pub so's to be nearer to her.' She gave a little laugh. 'He can't talk of anyone else.'

None of which was true. But how was the Professor to know that?

His busy week ended in an even busier weekend, so it wasn't until Monday morning that he got into the Bentley and drove to Nether Ditchling.

The Vicarage door, as usual, was half-open, and somewhere beyond it someone was Hoovering.

Mrs Selby came to the door when he rang. 'Oh, how nice to see you again. Come on in. Did you want to see the Vicar? He's in his study.'

'I wanted to see Philly.'

Mrs Selby shot him a quick look. 'She's in the garden, right at the end, hanging out the washing. Go and find her and I'll put the coffee on.'

Philly, in a cotton dress which was a bit faded, her hair tied back with a piece of string, was pegging sheets with the expertise of long practice.

The Professor didn't speak until he was close behind her, and then his, 'Good morning Philly,' was uttered very quietly.

Philly turned sharply round. 'Whatever are you doing here on a Monday morning? Shouldn't you be working?'

Which was hardly a good start to a conversation.

He said meekly, 'Sometimes I have a day off.'

He took a flapping sheet from her and pegged it neatly. 'I want to talk to you, Philly.'

She shook out a towel. 'Is Sybil with you?'

'No, this is something which concerns us.'

He took the towel from her and hung it up neatly.

Philly picked up a sheet and had it taken from her too.

'Will you listen, Philly?'

'No.' Then, much too brightly, she said, 'Gregory tells me that you and Sybil are to marry very soon. I hope you will both be very happy.'

'You believed him?'

'Of course.' She hadn't wanted to, but he had sounded so convincing. She had cried her eyes out that night, and then in the cold light of morning had resolved never to think of the Professor again.

The Professor sighed. 'Are you going to marry this Gregory?'

'I shan't tell you,' said Philly, turning her back smartly and hanging another sheet. 'And now, go away, do!'

He went, for there was no point in talking to her until she would listen.

At the house Mrs Selby met him as he went through the kitchen door.

'Coffee?' she offered, and then, seeing his face, added, 'Perhaps you would rather not stop?'

He smiled. 'I'll come again, if I may. Tell me, Mrs Selby, does Philly mean to marry Gregory Finch?'

'Marry him! Great goodness, no. She doesn't like him overmuch, and he certainly doesn't mean to marry her— although he's always on the doorstep. It's as though he's...' she paused to think '...acting a part.'

The Professor nodded; Philly had sent him away, but there was a reason for that and it certainly wasn't because she intended to marry Gregory. If it was because she thought that he and Sybil were to marry, then that was a misunderstanding he must put right.

He should have felt disappointed by her reception of him, but, driving back to London, he felt elated. Sybil and Gregory were somehow concerned in fabricating the man's assiduous courting of Philly; he must see them both as soon as possible.

He went straight to the hospital. Philly might be the love of his life, but his work was his life too.

It was several days before he had the good fortune to meet Sybil and Gregory together.

He had lunched with a colleague, and with an hour or so to spare was walking back to the hospital. Outside an elegant little café he saw Sybil and Gregory, their heads together over a small table.

Interesting, reflected the Professor; Sybil had phoned to say that she would be staying with friends in Wales for several days. She had also told him that Gregory was still in Nether Ditchling. 'I hear wedding bells,' she had said laughingly.

The Professor strolled across the pavement and took a chair between them. 'Am I interrupting something?' he asked pleasantly. 'Are you hatching another instalment of Gregory's love-life?' He turned a cold eye on him. 'If you so much as set foot in Nether Ditchling again I'll break every bone in your body. Now, tell me why you have been acting the eager bridegroom.'

Gregory had gone pale. He wasn't a brave man, and the Professor's nasty smile and the very size of him sent his heart into his boots.

'It was just a joke. I meant no harm. I did it to please Sybil.'

He ignored the curl of the Professor's lip and Sybil's quick, 'Shut up, Gregory.'

'She was afraid you'd gone off her; after all, no girl likes to see a comfortable future go down the drain. Only she wanted a bit of fun first. It was a good scheme; I'd put you off Philly and you'd forget her...' His voice trailed away. 'Well,' he mumbled, 'there's no harm done...'

'Don't believe a word of it,' said Sybil. 'I may have

mentioned that it would be rather a joke to get Philly interested, but that's all.'

The Professor got up, towering over them. 'What a despicable pair you are. If I ever meet you again, Finch, I'll not answer for my actions. And as for you, Sybil, there is a great deal that I would like to say, but what would be the point? I'm sure you will find yourself a husband without difficulty. I'll see that a notice goes into the right papers with the usual polite nonsense used for broken engagements.'

'You wouldn't,' gasped Sybil. 'I'll marry you when you want…'

'But I don't want.' He smiled coldly at them in turn, and then walked away.

It was almost another week before the Professor was free to drive to Nether Ditchling. It was early afternoon by the time he got there.

The Vicar was putting the finishing touches to his Sunday sermon and Mrs Selby was on the drawing-room sofa with her feet up. All five of her daughters were home, but they were all out, and an hour with a good book was something she had been looking forward to.

She frowned when she heard someone at the open front door and got unwillingly to her feet. But the frown disappeared when she saw the Professor standing there.

'I've disturbed you.' She was still clutching her book. 'I'm so sorry. I've come to see Philly.'

Mrs Selby beamed. 'She's in the church, doing the flowers.' She glanced at the hall clock. 'She must be almost finished.'

He nodded, smiled slowly at her, went back to the street and across to the church. She watched him going inside before going back to the sofa. Not to read this time but to make plans—the plans a bride's mother had such pleasure in making.

* * *

Philly was arranging a vase of flowers in one of the side chapels: lupins and phlox, sweet-smelling syringa and floribunda roses. James sat down quietly in a nearby pew and watched her.

When she had finished to her satisfaction he said quietly, 'Philly, will you leave your flowers for a minute and come with me?'

She turned to look at him, her face suddenly aglow with happiness, and went to him and put her hand in his. Together they went out of the church, across the quiet churchyard and into the narrow lane beyond.

'We will talk later,' said the Professor, and took her in his arms and kissed her in a masterful fashion.

Really, there was no need to say anything, reflected Philly, completely and utterly happy. When she was being kissed in such a way words were unnecessary. She looked up into his face and saw the love there. She smiled at him, and then stretched up to kiss him, too.

A PERFECT PROPOSAL

by
Liz Fielding

CHAPTER ONE

'MARK, what's happened? You were supposed to be at a meeting with the surveyors first thing. They just called from the site—'

'Jane...' Mark Hilliard sounded as if he'd come out of some dark place and needed a moment to gather himself. 'I'm sorry, I should have called... Ring them back and apologise for me, will you? I've got a bit of a crisis at home.'

'Crisis?' Jane Carmichael's heart turned over. 'Is Shuli sick?'

'No, she's fine. But she's just sacked another nanny.'

'*Shuli* sacked the nanny? I know she's bright, but isn't that rather advanced behaviour for a three-year-old? What did she do? Call her into the nursery, sit her down on Mr Fluffy and say, "I'm afraid you haven't lived up to the promise of your excellent references, Mrs Collins. I'm going to have to let you go?"'

'Mrs Collins was the nanny before last.'

'Oh, Mark!' Jane's amusement evaporated rapidly. She'd interviewed Sarah Collins herself and had been convinced she would be perfect for the job.

'She left last month. Some excuse about family problems. You tried so hard that I couldn't bring myself to tell you. The agency has been sending me temps in the meantime. It's given Shuli plenty of opportunity to practise the art of getting rid of them. This morning she just screamed the place down until the poor woman left the house. I don't know why; her references *were* excellent. She seemed perfect in every way to me.'

'Things look different from knee height. It wasn't you

103

she was giving a bath and tucking up in bed.' Then, grateful that he couldn't see her quick flush, 'Maybe you should try asking Shuli what she wants before you take on someone else. She might settle better with a live-in nanny.'

'She might. I wouldn't.'

They'd discussed it at length before, but he was clearly uncomfortable about sharing his house with a strange woman. She wasn't wild about the idea, either, but Shuli was more important than her own pathetic little jealousies. Getting him to acknowledge that his little girl was an individual who might have feelings of her own was an uphill battle, but someone had to try.

'Has she calmed down now?'

'Like any woman, Jane, she's perfectly happy now that she's got her own way.' Then, somewhat belatedly. 'I'm sorry, I didn't mean you...'

'No.' He didn't think of her as a woman at all.

'The agency is trying to find a replacement and in the meantime I'm calling everyone I can think of to have her.'

'No luck?'

'My mother is away at some conference and my sister moved to Strasbourg last month. They're not your average grandmother/aunt combination,' he said wearily. 'It looks as if I'm going to have to work from home until I can sort something out. At least for the rest of the week. Will you bring over the files on my desk, please? And the mail.'

'Are you sure? It'll be nearly lunchtime by the time I arrive. Maybe you should just take the day off and spend it with Shuli.' That was what the child wanted. A father who was there to give her a cuddle when she needed it. Who had time for her when she woke up eager to play; who made an effort to get home in time to read her a bed-time story. She didn't blame Shuli for sacking a series of strangers, no matter how well qualified, who were being paid to stand in for a mother she'd never known, for a father who found her presence a painful daily reminder of everything he'd lost. 'It's a lovely day,' she pointed out, trying again. 'You could take her to the country park.'

'Not today, Jane,' he said, briskly. 'If I don't get the Arts Centre designs finalised this week we'll fall behind programme.'

Heaven forbid that should happen. 'Of course. I'll be there as soon as I can.'

She called the surveyors to reschedule the meeting, then sat for a moment while she gathered her own protective shell about her. Shuli wasn't the only one who longed for Mark Hilliard to notice her. Love her.

But she was a grown-up, twenty-four years old, and, since she was also in her right mind, flinging herself onto the floor and screaming for attention wasn't an option.

She was good old Jane, who could always be relied on no matter what the crisis. The perfect secretary, hiding her love for her heartbreakingly handsome boss behind her owl-like spectacles. A total cliché.

Okay, forget the spectacles. But she might as well wear them for all the notice he took of her.

But Mark Hilliard was irresistible. Ever since she'd sat across his desk for the first time and seen him, newly bereaved, grief in every dark shadow of his ravaged face, with his baby daughter in a carry seat beside him, she'd known it would be a mistake to stay.

There had been an urgent phone call moments after she'd arrived for the interview. She'd picked up the noisy infant, taken her into Reception and played finger games with her while her father had dealt at length with some crisis.

When he'd finished, he'd come looking for her. 'You've got the job.'

The heart-leap of joy had been a warning and she'd heeded it. Much as she'd wanted the job, she knew that falling in love with the boss at first sight, any sight, was always going to end in tears. Hers.

'But you know nothing about me,' she'd said.

'I know that you see what needs to be done and do it. That's good enough for me. Can you start now?'

Shuli had been sitting on her lap, playing with the buttons on a smart new suit bought specially for the occasion. Well, it had looked smart in the shop. On her it didn't have quite the same stylish appearance. Nothing ever did; she just wasn't a standard size. Not tall enough. Not anything enough. And now it had dribble marks on the lapel.

'Not promising material. Lacks that touch of class.' That was what the woman at the secretarial agency had written on her application form. Jane was very good at reading upside down. Her skills were excellent but they hadn't even taken her on as one of their temps.

While she had been putting on her coat a call had come into Reception. Mark Hilliard, of Hilliard, Young and Lynch Architects, needed a first-class secretary urgently.

As soon as she'd reached the pavement she'd called him on her mobile phone. She sounded better than she looked and he'd asked her to come over right away.

He hadn't been put off by her appearance. She might have loved him just for that. Which was why, even though every sensible bone in her body had urged her to take a job that she wanted, needed, some internal alarm system had rung loud bells, warning her to turn him down, walk away.

There would be other jobs. Safer jobs. Jobs where her heart wouldn't be on the line every minute of every working day. But Mark had looked so desperate. And Shuli had smiled so winningly at her.

Which was why, for more than two and a half years, she'd seen what was needed and she'd done it, without waiting to be asked.

All except for Shuli, she thought.

She'd tried to engage his attention in his adorable daughter, but it was clear that he found it difficult to be near her, and for all those two and half years she'd watched helplessly as he'd done everything for the child but give himself. It just wasn't good enough. If he couldn't be a father to the child, he'd have to give her a mother. And, as always, having recognised the need, she would have to organise the solution.

She gathered the files Mark had asked for and picked up her laptop, stopping in Reception to have calls redirected.

Her reflection in a framed picture of Hilliard's most recent project warned her that her hair was escaping from the neat chignon the hairdresser had assured her would stay in place in a force ten gale.

She still needed to work on her presentation. Fortunately Mark wouldn't notice even if she shortened her skirts to her knickers and piled on the make-up. He just didn't see her that way. It was the one thing she had going for her.

'Read me a story, Daddy.'

Mark glanced irritably at his daughter, who was perfectly happy now that the nanny had gone and she'd disrupted his day.

'I'm busy, Shuli.'

She pushed the book she was holding onto the desk. It was old. Much read. 'This story,' she persisted.

Recognising the futility of resistance, he picked up the book. 'Where did this come from?'

'Jane gave it to me,' she said. 'I love Jane. I really, really love Jane.'

'Yes, yes, of course you do...' He opened the first page and saw, written in a round, childish hand, the words 'This book belongs to Jane Carmichael'. It was one of her own precious childhood books, brought into the office to amuse Shuli on those days when he had no choice but to take her in with him. It occurred to him that maybe that was what the child had wanted all along: to see Jane. He glanced at the clock, wondering what on earth was taking her so long.

Shuli crawled up onto his lap. 'Read it now, Daddy.'

'Please,' he said, automatically correcting her.

'Please, Daddy,' she said. And smiled. She was the very image of her mother. He could almost hear her voice pleading with him. *"Please, Mark*...let me go..."

The sound of a car pulling up in front of the house released him from the painful memory as, story forgotten, the child slid down and hurtled towards the door. He followed, opening it, and Shuli flung herself at Jane's knees, hugging them.

'You wouldn't consider swapping jobs would you? You'd be the best-paid nanny in the county.'

'No, thanks. Besides, she doesn't need a nanny.' Jane put down the files and her laptop and picked up the child to give her a proper hug. She got a big sticky kiss back. 'She needs a mother.' She put the child into his arms and took off her jacket. 'I'm sorry I was so long. The traffic was a nightmare. I need coffee. Urgently.'

'Help yourself. You know where everything is.'

She hooked the jacket over the newel post at the foot of the stairs and headed for the kitchen. Putting Shuli down, he followed her. 'What about you?' she asked, turning to him as she filled the kettle. 'Coffee? Or would you prefer tea?'

'Coffee, thanks.'

Shuli was at her knees again, and she looked down. 'What about you, sweetheart? Do you want something to drink?'

She giggled. 'Coffee, thanks,' she said, imitating her father.

'And would that be orange juice coffee, or apple juice coffee?' Shuli giggled as Jane opened her bag and produced a wrapped chocolate biscuit finger. 'And how about this?'

'Is she supposed to have stuff like that?' Mark asked.

Jane glanced up, surprised. 'You don't ever buy her chocolate?'

Her rebuke, mild though it was, took him by surprise.

'Of course not. It's bad for her teeth.' He and Caroline had read all the books. Theirs was going to be the perfectly raised child. No junk food. No eating between meals. No sweets... 'Isn't it?' he asked, suddenly less certain.

'I imagine she has a toothbrush?'

'Yes, yes, of course. I'll, um, be in the study.'

'We'll be right with you.'

Jane placed the tray on the desk out of Shuli's reach and then settled her at a table with a pile of paper and crayons. 'Daddy and I are going to be busy for a while. What I'd like you to do for me is draw a picture that I can pin up in my office. Will you do that?'

'Okay.'

'Good girl.' She turned and saw that Mark was watching her with a faintly baffled expression. She poured the coffee and they went quickly through the morning post. 'I've dealt with most of it.'

'As always. That's it?'

She took a moment to compose herself. She knew what she had to say. She'd nearly missed her exit on the motorway rehearsing her lines.

'Not quite.' He waited. 'There's this.' Heart hammering, she handed him a broadsheet newspaper folded back at an inside page.

'Connections?' he queried, looking up. 'What is this?'

He couldn't be that dense. Or then again... 'It's a dating column. I've prepared a draft advertisement for you.'

He took the sheet of paper she offered.

'"Widower, 34, with small daughter, WLTM warm, caring woman, N/S, GSOH, for LTR."' He looked up. 'WLTM?'

'Would like to meet.' Seeing his blank expression, she added, 'Non-smoker with good sense of humour for long-term relationship.'

'Oh.'

'On the day you hired me, Mark, you said I was someone who saw what needed to be done and got on with it. That's what I'm doing now. For Shuli's sake. I've written the ad for you. I'll even filter the replies if you want me to. All you have to do is tell me to go ahead and place it.'

He glanced at the newspaper again, read some of the ads. 'This one wants a "lady of class and intelligence for romance and precious moments".' He cocked a wry eyebrow in her direction. 'Does that mean what I think it means?'

'Undoubtedly,' she said, absolutely refusing to blush, or to laugh, which was what he hoped she'd do. Laugh and forget it, so that they could move on to the important business of life. Work. She cocked an eyebrow back at him. 'You can draft your own specifications if you'd prefer. Just don't forget the LTR.'

'Jane, please... You can't be serious.'

'No? Your daughter has rejected four perfectly competent, kind and caring nannies in as many months. She's trying to tell you, in the only way she can, that she needs more.'

'More?'

'More than you're giving her. Someone who puts her first. Someone who she knows is going to be there for her every morning when she wakes up, every night to read her a story.'

'I do what I can, but I have to work...' He wasn't laughing now. He couldn't even quite meet her gaze. 'People depend on me. My partners, everyone in the office—you, even. If I don't work, Jane, no one gets paid.'

It was more than that; they both knew it. But if he couldn't, or wouldn't, do the job himself, he must offer a surrogate. 'Then, I repeat, she needs a mother. You are the only person who can provide her with one. I appreciate that finding time to look for yourself is difficult, hence the ad. Or you could use an agency. Lots of people in your situation take this route.'

'Maybe they do. Maybe you're right.' He tossed the advertisement she'd drafted on the desk and then raised one hand in a gesture of helplessness at the silver frame containing a photograph of Shuli's mother. 'I appreciate your concern and I'll give it some thought, but can we move on, please?' He picked up a file.

'It's three years, Mark,' she said, refusing to let the subject drop. 'Caroline would expect you to move on. She'd want Shuli to have what all children need.'

He was beginning to look haunted. 'Where in the world would I find the kind of woman who'd take on someone else's child?'

'It's not that uncommon these days. With the high divorce rate.'

But that wasn't the problem and they both knew it. The problem was that no one could ever be as wonderful as Caroline...as perfect as Caroline...as beautiful as Caroline.

'Very well,' he conceded, finally accepting that she wasn't going to let the subject drop. 'The kind of woman who'd be prepared to accept the one-way relationship which is all I could offer?' That he'd said it out loud, admitted it, was the first step, Jane knew. He glanced at the child, quietly working at her drawing. 'I know you mean well, but I couldn't ask it of any woman. Certainly not one with all the great qualities I'd want for Shuli.'

Jane felt his pain, physically hurting for the man. She wanted to reach across the desk, take his dear face in her hands and tell him that everything would be fine if only he'd trust her...

Keeping her voice brisk and businesslike, she said, 'Don't underrate yourself, Mark. You can offer a lovely home, a comfortable life, friendship. A lot of women would be happy to settle for that.'

'Would they? And how would I know they weren't just doing it for the money? That a year on this ''warm, caring non-smoker with a good sense of humour'' wouldn't be suing for a divorce and a big fat chunk of my assets?'

He'd spotted the flaw in her suggestion. She'd been sure he would. Well, he'd look for any excuse to evade the issue.

'I think Shuli could be relied upon to see off any pretenders.'

That, at least, raised a smile. 'Yes, I suppose she would.' He sat back, regarded her across the broad desk. 'You've thought this through, haven't you?'

'Of course. I wouldn't come to you with some half-baked plan.'

'No.' He continued to regard her thoughtfully. 'Tell me, Jane, would *you* settle for a platonic marriage?'

This was it. The opening she'd been waiting for. She swallowed. 'Are you asking me?' she replied, her voice perfectly calm even while her heart was pounding loud enough to be heard in the next county.

'Yes,' he said. 'I want to know if you'd marry a man who wasn't in love with you?'

She shook her head. More hair slithered from the grip of pins unequal to the task. 'No, Mark. That wasn't my question.' He frowned, and she very nearly lost her nerve. It wasn't too late to bottle out... 'My question was...are you asking me if I'd marry you?'

CHAPTER TWO

THERE was a moment of perfect stillness while Mark Hilliard tried to decide if Jane was serious.

She was sitting opposite him, the way she did every working day of his life. She looked the same. Alert, a smile hovering behind her eyes and waiting to break out at the slightest provocation, totally in control of everything but her hair. And waiting for an answer to her question.

Was he asking her if she'd marry him?

The answer, of course, was yes. In a purely rhetorical sense. But Jane hadn't been speaking rhetorically. She was never anything but totally straightforward. She didn't play games, or tease, or do any of those tiresome female things to get what she wanted. He scarcely thought of her as a woman at all. Which was why she was so easy to work with. To be with.

She'd asked him a serious question and expected him to give her a serious answer. If he said no, she wouldn't be offended. This wasn't about feelings or emotions; it was about a practical solution to a problem that was beginning to affect not just his life but the success of his architectural practice.

And the longer he delayed before dismissing the idea out of hand the less inclined he felt to do so. It did, after all, make the most perfect sense.

He knew her so well. There'd be none of that awkwardness inevitable in any new relationship. None of the risk. She was hard-working, kind, loyal and beneath that serious exterior he knew she possessed in full measure that essential GSOH. She knew him, understood him perfectly,

wouldn't expect a thing from him except loyalty and friendship.

She'd be the perfect wife for him in every way. Whether
he'd be the husband she was looking for was something
else entirely.

'Would you consider moving in here?' he countered.

'Give up my job and look after Shuli for you full-time?
As what? I'm sorry, Mark. I can see what you'd get out of
such an arrangement, but, much as I love Shuli, I don't see
it as a great career move for me.' She didn't wait for him
to spell out the financial package he would be offering her
as his 'home' rather than his 'office' secretary. 'Maybe
we'd better stick with the advertisement.'

Shuli, hearing her name, looked up. 'I've nearly finished,
Jane.' And she held up her picture for them to see. Three
stick figures beside a house. 'Daddy, Jane and me,' she
said.

'It's lovely, poppet,' Jane said, amazed that the tremor
shaking her from the inside out wasn't evident in her voice.
'Are you going to draw some flowers in the garden?' she
asked.

Shuli at least knew what she wanted, and Mark had made
an opening offer, although what exactly he was offering he
clearly hadn't thought through.

Now she'd give him time to meet some of the women
who'd undoubtedly answer his advertisement by the truck-
load. She knew that no matter how nice they were he'd
recoil from getting sucked into a relationship he couldn't
control, with a woman who'd expect more from him than
he felt able to deliver.

When she returned to her seat Mark was flicking through
his diary, taking advantage of the interruption to change the
subject. It didn't matter, she told herself. She'd put the idea
in his mind. There would be another day, another upset.
She knew how to be patient.

'I've rescheduled the site meeting with the surveyors for

tomorrow,' she said, moving briskly on. 'Nine-thirty. Bring Shuli into the office and I'll take care of her.'

He made a note and then looked up. 'Would next Tuesday suit you?' he asked.

'Next Tuesday?'

'I shouldn't think the registrar will be busy mid-week.' Then, when she didn't answer. 'You don't want a big wedding, do you?'

'Wedding?' She felt the colour drain from her face. From being in control, driving the situation, she was suddenly way behind. She'd offered a solution, but she hadn't been thinking as far ahead as a wedding.

'You wanted to know if I was asking you to marry me. If the choice is you or the advertisement, I'll take you.' As a proposal it lacked just about everything. Except the man she loved with all her heart. 'You *were* serious?'

She tried to say yes, but nothing came out as her voice momentarily stuck in her throat somewhere. She cleared it. 'Yes. I was serious.'

'Then I see no point in waiting. I'm free on Tuesday morning, if that suits you?'

Jane had a fleeting vision of candlelight, red roses, a diamond ring. The perfect proposal, followed by the perfect wedding, with the long white dress and orange blossom by the cartload. There'd be a posse of little bridesmaids and her entire family watching in stunned amazement as her father walked her up the aisle to give her away to the man of her dreams. Of any woman's dreams. And then she let it all go. She'd look dreadful in white and the orange blossom would undoubtedly droop.

Mark had asked her to marry him. Sort of. How much more perfect could it get? And if his proposal lacked romance, well, that was the way she'd planned it. Common sense ruled.

'Tuesday will be fine,' she replied, as calmly as if they

were discussing a project meeting. 'Would you like me to handle the details?' *Please say no. That you'll do it...*

'If you would.'

'Do you want me to invite anyone? Colleagues? I imagine you'll want your family—'

'Is that necessary?' he asked, a small frown creasing his forehead as he looked up. 'I'd rather not have any fuss.'

He didn't want his mother or his sister there? It meant that little to him? She hadn't expected romance, but a certain amount of ceremony was usual to mark even the most low-key of weddings. She swallowed her hurt, her pride. 'No, it's not necessary. We'll just need a couple of witnesses. I'll see to it,' she said quickly, before he could ask her to find two total strangers to perform this service. Their marriage might not be made in heaven—more like the local DIY shop—but it wasn't going to be some hole-and-corner affair.

He nodded. 'You'd better find a replacement for yourself at the same time.' He offered a slightly rueful smile. 'Pity about that, but no plan is ever perfect.'

'No.' It wasn't perfect by a long way. But it was a work in progress. Having achieved her initial objective, she would have all the time in the world to go back to the drawing board and work on the fine details of how to get him to fall in love with her. 'There's Patsy,' she suggested. He looked blank. 'The girl in the planning department who covered for me while I was on holiday?'

'I didn't notice.'

Of course he hadn't. She'd worked very hard to make sure her absence didn't inconvenience him in any way. 'Then she's definitely the one. I'll sort it out tomorrow.'

'Right.' His brows came together in a frown and he looked at her sharply, as if he suspected he'd missed something. Then he let it go and said, 'Is that it? If you've finished straightening out my life can we look at that Maybridge contract?'

He didn't wait for her answer, just crumpled up the advertisement she'd typed out for him, tossed it in the wastepaper basket and reached for a file.

Working around a busy three-year-old was hard work, and Mark, after yet another interruption when Shuli had needed her supper, said, 'Look, why don't we take a break? I'll put her to bed, then we can do a couple of hours in peace.'

'I've got a better idea,' Jane said. 'Why don't I look after Shuli and leave you to get on with those figures?'

'Would you?' He pushed his fingers through his thick dark hair, leaving it sticking up at the crown. Just as he had the first time she'd seen him. Harassed and struggling to cope with the mess life had tossed in his lap. It had taken all her self-control not to reach out and smooth it for him then.

She still had to fight the impulse.

It was quiet. Blissfully quiet. Uninterrupted, he'd swiftly finished the calculations and now he needed Jane. She'd had more than enough time to bathe one small child and put her to bed. He walked out into the hall and listened. Nothing. About to call her, he realised he might wake Shuli and instead went upstairs.

The door to the nursery was open and Jane was sitting on the bed, gently stroking Shuli's fair curls. His heart turned over at the sweet intimacy of the scene. Jane was right. This was what his little girl needed more than anything.

Relief at how easy it had been with her here warred with guilt that he found it so difficult to cope with his own child. Relief won hands down. The thought of Jane taking care of things at home far outweighed the inconvenience of losing her in the office, and he suddenly felt as if a huge burden had been lifted from his shoulders.

Seeing him in the doorway, she put her finger to her lips,

set the listening device and then joined him, pulling the door partly closed behind her.

'You make it look so easy,' he said.

'I've had a lot of practise. I've got half a dozen nephews and nieces.' She had a family? He hadn't thought of that. 'You must be hungry. Shall we have something to eat now?' she asked. 'Or do you want to get straight back to work?'

'Let's eat. I'll get something sent in.' He headed for the stairs. 'What do you like?'

'Why don't I just make something quick? Some pasta or eggs?'

He glanced at her. 'You cook, too?'

'You're a very lucky man, Mark. I have an old-fashioned mother. She taught us all the basics.'

It occurred to him that he knew nothing of her background, her interests. He hadn't even asked her where she'd gone on holiday. For the past three years he'd used work to fill the emotional vacuum inside him. He'd cut himself off from everything human, vital. The only time he seemed to speak to his family these days was when he needed help with childcare. But he wasn't totally beyond redemption. 'How will she react to this wedding?'

'My mother? With considerable surprise, I imagine. Having given birth to four swans, she despaired of her little ugly duckling ever finding a mate.'

'You're kidding?'

Her eyes sparkled back at him. Of course she was.

'Why are you doing this, Jane? I can see the advantages from my point of view, but you're young. You have your life ahead of you. You should be looking for a man who can give you…' All of himself. That was what he'd been going to say. Her brows quirked up as he faltered. 'A little bit of romance,' he finished lamely.

'The girls in the office live for romance. As far as I can see it involves a great deal of weeping in the cloakroom followed by the consumption of chocolate in industrial quantities. It looks messy. Not to say a dietary nightmare.'

'Don't underrate it.'

'I don't underrate love,' she conceded, and a momentary sadness darkened her eyes. Then she shrugged. 'I just don't believe it's something you're likely to find in a club on a Saturday night.'

That was it, then. Her heart had been broken too. They'd make a perfect match. Even so... 'Will you promise me something?' She regarded him curiously from a pair of the darkest brown eyes, solemn now as she waited for him to continue. 'If you ever do fall in love—the real thing, one hundred per cent, no holds barred love—you must tell me. I wouldn't expect you to stay.'

Jane knew he was talking about the way it had been for him, with Caroline. She'd been treated to all the office gossip when she'd first joined the firm, heard how their marriage had been the perfect once-in-a-lifetime romance. How his wife's tragic death had nearly destroyed Mark, too.

And, despite her denial of a romantic nature, like the girls in the office she'd done her share of weeping. For him. And for herself. At home, in the privacy of her own bedroom. But this wasn't the moment to tell him that he was all the romance she'd ever need. Neither was it the moment to tell him that, like her mother, she was an old-fashioned girl who believed in taking her marriage vows seriously. Till death us do part.

'Jane?' he prompted, reaching out as if to keep her at his side, his hand beneath her arm, his look deeply intense.

'I promise,' she said.

'Thank you.'

And then she saw that in giving this promise she'd in some way absolved him from guilt about marrying her for his own selfish motives. Since her intention was to make his life easier, she tried to disregard the small stab of pain this caused, simply to be grateful that he hadn't thought to give her a similar promise from himself.

'Maybe you'd like to look around while you're up here,' he suggested brightly, shattering the quiet intimacy of the moment. 'You might like to have the suite overlooking the garden,' he added, opening a door and then standing back so that she could pass him and look around. 'Caroline designed it for guests and it's got pretty much everything.'

She was about to laugh and say that there was no need to take 'platonic' that far, when some inner sense of self-preservation warned her to hold her tongue. She already knew she'd have to wait for his heart. It seemed she'd have to wait for everything else, too.

CHAPTER THREE

'YOU'VE done what?'

Jane, curled up on her best friend's sofa, with a mug of tea clutched comfortingly between her hands, repeated her news. 'I've asked Mark Hilliard to marry me.' She lifted her shoulders, bunching them against her neck. This was harder than the actual deed. 'At least, I manoeuvred him into a position where he asked me, which is much the same thing.'

'How?' she demanded. 'I could use some help in levering Greg into a proposal.' Then she grinned. 'You're a dark horse, Janey. I knew you were potty about the man, but I didn't know things had progressed to hand-holding over the desk. Your mother must be over the moon—'

'She doesn't know. The ceremony is going to be on Tuesday at the register office. Just the two of us and a couple of witnesses. That's why I'm here. To ask if you and Greg will be our witnesses.'

'Are you out of your mind? Your mum expects these things to be done properly. The full fairy tale bit. Bells, choir, a three-tier cake and enough champagne to launch the *QE2*—'

'Yes, well, this isn't exactly a fairy tale wedding. Which is why I'm not telling them until Wednesday.'

'She'll kill you. No, she'll think you're pregnant and she'll send your father to kill him...' She stopped. 'Ohmigod! You are pregnant!'

Jane's hands were shaking so much with delayed reaction that she put down her mug before she slopped tea over the sofa. Her voice was steady enough though, even if her smile was wry. 'One step at a time, Laine. One step at a time. He has to kiss me first.'

'Actually that's not true…' Then, as the penny dropped, 'Oh, crumbs, Janey, I hope you know what you're doing.'

Did she? This morning she'd been absolutely certain, but suppose she was still in the guest suite when they were celebrating their silver wedding? Suppose he never saw her as anything other than 'good old Jane'?

'Janey?' Laine prompted, seeking reassurance.

'Mark doesn't want any fuss and neither do I,' she said, choosing to answer her concerns about the wedding arrangements rather than her concern about the marriage. 'Let's face it, Laine, I was never cut out to play the beautiful blushing bride.' But she crossed her fingers before she said, 'Trust me. It's my wedding and I know what I'm doing.'

There was a pause while Laine digested this statement. 'Well, you usually do, I'll grant you that,' she conceded eventually.

'I get the man I love, a darling little girl…'

'Do you? Get him?'

'I'm working on it.'

'Marriage is enough of a gamble even when you're head over heels.'

'Rather less so when both parties have so much to gain and know exactly what they're getting. There are none of those untidy emotions to mess things up.'

'I'm sure fate will find some way to throw a spanner in the works. The ghost of his first wife, for instance. You'll always be in her shadow.' When Jane didn't answer, Laine pushed harder. 'Wasn't she a famous beauty? One of the ''girls in pearls''? A perfect English Rose?'

While Jane was pure Celt. Dark-haired, dark-eyed, and struggling to make five foot three in her outdoor shoes. 'I'll have to get busy with the pruning shears, then, won't I?'

Laine didn't laugh. 'Well, if it's what you want, then of

course Greg and I will be your witnesses.' She waited, apparently expecting some response. 'It is what you want?'

'I love him, Laine.'

'I see.' She didn't respond with the obvious question—does he love you? Which suggested she did see. Only too clearly. But then Laine could read a three-volume novel from a tone of voice. 'So, Mark Hilliard gets a live-in nanny and a housekeeper. What do you get out of it?'

'To be needed.'

'Don't underrate yourself. You're worth more than that.'

Jane was getting a little tired of the word 'underrate'. She was underrating nothing, least of all herself. 'At ten o'clock this morning nothing was further from Mark's mind than getting married. By eleven o'clock he'd set the date.' She kinked an eyebrow at her friend. 'Just who is underrating whom, here?'

Laine regarded her thoughtfully for a moment, then she laughed. 'Right. So why are we drinking tea? Let's celebrate!' Then, as she took a bottle of wine from the fridge, 'Please, please, please can I help you shop for ''bad girl'' underwear?'

'I think the situation calls for subtlety rather than a sledgehammer.'

'Silk French knickers are subtle. Satin camisoles are subtle.' Then, 'You've got this all worked out, haven't you?'

'Down to the last detail,' she said. 'I've even got my mother sorted. She'll be so delighted to get her youngest daughter off the shelf that she'll happily forgo the fancy wedding.'

Laine grinned. 'You can hope.'

'No, honestly,' she said, her face deadpan. 'And if you'd ever seen my dad's reaction to the announcement that yet another daughter was getting married, heard his pitiful pleas for her to elope, you'd understand that I'm doing them a kindness.'

'Your dad didn't mean it.'

'No?' Then she grinned, too. 'And I always thought he was serious. Oh, dear. But it'll be too late by then.'

'I wouldn't be in your shoes when your mother finds out. You'll have to flee the country. Go on an extended honeymoon until the dust settles...' Laine glanced at her. 'Is there going to be a honeymoon?'

'Not until the design contract for the Maybridge Arts Centre is signed. Maybe my parents could go away instead? They could console themselves with a luxury cruise on the money I'm saving them.' She took the glass of wine. 'I do have one problem, though. What am I going to wear on Tuesday?'

'Something elegant.'

'But simple.' She didn't want to turn up in some fancy outfit that would startle Mark. He saw the occasion as nothing more exciting than taking an hour out of the office to marry his plain, comfortable Jane; if she turned up in 'bride' clothes he'd probably take one look and run a mile.

But even with just a couple of witnesses it had to look like a wedding, feel like a wedding. He needed to be reminded that this wasn't just some job promotion with 'living in' privileges. The ceremony might be little more than a pared-to-the-bone formality, but they were both going to be making some solemn vows on Tuesday morning.

He was taking her as his wife.

Whatever anyone else might think, she wanted Mark left in no doubt about that.

'I'm sorry I had to bother you with that, Mark,' Jane said, as they left the register office. 'I should have realised you'd have to sign the form personally.'

'It's not a bother. We'd have had to go into town anyway. The banks want your signatures for the accounts you'll need—credit cards, that sort of thing.'

'Accounts?'

'Personal, housekeeping.'

'Oh.'

'You won't be working, so I thought if I gave you the same allowance as your salary? If you need more—'

'No! No,' she repeated, her nails digging into the palms of her hands. She hadn't given much thought to what she'd do for personal money, but it had never occurred to her that he'd just keep paying her a salary. But why not? That was the way he saw her. Laine was right. This was a mistake. 'Mark—'

'And you're going to need a ring.'

Her heart turned over. 'A ring?'

'A wedding ring.' She bit on her lip, fighting an overwhelming urge to weep with joy. All morning he'd been distant, absolutely businesslike, and her heart had been shrivelling up inside her. Suddenly the world felt wonderful. 'We might as well get it now,' he said, matter-of-factly. It didn't matter. He'd been thinking about it.

'Wedding rings?' The jeweller beamed. 'Congratulations.'

'Thank you,' Jane said quickly, when Mark looked slightly bemused.

'What are you looking for? Something classic in gold? Or platinum's very fashionable now,' the man said. 'And there seems to be something of a trend towards wedding rings set with precious stones.'

Mark turned to her. 'Choose whatever you want, Jane,' he said, apparently under the impression that it had nothing whatever to do with him.

'A wedding ring shouldn't be a fashion statement. It should be practical. It has to take a lot of hard knocks.' She smiled at the man. One of them should be smiling. 'I want something in gold, absolutely plain, not too wide.' Her finger was measured and then she was brought a selection of rings to look at. It wasn't difficult to choose. 'This one,' she said, picking out the kind of ring a woman could live with for a lifetime. She realised the jeweller was waiting for her to try it on and rather self-consciously slipped it onto her finger. 'Yes, it's fine. Mark?'

She expected him to nod and reach for his credit card. Instead he reached for her hand, holding it so that her fingers were stretched across his palm, and looked at it for what seemed a lifetime.

It was the nearest he'd come in the two and a half years she'd known him to an intimate gesture.

Did this count as 'hand-holding'?

His long, elegant, fingers, vibrant and warm against hers, seemed to spark a chain reaction of warmth that raced through her body, just as it had a thousand times in her imagination. Her imagination had been light years from reality.

Oh, yes. This was hand-holding on an epic scale.

'You're absolutely sure?' he asked, finally looking up at her.

As her hand began to tremble, betraying her calm exterior for the act it was, she snatched it back, pretending to take a closer look at the ring.

His touch had meant nothing; she must read nothing into it. He was simply concerned that she was choosing the plainest ring in the tray out of some misplaced reticence.

Utility wife, utility ring.

She reassured him. 'Mark, this is the ring I'd choose if I were marrying the Sultan of Zanzibar.'

He continued to regard her with his steady grey eyes. 'Are you telling me I've got competition?'

'Absolutely,' she replied, matching his serious expression. 'He calls me day and night, begging me to join his harem.'

'Is that right? Well, next time he calls, tell him you're spoken for.' He turned to the jeweller with a smile. 'That was surprisingly easy.'

'The young lady certainly seems to know her own mind.

A classic choice, if I may say so. Now, if I can just check your size, sir, I'll bring a matching ring for you to try.'

'Oh, but—'

Jane felt rather than saw Mark's small instinctive gesture as he curled his fingers, lifting his hand back no more than an inch. It was enough for her to see that he was still wearing the ring that Caroline had placed there.

'There's no time right now, Mark,' she said quickly. 'We have to get to the bank.' It was the first thing that came into her head. That and regret that she hadn't kept to her original plan to tell him that she wanted to wear her great-grandmother's ring. This was exactly the kind of situation she'd been hoping to avoid. She wanted everything to go as smoothly as possible. She didn't want him jerked into painful reminders at every turn. But she'd been betrayed by the need to be noticed, recognised. By her singing pleasure that he'd been thinking about her. 'And Shuli will be getting hungry.'

Once outside, he stopped and said, 'I'm sorry, Jane.' She covered his left hand briefly with her own in a wordless gesture of comfort. She could not bring herself to say that it didn't matter.

It did.

Back in the office, she ensured that her replacement was coping and then collected Shuli from the care of a curious receptionist so that everyone could work in peace.

'Is it true that you're leaving?'

With Patsy installed at her desk, already busy organising her own replacement, she could hardly deny it. Why would she want to deny it? 'Yes, it's true. Patsy's taking over from today, although I'll be in and out for the rest of the week,' she said, fastening the little girl into her pushchair.

'It's a bit sudden, isn't it? There's a wild rumour going around that you're marrying Mark Hilliard.' She said it as if it had to be some kind of joke, but Jane wasn't in the mood to be patronised, and since Mark had already informed his doubtless much relieved partners of the imminent improvement in his domestic situation it was scarcely a secret.

'Is there? Well, even a wild rumour has to be right once in a blue moon,' she said. And came close to adding that the speed of the wedding was due entirely to the fact that she was pregnant. With triplets.

She restrained herself in the sure and certain knowledge that the rumour machine was already way ahead of her with that one. Instead she contented herself with a smile, adding, 'If anyone is looking for me, I'm taking Shuli shopping for something totally gorgeous to wear for the occasion.' She didn't say which of them the 'totally gorgeous' something was for.

Mark returned to his office, but couldn't concentrate on work. Instead he sat at his desk, turning the wedding ring round and round on his finger. It was so much a part of him that it hadn't occurred to him that he would be expected to wear a new one. It did occur to him that he wasn't thinking about anything very much except his own feelings.

Jane had covered for him when he'd instinctively recoiled from the thought of a new ring. She had reached out to him offering instant reassurance rather than the reproach he'd deserved. The warmth of her touch still lingered comfortingly against his skin.

Only her eyes, huge and brown, had momentarily betrayed her hurt at his thoughtlessness.

He took one last look at the ring before slipping it from his finger, then, uncertain what to do with it, he tucked it away in his wallet before reaching for the intercom. 'Penny?' No, that wasn't right. 'Pansy?'

'Try Patsy,' a disembodied voice advised.

'Patsy. Of course. Sorry. I have to go out for half an hour. Can you ring round and put back the weekly progress meeting?'

'No problem. Everyone will understand.' Then, 'Look, I don't know if I did the right thing, but I've made a provisional booking at the Waterside for lunch on Tuesday.'

About to ask why she'd thought that necessary, he just managed to stop himself in time. 'Did Jane ask you to do that?'

'No, I used my own initiative. She said you'd want me to.' After another pause, 'If you've made other plans I can cancel, but Jane said you weren't going away. I thought you might like to surprise her.'

'And your initiative suggested lunch at the Waterside would be a suitable surprise?'

'Absolutely. If I'd just been swept off my feet with a whirlwind wedding I'd want a romantic lunch somewhere quiet by the river. Well, short of Paris in the spring.'

Paris? Jane wouldn't expect to be taken away, would she? He tried to imagine walking along the banks of the Seine at night with Jane. The picture wouldn't come into focus. 'Paris will have to wait until we've signed the Maybridge contract, I'm afraid. And when you confirm the reservation at the Waterside make sure they've got a highchair, will you?'

'Is Shuli going to be a bridesmaid? How sweet. Do you want me to organise flowers?'

Rings, flowers, bridesmaids. What had happened to the simple no-nonsense ceremony he'd envisaged? He recalled the uneasy feeling he'd had that it couldn't be that easy. And wondered what else he'd overlooked.

As he tensed his hand he could still feel the ring that until a few minutes ago had been part of him. Could still see the mark, feel the weight of it.

Could still feel the warmth of Jane's reassuring touch.

Then, realising that Patsy was still waiting, he said, 'No. Thank you. I'd rather organise the flowers myself. I'll be out of the office for about half an hour.'

Choosing the flowers was a pleasure, he discovered, un-

til, opening his wallet to get out his charge card, he saw
the wedding ring glinting in its depths. It brought back the
flash of hurt in Jane's eyes and he tried to imagine how
she'd feel if she ever saw the ring. Or found it in the back
of a drawer.

He didn't want, ever, to make her look like that again.
She deserved his total loyalty.

Which was why, on his way back to the office, he took
a detour by the river and dropped the ring into the deep-
est part.

CHAPTER FOUR

MARK was waiting on the steps of the Town Hall, the white rosebud in his buttonhole drawing indulgent glances from people passing in and out of the building. Shuli, wearing her new dress, a ribbon-tied posy clutched in her chubby hand, was fidgeting at his side. He was looking at his watch.

'I told you we shouldn't be late,' Jane said, as the taxi came to halt.

'Nonsense,' Laine declared. 'You have to give a man time to look into the void. Consider what life would be like if you didn't turn up. You're Miss Cool. You know that.'

She knew nothing. She'd spent the night looking into her own dark void, considering what life would be like if she'd got it wrong. Then this morning the florist had arrived with a spray of rosebuds and white freesias arranged in a silver Victorian flower holder, with a card from Mark that simply said 'Thank you.' And her cool façade had been washed away on a hot tide of tears.

It had taken a ton of concealer to cover the black rings and blotchy skin before Laine had arrived to put the finishing touches, help her with her hair. Help her dress in the fine cashmere *shalwar kameez* that had cost a month's salary.

Laine had whisked her to the boutique and wouldn't let her leave until she'd bought it. 'It's a wonderful compromise. Really special, but you'll be able to wear it anywhere…'

Now, after adjusting the long chiffon silk scarf Jane had wound once around her neck, leaving the long tails to trail behind her in the merest suggestion of a bridal veil, Laine handed her the spray of flowers and said, 'Well, what are you waiting for? He'll take one look and won't believe just how clever he's been.'

Was 'clever' going to be enough? Stepping out of the taxi, Jane couldn't quite meet Mark's eyes, afraid of what she might see there. Or rather not see there. Instead she swooped to gather the little girl into her arms. 'Darling, don't you look just good enough to eat!'

'You're supposed to say that to the groom, Jane.' Laine offered her hand to Mark, introduced herself. 'I'm Jane's best woman. We've been friends since nursery school.' She turned to the man behind her. 'And this is Greg,' she said, linking her arm with his. 'He's my best man and I'm hoping he'll be sufficiently inspired by today's simple and painless ceremony to follow your great example to pusillanimous men everywhere.'

'Sorry, Laine, but I don't think I can help you there. My heart is as faint as the next man's.'

Jane, already a bundle of nerves, thought she was the one who'd faint. He'd got cold feet. Decided this was all a huge mistake. She'd have to leave the town. The county. Possibly the country.

'It seems to be taking all my time to remember to breathe,' he said. 'Inspiration is quite beyond me. It's all Jane's fault.' Putting Shuli down before she dropped her, Jane looked up sharply. 'I've spent the last five minutes convinced that you'd changed your mind.'

'I wouldn't leave you standing here, Mark,' she said, hurt that he'd believe her capable of such cruelty.

Laine, behind him, lifted one expressive brow, then said, 'The traffic was terrible.'

This was a nightmare. So stiff, so formal. 'Thank you for the flowers...' Jane's voice failed her, dying away to leave an awkward silence.

'Look, I don't want to rush you two,' Greg said, coming

to the rescue, 'but I think that's the next wedding party arriving.'

Jane turned and saw two young people surrounded by friends, all of them laughing, happy.

'Are you ready?' Mark asked. And she nodded, her throat too stuffed with what felt like hot rocks to speak. Would she be able to say her vows? Would nodding count?

'She's ready,' Laine said, taking Shuli's hand and leading the way, turning back to add flippantly, 'I just hope you haven't forgotten the rings.'

Jane flinched and, looking anywhere but at the man she was about to marry, she blinked back a tear. Laine was right. It wasn't supposed to be like this.

If anyone had asked him to describe Jane Carmichael, Mark knew he would have been pressed to say much more than that she was a plain little thing. That the black suits she habitually wore never quite seemed right and she fought a constant battle to control a mass of hair that was neither black nor properly brown. That she had kind eyes. Smiled easily. Was comfortable to be with.

Her arrival outside the Town Hall had shattered that image of her.

'...I, Mark Edward Hilliard, take you, Jane Louise Carmichael...' Jane listened to his low, steady voice as he made the solemn vow. Then it was her turn to repeat the words after the registrar.

'...I, Jane Louise Carmichael...' Her voice had never seemed so faint, but she made it through without a mistake.

The registrar smiled at Mark. 'Do you have the rings?'

He produced the ring she'd chosen from his pocket and placed it on her finger, again repeating the solemn words. But when she would have turned back to the registrar he opened his hand. Lying in his palm was another ring, bright and new as the one he'd just placed on her own finger. A matching pair.

Only then did she realise that his left hand was bare, with just a lighter band of skin to show where another ring had once been.

The registrar, noticing nothing odd, prompted her promise. But her fingers were shaking as she took the ring and placed it on his finger. Her voice was shaking, too, as she made her promise. Had he thought of the meaning as he'd said his vows?

'You may kiss the bride.'

The momentary hesitation before he brushed his lips lightly against her own answered that particular question.

'Daddy!' He looked down at Shuli. 'Can I have a baby brother now?'

'Shh! Not now, sweetie,' Jane said, scooping her up to distract her while Mark signed the register. Then she did the same, her signature shakier than usual.

'Would you like to join us for lunch?' Mark asked Laine and Greg as they all left the registrar's office. 'I've got a table at the Waterside.'

Jane turned, astonished, to look up at him. 'The Waterside? When did you organise that?'

'I didn't. It was Patsy's idea. She was practising using her initiative.'

'Really? I didn't think she was *that* good,' she joked. Joked! Inside, she was shrivelling up at the make-believe of a romantic lunch together, and she turned to Laine. 'Of course you must come.'

Her friend, apparently reading the panic signal loud and clear, said, 'Try and stop us.'

'She arranged a car, too.' Mark offered a half-smile. 'Maybe she thought I'd be too nervous to drive myself.'

'Maybe she thought you'd be swimming in champagne,' Greg suggested.

'If that's the case I imagine it's already on ice.'

'Well, I sincerely hope so,' Laine said. 'This is Jane's big day.'

'I wonder if you'd go and see if the driver is there?' he asked, without comment. 'I said to come back at twelve. And could you take Shuli with you? We'll be along in a minute.'

'It'll be back to normal tomorrow,' Jane said quickly as he turned to her.

'I do hope not. "Normal" has been a nightmare.'

'Not any more.'

'No.'

She waited.

'I just wanted to tell you how lovely you look. I've never seen your hair loose before.'

She didn't wear it loose very often. It took an entire bottle of conditioner to tame it. But for today she'd made the effort, catching it at her nape with an ebony clasp and leaving it to hang down her back. 'It would be a nuisance in the office.'

'That won't be a problem any more.' He lifted her hand, looked at the ring he'd so recently placed on her finger. 'It looks a bit lonely all by itself, don't you think?' But he clearly didn't expect an answer because he reached into his jacket pocket and, spreading her fingers, slipped another ring beside the gold band.

The diamonds flashed back at her in the sunlight. Three considerable diamonds that had been set gypsy-style, almost flush in the gold. 'I'm sure the Sultan of Zanzibar would have given you a diamond as big as a paperweight. But, since you won't be sitting in a harem with nothing to do but your nails, I thought this would be more…practical.'

'They're industrial diamonds?' His head came up sharply and her hand flew to her mouth. 'No—sorry. Please forget I said that. It's nerves.'

'Nerves?' He looked astonished. 'I don't believe it. I've never seen anyone looking less flustered.'

'That's because I'm numb with terror.' Then, realising that it probably wasn't the most tactful thing she could have said, she rushed on. 'I was sure I'd make a total hash of it. Get my name wrong. Get *your* name wrong.' She was babbling. Big breath. Look at the ring. Say something sensible. Except how could she be cool and sensible when he'd just given her the most perfect, most exquisite ring? That was it. Thank him for the ring.

'The ring is beautiful, Mark. Absolutely, incredibly, wonderfully...practical.' She blinked back a tear. 'Thank you.'

'I'm glad you like it.'

Like it? If he'd read her mind he couldn't have chosen anything she'd like more, but she mustn't cry. It would embarrass him terribly.

If she concentrated really hard on the hideous mess it would make of all Laine's careful make-up, she'd get through it.

'I love it.' The nearest she could come to saying I love you. Oh, hell! Think of something else. Anything else. 'But I have a confession to make.' He waited for her to go on. 'I lied about the Sultan.'

'You mean he doesn't phone you day and night?' Mark didn't sound totally surprised.

'Actually he was deposed in 1964.'

'Well, I'm glad you told me,' he said, then added solemnly, 'I was afraid I'd have to let you down gently, warn you that someone was pulling your leg.' Only the small creases at the corners of his eyes suggested that, while somewhat under-used in recent years, Mark's GSOH was still in good working order. 'Shall we move, before Laine and Greg think we've ducked out of buying them lunch?'

Patsy had let her romantic nature run away with her and rented a limousine for the day, so there was plenty of room for the five of them. As Mark was distracted by Shuli's insistence on climbing onto his lap, Laine raised a querying eyebrow.

Jane just wiggled her fingers in reply and waited for Laine's jaw to drop. Her friend obliged and clearly couldn't wait to get her alone in the powder room at the Waterside in order to demand a full account of what had just happened.

She had to wait. They walked into the intimate little reception bar of the restaurant to be greeted by a loud cheer. Mark's partners and all their staff were there before them, presents piled high, champagne standing by, eager to wish them every happiness.

'I should have guessed,' Jane murmured to Laine as all the girls surged round her to look at the ring, all the men to kiss the bride. 'I *knew* Patsy couldn't have done all this without someone authorising it.'

'Mark?'

'No, one of his partners…' For a moment she'd thought it might have been him…hoped it might have been. But when she'd turned to look up at him, it had been obvious he was as surprised as she was. 'This is Charlie Young's idea, I imagine.'

By way of confirmation the man himself called for order. 'Jane, Mark—I know you both thought you were going to have a quiet romantic lunch together and are probably horrified to discover you're going to be sharing your special day with this unruly bunch. But we couldn't let the moment pass without letting you know how happy we are for you both.' There was a hum of approval. 'And maybe pick up a few hints on how to keep an office romance that quiet.' Amidst the laughter, he raised his glass. 'To Jane and Mark.'

'To Jane and Mark.'

Then someone called out, 'Well, go on, Mark, give her a kiss.'

Beside her Jane felt him tense, and instinctively she

reached for his hand. One thing to kiss her at the register office, witnessed by strangers. Quite another in front of people who knew them both. Who'd known Caroline.

For a moment he gripped her fingers, then he turned to her and, with his eyes fixed upon hers, lifted her hand to his lips. And the only sound in the room was a soft sigh from the women.

The party broke up just after four, when an exhausted Shuli dropped asleep on Mark's shoulder.

He leaned back against the soft leather upholstery of the limousine and said, 'That was surprisingly good fun.'

'Yes, it was kind of them. I'll write thank-you notes to Charlie and everyone for the presents tomorrow.'

'Totally efficient as always?'

She turned sharply, but he was teasing. 'Not totally efficient. That would suggest I'd discovered some way of telling my mother about today and surviving.'

He looked perplexed. 'You didn't tell your mother that you were getting married?'

'Did you tell yours?'

'Well, no. But she's at an environmental conference in New York. And Portia's deeply involved in some legal wrangle at the European Parliament.'

And it wasn't as if he was marrying a glittering society beauty this time round. Just good old platonic Jane. Nothing to get excited about.

'It's a pity they don't make cards,' Jane said.

He frowned. 'Cards?'

'Greetings cards. ''Just to let you know that blank and blank were married on the blank.'''

'Maybe they do.' Then, when she gave him an old-fashioned look, 'No, I don't suppose there's much call for that sort of thing. Do you want me to ring her? Explain—?'

'No!' Explanations were the last thing she wanted.

'Explain why we didn't wait and do the whole banns and church bit,' he finished gently. 'Because of Shuli.'

And have her mother speculate on whether she'd married for Mark's convenience rather than her own? Besides, that wasn't why they'd opted for the fast-track wedding and he knew it. 'No,' she said. 'Really. I can handle it. But not until tomorrow.'

The evening, which she'd been so certain would be full of awkward moments, passed in a whirl of Shuli's needs. Exhausted, it was a relief for Jane to stretch out beside the child, cuddling up to her as she read her a long fairy story. She was in no hurry to go downstairs and face reality.

Shuli had been insistent that Jane bath her, so Mark had changed into a pair of comfortable chinos and a polo shirt, opened a bottle of wine, looked at the labels on the wedding presents and eventually, when he'd been able to wait no longer, had gone to look for her.

He found her, fast asleep and curled up beside Shuli, looking like a child herself in soft grey sweats. He picked up the book she'd been reading, put it on the night table. Then he carefully picked up Jane and carried her to the guest room, removing her shoes before covering her up, the way he'd done for Shuli more times than he could remember.

She didn't stir. Probably hadn't slept a wink the night before. Well, neither had he. But he was used to it.

He drew the curtains, then lingered, not wanting to leave, reliving that astonishing moment when his lips had touched hers. It had been the barest touch and yet, like the touch of her hand against his in the jeweller's, the heat lingered. And on an impulse he bent to kiss her again.

CHAPTER FIVE

JANE woke with a start and sat up in the dense dark, not knowing where she was. Then it all came back to her with a rush. The wedding, the reception, the champagne. The guest room.

She fell back against the pillow. Then she sat up again as it occurred to her that maybe Shuli had cried out, her sleep disturbed by too much excitement. She hadn't been plied with champagne, but she had eaten an awful lot of ice cream.

She reached for the bedside lamp, missed and knocked it flying. 'Oh, sugar...' If the child wasn't already awake she soon would be. She crawled about on the floor until she found the lamp, then switched it on. That was when she realised she was still wearing the clothes she'd changed into before she'd bathed Shuli.

She sat back on her heels and frowned. The last thing she could remember was reading Shuli a bedtime story. The combination of a sleepless night, stress and vintage fizz had clearly knocked her out as effectively as a sleeping pill. She had the headache to prove it.

Great start. So much for totally efficient, totally in control Jane Carmichael.

The light caught the diamonds on her hand and they flashed a reminder that it wasn't only the calm and order that were things of the past. She was no longer Jane Carmichael, but Mrs Mark Hilliard.

She gave a little shiver, not from cold, but apprehension. The word 'home' had come naturally to her thoughts, yet as she put the lamp back on the table and looked around the exquisite suite she knew she could never call it that. Not while she stayed in the guest room.

This was Caroline's house: every perfect inch of it. She'd chosen the furniture, the wallpaper, the colour of the paint. There were even some of her clothes, still in dry cleaners' bags, hanging in the guest room wardrobe where someone had put them, out of the way.

She was here on the sufferance of a ghost. Feeling suffocated, choked, she pulled back the curtains to breathe in the sweet fresh air pouring in at the window.

The sky was the pearlescent grey of the pre-dawn, and she glanced at her watch to check the time. Not quite five. She'd heard no sound from Shuli, but she checked anyway. Anything to get out of that room. The child was fast asleep, her curls a tumbled halo on her pillow.

It must have been her own uneasy thoughts that had disturbed her, then.

She'd allowed Laine to believe that she had everything under control, that marriage had simply been the first step in her master plan. Ha! Some plan.

Here she was on the first morning of her married life, alone in the guest suite and still wearing the clothes she'd changed into when she'd gone to bath Shuli. It had been her wedding night, and the seductive nightgown that had been Laine's gift was still packed up in a suitcase somewhere; the only clothes she'd shed had been her shoes.

That was no way to set about reminding a man that he was made of flesh and blood. No way to infiltrate herself into his mind, exorcise the past.

Not that she'd have lingered on the landing to flash a bare shoulder as Mark followed her up the stairs—Laine's parting suggestion. Like the bad-girl underwear, it just wasn't her.

No, she'd had it all worked out. She was going to be the perfect wife, taking the strain, easing the burden. And hopefully reminding him that he could still laugh. And, starting as she meant to go on, she'd stocked the fridge in readiness to cook a perfect wedding-night supper.

Talk about falling asleep on the job!

But now, at five in the morning, her alter ego was wide awake and whispering sedition, suggesting that *he'd* got it made, but questioning what was in this marriage for her.

Confused, but certain that she wasn't going to get any more sleep, she decided to go downstairs and make herself a cup of tea.

Mark, used to sleeping with one ear listening for Shuli, woke on full alert. It wasn't Shuli, but something had woken him, and after a moment straining to identify any unusual sound he heard a door being opened with infinite care.

Jane. As he lay there, listening to her move quietly across the hall to look in on the sleeping child, he felt an unexpected surge of pleasure in the realisation that he was no longer on his own. That for the first time since he'd become a father he had someone to share the responsibility, the broken nights when she had a cold, the fear that he wouldn't be good enough.

Someone who cared.

Not wanting her to think he was abandoning all responsibility for Shuli to her, he swung out of bed and headed for the door. Then, realising that he probably needed to be wearing more than a pair of boxers, he picked up a robe and tied it about him.

He was too late. Shuli was fast asleep and Jane had returned to her own bed. Feeling oddly disappointed, he stood for a little while watching his daughter. The source of so much delight and so much pain. She was sleeping more peacefully than he could recall in a long time.

He lifted the cover over her shoulder, gently kissed her curly head and was returning to his room when he saw the glow of a light spilling from the kitchen. Had Jane gone downstairs?

Concerned that she might be suffering from the after-effects of Charlie Young's boisterous hospitality, he went to see if she needed anything. And came to an abrupt halt as he turned at the foot of the stairs.

Jane was sitting at the breakfast island, her legs wrapped around a stool, dunking a teabag in a mug, her shadowy figure backlit by a single downlighter.

Her hair had exploded into a thick mass of waves and curls, while her mouth, far too large for her face and usually tucked up tidily into a smile, had drooped into a soft, pensive pout.

Yesterday, arriving for the wedding, he'd been startled at how different she looked out of the stark black suits she wore in the office. But this was a Jane he'd never even suspected existed. And as he stood there his body disturbingly reminded him that he was a man.

'Jane? Is anything wrong?' His voice came out more sharply than he'd intended and she jumped, sending the mug crashing on its side so that hot tea cascaded over the edge of the worktop onto her legs. Without thinking he rushed to grab her, pull her from the stool and away from the scalding liquid. 'Are you hurt?' he demanded. 'Get those things off...' He tugged at her jog-pants, pulling the wet fabric away from her skin, and discovered somewhat late in the day that her eyes could spit fire as easily as they smiled.

'What the hell do you think you're doing?'

Realising, belatedly, how his reaction to the drama could be misinterpreted, he released her. 'I was just trying to minimise the damage. You need to get out of those pants—'

'I know, but I'm not helpless.' She turned away from him and peeled down the jog-pants, kicking them off.

'And get them under cold water,' he added, heading for the fridge.

'I know that, too! I'm not a complete idiot.' She turned on the tap and, grabbing a towel, held it beneath the flow to soak it. 'I was a Girl Guide—'

'Turn round.'

She turned, but only to berate him further. 'I did first—' Her verbal onslaught came to an abrupt halt as he slowly and carefully poured the contents of the water container he'd taken from the fridge over the pink patches on her thighs. It was a big container and it was a long time before she could draw in sufficient breath to gasp out, 'That's enough! I'm fine… Please… Stop…'

He looked up. 'Sure?' She nodded wordlessly. 'How does it feel?'

'Totally numb. I think I'm in more danger of frostbite than blistering.'

He switched on the main light and took a closer look. Her legs were still pink but he suspected that she was right. It was from the cold water rather than the scald. He looked up. 'Fortunately the jog-pants saved you from any serious damage.'

Jane looked around; yes, well, he could quite understand why she wouldn't want to look at him. If anyone was an idiot it was him. Startling her that way—

'Whoever would have thought so little water would go such a long way?' she said. 'I'd better mop it up.' She lifted her shoulders in an awkward little shrug. 'If you'll tell me where the mop is.'

'Not a chance. You're going to sit down while I make you a fresh cup of tea.' Paddling through the iced water, he led her back to the stool, but, since her legs were already sparking libidinous ideas, he thought it wiser not to attempt to lift her onto it. 'And this time try not to throw it over yourself.'

'I did not do any such thing! You startled me!'

Lord, but she was jumpy. 'I was pulling your leg, Jane. For heaven's sake, relax.'

She looked as if she was about to tell him what he could do with his leg-pulling, too. Then she gave a little shiver. 'I'm sorry, Mark. I'm not usually so jumpy. And I'm sorry I shouted at you for trying to help.'

'Shout away. You had every right.' Her reaction had revealed a side of his unflappable secretary that he'd never witnessed before; it had been worth a scolding. 'I'm the one who should be apologising. I heard you come down and I thought you might be…' Sick. Or maybe just sleepless, lying awake and wondering how she could ever have made such a big mistake. The thought was enough to make him feel ill.

During the last few days he'd felt as if he was reaching light at the end of some long tunnel. He'd scarcely given a second thought to how she was feeling. After all, this had been her idea. She'd been pushing him to find someone, a partner, a mother for Shuli, and when it came right down to it there was no escaping the fact that she'd put the idea of marrying her into his head.

And he'd grabbed it with both hands.

Because it had been the easiest thing to do? An answer to all his prayers? When had he become so selfish? So self-centred? It was too late to suggest she think again. All he could do was make sure she never regretted her generous impulse. Do everything within his power to make her happy.

He realised she was still waiting for him to complete the sentence. 'I thought you might be worrying about how your mother will react the your news.'

'My mother, my father, my four big sisters and their husbands, as well as several dozen cousins. Oh, and a parcel of nieces who'll be furious that they didn't get to be bridesmaids,' she said. 'They are going to be really fed up.' Her answer was undoubtedly true, but had been seized on with such enthusiasm that he suspected he might have offered an excuse that was a lot easier to admit to than the truth.

'Maybe we should leave the country,' he suggested.

She finally smiled. 'Good plan. Unfortunately you've got a tight deadline on the Maybridge project.'

'I know, but if your father's going to come after me with shotgun—'

'Why would he do that? It isn't as if you've done me wrong. This was all my idea...' She suddenly found it necessary to check on her legs.

'How are they?'

She looked up.

'Your legs?'

'Fine. That was quick thinking—if out of the cruel-to-be-kind school of nursing. I bet you rip sticky plasters off hairy limbs, too.'

'Is there another way?' Her legs, he realised, were not just fine. They were very fine. Jane might not be tall, but her legs left nothing to be desired: proportionately long, shapely, with a pair of very fetching ankles. His treacherous body found an ally in a mind quick to offer an alternative occupation to tea-drinking for two newlyweds awake in the early hours of the morning.

He couldn't understand it. His libido had lain dormant for years. Last week, when they'd agreed that this was a sensible, logical and totally platonic marriage, nothing had been further from his mind than making love to his new wife.

Certainly nothing had been further from hers or she'd never have agreed to it. And he couldn't change the rules now, just because he was unexpectedly aroused. He wasn't that selfish. Realising that he was staring, he said, 'I thought you were going to sit down while I made us both a cup of tea.' It would occupy his hands.

Jane, feeling suddenly naked, was about to refuse, rush away and cover herself up. But Mark didn't seem in the least bit bothered by the fact that her sweat top barely covered her knickers. Not nearly bothered enough, if all he could think of was making a cup of tea.

So much for Laine urging a little provocative shoulder display. It didn't seem at all fair that a glimpse of his naked chest could leave her feeling weak with lust, while her entire legs were apparently not worth a second glance.

Forget naked anything; she'd be wiser to stick to her first plan. Which was why, eschewing modesty, she did what any perfect wife would do under the circumstances. She ignored the stool and instead found the mop for herself and dried the floor. Then she cleaned up the mess made by the tea.

'You didn't have to do that,' Mark said, carrying across a couple of mugs of tea and sliding onto a stool beside her. 'A couple of people come in a van three times a week and clean from top to bottom.'

To distract herself from the body heat leaping the small space between them so that the tiny hairs on her thighs stood on end, she said, 'Maybe we should cut their visits back to once a week or I won't have anything to do.'

'Caroline never had any trouble filling her time. Upper Haughton has a busy social life, apparently.'

'Do you mean there are a lot of coffee mornings, jumble sales and other time-consuming ways of raising money for worthy causes as an excuse for catching up with the gossip?'

'Don't forget the village fête.' He turned and looked down at her, a wry smile pulling at the corners of his mouth. 'You're right. It doesn't sound that exciting.'

'I might think that, but, since this is all new to me, I'll reserve judgement.'

'Shuli will keep you on the run.'

'Undoubtedly. Does she go to a playgroup?'

'One of her nannies took her to something called Tiny Tots at the village hall.' He turned away, his jaw tightening, and suddenly found something of enormous interest in his mug. 'It was there that Shuli discovered other children didn't have nannies, they had mummies. That's when she started getting so difficult.'

Jane made a move to reach out, cover his hand with her own. He was so close. It would be so easy to offer that simple, wordless assurance that everything was going to be put right. That from this day forward he wouldn't have to worry about a thing.

He might not, but she was beginning to get an inkling of just how far out on an emotional limb she'd crawled. So she restrained herself, instead picking up the mug of tea and cradling it for a little personal comfort between her fingers. 'Well, she's got one now,' she said. 'I hope she won't be disappointed.'

'No.' He turned to her. 'I think she's been telling me for some time that she'd chosen you.'

She frowned.

'Think about it. Every time she played up and I had to bring her into the office she spent the day with you. She adores you, Jane. She hasn't stopped talking about you all weekend. I should have realised sooner, but I guess I just wasn't listening.'

Who would blame him? It was obvious that such a sacrifice would be above and beyond the call of duty unless desperation drove you to it. She put down the mug before she had another accident.

'She'll be waking up any minute. I'd better go and take a shower, see if I can find something to wear. I packed so quickly that it'll take me days to sort everything out.'

She slipped down from the stool and Mark watched her as she crossed the kitchen, vaguely troubled by his unexpected reaction to a woman he'd thought he knew so well. He knew what he was getting out of this marriage, but what had driven her to make such a choice? Not for the 'lovely home' or the 'comfortable life', he was certain. Or to avoid the tears and chocolate that went with conventional match-making. Had her heart been broken by some careless man too stupid to recognise what he'd got? Afraid of being hurt again, had she opted out and settled for friendship?

He promised himself that she wouldn't be sorry with her bargain. That he would be the best friend she'd ever had.

'I promise you,' she said, echoing his thoughts as she bent to pick up her tea-soaked jog-pants, 'I'm not in a habit of sleeping in the clothes I'm wearing.'

'That was entirely my fault. Maybe I should have woken you, but you looked so peaceful.'

'Woken me?' She straightened, slowly turned around. 'Peaceful?' She said the word as if it were unknown to her.

'You were reading to Shuli,' he said. 'Remember? It must have been one heck of a boring story because it put you both to sleep. I thought you'd be more comfortable in your own bed.' A deep flush flamed her cheeks. She was embarrassed? Because he'd picked her up and put her to bed? It wasn't as if he'd taken her to his. Or even undressed her. This probably wasn't the moment to admit that he'd kissed her goodnight. 'I thought I'd better take off your shoes, though. I hope you don't mind?'

She swallowed. 'Why should I mind?'

'You seem a little...disconcerted.' Then, 'Has anyone ever told you that you've got very pretty feet?' The desire to tease her, just a little, was a wicked temptation. But irresistible. He'd never seen a woman blush like that before.

'All the time,' she said, then added airily, 'People stop me in the street to remark on them.'

'And they say the British are a reserved people.' He shook his head, hiding a smile. 'I hadn't noticed how small they are. Your feet.' He hadn't been noticing much at all, he thought. Not for a long time.

Unable to shuffle them out of sight, hide the pretty pink toenails, she backed towards the door. 'I'd better take that shower.'

'Better make it a cool one.' Her eyes widened. 'Hot water will make your legs sting,' he explained. What the heck had she thought he meant?

'Oh, right. I'd forgotten all about them.' She took another step backwards. 'Great first aid.'

Mark watched her retreat all the way to the hall, where she gave up any pretence of dignity, and turned to bolt up the stairs.

He remained where he was for a long time, just smiling and thinking that this was a great way to start the day.

Then, hearing Shuli squealing with pleasure as Jane went to see if she was awake, he realised that it was time he thought about getting ready for work. And that he might benefit from taking his own advice regarding the temperature of his shower.

CHAPTER SIX

MARK put his head around the nursery door. 'Jane, I've got an early meeting with the project team, so I'll get off now. I should be home by seven.'

Jane, who'd discovered that dressing a wriggling three-year-old who would much rather play took a lot longer than she'd anticipated, leapt to her feet. 'But what about breakfast?' The whole essential coffee, fresh orange juice, cereals and egg thing that every perfect wife provided for her man. That her mother had provided for her family without apparent effort every morning of her life. 'It's the most important meal of the day.'

Mark just grinned, picked up his daughter and kissed her. The dungarees fell off. 'I'm used to getting my own breakfast. And Shuli's too.' He turned to her, still holding his little girl. 'This morning has been a piece of cake.' For a moment she thought he was going to kiss her, too, but then he put Shuli down and said, 'If I'm going to be late I'll ring you. Bye, Shuli. Be good.'

'Be good,' Shuli called back.

'Take care,' Jane whispered. Then, when the sound of Mark's car had faded into the distance, she picked up the little pair of dungarees and started again.

Breakfast took an age. And then, on the dot of nine, two ladies arrived in a bright yellow van and set about dusting and polishing the house with frightening efficiency. They seemed to be everywhere, and Jane didn't need much tempting to leave the call to her mother for a quieter moment.

Besides, a walk would clear her head, give her time to

151

think through exactly what she'd say. Fastening Shuli into her buggy, she set off to explore the village.

Patsy put her head around the drawing office door. 'Mark, there's a personal call for you. Shall I put it through to you here?'

'Sure.' Anticipating Jane's voice, he tucked the phone against his shoulder and carried on hatching in an area to be detailed by a draughtsman. 'What's the problem?' he asked.

'I don't know, Mr Hilliard,' a woman's voice replied briskly. 'That's why I'm calling you. To get some answers.'

'Sorry?' He straightened. 'Who is this?'

'Jennifer Carmichael. Your mother-in-law?' she prompted.

The pencil point snapped as Mark pressed down too hard. 'Jane rang you.'

'No, Mr Hilliard, she did not. And since I have no way of contacting her to confirm the astonishing news that my youngest daughter was married yesterday, I'm calling you.'

'Mrs Carmichael—'

'Is it true?'

'Well, yes, but I really think—' He really thought she should be having this conversation with Jane, but Mrs Carmichael was not in the mood to listen to his thoughts.

'Is she pregnant?'

That at least he could answer. 'No...' Realising that twenty pairs of ears, having caught the name, were straining to hear what he had to say, he cut short the sentence. 'No,' he repeated firmly.

'Then maybe you can offer some other explanation as to why she chose to marry in what appears to be unseemly haste and without a single member of her family present?'

'She was going to call you this morning,' he hedged, wondering what on earth had happened to stop her. He was certain something had, because Jane wasn't the kind of woman to duck a difficult task, no matter how thorny. 'First thing,' he added.

'I'll talk to Jane later. Right now I'm asking you, Mr Hilliard.'

'Mark,' he said, inviting her to use his given name.

Jane's mother made no indication that she was prepared to make any concession to familiarity until she'd heard his explanation, but he wasn't about to tell her anything with an audience. 'I'm not in my office right now, Mrs Carmichael. May I call you back in a couple of minutes?'

'Please do.'

He didn't exactly race back to his office, taking the time to call home on his mobile and find out what Jane wanted him to say. He got the answering machine.

Mark arrived home minus the warm feeling with which he'd started the day. In fact he was in a mood to chew rocks. He'd been forced to cancel two meetings and leave a deputy to stand in at a third. In two and a half years as his secretary Jane had never let him down. They'd been married for one day and Miss Jekyll had suddenly turned into Mrs Hyde.

The side gate to the garden was locked, so he let himself in through the front door and immediately heard the sound of childish laughter coming from the kitchen. He felt a rush of relief and was forced to acknowledge that it wasn't just anger at having his day wrecked that had brought him home in the middle of the afternoon. Each time he'd phoned and got no answer his unease had increased. He'd been here before.

He stopped the thought. Clearly no disaster had befallen either of them.

Then, as he opened the kitchen door, he was forced to revise that conclusion. 'Disaster' might be overstating it, but Jane, looking as if she been dragged through a muddy pond by her hair, was down on her knees scrubbing at the tiles with a hard brush. Lying on an old blanket, his nose flat to the floor and looking decidedly sheepish, was a shaggy half-grown pup of doubtful parentage. Shuli, sitting high above the mess, fastened safely in her old high chair, was laughing delightedly.

'Daddy!' she cried, reaching out her chubby little arms to him.

Jane, up to her arms in hot soapsuds, shuddered. 'Not yet, sweetheart,' she said, looking up at the child. 'Not for hours. Please,' she added fervently.

Then, realising that Shuli wasn't looking at her, but at something or someone behind her, she turned and saw him. Six foot plus of elegant, three-piece-suited and perfectly groomed manhood standing in the kitchen doorway, looking as if he'd just been hit with a brick. Her heart, which was already struggling to maintain an optimistic beat, gave up the effort and hit her boots. 'Oh…sugar.'

'It's great to see you, too,' Mark said, crossing the kitchen to Shuli.

This was her worst nightmare. The dog. The mess. And Mark arriving home to find his beautiful home not the haven of peace he had anticipated, he'd bargained for, she'd promised, but in uproar.

It shouldn't have happened. It wouldn't have happened if he'd stuck to his usual routine. She'd never known him leave the office before six. She should have had plenty of time to clean up the house—and herself—and prepare the quiet, relaxed evening she'd planned. First some quality time, while Mark played with Shuli before bedtime. Then a drink while she was putting the last-minute touches to dinner. Only then had she planned to admit to the puppy. When he was in a relaxed and receptive mood.

Some plan. She hadn't even taken the meat out of the freezer.

'I've been trying to get hold of you all day,' he said,

unfastening Shuli from the safety restraints. 'Where on earth have you been?'

Jane belatedly discovered that she wasn't perfect wife material. She found herself wanting to ask him where he got off, talking to her like that. She wasn't his secretary any more. He wasn't paying for her time by the hour.

By reminding herself that he might, just might, have a point, she managed to restrain herself. 'Do you want the whole story, or just the edited highlights?' she asked, finally getting to her feet and pushing back the damp strands of hair that were clinging untidily to her face. She didn't wait for an answer, preferring not to confront his shocked expression at her appearance, but took the bucket through to the utility room and tipped the water down the drain.

'I think we'd better stick to the highlights for now,' he said, following her but remaining in the doorway, presumably to avoid contamination.

'Right.' She dried her hands and turned to face him. She didn't think this was the moment to tell him that Shuli had left a sticky handprint on the lapel of his dark suit. 'Well, let's see,' she began. 'This morning, after breakfast, the cleaning team arrived. What with the noise of the vacuum cleaner and being underfoot no matter where I went, it seemed like a good idea to take Shuli for a walk—explore the village, check out the post office and the village shop. You know—show myself, give people something to talk about.'

'You certainly know how to make yourself popular.'

She glanced at him uncertainly. Was that supposed to be funny? There was nothing in his expression to suggest he was clamouring to join her fan club. 'I didn't get very far before this walking hearthrug decided he wanted to come along.' He glanced at the dog but made no comment on his appearance. 'I tried to discourage him, but he would keep running out into the road so I had no choice,' Jane said, just a little desperately. 'I had to grab hold of him.'

He didn't commend her public spirit, either. 'There might have been an accident, Mark.'

'That's why you brought him home?'

'No!' Then, 'Well, yes, but that was later. When I needed the car. He didn't have a collar, you see.'

'He's got one now.'

This was like wading through treacle, Jane thought, but she refused to get upset. This was Mark's home. She'd never seen it looking less than pristine. He had every right to be angry, she reminded herself. 'I asked at the village shop and the post office and the pub but no one recognised him.'

'This tends to be a pedigree dog neighbourhood. Good-looking dalmatians and Labradors, mostly. I shouldn't think too many people around here would admit to owning this apology for a dog.'

'He's got a lovely nature,' she declared defensively. Then, realising that she was not helping things, she said, 'Yes, well, I took him to the police station. They thought he'd probably been abandoned overnight. That someone had just dumped him from a car. How could anyone do that?' she demanded.

'It beats me.' The puppy shuffled closer so that his nose was touching the toe of Mark's shoe.

'They suggested I take him to the RSPCA,' Jane said, 'but he cried so when we walked away. And then Shuli cried.'

Mark looked up. 'And then you cried?' he suggested.

'Of course not.' She blinked rapidly. She did not get sentimental over abandoned animals.

'Of course not,' he repeated, clearly unconvinced. 'So, what this short version comes right down to is that we now have a dog?'

'I don't know what else I could have done, Mark.' He shook his head as if he couldn't believe his ears. 'Are you very angry?'

'Angry?' Mark regarded the sweet, caring woman who was looking at him as if he might throw her and the dog out of the house. And felt like a heel. 'How can I be angry? You did what you always do. You saw a need and dealt with it. First Shuli, then me, then the dog.' Which sort of put him in his place.

'He's a nice dog, Daddy,' Shuli said helpfully, reaching down, wanting to touch. The dog sat up hopefully.

'It's only temporary. Until his owners turn up,' Jane offered optimistically. 'I left a phone number with the police and the RSPCA.'

'I won't hold my breath.'

'No,' she admitted. 'That probably wouldn't be wise. Is it a terrible imposition, Mark? I will find a new home for him.' She didn't actually say, If you insist, but he saw the words in her eyes.

Mark felt the tension of his own bad day melting beneath the twin assaults of two pairs of brown pleading eyes. Putting off the inevitable moment, clinging to the pretence that this would be his decision, he bent to ruffle the fur behind the pup's ears.

'He's a really nice dog, Daddy,' Shuli said, her little face furrowed with anxiety.

'I'm sure he's a very nice dog.' The dog, his immediate slave, licked his fingers. 'Have you given him a name yet?'

'Name?' Jane repeated, as if such a thing had never entered her head.

'His name is Bob,' Shuli said. 'Bob the dog. Here, Bob!' The pup wiggled ecstatically at so much attention.

Mark looked up. 'Bob?'

'It doesn't mean anything.' Jane, pink and flustered at being caught out in this act of gross sentimentality, rushed to defend herself. Things had been going so well; she didn't want to ruin it now. 'We—Shuli and I—thought he looked like a Bob. That's all.'

'Yes,' he agreed, straightening. 'He does.'

Oh, heck, he was not amused. Well, why would he be? One day—he'd been married to her for just one day—and instead of peace and tranquillity he'd got Bob. And no dinner.

'He'll need a collar and lead. And some shots,' he said. She made a sort of noise in the back of her throat. 'He's already had them?'

'The RSPCA gave him his shots and a health check before I brought him home.' For a small fee.

'Along with the collar?'

'And lead. He's been well looked after. No fleas—'

'Just surplus to requirements?'

'And a bit muddy after a night on the common.'

'And he chased a duck, Daddy. Right into the pond. There was mud—' she flung her little hands wide in a vivid demonstration '—everywhere.'

'Thank you, Shuli,' Jane said, wondering if it could get any worse. 'I can't imagine how I forgot that part.' Then she realised that, contrary to expectations, Mark was struggling not to laugh. 'I bathed him outside, but he escaped before I'd quite finished.'

'He ran inside and shook himself all over the kitchen,' Shuli added, quite unnecessarily. 'See, Daddy?' And she very kindly pointed to a splatter of mud that Jane had missed. Because it was halfway up one of the pristine white walls.

'You're sure *you* bathed *him*?'

Mark reached out and wiped his fingertips over her cheek. His hand was cool, his touch sweet bliss against her hot and bothered skin. It was all she could do not to rub herself against him and purr, say, Thank you for understanding. He held it up his fingers for her to see. 'It looks more as if he transferred the mud to you.'

She looked down at herself and groaned. So much for the well-groomed wife, the angelic infant and the exquisitely prepared dinner waiting for her hero at the end of a hard day slaying dragons.

'Don't worry, it'll wash off.' He looked around. 'Probably.' Then, 'It certainly explains why you haven't had time to check the answering machine for messages.'

'Oh, Lord! You said you'd been trying to ring me. Is something wrong?'

'You were going to ring your mother?' She clapped a hand over her mouth. 'I can see you had more important things on your mind.'

'I'll do it now. As soon as I've had a shower—'

'Too late, Jane. She called me first thing this morning. Apparently she rang you for a chat last night. One of your sisters is expecting a baby. Elizabeth?'

'Is she? That's wonderful, they've been trying for ages…' She stopped. 'Sorry. What else?'

'Oh, pretty much everything. The woman from Accounts who's leased your flat told your mother how surprised everyone was, how no one had suspected a thing. How romantic she thought it was that you'd married your boss.'

'Oh, Mark! I'm so sorry.' Then, 'What did you say?'

'What *could* I say? I told her the truth.' Jane felt the blood drain from her face. 'I told her I asked you to move in with me, but you wouldn't. So we got married.'

'Oh.' Then, 'You didn't say anything else?'

'Anything else, Jane, is our business.'

'Yes, yes, of course.' She swallowed hard. 'And she, um, accepted that?'

'That's probably overstating the case, but I explained about Shuli and that appeared to pacify her.'

He wasn't telling her everything. 'And?'

'And I suggested she and your father come to dinner so that we can get acquainted.'

CHAPTER SEVEN

'DINNER?' Jane swallowed nervously. *'Some time,'* she said. 'You asked them to come to dinner *some time* so that you could get acquainted.' He didn't answer. 'Please tell me that you didn't ask my parents to dinner tonight.'

'Well, I will if you insist. But they'll still be here at six-thirty.' He put Shuli down so that she could stroke the dog. 'I wouldn't have asked them, Jane, but it was clear that your mother thought I had something to hide.'

'No! Why on earth would she think that?' But it explained why Mark had come home early. He hadn't been able to raise her on the phone so he'd been forced to come home to ensure there'd be something to eat. No wonder he'd been mad. She wasn't exactly over the moon herself. 'What could we possibly have to hide?' she asked, the edge to her voice sharp enough to cut glass. Then, with a little wail of anguish, 'Did you say *six-thirty*?'

'I did.'

'But that's…' She couldn't voice what she thought. Not with Shuli listening. 'That's so early!'

'The plan was to let Shuli win them round.' He looked down at the child, who was sitting on the floor chattering away to Bob. 'If they fall for her—'

'Oh, they will.' Who wouldn't love the child on sight? 'I'm sorry. I didn't mean to complain. It's really sweet of you to make such an effort, especially when I've dropped you in it so comprehensively.'

'But?' he prompted. 'I'm sure I sensed a "but" in there somewhere.'

She gave a little shrug. 'Well, just for future reference

you might like to make a note that I need a minimum of two weeks' notice to cook for my mother.'

'Two weeks?'

'One week to plan and one week to panic.'

'For heaven's sake, what kind of man do you take me for? I had Patsy call a caterer and order dinner for four at eight.'

'A caterer?' Jane covered her face with her hands and moaned pitifully. How could so much go wrong in one day?

'Of course. Caroline always used a caterer—'

Caroline? This marriage might not be the romance of the century but she was a person in her own right, not some pale stand-in for his dead wife. 'I am not Caroline,' she said, through gritted teeth.

'No,' he said. And with a sweeping glance that took in mud, dog and the cut-off jeans she'd worn to bath him, he made it clear that she would never measure up.

She wasn't about to try. She was her own woman.

'Caroline would never have wasted half an hour, let alone half a day, on a mongrel pup.'

'No? Well, I did tell you to advertise for the perfect woman, but you couldn't face the hassle so you settled for me. Live with it.' She tugged on her bottom lip with her teeth to stop the hot tears that threatened to overwhelm her. 'Just as I'll have to live with my mother telling me, at length, how my four beautiful sisters can cope with their children, their sparkling careers and a positive menagerie of pets and still manage to cook dinner for their parents.'

'Your sisters haven't been married for little more than twenty-four hours,' Mark returned sharply. 'Even your mother must suspect that you'd have more interesting things to do than cook.'

'Why? You went to work this morning. Business as usual.'

Mark felt as if he'd been sandbagged. What had he said

to provoke that reaction? They'd discussed what they'd do and they'd done it. Hadn't they? It occurred to him that perhaps 'discussed' was rather overstating the case. He'd said how it would be and she hadn't demurred. That didn't mean she was totally happy with the situation.

And, remembering how her face had lit up when he'd told her about her sister's baby, he wondered just how many assumptions he'd been guilty of making.

Maybe he should have spent a little more time working on the details of this arrangement and less time congratulating himself on his good fortune.

'Oka-a-ay…' he said. 'Why don't we try that again? Start from the beginning? I'll go out, drive around the village and then, when I come back, I'll say, Hi, honey, I'm home. Had a nice day? And you'll say, Don't ask, and then you'll tell me anyway, and I'll say, You think you've had a bad day? Just wait until you hear what happened to me…' He reached out and cradled her cheek, turning her face towards him. 'You wouldn't be laughing by any chance?' he asked hopefully.

'No…I mean yes…' Her cheeks flushed a hot pink. 'Actually, I don't know what I mean.' Then, 'Mark?' He waited. 'I'm really sorry about the dog.' She gestured at the kitchen. 'The mess in here.' She took a shaky breath. 'He dug a hole in your lovely garden, too.' She pulled her lips against her teeth, clearly afraid that this would be the final straw.

His garden. His kitchen. His house. And he hadn't exactly helped by walking in and demanding why she hadn't been there to answer the phone. She was his wife, not his secretary. It was time he started treating her like one.

'*Our* lovely garden, Jane. This is our home. And our dog.'

'You mean it?' Her eyes lit up. 'He can stay?'

'Whatever you want is fine by me. Honestly.' He bent

and ruffled the pup's ears. 'He is a very nice dog. Different. A slightly eccentric choice, perhaps—'

'He chose us.'

'So he did.'

'It's rather like that old nursery rhyme. The farmer needs a wife…the wife needs a dog…' She stopped, realising just in time that the rhyme didn't go quite like that. 'First you get an ugly duckling wife, and then you get a dog to match.'

He looked up, irritated by the way she'd put herself down. 'I didn't say that, nor should you. So what if neither of you ever fledge into swans? You'll make very fine ducks.'

'Well, thanks. I think.'

'Swans hiss and bite, Jane. Ducks are friendly and eager to please. I know which I'd rather live with.'

She took a deep breath, as if she might argue, then she said, 'Okay, you win the bunch of onions for the weirdest compliment of the month. But be very sure about the dog. Say the word and I'll take him back to the RSPCA right now. They'll find him a home, I'm sure. Eventually. But if he stays, he stays for good.'

Like the wife? 'He's got a home.' Mark looked around at the disordered kitchen. 'I've got a home.'

'But—'

'But nothing.' Her forehead had puckered in an anxious little frown and instinctively he reached out to smooth it away with the pad of his thumb. He didn't want her anxious, or worried. He certainly didn't want her in a stew because the kitchen, for once in its immaculate life, didn't look like a feature from some glossy magazine. On an impulse he placed a light kiss in the wide space between her eyes. 'A tidy house is a place where nothing happens, Jane,' he said, close enough to see the faint gold freckles that dusted her nose. 'Believe me. I know.'

*   *   *

The dining room was ready for their guests. Bob was be-having like a graduate from obedience school. Shuli had been fed, bathed and dressed in her pretty new frock.

Clipping back her hair in the ebony clasp, Jane critically regarded her appearance in a long mirror, smoothing the simple, unadorned grey dress over her hips before slipping the diamond ring Mark had bought her in place next to her wedding ring.

It wouldn't be enough. Her mother, already suspicious, was as sharp as knives. And her father, having spent thirty-five years in medical practice, had developed an intuitive gift for spotting when something was not quite as it should be. Which was why she'd spent the last fifteen minutes carefully eradicating any trace of her presence from the guest suite.

But she'd need to do a lot more than that to create the right impression when her mother asked to see around the house. As she undoubtedly would.

She could hear Mark outside, playing with Shuli and the puppy. She slipped into his bedroom, heart beating over-time and feeling like a guilty trespasser. But she had no time to waste worrying about that.

She put the silver-backed hairbrush she'd inherited from her grandmother on the heavy antique dressing table, add-ing a few hairpins and a jar of moisturiser for effect. The electric toothbrush her mother had bought her, but she'd never used, was propped conspicuously beside Mark's own toothbrush in his bathroom. Her new white towelling bath-robe was hung on the door beside its twin. His and hers.

Then she turned to the bed. The tender little kiss he'd given her had fired her imagination, and for a moment she held the slinky silk nightdress against her cheek, imagining herself wearing it. Imagining how it would feel to have Mark slip the shoestring straps from her shoulders so that it fell to the carpet, to puddle around her feet. She imagined him touching her, lifting her onto the huge bed that dominated the room—

Jolted from her dreams by the crunch of her father's car tyres against the gravel, she quickly tucked the nightdress beneath one of the pillows, leaving just a tiny trail of black silk visible to catch the alert eye. Even then she lingered, her hand against the cool fresh linen, before the sound of the doorbell sent her racing downstairs.

Mark looked up as Jane hurried down the stairs. She'd been a bundle of nerves and he was convinced that she was going to look so pale and guilty that her parents would think he was some kind of fiend. Instead her cheeks were faintly flushed, her eyes dark and sparkling—the perfect picture of a new bride.

For a moment he experienced again the same moment of shocked surprise that had seized his breath when he'd seen her first thing that morning. Before she'd realised he was there. Of looking at someone he'd worked with five days a week for the last two and a half years, a person he'd thought he knew, and realising that there was an undiscovered woman beneath the façade of the efficient secretary he'd taken for granted.

He wanted to tell her that, to let her know. He wanted to say how lovely she looked. But if he said that she'd think he was simply being kind. Nothing could be further from the truth.

'You look…special,' he said. Then, 'I thought you might have worn the same outfit as yesterday.'

'Yesterday's outfit wouldn't do, Mark. It offers too much scope for speculation. Now, this dull little dress serves a dual purpose.' She ran a hand over the flat surface of her abdomen, drawing attention to her body. The gesture was innocent of provocation and yet it concentrated his mind totally on her slender waist, the gentle flare of her hips. 'It hides nothing, comprehensively proving that you were speaking the plain, unvarnished truth when you told my mother that I'm not pregnant.'

'What? Oh, right.' He forced himself to concentrate. 'You said a dual purpose?'

'There is nothing to distract from this.' She held up her left hand and moved it so that the diamonds flashed in a beam of sunlight. 'As far as the outside world is concerned there's nothing more convincing of a man's sincerity than his generosity with pure carbon.' The doorbell sounded again but he didn't move. 'I don't think they're going away, Mark,' she prompted. Still he didn't move. 'You're really going to have to open the door.'

'I can't fool you, can I?' He stretched out his hand. 'You know I'm scared to death. Will you hold my hand?'

'Like this?' She placed her fingers on his.

'No, I think we should make it really convincing.' And he tightened his grip and pulled her close, then put his arm around her before throwing open the door.

Pressed against Mark's freshly ironed shirt, bombarded with the shock of his body hard against hers, an elusive hint of aftershave, the warmth of his hand keeping her close, Jane had to struggle for breath. 'Mum, Dad…this is Mark…'

CHAPTER EIGHT

THERE was a moment of brittle tension while Mark shook hands with her parents. Then her mother said, 'Oh, come here.' And, gathering her up, gave her a big hug before holding her at arm's length. 'You look wonderful. And who's this?'

Shuli, hiding behind her father's legs, had to be coaxed to say hello. But then Bob hurtled through from the back of the house, wiggling with such excitement that Jane rushed him out into the garden, calling back, 'He's going to have an accident if I don't...' and grabbing the excuse to catch her breath.

Her father followed her. 'Your mother was worried, Jane,' he said, as they watched Bob chase a starling. 'I can see there was no need. I've never seen you look so happy.'

She was. It was totally pathetic that that one little kiss, Mark's arm around her waist, should make the world seem brand-new. But they had. 'Everything's—' she lifted her hands in a gesture designed to indicate that the world was a wonderful place '—perfect.'

'Then I'm delighted. I was looking forward to walking my little girl up the aisle, though.'

Fortunately Bob chose that moment to race back and show them how happy he was. 'No! Down, Bob!' She pulled him off. 'Sorry, but he's new. A stray.'

'He's going to be a handful.'

'Just a bit excited to have a new family,' Mark said, bringing out a tray with glasses and a bottle of champagne. 'I know how he feels.' He opened the bottle, poured out the wine. 'Jennifer.' Jane blinked to hear her mother addressed by her first name on such short acquaintance. 'Harry.'

'Thanks. I was just telling Jane that I'm sorry to have missed out on walking her up the aisle the way I did her sisters.'

Mark handed her a glass with a look that fried her insides. 'I just couldn't wait,' he said, and grinned broadly.

Seriously convincing if you didn't know that it was all play-acting. Like the arm about her waist, she realised.

And the evening suddenly lost its sparkle. She responded on automatic to her father's toast, just sipping the champagne before putting the glass down to pick up Shuli, make a fuss of her.

'Jane?' She looked up to discover everyone was looking at her.

'Sorry, did you say something?'

'I suggested that your parents should stay over. Back me up, here. Tell them we've got plenty of room. That it's crazy to drive all the way home tonight.'

Jane nearly choked on her champagne. Did he realise what he was doing? There was convincing, she thought, and then there was asking for trouble.

'Really, we can't,' her father said quickly, before her mother allowed herself to be persuaded. 'I have a clinic tomorrow morning. But you must come down for a weekend very soon so that you can meet the rest of the family and we can have a proper celebration. Shuli will love it. There are lots of children and we're right by the sea.'

'We can't leave Bob,' Jane said, before Mark could do something stupid like say yes.

'Bring him with you. I don't suppose one more dog will be noticed, do you? We'll soon wear him out on the beach. What about the weekend after next?'

'That sounds wonderful,' Mark said, before she could leap in with some unbeatable excuse. She was fast running out of excuses. In fact her brain had stopped functioning right after she'd worked out what the arm about the waist had really meant. 'Shuli has no cousins of her own. It'll be a whole new world for her. Just what she needs, wouldn't you say, Jane?'

It was exactly what she'd been saying. Shuli needed a family and her family was the one she'd had in mind. It would have been perfect, but for one small detail.

Fortunately her father made any reply unnecessary. 'You have no immediate family, Mark?' he asked.

'A mother and sister, both too busy putting the world to rights to have much time to spare for mundane things like family life. Shuli's mother was an only child. Her parents were killed when she was a baby; her grandmother raised her. So it's just been the two of us.' He glanced at Jane. 'Until now.'

'Well, maybe Shuli will have a new brother or sister of her own very soon,' her mother suggested.

'For heaven's sake, Jennifer, let the girl catch her breath.' And her lovely, lovely father, well-practised in the art of changing the subject, said, 'This is a lovely old house, Mark. Not what I'd expected at all. I've seen some of your designs and I imagined you'd be living in some minimalist ultra-modern affair constructed from glass and steel. A functional advertisement for your work.'

Only Jane was situated to see the briefest look of pain flicker across Mark's features before he said, 'If you'll excuse me, I'll go and see what's happening about dinner.'

'And I'll put Shuli to bed. Mum, do you want to come and give me a hand? See the house?'

Jane leaned back against the door. 'Well, that was different.'

'I enjoyed myself,' Mark said. 'They're nice people.'

'I never suggested they weren't. Just that my mother has high expectations that I've never quite lived up to. But what would you have done if they'd accepted your invitation to stay overnight? Since the guest suite is occupied?'

She didn't wait for his answer. He'd undoubtedly got it all worked out and she didn't want to hear how she could so easily have hidden out in one of the small rooms on the top floor for tonight and no one would have known a thing about it. Instead, she kicked off her shoes and padded barefoot into the living room to set about gathering the coffee cups.

'Leave that. Come and put your feet up for a minute.' He settled on the sofa, patting the seat beside him. But Jane wasn't in the mood to get cosy. They were on their own; there was no one around he had to convince with his happy families act.

The small touches, the quick conspiratorial smiles. He'd been so good at it. Her parents hadn't suspected a thing. Now it was just the two of them. Platonically linked, until death did them part. No more need to pretend.

Until the weekend after next.

'More to the point,' she continued scratchily, her throat aching from a totally stupid desire to cry. She'd brought this entirely upon herself, after all. 'What are you going to do on our long meet-the-family weekend? You do realise that we'll be installed in state in the guest bedroom?'

He took his time, apparently giving the matter considerable thought. 'Wear pyjamas?' he offered finally.

That was it. She'd had enough. 'You're right, this can wait until the morning. I'm going to bed. Don't forget to let Bob out for a run.'

She was halfway to the door before it occurred to her that she sounded exactly like a wife. One whose husband needn't think that she'd be awake when he followed her up the stairs.

Very apt.

'Jane—' She turned in the doorway. Mark had put his

feet up on the sofa and with his hands laced behind his head was stretched out with his eyes closed. 'Sleep well.'

Mark couldn't sleep. He'd forgotten how it felt to have a woman burning mad at him. The boiling mixture of emotions that could be blown away in the kind of sex that started as a fight and ended in hot, sweet, forgive-me lovemaking.

And the only woman he had in his head was Jane.

He didn't understand it. A week ago he'd scarcely been aware of Jane as a woman at all. Now her scent clung to him, even here in his own bed, evoking the silk of her skin against his fingers.

That flash of anger in her eyes when he'd mentioned Caroline. The soft, dark look of surprise when he'd kissed the frown from her forehead. And his mind just wouldn't let go of that early-morning picture, of full soft lips just begging to be kissed.

How many times today had he come close to kissing her? Just taking her in his arms and kissing her with no thought of the past? Half a dozen times. And when she'd stormed up to bed it had taken every ounce of will-power not to follow her and suggest they give the double bed a practise run.

He gave up on sleep and flung himself out of bed to pace the carpet.

That kind of response didn't happen overnight. Not with someone you'd known for years. It had to have been there, growing unseen, like bulbs forced into flower for Christmas. Kept in the dark while they built up a strong root system, they burst into flower within days of being brought into the light.

Jane wasn't conventionally beautiful. She wasn't the kind of girl who'd ever turn heads. But her kindness and generosity were qualities that touched even the most moribund of hearts and, unlike beauty, would never fade. They already had the LTR, a long-term relationship based on trust and respect. It had simply needed light to flower into something deeper.

Now all he had to do was find some way to demonstrate his feelings. And to help Jane forget whatever pain had driven her to contemplate a platonic marriage.

He remembered what she'd said about diamonds. Guaranteed to convince. But that was to convince other people. No, it needed a larger, more personal gesture, something that she couldn't possibly misinterpret.

As he turned he stepped on something sharp. A hairpin. He bent and picked it up. Then looked around. Jane had been in here? That was why her scent lingered in the air?

He groaned as he realised that she must have scattered her possessions around to convince her mother. Her brush, her hairpins. He crossed swiftly to the bed and, pulling off the pillows, was assailed by the delicate scent she'd been wearing. Her nightdress. Her nightdress had been here in his bed. The very thought of it inflamed a passion he'd thought long dead.

Reaching for his robe, he went down to his study. He might as well catch up with work. There was no way he was sleeping tonight.

CHAPTER NINE

'MARRIED life is a lot tougher than it looks,' Jane said in response to Laine's question. She tucked the telephone into her shoulder, taking advantage of Shuli's absence at play-group to tidy Mark's office as she talked. He must have been looking for something to show her father because there were blueprints heaped up everywhere. 'My parents came to dinner last night.'

'I know. Your mother rang my mother and I'm seriously in the doghouse for not spilling the beans. I hope it's worth it.' Then, when Jane didn't respond with instant glee, 'From the resounding silence I take it you're still in the spare room?'

'Please! The guest suite. But you're right; it isn't going to happen overnight. In fact my plan of proving myself the perfect wife didn't survive the first day.'

'You've had a row?'

'Yes. No. Maybe.'

'That was decisive.'

'It wasn't about anything personal.' Well, it had felt pretty personal when she'd been compared to Caroline and found wanting, but that was her business. 'It all began when I found this stray dog.'

'Crumbs, Jane. Whatever possessed you?' Laine demanded, when she'd finished telling her the entire story. 'Can't you ever just look the other way?'

Like Caroline? 'Apparently not.'

'Well, I think your Mark is a hero and you can tell him so from me. Give him a great big kiss as well.'

'You haven't heard the worst, yet. We've been invited home for the weekend. A full-dress family affair.'

'Is that a problem?'

'Think about it, Laine.'

'Oh, you mean you're going to have to share that great big double bed. Some problem. Why are you waiting until next weekend? Drag him down there tomorrow. And don't forget to pack your sexy black nightdress.'

'I don't just want sex, Laine. I want him to love me.'

'Darling, you wear the nightdress, you let your hair hang loose and you just stand there. He won't be able to help himself. Trust me.' Then, 'How's that sweet little girl?'

'Totally gorgeous. She's at playgroup right now.' Then, 'She woke me up this morning to ask if she could call me Mummy.'

'Oh, Jane!' Then, 'Did you cry?'

She sniffed. 'I'm crying right now.'

'So am I.'

Promising to ring again soon, Jane replaced the receiver on the handset and bent down to pick up a piece of blueprint that had been ripped up and tossed in the bin.

It wasn't for anything very big. It didn't have a project number or name, only 'Detached House, Upper Haughton' printed in the corner. And the date. It was five, no, six years old.

Jane retrieved the rest of it, but she knew where it was even before she'd pieced together the drawing of the front elevation. She'd passed it that morning as she'd taken Shuli to the village hall.

She might not have noticed the house at all, hidden behind an old weathered brick wall, but as she'd passed the gate the woman who lived there had come out with her own two little ones and had stopped to say hello. And then Jane had seen the house and admired it.

'We were so lucky. It was exactly what we were looking for, although I suppose it's not to everyone's taste. It was built specially as a surprise for the architect's bride-to-be, but she'd set her heart on a Georgian rectory she'd seen. And that apparently was that.'

She'd known even then that it must have been designed by Mark. Now, looking at the drawing he'd poured his heart into, Jane wanted to weep all over again.

'The playgroup is holding a jumble sale on Saturday, Mark. I've sorted through my things, but I wondered if you'd got anything past its wear-by date in your wardrobe. It's for a good cause. We're raising money for some outdoor play equipment.'

Mark glanced up. For days there had been a brittle, touch-me-not distance about Jane. Everything she did was pitch-perfect, there had been no more incidents with stray dogs, or mud on the kitchen walls, but something was wrong. He just couldn't pin her down long enough to find out what it was. Every time he tried to talk to her she leapt up to do something that apparently couldn't wait a second.

He'd hoped that prompting Shuli to call her Mummy would have opened the emotional barriers. She'd been affected by it, he knew; he'd seen the tears. But it hadn't been enough. Even now she could hardly wait for his answer so that she could race off and be doing something, anything, rather than putting her feet up and spending the evening with him.

'Don't say I didn't warn you. Once you're on the jumble sale rota your life will never be your own. Have they got you on the village hall committee yet?'

'I'm not helping, Mark. Not this time,' she said, avoiding a direct answer. 'We're going away for the weekend. Remember?'

'Of course. Better hang on to any pyjamas you find, then,' he added. He knew he shouldn't, but he just couldn't stop himself.

'You've actually got some?' she enquired, ultra-polite.

'I couldn't swear to it.'

Jane was struggling to hold herself together. Until she'd seen that plan she hadn't had any idea of what she was up against. How much he'd loved Caroline. How utterly futile it was to imagine he would ever love her. And nothing less would do. 'We don't have to go, Mark,' she said, hoping that he would grab the lifeline. 'I could make up some excuse.'

'No, they're expecting us. It's supposed to be a secret but they're planning a huge party.' He'd been talking to her parents? He must have seen her confusion because he added, 'Harry phoned and asked if I wanted to go fishing.'

'Oh.'

'Don't look so tragic,' he said. 'I promise I won't snore—'

She snatched the paper out of his hands. 'Stop it! Will you stop being flip and take this seriously?'

'It's *serious*? I thought it was just a jumble sale. Okay, well, you'll find a load of Caroline's clothes in one of the spare rooms. Take those. I'm sure they'll cause a lot more excitement than my old shirts.'

She looked stunned. She might well do. He was fairly stunned himself. That had come out of nowhere. It was right—he should have done it a long time ago—but the fact that he could do it so easily now was faintly shocking.

'Is that serious enough for you?'

For a moment she just stood there, and then she turned and walked away. He heard her mount the stairs, then go up again to the top floor, where there were half a dozen small rooms that were mostly used for storage. He heard her opening doors until she found the one with the rails of designer clothes that had belonged to Caroline.

He poured two large drinks and then went after her.

'Jane?' She'd pulled the dust covers from the rails and was looking at the clothes. He offered her a glass. She took it without saying a word, didn't even appear to notice that their fingers had touched. Didn't so much as twitch, let alone jump like the nervous kitten she'd been all week. He was the one who felt as if his skin had been seared. She swallowed a mouthful of brandy and shuddered. 'This lot should cause a bit of a stir in jumble sale circles,' he offered.

Jane had expected a few bags of clothes. Designer labels, of course. There'd been nothing 'chainstore' about Caroline Hilliard. Tall, slender, with a personal fortune that had allowed her to indulge her taste in fine things, she'd caused a stir wherever she went, apparently. But it was a shock to confront the reality. She couldn't conceive of any woman owning so many beautiful clothes.

'You can't...I can't...' She gave up. She didn't know what to say.

'Can't what? They're just clothes. Would you wear any of them?' Jane shook her head. Took a step back. 'Of course you wouldn't.'

Afraid she'd offended him in some way, Jane said, 'They wouldn't fit me, Mark.' Not in any sense, she thought.

'No,' he said. And she shrank inwardly. She was way out of her depth here. And in grave danger of making a fool of herself. He must never know how she felt about him. That scrap of dignity was all she had left. 'She was a lot taller than you.' A lot more everything, Jane thought as he bent to pick up a shoe. 'And she had feet to match.' Long, narrow, elegant feet.

'Talk about her, Mark. Tell me about her.' *Lay the ghost.*

'You want to know about Caroline?' She didn't want to know about her. She didn't want to ever hear her name on his lips. But until his first wife was out in the open, all the dark shadows exposed to the light, their marriage would remain a sham. 'Caroline is what you see about you, Jane,' he said at last. 'The house, the clothes. Perfection in everything. It was, in the end, her need for perfection that killed her.'

Jane frowned. 'But she drowned...'

'She was suffering from post-natal depression, Jane. It wasn't an accident.'

'Oh…' She shivered. 'I had no idea. Poor woman. Poor Shuli.' And then, 'Poor you.'

He replaced the shoe and then put an arm around her shoulder and said, 'Come on, let's go back downstairs.' He paused in the doorway, looked back, then turned out the light. 'I'll get this lot cleared out tomorrow.'

'No.' She looked up at him. 'Leave it to me. I'll do it. But not to the jumble sale. I don't want Caroline talked about, her things picked over.' Having Mark meet someone in the village wearing her clothes. 'It wouldn't be…proper.'

'I'm not sure either of us deserve such thoughtfulness from you, Jane. But thank you.'

Back in the softly lit drawing room, Mark topped up their glasses. 'We were the golden couple, did you know that?' he asked, with just a trace of bitterness. He didn't expect an answer because he went on, 'We had everything. Money, recognition, style. And for a while it was enough. Then Caroline decided she had to have a baby, too. All her friends had babies. It was the ultimate accessory. They glowed, they gave birth and then passed the result to a nanny to care for. They made it look so easy.'

Jane shivered, stirred, looked at Mark. 'What about you?'

'Me? I was delighted, over the moon. It was like the world had been made over just for me.' He took a long drink. 'The first few months were fine. She told all her friends, basked in the attention, read all the books. She was going to be the perfect mother. Then—' he shook his head. 'I don't know. She just seemed to panic. It had been ex-citing for a while, but then reality kicked in and she wanted to turn it all off. She couldn't.'

'What a nightmare.'

'She blamed me, of course. And she was right. She was like a beautiful piece of perfect glass. Exquisite, but fragile.

I should have known she'd never cope. That she was just
playing—'

'Mark…' she warned. She was sure he didn't mean to
be saying this. But he didn't seem to hear her. Maybe it
had all been bottled up so long that it was unstoppable.

'She hadn't had much morning sickness to speak off, but
suddenly she started to be sick with nerves. I've never felt
so helpless in my life.' He stared into the depths of his
glass. 'The last three months were undiluted hell, but I
thought once the baby arrived everything would be better.
If anything they were worse. She just lost interest in everything. I even had to wash her hair…'

Jane fought the lump in her throat. She must not cry. He
needed her to be strong. To listen and absolve him…

'She wouldn't touch Shuli. Could hardly bear to look at
her. She had a maternity nurse, but she couldn't be on call
twenty-four hours a day. I did what I could but the work
was piling up. Maybe if she'd had a mother it would have
been different.'

Jane thought of her own capable mother, how she'd been
there for her sisters. Was always there. A lifeline. 'Yes,'
she said. 'A mother makes all the difference.'

'She was totally unable to cope with this small helpless
creature who was totally dependent upon her. She was desperate to escape. When some friends suggested she join
them for a couple of weeks in the Mediterranean she
begged to go with them. God help me, I thought it would
do her good. The sun, swimming… She loved to swim.'

'It could have been an accident, Mark. Even the strongest
swimmers get into difficulty.'

'That was the Coroner's verdict,' he conceded. 'But
she'd sent me a letter. Taken it to the post office and sent
it by special delivery so that she could be sure it would
arrive. By the time I got it, she was dead.'

'Mark, I'm so sorry.'

He acknowledged her sympathy, but his smile never

reached his eyes. 'It was the last act of a perfectionist. Leaving a note would have been far too messy. It would have meant everyone knowing that she'd failed the ultimate test for a woman. Motherhood. The letter was not for public consumption, just to say sorry...'

'Mark, she didn't fail. She needed help—'

'Not a holiday?' He stood up. 'Yes. I'm making no excuses, the failure was mine. As a husband.' He reached out, grasped her hand. 'I promise I'll try harder this time, Jane.'

For a moment she believed he was going to reach out for her, hold on to her, seeking some kind of reassurance, forgiveness. If he did that, anything was possible. But he turned away—almost, she thought, with relief—as Shuli called out from her room. 'She's excited about tomorrow. Meeting all her new cousins. Would you mind going up to her? I'll take Bob for a walk.'

She wanted to scream with frustration, but she could see that he needed to be alone for a while with his thoughts. So she just said, 'Try and keep him out of the pond.'

CHAPTER TEN

JANE sat at the window seat by the open window. The night was soft and warm, and beneath her the honeysuckle and night-scented stocks filled her mother's moon-silvered garden with sweetness.

Mark had stayed tactfully downstairs, using the excuse of taking Bob out for a walk before joining her. Giving her an opportunity to get into bed, close her eyes and pretend to be asleep. He couldn't believe she'd manage the real thing.

She'd scarcely had a moment to talk with him all day. She'd waited last night for him to come back, but he must have walked for a long time with his memories for company. Bob had been worn out, totally ignoring the jangling of his lead when she'd taken Shuli to playgroup that morning.

And the child had claimed all her attention in the car on their way to her parents'. Stories, games—the journey had passed in a flash. And once they'd arrived—well, there had been dinner and family news to catch up on. Elizabeth's news to wonder over. A dozen people for Mark to meet.

Finally, though, they were to be alone. She had it all planned. All he had to do was kiss her. She'd do the rest. She started slightly as she heard the lightest warning tap on the door before he opened it. Her heart was pounding like a road drill, her skin heating up...

'Are you asleep?' And then, as he saw her, 'Oh...'

'Don't turn the light on,' she murmured. She didn't turn around. 'There's a fox in the garden.' She reached back, holding out her hand to him. 'Come and see.'

For a long moment she thought he wouldn't come, but

then his hand grasped hers and he put a knee on the seat beside her to look out of the small casement window and search the shadows. 'Where?'

'Just there.' He leaned closer, his chest pressed against her back, his soft twill shirt against her skin. He smelled so good, felt so strong… 'She's got her cubs with her.' She retrieved her hand to point to the dark patch on the grass where they were playing and he put his hand on her shoulder. Palm against naked skin. Surely he could hear the sizzle? She turned to look up at him. 'Do you see, Mark?' she said.

His face was unreadable in the moonlight, just black and white shadows like the negative of an old picture that might be anybody… 'Yes,' he said. 'I see.' Then he bent and kissed her, so gently, so tenderly, so briefly that before she could respond it was over. 'Go to bed, Jane.'

'Mark…'

'Tomorrow, Jane. Go. I won't disturb you.'

Too late for that. She was disturbed beyond endurance. But she didn't need telling twice. Grateful for the darkness to hide her hot shame, she scrambled from the window seat and into bed, lying on the farthest edge, her back turned towards him. But she needn't have bothered; he kept his word, sitting at the window, staring out into the night.

As for tomorrow—what difference would a day make? He'd made his position clear right from the beginning while she, in her vanity, had believed she could win his heart.

'Mum, can I talk to you?'

'Goodness, Jane, aren't you ready? We're meeting the girls in less than an hour.'

'It's Saturday lunchtime down the pub. It hardly calls for designer dressing.' She realised belatedly that mother was, in fact, dressed to kill. 'Isn't it?'

'We haven't gone to all the trouble of getting the men and the children out of our hair just for an hour at the pub, sweetheart. Elizabeth has found an absolutely wonderful new restaurant for our own little hen party treat and it's definitely not a jeans kind of place. Why don't you wear that lovely outfit you wore for your wedding?'

'No…'

'Please, make an effort, Jane. Your sisters always do.'

'For heaven's sake, Mum! I've probably made the biggest mistake in my life and all you're interested in is whether I can hold my own in the fashion stakes with my sisters. We both know it's a waste of time even trying.'

'Mistake?'

'Mark doesn't love me. I thought I could make him…' As her mother reached for her the whole truth spilled out in a torrent of anguished self-pity. 'What on earth am I going to do?'

'Do?' Her mother touched her cheek. 'You don't need me to tell you what you have to do, darling. You're going to go upstairs right now, put on your make-up and your pretty new clothes—'

'I can't—'

'Yes, Jane. You can. You have no choice. They need you. Mark made an honest bargain with you, and you have taken on a little girl who loves you—'

'And I love her.'

'Of course you do. As I love you. And I know you won't let either of them down.'

'No.'

'This might not be a great romance, Jane, but marriage takes a lot more than romance. It takes hard work and commitment. And sometimes a brave face.'

'I hope I'm as good a mother to Shuli as you have always been to us.'

'I used to worry about you so much, but I must have done something right. You're strong, Jane. Inside—where it matters. You'll be a wonderful mother to Shuli. And you'll have babies of your own, too. Just give it time.'

'How long?'

'How long is a piece of string?' Her mother looked at her watch and gave a little yelp of panic. 'Let's take this one step at a time. Right now, you've got twenty minutes.'

'Why are we stopping?' Jane looked around as her mother pulled into a space in front of the church. 'Why are all these cars here?'

'The Women's Institute...' she said vaguely, as if that were explanation enough. 'I've just remembered that I promised to pass on a message. I won't be a minute. Why don't you go and have a little chat to your grandmother? You always used to tell her your troubles when you were little.'

'You think she'll have the answer?'

Her mother, about to climb out of the car, paused and put her hand over Jane's. 'It wouldn't hurt to ask.'

'No.' Jane got out of the car and walked around the church to the quiet spot where her grandmother was buried.

Someone else was there before her.

'Mark?' He turned as she approached. 'I thought you'd all gone down to the beach.' But he wasn't dressed for the beach. He was wearing a cream suit. A shirt the same colour as her *shalwar kameez*. A new tie she'd bought him. 'What are you doing here? What's going on?'

'Last night—'

'Don't!'

'Last night I wanted to make love with you, Jane. More than anything in the world. I ached with a depth of longing, desire, that I was certain I'd never feel for any woman ever again.'

That wasn't an answer. But she'd lost interest in her original question. 'Then why didn't you? I couldn't have made myself plainer—'

'Because I'd done everything wrong.'

'No!'

'Oh, yes. I'd seized your selfless offer with both hands without a second thought. That should have told me something, don't you think? What man would marry a girl he didn't care for? I could have hired a housekeeper or a live-in nanny any time in the last two and a·half years, but I didn't want to share my house with anyone. Yet from the moment you said ''Are you asking me if I'd marry you?'' I never considered anything else. It seemed so…right.'

'I pushed you into it. I knew you'd never advertise, but I thought if I put the idea into your head—'

'I was so sure it was the right thing to do, and I told myself that you must have a good reason to settle for something less than perfect. I imagined that someone had broken your heart, too, and you couldn't ever face the pain again.' He took her hand. 'That wasn't the reason, was it?'

Jane was without defences. Only the truth would serve her now. 'There has only ever been one love in my life, Mark. I've loved you from the first moment I saw you.'

'And I think I must have loved you for a long time. Maybe from that first day when you walked into my life, picked up Shuli and cuddled her, stopped her fretting.'

He remembered? 'A helpless, needy man and his baby,' she said softly. 'I knew you'd both break my heart even then. Well, last night I finally felt the pain.'

'Last night was different.'

'How, Mark? How was it different?'

'Because I wanted to make a gesture. Show you how much you really mean to me. Make a new start. Not as some couple who married out of convenience and fell into bed because it was there…' He took both her hands and clasped them in his. 'Everyone we both know and care for is waiting in the church. To hear us say our vows before God. To bless our marriage not as an expedient but as a partnership, in every sense of the word.'

'A blessing?' She looked around at all the cars. 'You've arranged all this?'

'With the help of your parents, your sisters, and Laine. I've even managed to drag my mother and sister here for the occasion. I love you, Jane, and I want everyone to know it. You're my wife in name. Now I'm asking you will you be my wife...' he paused briefly, as if searching for the right words '...heart, body and soul?'

She reached up, touched his face. 'I always was, my love. I've just been waiting for you to notice.'

'Then let's not keep the vicar waiting.'

Laine and Shuli were waiting for them in the porch. Laine hugged her and handed her a bouquet of flowers. Shuli had a velvet cushion waiting to carry their wedding rings.

And when, after they'd exchanged their vows, the vicar said, 'You may kiss the bride,' Mark's tender, lingering kiss held a promise that this was the real beginning of their marriage.

Jane turned and picked up Shuli. Mark took her, and with his hand in hers walked her down the aisle. At the church door he stopped to kiss her again. 'You know,' he murmured, 'I really like your family, but I don't think I want to spend my honeymoon with them.'

'We could go home.'

'We could,' he agreed. 'Or we could leave Shuli and Bob with your parents while we go to Paris for a few days.' And he opened his jacket so that she alone could see the airline tickets in his inside pocket. 'What do you think, Mrs Hilliard?'

'I think I'm the luckiest woman in the world.'

He reached up, brushed a tear from her cheek. 'No. The bravest, truest, strongest woman. The luck is all mine.'

'Daddy?'

'Yes, angel?'

'*Now* can I have a baby brother?'

Mark glanced at Jane, lifting his eyebrow, and she blushed. 'We'll work on it, sweetheart. I promise you, we'll work on it.'

À Taw, le mien.

R.D.

ETIENNE

PAULINE

JUSTINE

ARISTIDE

noa

SELIE

THOMAS
(le petit)

THOMAS
(le grand)

MARIUS

ABEL

CELESTE

emilie

L'amoureux

Rébecca Dautremer
AVEC LA COLLABORATION DE MONA LE THANH

ERNEST

SALOMÉ

Gautier·Languereau

Il y avait Ernest, le petit garçon
qui aimait beaucoup (embêter) les filles...

... et surtout Salomé.

Et il y avait Salomé,
la petite fille qui a rapporté
à sa maman tout ce qu'Ernest
lui avait fait. **Tout** :
tiré les cheveux,
attrapé sa capuche,
fait tomber ses lunettes **exprès**...
Alors la maman a dit
qu'Ernest avait **sûrement**
voulu jouer avec Salomé,
mais qu'il ne savait pas
comment le lui demander.

Et la maman a dit aussi que, sans doute,
Ernest voulait être **l'amoureux** de Salomé...

À l'école, Pauline a demandé :
« L' amoureux de Salomé !
C'est quoi ça, **l'amoureux** ? »

Salomé non plus ne savait pas ce que c'était, cette moureu...

Abel, lui,
savait
qu'on tombait.

On tombait
amoureux.

Salomé était souvent tombée à vélo, mais à Moureu, **jamais !**

« Les amoureux,
c'est dans les histoires !
a dit Étienne.
– Ah oui !
Pour les princes
et les princesses ?
– Avec des belles robes ?
– Des épées ?
– Des rois, des reines ?
– Et des dragons ?

« – Alors, les amoureux, c'est seulement pour de **faux** ? » a demandé Salomé.

Justine pensait qu'on est amoureux
parce qu'on est triste...
ou **quand** on est timide...
ou plutôt **si** on est tout rouge.
« Quand on est **hypnotisé !** »

Salomé a compris finalement qu'on est **un peu fou** quand on est amoureux !

La petite Noa
avait entendu parler
du **coude-foudre**...
« Amoureux, c'est du feu !
– Ça brûle ?
– Comme un éclair !
– C'est l'orage.
– Il pleut alors ? »

Et Salomé s'est dit qu'il **valait mieux** avoir un parapluie pour être amoureux !

Mais Aristide a dit qu'amoureux,
c'est **dans le cœur**.
« Tu veux dire mal au cœur ?
– Et de la fièvre aussi ?
– Et tout mou ?
– On est **malade ?**

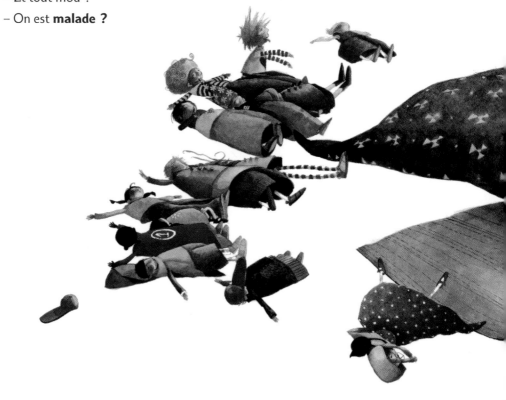

– Comme c'est fatigant d'être amoureux ! » a soupiré Salomé.

« Il faut être **deux**

pour être amoureux !

a affirmé Céleste.

– Tout seul, on peut aussi ?

– Ou trois ?

– Ou quatre ?

– Ah ! Aaah ! Tous des amoureux ! »

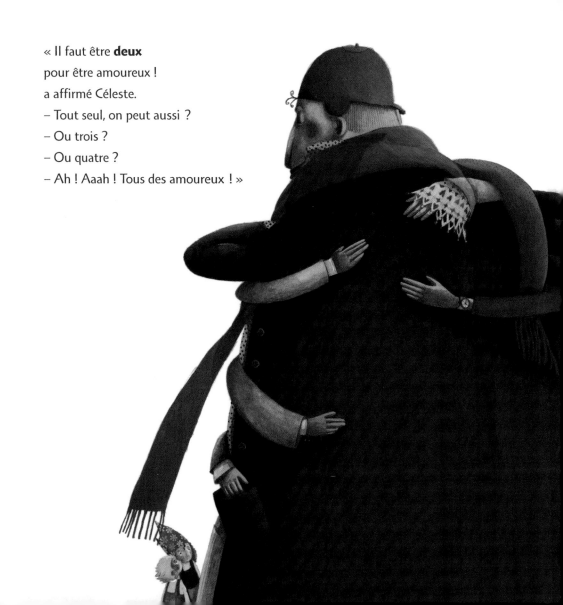

3 4 5 6 7 8 9 10 11 12 13 14 15 16 17 18 19 20 21 22 23 24 25 26 27 28 29 30 31

« Alors, il vaut mieux être **combien**, finalement ? » s'est demandé Salomé.

La grande Zélie
savait qu'amoureux
c'est pour se marier, **forcément**.
« C'est pour les messieurs.
– Et pour les dames !
– Pour les parents !
– Pas pour les petits !

« – Donc il faut être **grand** pour être amoureux ! » a ajouté Salomé.

« Pfff ! Amoureux,
ça n'arrive jamais,
a soupiré Marius.
– Si, ça arrive toujours !
– Et pour toujours !
– Ou pour cinq minutes ?
– Pour toute la vie !

– Oooh... mais c'est un peu **long**, non ? » a soufflé Salomé.

« Amoureux,

c'est **très important !**

a décrété Thomas (le grand).

– C'est pour la maîtresse.

– Pour ta meilleure copine !

– Que pour les filles, alors ?

– Mais non !

– Non ! C'est **que** pour les garçons ! » a crié Salomé.

Émilie a ri
parce qu'il faut **s'embrasser**
quand on est amoureux !
« Se donner la main !
– Amoureux, c'est pour faire les bébés !
– Oouuh ! Ouuuh !

– Il ne faudrait pas être **tout nu**, par hasard, pour faire l'amoureux ? » a suggéré Salomé.

« Amoureux,
c'est comme un rêve !
a dit Thomas (le petit).
– On vole dans le ciel !
– Avec des fleurs...
– On plane ! Pfffouuuuitt ! »

Et Salomé a conclu qu'on est **un ange** quand on est amoureux.

Mais quand Ernest (l'amoureux) est revenu
pour bousculer Salomé **très fort** encore une fois,
qu'il a tapé son cartable et marché sur son manteau,
exprès...

... plus personne n'a rien dit !

Et Salomé a pensé qu'ils ne connaissaient rien aux amoureux, tous ceux-là !

TRAFFIC JAM

A play by Geraldine McCaughrean

Illustrated by Alvaro Fernandez Villa

Characters

Pickle

Police Officer

Robot

Lorry Driver

Van Driver

VIP

(Very Important Person)

Children

(Children on the bus -
played by all the readers)

Children:	ARE WE NEARLY THERE YET?
Pickle:	We're stuck in a traffic jam.
Lorry Driver:	An extra sticky traffic jam.
Pickle:	Will we ever get to the zoo?
Children:	ARE WE NEARLY THERE YET?
Pickle:	There's a white van next to us.
Van Driver:	Why have we stopped?

Pickle:	There's a lorry ahead of us, full of fruit.
Lorry Driver:	Is it road works again?
Pickle:	There's a shiny new limo, tooting.
VIP:	Come on, come on, come on, come on!
Pickle:	The queue is miles long.

VIP: At last, a police officer. Officer! Tell us at once. What's happening?

Police Officer: Some kind of problem; stay where you are. Try to be patient. Stay in your car.

Van Driver: Is it an accident?

Police Officer: We're sorting things out as fast as we can. Just stay where you are: don't get out of your van.

Lorry Driver: Can I turn my lorry around and go home?

Police Officer: Certainly not. I'm very sorry. Kindly stay calm and remain in your lorry.

Children: ARE WE NEARLY THERE YET?

Police Officer: Sit in your seats, kids.

Don't make a fuss.

Do as you're told;

don't get out of the bus.

VIP: Never mind them. I'm an important person! You must clear a path for me!

Police Officer: Oh, must I indeed?
You stay where you are.
Stay tucked up warm
in your big comfy car.
(Her phone goes.)
Yes, sir? NO! Again? Well, well!

The VIP, Van Driver, Lorry Driver and Pickle come over.

VIP: Well?

Van Driver: Well?

Lorry Driver: Well?

Pickle: What did they say?

VIP: Just tell us!

Police Officer: A robot.

Pickle: A robot?

Police Officer: Yes. A giant robot. Sitting in the road.

Pickle: Wow!

Van Driver: Never!

Lorry Driver: Are you serious?

9

VIP: Well, go and move him out of the road! I'm a busy man.

Police Officer: That's easier said than done, sir.

VIP: Nonsense! Use a bulldozer. Use a crane!

Police Officer: We tried that last time.

Pickle: Last time?

Police Officer: The robot ate the bulldozer, and picked his teeth with the crane.

Children:	WHERE IS PICKLE GOING?
Pickle:	I've never seen a robot before.
Van Driver:	You can't go visiting strange robots on your own!
Lorry Driver:	Wait for us.
Police Officer:	Come back, little boy. You must stay here with us. Do as you're told and get back on your — Oh no ...

11

The Lorry Driver, Van Driver, Police Officer and VIP follow Pickle.

Pickle: Hello, Robot.

Robot: Hello, Small Thing.

Pickle: Why are you sitting in the road?

Robot: I'm making sandwiches.

Pickle: Yum. What sort of sandwiches?

Robot: Jam sandwiches.

Van Driver: Nice.

Lorry Driver: What sort of jam?

Robot: TRAFFIC JAM! I shake all the people out of their cars. Then I mish them and mash them and squash them and squish them. That's the filling.

Lorry Driver: What's the outside?

Robot: Two cars squashed flat. White ones are best.

Van Driver: Hang on! My van is white!

Pickle: So is my school bus. Er ... brown cars are better for you, didn't you know?

VIP: What do you mean? My car is brown ...

Robot: I'll put you in my jam, Small Thing. You look nice and squidgy.

Pickle: That's kind. But you wouldn't like me. I taste yucky, don't I, Mr Van Driver?

Van Driver: What? Oh. True. And so do I.

Lorry Driver: Me too.

VIP: I'm not surprised. You have no taste!

15

Police Officer: One thing I must tell you, one thing must be said: It's wrong to mash people and eat them on bread.

Robot: But I get hungry.

Lorry Driver: I quite understand. You're very big. It takes a lot of fruit to fill up my lorry, and you're much bigger than that. Of course you get hungry.

Robot: And I like traffic-jam.

Van Driver: Have you tried any other kind? I like jam-jam, myself.

Pickle: I'll tell you what! Let us make you lunch today, Mr Robot.

Robot: Well ...

Pickle climbs back onto the bus.

Children: ARE WE NEARLY THERE YET?

Pickle: Listen up, everyone. I need your packed lunches – and all your snacks.

Children: OO-BOOOO-NO-WAY.

18

Pickle: I'll take your photograph standing beside a robot.

Children: Okay!

Pickle gets off the bus.

Pickle: Give me your load of fresh fruit, Mrs Lorry Driver.

Lorry Driver: Okay.

Pickle: Give me your sandwiches, Mr Van Driver.

Van Driver: I don't have any ... I've already eaten them!

Pickle: What are those dangly things hanging from the mirror?

Van Driver: They keep my van fresh.

Pickle: Okay, give me those. Mrs Police Officer?

Police Officer: I don't have a packed lunch, but you can have my whistle and notebook and the silver pips off my jacket.

Pickle: *(To the VIP)* Can you spare any food for the robot, sir?

VIP: No! Certainly not! I don't **do** giving.

Pickle: Here is your traffic-jam sandwich, Mr Robot.

Robot:	Does it have people-jam in it?
Van Driver:	No – it's much better than that.
Pickle:	It has 40 packed-lunches and all sorts of yummy snacks.
Lorry Driver:	And fresh fruit ...
Van Driver:	Dangly things from my van ...
Police Officer:	And a whistle and pips!

Robot:	Where's the bread?
Pickle:	I —
Lorry Driver:	We —
Police Officer:	Oh dear.
VIP:	Oi! Stop that! Put me down! Do you know who I am? Aaaaaaargh!
Robot:	I've got bread, look.
Pickle:	That's very shiny bread.
Robot:	I squished a very shiny car.
Police Officer:	Oh dear. What happened to the shiny driver?
Robot:	I'm keeping him here. In my jam jar.
Pickle:	What for? A pet?
Robot:	No. For LATER.

Police Officer: Ladies – gentlemen – kids.
There's no further delay.
Kindly get in your cars
And set off on your way.

Children: ARE WE NEARLY THERE YET?